THE WORKS OF CHRISTINA STEAD

The Salzburg Tales (1934)
Seven Poor Men of Sydney (1935)
The Beauties and Furies (1936)
House of All Nations (1938)
The Man Who Loved Children (1940)
For Love Alone (1944)
Letty Fox: Her Luck (1946)
A Little Tea, A Little Chat (1948)
The People with the Dogs (1952)
Dark Places of the Heart (Cotter's England) (1966)
The Puzzleheaded Girl: Four Novellas (1967)
The Little Hotel (1975)
Miss Herbert (The Suburban Wife) (1976)

A
CHRISTINA
STEAD
READER

A CHRISTINA STEAD READER

Selected by
Jean B. Read

Random House New York

Library of Congress Cataloging in Publication Data
Stead, Christina, 1902–
A Christina Stead reader.
I. Read, Jean B. II. Title.
PZ3.S7986Ch 1978   [PR9619.3.S75] 823   78–57134
ISBN 0–394–50095–4

Manufactured in the United States of America
2 4 6 8 9 7 5 3
First Edition

Editor's Note:

In making the selections for this book, we have been fortunate to be able to draw on all of Christina Stead's published works, with the exception of *The Man Who Loved Children*, her well-known masterpiece, and *The Little Hotel*, which was published in 1975.

The selections are arranged in chronological order according to the publication dates of the books from which they were taken. They begin with the author's first work, *The Salzburg Tales* (1932) and end with her most recently published novel, *Miss Herbert* (1976), covering the more than forty years of her career as a writer.

During these years Miss Stead has lived in Australia (where she was born and recently returned to live), in Europe, England and the United States. These places have shaped and informed the background of her novels: the island life on the fringes of Sydney in *For Love Alone*; the bleak, impoverished mining village in the north of England in *Dark Places of the Heart*; the world of New York City in *Letty Fox*; the beauty and serenity of rural America in the section called "Whitehouse" in *The People with the Dogs*.

When *The Man Who Loved Children* appeared in 1940, Rebecca West said that Christina Stead was "one of the few people really original we have produced since the First World War." In an essay on her novels, Elizabeth Hardwick speaks of her "prodigious talent for fiction" and her "storytelling abundance"; she describes her style as one "of remarkable uniqueness and strength, of truly radical power and authenticity." With the publication of *House of All Nations* in 1972, a reviewer said of Miss Stead: "She is one of the important modern novelists and everything she has written should immediately be made available."

In his introduction to the reissue of *The Man Who Loved Children*, Randall Jarrell wrote: "Christina Stead's way of seeing and representing the world is so plainly different from anyone else's that after a while you take this for granted." More recently, in the *New York Times Book Review*, Helen Yglesias wrote: "Her works are great to read —long, rich, funny, moving . . . the whole built solidly on ground chosen and controlled by a master."

Having to choose between one passage from an author's work and another is always painful. But it has helped to remember that a great deal of the work represented here is out of print and that half a loaf, or even a slice of it, is better than none. Cuts have been made wherever the names of characters and past events alluded to are not necessary to a particular passage, and where their inclusion would be confusing in the excerpt. These cuts are indicated by the conventional sign for a deletion (. . .). Some cutting has also been done in the interest of space—to make this collection as representative as possible of the author's work. The separation between passages is marked by a roman numeral.

It is hoped that what has been chosen will express the richness and diversity of the author's mind and imagination, the character of her convictions, and above all, her originality.

JEAN B. READ

Contents

THE SALZBURG TALES   3

SEVEN POOR MEN OF SYDNEY   15

THE BEAUTIES AND FURIES   59

HOUSE OF ALL NATIONS   71

FOR LOVE ALONE   105

LETTY FOX: HER LUCK   161

A LITTLE TEA, A LITTLE CHAT   189

THE PEOPLE WITH THE DOGS   199

DARK PLACES OF THE HEART (COTTER'S ENGLAND)   241

THE RIGHTANGLED CREEK: A SORT OF GHOST STORY   293

MISS HERBERT (THE SUBURBAN WIFE)   349

THE
SALZBURG
TALES

"The Sensitive Goldfish" comes from Christina Stead's first published work, *The Salzburg Tales,* which appeared in 1934. This collection of tales is in the form of a modern Decameron, told by an assembly of visitors to the Salzburg Festival.

I

THE SENSITIVE GOLDFISH

Henry, the securities clerk, was born under the sign of Pisces, but he had not learned swimming, for all the water he had seen had been in London Pool and in the goldfish pond on the roof-terrace of the Bank of Central Honduras. The Bank of Central Honduras, I have no need to say, is the Bastille of the City: the humble citizen who passes its buttressed, unpierced walls, thinks of the mountains of gold under the mined pavement, and for a moment comes into his pale eye an imperial glint, the look of the slave-driver, the frontiersman, the dragoon.

The yellow-vested porters have the composed mien and slow speech formerly associated with a five-thousand-acre pheasant shoot. At sunset, the flag is struck, and the Bank's private band plays soft martial music while the steel doors within, all over the building, automatically swing to: the yellow day porters go off and the sable night watchmen come on.

Henry smiled each morning when, arriving at the Bank, the auroral liveries of the porters put him in mind of the goldfish in their Chinese sleeves and skirts. He was called a securities clerk, but his function was to aërate and feed the fish; and a large part of each day he spent in a stone cabin on top of the building listening to the voices, motor-horns and sirens ascending through the fog which often covered the City's business; or, on a clearish day, following with shaded eyes the barges moving slowly down the sluggish golden flood which at noonday rolls under London Bridge. Often, too, on a moony, brown night, he leaned on the kerb of the goldfish pond and listened to the soft voices of the goldfish, then gambolling, white, dark and silver, in the basin. How many of them were there? He had never counted: they were like leaves.

Henry had discovered long ago that his fish were temperamental. On certain days, quite apart from the occasional sad tinges lent them by soot, fog or nightfall, the fish appeared to change colour, hourly, and even momently, due to secret and invisible movements of the water, or its animalculæ, or to the filtration of light through the plankton, or to the thoughts of those finned images themselves. Sometimes, their bars and mottlings, their scars, freckles and wine-marks would glow and burn, redden, blacken, glower: sometimes, the fish would turn paler and the outlines of their beauties fade.

Henry dreamed of other climes and postulated to himself other habits. He saw goldfish swimming in the sunken tarns of impassable mountains, goldfish in brimming rivers floating through the reeds, goldfish in the shape of a wild boar's head pressing through the packed flood-waters of the Yellow River, goldfish in the one-franc glass bowls of the Paris bird-market, goldfish in bamboo cages and oiled-paper tanks, goldfish momentarily glinting behind a rattan screen in the Maughamy air of some Eurasian bungalow, with milk-fed feline clumsily pawing and the shriek of overturned globe. He pondered so deep that often he thought he heard a voice arising from the depths of the artificial pool, as if he were in the thicket by Melisande's glade, and a fatal voice foretelling harm smote his heart: then whistles, as of distant wild geese affecting that imagined sky, seemed to drop to him from the vaporous circles of the moon, moving rheumily over the sky in its crinolines of mist, shadowing, with its morbid light, airy spites and watery turbulences.

Thus he dreamed: but never, day or night, forgot to feed the fish on powdered liver, which swelled their mandarin bellies and reddened their metal coats.

He, at other times, seemed to himself that ancient mandarin whose loving-cup, in jellied alabaster, painted with twin carps in Chinese red, was now preserved by the heaven-descended professor of ichthyology in an inferior Canton College, and catalogued in a shop in Piccadilly. The marble basin stood in his hand, he offered it full of wine to some beautiful girl bought for a phenomenal price—a beauty of such high birth that her full eyes were scarcely almond, and her complexion the colour of the cup with two red carps floating in her cheeks.

He kissed the flat-tasting water of the pool, lying in the shadow of the Bank's parapet, and a goldfish, rising suddenly, presented a viscous, cool surface to his lips. Ungrateful for this caress, the youth wished for the day to come when he could take service in foreign branches, and look down from the glass top of his table upon the silent steps of some masted sea-port, and the swilling quays, grown with seaweed of a foreign sort, in a land of coral. He blamed himself again, looking at the fish sporting their unmerchantable plates of gold, that he could think of no scheme for making money; with his opportunities (as his sister said). Looking through the goldfish and through the bottom of the pool, he transpierced the beamed rooms, the mahogany, marble, plush and shagrin, into the vaults of the bank, where (he believed) attendants dressed like Phantomas glided above a vast honeycomb of gold, sealed in cold chambers, along slippery corridors, guarded by impenetrable steel doors, full of wheels and cogs, and bombs of tear-gas, and subterranean lakes in cement basins.

The City is a machine miraculously organised for extracting gold from the seas, airs, clouds, from barren lands, holds of ships, mines, plantations, cottage hearth-stones, trees and rocks; and he, wretchedly waiting in the exterior halls, like the porters, or the newsboys, could not even get his finger on one tiny, tiny lever. More, newsboys proverbially became noble lords, but what known bank-clerk had done so? Newsboys got tips, telephone-operators tuned in on important calls, cashiers —sometimes—got away, but the road before him was long, slow, footworn and desperately unspeculative. He saw himself like a sparrow on the Bank-top; sitting on the wherewithal for a thousand, thousand meals and dropping dead from hunger the first day of winter. The fish had liver, the fish had marble, the fish changed their colour from day to day, and were a matter of concern to the Baron; but what was he?

As the securities clerk despaired one day, in this style, the chief director, Baron Franz-August de Geldreich, came out in the pallid late sunlight and peered through the mist at the goldfish now coloured like brass showing through rubbed silver. The clerk gazed at the Baron, at his superiorly stolid, red phiz, his sad-coloured eyes and pensive moustache: the Baron had his shoes patched once a month and never took a taxi, even when it rained. In the last two matters Henry resembled the Baron.

The Baron said in his deliberate, impeccably-accented voice,

"Look after these fish carefully for me, like a good fellow. They have a curious colour: did you feed them this morning?"

"Yes," said Henry.

"These fish are most valuable, most extraordinary," said the Baron; "watch them carefully. I had them, you know," he continued, turning pleasantly to the youth, "from an old Chinaman, politician, sage and poet. He poisoned his wife and sold his sister, but was a good friend to his friends, did well by his fifteen illegitimate sons, and was said to have been altogether in the sway of his last mistress, a child he found sailing paper boats in a fountain in the hills.

"These fish are over two hundred years old; and were said, by the informants of my sage, to have come from the cataracts of Kin-Saï, in a miraculous tempest which raged over Pekin all one night. It was so fierce that when morning drew near, the coolies were afraid to go out to work, but did so, and found the ground moist only with dew, and thick with unsmirched flowers. On that night, these fish and others like them appeared in the fountains of the Emperor, a holy prince who waged war continually with the enemies of the State and whose treasury was drained to the last ounce of gold-dust. Immediately after the appearance of these fish, the Emperor was granted an enormous loan on most favourable terms by our own country, and although he himself was poisoned, with his uncle and son, by his mother, shortly after, the next Emperor, his mother's son by a second marriage, was enabled to live long and abdicate in time, by a discovery and study of the secret virtues of the fish. This is, of course, the tale told me by the donor of the fish. Have you an ichthyological turn? While taking this freshwater story with what salt you think necessary, you may be sure the fish are of the rarest breed—are, indeed, unique! Watch them carefully," said the Baron Franz-August; "if anything should ever happen to them, let me know at once, personally." He smiled at the curator, and departed with the delicate, pointed tread of a quick-witted stout man.

The youth peered at the ancient fish, sons of Kin-Saï, who turned like scythes round the coppery spindles of the fog-sifted sunlight. It even seemed to him that on their great caudal and pectoral fins the black, orange, rose and silver markings took curious shapes: here was a blue willow, there a cluster of lanterns, there, weeping night-blue hair, garment of a sallow face.

He cautiously drew from his inside coat-pocket at last, preparatory to going downstairs, the day's copy of "The Speculative Times." He did not care for the true nature of the Junonian milk, the curvature of the earth's, or infantile, spines, Sir James Jeans's cosmogony, or the flights of contemporary Teutonic statecraft: his speculations concerned Spratt & Brown's Brewing Process, Emprunt & Borrow's new share capital and the North Atlantis Gold Mining and Diamond Syndicate, Ltd.

Henry's study of this paper was necessarily furtive, for no one in the Bank would have been seen reading anything inferior to the "Commercial & Financial Chronicle." Indeed, "The Speculative Times," which habitually took an unhappy and morose, no, even malcontent view of most things that happened in what it was pleased to call "that adamantine, floating, faery isle, the City," was scarcely a paper to be seen about with. It marked a man as having no vision, no future, no honorific qualities, but as having the nature of a tick, termite or hookworm, and a taste for whispering behind hands concerning men of high principle, of battening on the battener. Henry had seen the wretched office where this prophetic sheet was printed, and yet he hoped that (with his opportunities) he would be one day able to tell a bargain from a ramp, make a scoop, and rapidly advance up the rungs that led to the East, the West, and directors' participations.

He looked at the goldfish, which seemed flushed with emotion. Did they bring fortune? For the Baron, for the Bank, or for whom? He wished he could have one of all those fish to predict fortune for him, and to bring him good luck. In a romantic head, temptation germinates fearfully fast. The next day Henry slipped into the Bank with an air of virtue, because he had brought with him a goldfish bowl the size of a cricket-ball in which he intended to carry home, just for one night, one of the Baron's miraculous goldfish, the smallest, the plainest. There were one hundred and twenty-five goldfish that he counted before he abstracted his small one, and all were red as paint. When he got home and showed his small fish to his loving sister, he was dismayed to see that it was very pale, although quite healthy, and he took it for a bad omen, tossing all night, and hardly able to wait for daylight, so that he could get up and take the fish back to the Bank.

His sister came in to wake him, from the heavy sleep into which he had at length fallen, and whispered to him that the fish had gone: it was not in the bowl—perhaps the cat had taken it. They beat the cat, and Henry went to work without any breakfast, feeling like death. He dragged himself up to the roof and looked dismally at his wards. He saw in the basin a very small fish. He counted the fish, and found there were still one hundred and twenty-five. He rubbed his eyes. That night, trembling with his daring and folly, he took home again, in a new and larger glass bowl, another goldfish, after carefully counting them all again. The next morning his bowl was empty but the tale at the Bank was complete. To have evidence of the miracle he, next night, put a gold wire delicately round the tail of a goldfish and carried it home. On the way home he looked in at the offices of the North Atlantis Gold Mining Syndicate to see what he could see, but the offices were shut up, with thick doors, barred windows and padlocks like a gaol, and when he knocked, a little suspicious man popped up a tiny slot in the pane of a door and asked him rudely what was his business. Henry asked for the last annual balance-sheet of the North Atlantis Syndicate, and when, after a prolonged cross-examination, it was grudgingly handed to him, he was so upset that he asked the janitor's leave to sit a minute on the stool placed in the frigid iron-barred corridor. There he took out his fish to see if it was still with him, and found it not only there but brilliantly red. He got up and walked across to the grim door of the North Atlantis Gold Mining, watching his fish. The fish was now red as blood. Henry, to save it from bursting from apoplexy, turned on his heel and hurried out of the building. The janitor shook his head in astonishment.

Henry and his sister spent the whole evening looking at the goldfish. A visitor disturbed them, a young bank-clerk from a branch bank, the suitor of Henry's sister: under the seal of secrecy, he was told the marvellous tale of Kin-Saï and the temperamental goldfish, and he offered to buy the fish from Henry. Henry refused, but as the clerk raised his bid for the fish (for he intended to promenade it round all the speculative companies of the City the next day) Henry suddenly remembered that the ingenious youth might well buy it and take it home, it would be at the Bank again in the morning, whatever happened. He accepted the offer. The youth made off almost at once and Henry, when he heard the front-door close, went pale and dashed out after him. But the youth was nowhere to be seen. "What if the fish, once sold, stays with its buyer?" he asked his sister, trembling: "and can Herbert be trusted?"

"Herbert could be trusted with a million pounds, or secrets of state," said Henry's sister indignantly. Henry sighed.

The next morning, the fish with the gold wire on its tail was back in the pool. It is sad to relate that during the next few weeks Henry sold the same fish to one hundred ambitious bank-clerks, and the legend of Kin-Saï had become one of the most widely-spread legends of the City. Henry, likewise, had, to console the desolated and mystified Herbert, gone shares with him in a small flutter in North Atlantis shares: they bought the shares at 7/6 and they rose to 12/6, at which price the youths sold out and took their profit.

Now, to the end of my tale.

One morning, a year or so ago, the clerk mounted the stairs on a Friday morning and perceived a marked agitation in the building. When he asked questions, a hundred answers were given him, and one of the clerks, sniggering, said, "It is the Lord fluttering his account-books of his chosen." It was, in fact, not only the day before the Jewish Sabbath, but the most dismal Friday in all the year, the one which precedes the Day of Atonement, when all Israël mourns: it is then that the Lord makes up his accounts of good and evil for the year, and closes, after a brief respite, that journal for ever. The chief director, Baron Franz-August, necessarily, was not at the Bank, but was attending to his spiritual business.

Nevertheless, at eleven o'clock the directors of the Bank assembled hurriedly, and there was a going and coming all day. Henry, in the exceptional rumours of the day, had neglected his goldfish for a few hours. At eleven o'clock he took the lift to the roof and the most dreadful sight met his apprehensive eyes. The pool was strewn with fish, which were not only past gasping, but were all of a shocking colour, and limp and blown-up, as if they had been dead a week, at least: the scales had fallen off in places, the eyes were completely clouded, the gills pale, fungus had appeared on the bodies and the fins were eaten. Henry thought of putting his head in the pool along with the valuable dead, and cutting short a breath much less prized by man. Next, he considered that the water might be poisoned, and like us all, he did not wish to meet an unknown death, but only the one chosen. He ran to the lift, trembling violently, almost running out at every floor, and making a mistake in the end, and getting out at the sixth instead of the fourth floor.

Here, as luck would have it, a director hailed him, gave him a sealed note and said in the gravest and most peremptory way, "Henry, run as quickly as you can, take a taxi, to the Duke Street synagogue, and give this note to the Baron Franz-August: tell the attendant that nothing could be more important."

The jaws of fate presented themselves: he rushed in. He was now convinced that in one of its journeys his stolen fish had caught some inimical germ, communicated it to all the fish, and that he, in fact, had killed them. The world whirled away past him like the waves of the ocean rushing innumerably past a ship. He reached the synagogue, was admitted, and there, touching the shoulder of the mourner, he whispered, "Baron, Baron, I don't know how to tell you, but the goldfish are dead!" The Baron followed him quickly from the synagogue, and took the letter from his hand, saying "Dead? All? Just now? You were right to tell me! What time is it?" and he followed the palpitating youth into a taxi. He had been followed by the inquisitive and anxious looks and was now followed by the inquisitive and anxious persons of such other business men of wealth as found themselves in the temple.

At the Bank, Henry, wonderfully elated at being seen with the Baron, paid the taxi-driver, and when he turned, found the Baron out of sight. He had already reached his broker's office. Henry waited all day for the Baron to go and look at the fish. In the evening, he regretfully picked them out of the foul water, gutted them, cleaned them and put them in his cabin while he went and fetched glass jars, white slides, formalin and paraffin. He then put each fish in a separate jar with the label, "Goldfish from Kin-Saï" with a word of history and the date of decease, put in formalin, closed the jars with paraffin and set up his funereal museum on the roof for the Baron to see when he arrived.

He spent a sad week-end. The Saturday afternoon came with electric warnings in the air, and a stir in the City. He passed Sunday rather sadly looking at the columns of "Positions Vacant." He awakened on Monday to a changed world! That was the morning on which our country declared publicly an embargo on the export of gold, "went off the gold standard" as they said. I trust the ladies will forgive my mentioning these details.

In the afternoon of this day Henry found the Baron on the roof-terrace. "Where are the fish?" said the Baron. Henry showed him. The Baron laughed and said, "Pickle; never inter!" He took the young man's arm and walked him into the lift, still holding his arm till he reached the sixth floor, where he went out and left Henry to the lift-attendant's respectful congratulations.

"What the Baron touches," said the lift-man, "turns to gold: and he has only to shake hands with a man for him to make money: I believe in you, sir: I'll make you a proposition. You pick out a stock and I'll put up the money: we share fifty-fifty, either way, but you do the business."

Henry was impressed by the lift-man's words, took the money and bought one hundred shares of North Atlantis Gold Mining and Diamond Syndicate Ltd. at 17/6, and sold them at a shade less than 39/9, the best price this company's shares ever saw in the market. At the price just mentioned the lamentable discovery was made that diamonds were a drug in the market, and gold absent from the North Atlantis workings, at least in the northern parts, that the directors were taking rest-cures on the Continent and the hyperbolic geologist who had made the reports was cruising along the Dalmatian coast. Henry, who had received a jar containing one of the sensitive goldfish, as a personal present from the Baron, and who always kept this souvenir on his mantelpiece, one morning began speculating to himself and said aloud, "Now if North Atlantis goes up again . . ." when he noticed the goldfish go as pale as a sheet. Experimentally, he said, as if still thinking aloud, "Perhaps, though, I should *sell* North Atlantis . . ." and he observed that the dead goldfish became red again. The same day he took an option on the sale of 1,000 North Atlantis and before the end of the month had realised a large profit on the downgrade.

Except for this singular accident, Henry would never have made any money. But now we can safely leave him with his foot well advanced for the slipper of fortune, and pursue no farther than today the remarkable and true, yet fantastic story of the Sensitive Goldfish. I should say that the rest of the goldfish have been secreted by the Baron, for they are not always exactly of the same shade of opinion, and he is then obliged to take a majority ruling.

SEVEN
POOR MEN
OF SYDNEY

Written in 1935, *Seven Poor Men of Sydney* is Christina Stead's first novel, set in her native city in Australia.

In the five passages from the novel that follow, we get a rich sense of the city's character and color, and see the lives of several of the poor men who live there: Joseph Baguenault, a working-class Catholic boy; his radical American friend, Baruch Mendelssohn, who works with Joseph in a printing shop and goes to night school; and Michael, Baguenault's cousin, a misfit who can no longer find solutions to his problems in the world around him.

The first excerpt describes Fisherman's Bay, the settlement where Joseph lives and where he takes the ferry to his job to Sydney. The second takes place in the printing shop in the city and the third as Joseph and Baruch go window-shopping after work. In the fourth excerpt we see another section of Sydney where Baruch lives among the native and immigrant poor. In the final passage Catherine, Michael's sister, looks back on the life of her brother, who has committed suicide, and describes the relationship between them. This theme of the relationship between a sister and brother appears in several of Stead's novels.

I

Fisherman's Bay

The hideous low scarred yellow horny and barren headland lies curled like a scorpion in a blinding sea and sky. At night, houselamps and ships' lanterns burn with a rousing shine, and the headlights of cars swing over Fisherman's Bay. In the day, the traffic of the village crawls along the skyline, past the lighthouse and signal station, and drops by cleft and volcanic gully to the old village that has a bare footing on the edge of the bay. It was, and remains, a military and maritime settlement. When the gunners are in camp, searchlights sweep over the bay all night, lighting bedrooms and the china on dressers, discolouring the foliage and making seagulls fly; in the daytime, when the red signal is flown over the barracks, the plates and windows rattle with the report of guns at target practice. From the signal station messages come down of the movements of ships and storms. Flags flutter and red globes swing on its great mast, which is higher than the Catholic Church, higher than the Norfolk Island pines, higher than the lighthouse and than anything else which is between the rocky cornice and the sandy sea-floor. In dark nights, from the base of that enormous spectral pole which points up any distance into the starry world, one looks down on the city and northern harbour settlements, on the pilot-lights in the eastern and western channels, and on the unseen dark sea, where the lighthouse ray is lost beyond the horizon and where ships appear through the waves, far out, lighted like a Christmas Tree, small, and disappearing momentarily; and where, after half an hour of increasing radiance, the yellow rim of the great sub-tropical moon comes up like a lantern from underneath.

Early in the morning, through the open window, the people hear the clatter of anchors falling into the bay, and the little boys run out to name the liners waiting there for the port doctor, liners from Singapore, Shanghai, Nagasaki, Wellington, Hawaii, San Francisco, Naples, Brindisi, Dunkirk and London, in the face of all these old stone houses, decayed weatherboard cottages, ruinous fences, boathouses and fishermen's shanties. Presently a toot, the port doctor puts out in the *Hygeia;* a whistle, the Customs launch goes alongside; a hoot from the Point, and that is the pilot-ship returning to its anchorage. A bell jangles on the wharf where the relief pilot waits for his dinghy, and the ferry whistles to clear the dinghies, rowing-boats and children's canoes from its path. The fishermen murmur round the beach-path, fishing-nets dry in the sun, a bugle blows in the camp, the inspected ships draw up their anchors and go off up the harbour, superb with sloping masts, or else, in disgrace, flying the yellow flag, to the rightabout, with nose in air, to Quarantine, under North Head and its bleak graveyard. Butchers' and bakers' carts rattle, an original milkman yodels, little girls gabble on the way to school, the wind with hands in pockets whistles a tune, and the day goes gaily and blatantly forward.

There is no place in the estuary, though, so suited for an old tale as this fish-smelling bay, first in the port. Life is poor and unpretentious, life can be quiet. The sun rises just over the cliff, and sailing vessels roll in and out as they have done for a hundred years, and a quarter of a mile away unfurl their full sails to catch the Pacific winds.

There was a family there named Baguenault, which had settled in the bay directly after its arrival from Ireland thirty years before . . .

II

A hot morning in Fisherman's Bay. We find four of our heroes at work in a devil's kitchen where the word is made bread.

On a spring morning in September Joseph Baguenault came down to breakfast late and found his mother already seated near the window, wearing her red shawl. The crickets trilled in the dewy grass and there was a smell of new perspiration in the room. Joseph kissed her dry cheek: her eyes were full and light.

"Did you sleep well, son?"

"Yes, after I got to sleep, but it was so wild when I got in that I lay awake listening to the house creaking. I did not get in till after eleven from college, because the ferry was late. They broke two ropes trying to tie up at Nielsen Park, with the swell that came from George's Head. And then the window blew in, in the attic, and I had to put a board over it before I finally got to sleep. Though, you know, I like a wind late at night, when the tide is up and every one is at home. You feel that something strange is going on."

"I thought I heard you call out once?"

"No, Mother."

"I was sure you called. It must have been a dream. I was worried— I thought you were spending the evening with your cousin Michael. He has such strange friends—I don't think he quite realises what they are. He has a good heart, and since he came home with shell-shock, or whatever it was, he has not been quite the same. Poor boys, I saw only yesterday in the paper, where a shell-shocked soldier killed his wife and two little children. Terrible, terrible, and he had been given a farm by the Government, too. It is terrible. I did hope, Joseph, at the beginning, that you would influence Michael; he used to be fond of you. Poor boy—funny, you know, you're boys to me still, even though poor Michael's thirty-two and you twenty-one . . ."

"Twenty-two."

". . . but now I only think of you. I am too old to worry about others. I think, my baby is not home, and such a storm! Anything may have happened to him. Well, at last the storm is gone."

"Time enough—nice spring weather! But, by the sound in the cove, it will come back."

"Will you say grace, my dear? I have not had my tea yet."

The tea steamed in the sun and skin came over the surface. Joseph said grace, and eyes were shut. He finished: Mrs. Baguenault filled her mouth with the steaming tea—a rude pleasure; her eyes got moist, her lips red, her gullet was burned and rejoiced. The breakfast clatter began like a chorus of crickets. Mr. Baguenault came in in an apron and laid his boots and a blacking-brush on a chair. The mother discoursed on an infinity of local matters, with the preoccupation of housewives with their five senses.

"I heard yesterday—the radio is so loud—margarine not butter—mine taste better—I said, Where is the smell coming from?—that cheap eau-de-cologne—I saw her hair had been peroxided—you could write your name in the dust—all real silk," and the sixth, "I had an *intuition* her husband . . ." The father read the leading article in the *Telegraph,* through his silver-rimmed glasses, but Joseph listened to his mother's conversation with interest. She was a plain woman. Hearing her speak, the tongue clung to the palate and the throat whirred, one's own ideas dried up, in sympathy. That was the effect of a dull youth, a devout life, an intelligence developed between smoky kitchen-walls, a slow remastication of ancient events to amuse the long tediums. Sixty years of poverty had extinguished that fountain of life which lives in infant flesh and ejects experiment and improvisation out of the mouth. The cheap print which hung over the piano showing Jesus with his sacred heart, in three colours out of register, blood, thorns, a night-gown, worn hands and tears, represented her own life as she knew it and as she was not ashamed to record it. Then, she went to church to know what was going on in the world, to know what view to take, as people used to go to panoramas, bad paintings artificially lighted in a little round hall, to find out what the country was like that lay about them. She saw the workaday world through a confessional grille, as a weevil through the hole he has gnawed in a nut. It might have opened to the thrust, that grille, if she had had the will, or if her husband had had the patience to teach her; but he had not, he thought too little of her brains.

Within, her heart was a stuffed chasuble continually repeating "Om, Om," with censers swinging and the tin cash-box clinking, making a sort of perpetual low mass in her soul—if she had a soul; but it was no soul, it was a dried leaf. It had once fluttered on the tree, but that was in spring; now it was winter. Daily events and catastrophes treading on each other's heels over that dried leaf made a faint crepitation and rustling, like a handkerchief wet with tears slipping into a high calico bosom, the prayer of the sacerdotal minister muttering smoke and incantations, the rustle of the assembly crossing itself and jingling rosaries at the name of the Father, or the slow beating of old sleepless blood on the pillow at night. Who can explain how superstition, proverbs, prejudices lay together, taking the place of sense in this simple old head? The face was wrinkled, blackened by age in the folds, but it hung together well, for the body was firmly moulded on the pattern of peasant ancestors bred to survive starvation, fireless winters and the scratching for crops in Irish tenant farms. But her pock-marked face folded most kindly when Joseph ate at table. The mother's liquid eyes saw that his hair was awry, his tie badly knotted. Her hand, already withered with thousands of household and maternal labours, stretched for the clothes-brush to rub the fluff from his ravelling sleeve. She moved towards Joseph with a fuller motion and she was more graceful with him, she had a faint charm, speaking to him, because he also was dried up and gnarled, but that much before his time. He was the solitary woody pear that sprouted late on the old tree, but he was the very seed of that tree. And she looks at him sentimentally, her blue eyes filmy. Heavens, he thought, comparing her and himself, how can so small a pear carry so grand a universe of suffering in its heart? The reason is, the pear had a thousand, thousand ancestors. In Joseph some of those ancestors, seed of other trees, appeared somewhat different, half-blotted out, by a freak of generation. He had musical undertones in his voice, a pale skin, unbroken patience. But he was dwarfed and seemed to scramble along the street even when he walked straight ahead; and his face was as narrow and feebly-lighted as the evening window of their weatherboard cottage.

Joseph looked at the clock, pushed his chair aside, and put on his hat. His father spoke for the first time.

"I'm not going in till eleven-thirty; Simpson's taking the morning shift. It's Wednesday, school half-holiday; that means there'll be students all over the Art Gallery this afternoon. Personally, I prefer it to sitting all the week, without seeing a fly, not a fly, but Simpson don't like them. He says they clutter up the place. I said to him, They're students, it's for them. It makes no difference, he said, they clutter up the place; it's nice when it's quiet. So on Wednesdays I've arranged to take the afternoons."

"Well, good-bye," said Joseph.

"Jo—your uncle Baguenault wrote to me this morning about your cousin Michael. Because you go out with him, your uncle reckons we see more of him than his own home. At any rate, he wants to know if any of your friends can get him into journalism, or as a proof-reader. He wants something quiet, because Michael can't stand the rough-and-tumble. Do you want a proof-reader or something?"

"No, I told you before, we don't want any one, we're practically overstaffed, and Baguenault wouldn't thank you for getting Michael into a place like ours. Besides, he's too old to begin in our game: and they've got lots in all the places to do proof-reading, doctors of philosophy, M.B.'s, engineers, lots without a job. A journalist—I don't know if he's got the style. At any rate, he knows more journalists than I do. The Folliots—"

"Not a rag like their sheet—a paper like the *Telegraph* or *Smith's*. Your uncle's an alderman, don't forget. In any case, you should try to get Michael away from that set of trouble-makers, it'll get him nowhere, and your uncle blames you. He says, Jo takes him into a set of rascally working-men, without home or religion, foreigners, and even Communists, from what I hear. Now, Jo, I don't like your uncle to have any basis for saying that, however wrong-headed he may be. I know it's not true, myself. You had better give up seeing Michael."

"I don't see him. And if I did—he's ten years older than me, and he's seen plenty more than me: it's rot. But I'll see if I can find out where he's staying if they're anxious. Though why his sister Catherine can't locate him better than me, I don't know; she knows the same crowd. But I know Uncle Jim, he doesn't know what it's all about. It's his fault that Michael and Catherine are always away from home. Anyhow, I've got to go."

"Have you spoken to your boss about your back pay yet?"

"Not this week."

"Tell him you've got to have it: two months—it's a disgrace. Suppose you weren't living at home?"

Joseph kissed his mother mechanically and went out. The gloom of the interior dropped from him. He walked smartly round the beach-path while the coral-trees along the shore, wrapped up in themselves, murmured without wind and dropped dead calyces on his hat. It was low water; a transparent wave two inches high rang its air-bells along the sand. The receding tide had left dark lines of flotsam along the beach. The poor children of the district and their mothers, with sacks in their hands, were raking through the deposit with their fingers, gathering coke, chips, and even vegetables thrown overboard in port from the vessels. Temperate sun and cool shadow divided the air. The sea-gulls paddled in and out of the water without a cry, and the fishermen pottered about sluicing and scraping their boats. During the night, the tide had risen over the path; there was a broken oar, a boathouse cradle, and part of the gates of a harbour-side bathing-pool. Miles away, south-west, between the side-drops of Bradley's Head and Shark Point, the city sat in miniature, glittering, without a trace of smoke. Blue-blooded spring was everywhere.

The ferry had not yet come in. Joseph waited outside the Italian fruit-shop at the end of the wharf, looking at a dead shark drawn up on the beach. It was responsible for the first bathing casualty of the season. It had torn off the buttocks and right leg of a bather the day before, and had been caught with a meathook on a clothes-line tied to a buoy, during the night; the bell on the buoy had rung for over an hour. The fishermen were all gathered there, with clusters of school-children and a barman from the hotel. They stood talking amiably and endlessly, like a collection of blue-bottle flies. As Joseph lounged on the railing, Black Jack, the negro fisherman, came up flat-footed, dropped a word in one of the groups and shrugged his shoulders towards the sea-cliffs. A fisherman in the group scratched his chin, hitched up his belt, and planting both broad bare feet on the beach-path spat into the sand. Then he strolled up the shady side of the short street leading to the cliff. There is the Gap, an indentation in the sea-wall, at the foot of which is a shale platform standing out in the waves, a place for fishing at low tide. The Gap is dangerous for shipping on a dark night, because it looks like an opening in the cliffs. Iron hooks in the rocks permit lines to be thrown down, and fishermen climb up and down in any weather. Here have been wrecks, and here is the favourite suicide spot of the city.

Two more fishermen plodded up the street some hundred yards after the first. The school-children pushed and jostled with upturned faces. Another fisherman left them and went up the street, walking on the same side, with his eyes on the ground, meditating and limping on his swollen bare foot, poisoned by a puncture from a stingray spine. The school-children milled round Black Jack, who was spinning out his tale with pleasure; a moment more, and all the little boys had left him and ran shouting towards the Gap, with the little girls at their tails. The pilot-ship gave a long shriek and started for the Heads. Soon they all appeared against the skyline on the edge of the Gap, motionless, except for a couple of boys pushing their way in to a better place, and all looked downwards at the sea. Amongst them stood three nuns in black. Black Jack sat on the shark's head and bit into his plug. It was a sort of dumb-show, the lazy men walking with heads dropped, their time- and weather-beaten faces, naturally sad and grotesque, now creased with interest as if they went to an entertainment, but not a new one.

The ferry whistled and Joseph had to run down the wharf. The school-children came tumbling down from the Gap, and a boy shouted to the deck-hand, "Hey, Nosey, a man committed suicide: there's a man over the Gap." The passengers looked round and then took out their papers and began talking cheerfully to their usual companions. A suicide at the Gap was a commonplace affair. Every one knew why a person committed suicide: if it was a man, because he couldn't pay his bills or had no job; if a woman, because she was going to have a baby. . . .

The ferries flock into Circular Quay each morning at eight and nine o'clock. The people burst out of the turnstiles in streams which go twisting uptown through the narrow streets. Some walk in the cool and some choose the sun. The office-boys in worn school jackets, the clerks in unpressed slop suits, the girls in light blouses and thin floating dresses, are already sweating and flushing with the heat. Near the quays is Lachlan Place, where there is a small triangular park, generally filled with sunlight, where all day starlings and occasional flocks of mountain magpies chatter in the trees. The place is cool and old, surrounded with old bonds, warehouses and shipping offices, in part let out for shops, and bounded on one side by a large sombre Government building.

Joseph came up the place this spring morning taking short steps and putting his feet down flat to hide the holes in his soles, with legs slightly apart so that the trousers-cuffs should not be further rubbed, but doing this as a matter of habit and all the time glancing up at the blue sky over the new bank buildings. Several times he bumped into people.

"Sorry," said he, and "Sorry," said they.

The air was still and warm. The red flannel which his mother still made him wear was too hot, and prickled. Already office-boys loitered in the park, and the tobacconist stood at the door of his shop fixing the awning and whistling, "Funiculi, funicula." The hyacinths, roses and sweet-peas in the florist's window reminded him of his mother's garden. The boxed luncheons, with sandwiches, a cheese tart and a piece of fruit, priced one shilling, seemed expensive delicacies to him who had, as usual, his hunks of bread and meat-paste wrapped in newspaper in his pockets.

A wide old doorway opened beside the tobacconist's shop, and over it was a name, white on blue, "Tank Steam Press, Ground Floor." The tobacconist owned the old single-storey building and rented out to several establishments the mouldy apartments of the ground and first floor. In the attic was a man who did heliogravure. The building had once been a private house. Its court was now a cart-dock and opened into the other street. Its first-floor bathroom at the head of the stairs contained the old water-closet, used by all the workers in the house, a gas-ring to make tea, and the usual broken chairs and out-of-date telephone directories. The distinctive smell of the building came from this closet and from the printing-ink.

Joseph asked the tobacconist for the key, and when he was told, "Old Williams has it," he bought a packet of used razor-blades for twopence. The tobacconist, who was also a barber, looked at his bristly chin and said:

"Shaving soap?"

"No, thanks; I have some."

Joseph walked through the old doorway, went by a staircase and entered the large airy double room occupied by the Press. He opened the glass back-door and moved about among the presses, curiously inspecting the jobs in their various stages, picking up a paper, looking through the bills on a bill-hook, putting his finger in the dust in the little glassed-in office of Chamberlain, the owner, and shutting off the stove, lighted by the cleaner, because the day was warm enough.

He hardly allowed himself a minute's glance into the sunlit place, yellow through the dark passage and door, blue through the high windows in front. He went about the room with the unhurried motions of one who has worked for a long time without pleasure at the same tasks in the same place. He carefully hung up his coat, grown yellowish, a schoolboy's Norfolk jacket with short sleeves, and wiped the band of his hat. The warm air drifted in through the street-door bearing odours from the park and the Botanic Gardens. His mother's garden and the yellow pumpkin flowers in the grass, thick with bees, swam back into his half-adjusted mind: there was a tall paling fence beside which he lay all Saturday afternoon.

"God, I wish I had a holiday: you can't go on for ever!"

He heard old Williams sluicing down the yard. He stood looking at a German printers' catalogue of papers and inks brought in since yesterday, no doubt by Mendelssohn, one of the printers. There was a great A in red, shovelling coal into a furnace-mouth made of a black M, and G in blue was marching off the page: "Wo gehst du, G?" He was going to get Mueller A. G. coal, although it didn't say so. It was a beautiful job done on an offset press on thick paper. If you had travelled like Mendelssohn, even as a tramp, even with I.W.W.'s, even riding the sleepers, you could find amusement in any hole and corner. You had to be a flathead like him to stay in one hole for seven years; and that without even a holiday. A mug.

Chamberlain drew up outside in his Bentley with a frightful whine of brakes. He ran into the office lugging a suit-case which split open in the doorway. Jo helped him put back his ties, underpants and so forth, all crushed in anyhow, and nothing freshly laundered. Chamberlain plumped the bag in his office, while Effie, his daughter, a childish coquette of seventeen, took off her fur coat and put a bunch of violets in a glass. Chamberlain hung up his hat beside Joseph's, damped his hair which always fell into his eye, and which he viewed now with love in a blighted jag of glass; he rolled his sleeves over his round hairless white arms, adjusted his eye-shade and called irritably:

"Williams, give my desk a wipe, can't you? Morning, Baguenault. Oh, morning, Mendelssohn. What have we ahead of us this morning?"

The girls were arriving and hanging up their hats.

"Finish printing and bind Jones's catalogue: cover in colours of the wire-netting magazine."

"Are the pages done?"

"No, we're waiting on the blocks that were sent back; we ought to change blockmakers, I've never got blocks on time," said Joseph.

"Ring them up: I'll ring myself. That's sabotage: I know that little red-faced Benson, the foreman, takes a pleasure in disobliging me, because I'm not a mason. I told him, I'll take my business away, last time. I'll break the contract: there's sufficient cause. Where's the telephone? I'll ring him up, I'll tell him . . ."

"If you want another lawsuit, but you're the lawsuit king," said Effie.

"They're coming right away," cried Danny, the boy of fourteen, who came in at this moment. "I remembered to call in on my way here." He had called in at the blockmakers as an excuse for being late.

"Good, good, that's the ticket; now, boys, whistle and ride. You ought to be through by about eleven, eh, Jo? You don't need me, do you?"

"I need help," said Joseph tartly; "Mr. Withers is out all day. There was no one here yesterday afternoon but Danny and Mendelssohn."

"I was damned busy yesterday afternoon. Clients, clients, complaints, complaints, all day. I often wish they'd be here one morning to see how the demon gets into the works; everything tuned to concert pitch and nothing working. Then, after they give an order or two, the very office-girls become experts in printing: should I change the paper, don't the blocks cost too much? I got orders too: I may get the business from a new publishing firm that Montagu knows. Little books of poetry, belles-lettres. The money's safe, because the authors pay for their own printing costs. Well, no cheques at any rate in this morning's mail, Effie? That's our style, isn't it? You've known me for seven years, Jo; you've seen me in my ups and downs. Money only flows to mercenary types, and I'm not that. There's more of the workman, artisan, artist, faber, in me. Well, we'll see each other through. And now, what are you waiting for? I don't know what those travellers do. Oh no, they don't need to produce any references, they're so smart, a week's trial will convince—only they need an advance on the first week's commissions. They must see I'm a soft-hearted duffer. Then, good-bye, it don't suit. If I only could spend all my time drumming up business, it would be different. There's something in me gives people confidence: it's that very lack of avarice I mentioned. I've never had a business relation for a long time where my partner didn't actually love me; they realise I'd do anything for them. But you can't be the whole works, 'The bo'sun, the cap'n, the midshipmite and the crew of the captain's gig'—you know the old song."

"Give it a breeze," said Effie.

"Put your lipstick away and do some typing."

Joseph's face had a stone-deaf expression.

"Let's see: what have you got there? the wire-netting magazine?"

The presses worked with a low grunting and soft click-click.

"No, we're waiting on the blocks."

"Of course, of course." Chamberlain came and stood by Joseph. "Yes, of course. How is that new ink? . . ."

Joseph said nothing. Chamberlain looked at him on top of the ladder loosening a screw in the paper-feeding rollers. It was the new press imported from England at a cost of about £4,500, and only allowed through the Customs because Chamberlain had agreed to give the pattern to a local engineer. It was cemented in the floor and stood in an oil-bath: it could turn out forty thousand impressions the hour at top speed. It was Chamberlain's pride and he had already based two overdrafts on it. Chamberlain watched Jo's expression, and anxiously repeated, "Eh?" Jo remained silent. Chamberlain frowned. Joseph climbed down the ladder, released a lever, and the bed of the press began to move indolently back and forth. Danny, the devil, seated in front of the machine, took a sheet or two as it settled in place, and then pulled the string which stopped the press.

"What is it?" asked Joseph calmly.

"Over-inked on the top right-hand block."

They went on for over an hour on the large press, making proofs and frittering away time, before it ran smoothly. Towards eleven, when Effie was making tea in the lavatory upstairs, Chamberlain, who had been trying to go through his accounts, came and stood beside Joseph and said, quite low:

"I must tell you, personally, that things are bad with us. I like to confide in my workmen; and then it concerns you. I'm trying to find a buyer; some one to run things and take the financial worry off my shoulders, to keep me as manager. . . . I'm the practical workman, nothing mechanical beats me, there's nothing in printing I don't know, but I'm beat by the banks, the mortgages, the interest: money should be free. Now, if any one comes and asks about our financial situation, don't say anything about the overdraft, and tell 'em business is boom-ing, because they always poke around amongst the workmen—see? But, of course, if another chief wanted to change round the staff I'd have nothing to do with it; there'd be no telling. But you live at home, Jo, don't you? So you're all right. And take my tip, a little change does no one any harm; it's no tragedy. You ought to get all the experience you can when you're young. If I were your age, well, never mind. But perhaps you're counting on buying me out, eh, Jo? You're a quiet one, you're a canny one?" He chuckled at the dig. Joseph got very pale.

"I have no money, and although I live with my people, I need a steady job like the others. We are poor; I need my money terribly bad, sir, joking apart." He blushed; his legs trembled so that he could hardly stand. If it came to giving them the sack now, with their pay two months in arrears, and so many out of work, he would not know what to do. In an instant of terror, he reviewed all his relatives and friends, all his possessions: he could not raise any money at all. He could not face the prospect of tramping the city, as he was, dressed like a tramp, and personally, far from engaging.

Chamberlain looked at him demurely.

"We're all poor, old boy; but I'll see what I can do this week. It's a bargain: any money that comes in we split *pro rata.*"

. . . Joseph's mind began to wander with the regular sound and the approach of lunch-time. He remarked to himself, "Contra audentior ito qua tua te fortuna sinet," a motto the priest had written for him in his prize at school, the only prize he ever got—one for handwriting. When he was alone as now, in the noise of the machines, in his room, on the boat amid the rush of wind and water, on Saturday afternoons lying in the grass, he liked to go over his little store of recitations. He had picked them up from the church service, from his Latin grammar at school, and from three little books bound in silk and stamped leather which his mother kept on the round table in the front room when visitors came for dinner. He had picked some up from Christmas cards and some from the title-pages of books. The great charm of his phrases, which were all in foreign languages, was the uncertainty of their meaning, the adumbrations and suggestions which hovered round them in his mind. Where he understood them, they had the same axiomatic standing as proverbs have for old women; and where he did not understand, they were abracadabra to show him he had power too, whenever he felt saddened by his smallness and weakness. He said now, "Labor omnia vincit."

He had spent innumerable long hours of his infancy alone, by the sea, among the bushes on the cliffs, staring at things from a distance, the fishing-boats like peanut-shells, the foam on distant bluffs, sea-gulls and sea-eagles deep in the sky. He had got used to talking to himself, and conversed only at odd intervals with poor and old-fashioned people, like the brothers at the school, the priest, his mother and father. Even when the little boys came together for catechism and skylarked round the church, he always stood aloof. The headmaster of the Catholic school refused to have any notions of modern science taught in the lower classes. Joseph, leaving school at twelve, moved all his life among old things; his Latin tags were even comforts to him, recalling those quiet, sad old days.

He had learned his catechism by heart easily. He loved music, resonant words, the greenish sunny light and shadows of his little hillside church, the wind as it passed outside in the grasses, the cricket which would begin to chirp and stop hearing a footfall on the road, the rattle of the milk-cart, the cry of a boy under the wall. He loved the Sunday masses, the respectable smiling people, the bustle of their clothes, the priest in his vestments and the repetition of the ritual that he knew so well. The ritual allowed its participants to enjoy the exaltation of inspiration, although they had none, as each phrase moved to its oft-rehearsed conclusion and the sacred words were born living on their lips. They were a second transubstantiation, the word becoming spirit. Different from his mother, who muttered her own prayers and plaints, he went through the service like a celebrant. Each moment of the mass perfectly absorbed the small amount of mental energy the quiet allowed him, and the end left him peaceful, quiescent, in a state of grace. The confessional purified him and made it possible for him to live without thinking at all. . . .

. . . Now while he worked with his hands, back at the machine, his mind floated out over the harbour and wove invisible skeins in the invisible fine air. He was busy fitting together his future like a jig-saw puzzle. He thought of sailing outside the heads and going to the old countries, where the morning sun gilded domes, palaces, royal parks and hives of cities, bigger ports, and where men had a history that looked through millenniums. He looked at the ugly letters on the yellow-and-blue cover of the magazine, and saw between them the bright features of an elzevir Utopia. Why, he was a man, it was not so bad. As the years go on one gets older, one is not so stupid as before; every one is out for himself, some predestined to high and low life, grouches only make it worse for themselves, and the poor in spirit inherit the kingdom of Heaven. So one graduates without knowing it into the adult world; mere living makes a man wise. The trouble we have had is not as bad as that we shall see before we die, so we must be prepared for it with a stiff upper lip. But Joseph wondered if it would be possible to stow-away, or get a job as steward on a ship. This had never occurred to his sleeping seaside brain before. There it came again, the mirage which leads people from country to country. His future was a procession of days, laying down line after line of clear print, with a few errors, no doubt, each year a sheet sidling into place and followed by others from the press of the Lord. And the whole printing-world is not like this miserable workshop. There are giant workshops with hundreds of men, artists, engravers, lithographers, electric etchers, superb lights blazing like suns in the roof, workers shut off in gauze covers, benches yards long covered with clean trays of brilliant cast lead, linotypes by the half-dozen. There are giant buildings for the printing of books and newspapers, where the lights burn all night, as if in a palace, and reporters and photographers run in in shoals; where the news goes in towards the editor through circles of decreasing diameter of rewrite men, the seven spheres of editing, and runs out again through the corridors of the monstrous newsprint machines, through which printers wander as through a forest. There are hundreds of kinds of printing-works—no industry in the world is so varied. Is it possible that he will stick for ever in one wretched place, where one learns nothing and is maltreated? . . .

At lunch-time, in the park, Joseph read the newspaper wrapping round his lunch while he ate. In this way he always got the news, although a few days or even a month late. Presently he unwillingly drew out his algebra book and worked through the examples set for the evening class. At night, if he had any difficulty in getting to sleep, he resolved $(a+b+c)^2$ in his head, and always found himself falling asleep before it was done; and he more often nodded with sleep than acquiescence in his night-class.

He was now joined by Baruch Mendelssohn, an American born of European parents, a young man a little over five feet in height, with a white skin, lively brown eyes, and a black stubble springing all over his round cheek. The excessive heat of the advanced spring on an empty stomach made him sick. When he sat down, Joseph observed large tears balancing themselves on his eyelids. Baruch did not wipe them away, but closed his eyes so that the tears ran down his cheeks and dried off in the sun. He opened his eyes unashamed.

"Sick again?" asked Joseph.

Baruch nodded. One would have thought that he did not intend to speak: not Joseph, who knew him. Joseph waited, with eyes roving in the distance, his ears open. Baruch opened his mouth and the words tumbled out:

"What a *fantasque* economic system! We all stand about helpless waiting for great Jupiter to descend in overalls on the stage and plaster his bricks into their courses; in the meantime, we act like common clay. Hum! you know the parables? The eldest son of the world goes off voluntarily and keeps pigs and lives on husks. When he decides to come home and get a square meal, his father wants to give him a veal cutlet, but his brother, who's been running things all the while and expected to see brother cut off, sulks. Gosh, what a morning! Chamberlain's not a bad egg, you know, but his weakness is vicious and . . . say what you will, he indulges his fantasies at our expense. A man goes mad but his wits are still with him, he knifes some one else: he hasn't forgotten how sharp a knife is. However weak-minded an amiable man is, he buys his own groceries first."

"It's his business," objected Jo, "he put the money into it."

"A philanthropist," exclaimed Baruch irascibly, "look at you! You can afford to keep Chamberlain in Corona Coronas. You pay for a fur coat for Effie without turning a hair: but you don't buy one for mother —that simply shows you're unfilial and hate your family. You save your pennies, don't you, Jo, to give a penny on Saturdays to the first beggar you see, and to put something in the box on Sundays? You can afford also to support the Church of Rome. You see a business so prosperous that it can afford to keep hundreds of square miles of uncultivated land, hundreds of giant buildings of the finest stone, richest workmanship, with priceless treasuries, laces and coloured windows, with paintings, carvings and woodwork, enough to say masses to all eternity for all the souls on earth, so rich that it can keep regiments of idle, big-footed lumpkins to tinkle bells and recite a few Latin words that you know as well as they, and has conveys of devout females to work for nothing all their lives, scrubbing, laundering, teaching, without a decent bite of food or a piece of soft linen to cover themselves; you see an institution that conducts prosperous businesses, has printing-presses of its own, ships at sea, casinos and expensive schools, that has laws enacted to protect its interests, that pays no taxes and levies an irregular toll on millions of people, mostly ignorant and wretched. And what do you do? You save your money to put something in the box on Sunday. Yes, the poor are charitable, the poor are religious, the poor have bottomless purses. They buy gold dishes and gold telephones for the Pope and fill the Vatican with priceless marbles that they will never in their lives see or appreciate. They keep silk-robed youths, fat and rosy, singing songs and learning pseudo-history, in all the proud seminaries of Rome. They keep Cardinals' mistresses and Pope's nephews on the Seven Hills. They buy satin banners for Santa Maria Maggiore and a broom for the Scala, possibly Santa, and before they pray for their own relatives in distress, pray Heaven to protect the Pope, some black-bearded dago who doesn't even know they exist and doesn't give a damn. Does the Pope keep beggars, or the Vatican police hand out alms? Not on your tintype! But you do, Jo. And you likewise give money on Hospital Saturday, and also, I believe, for the missions in China. There's a world-embracing philanthropy for a poor man who doesn't have enough to sole his own boots. What characters we all have, the poor! They tell you poverty keeps you from temptation; it certainly does: but what you need, my poor friend, is a little temptation. Items: pride, in belonging to a dominant class; covetousness, in respect of a new pair of pants; lust, enough to make an appointment with a pretty girl; wrath, when you find you're trod on; gluttony, for a beefsteak; envy, of the bounding health of rich children; sloth, the lying all day on a yellow beach staring into vacancy and getting brown. But the Church has cleansed your heart of the seven deadly sins for working-men. You have pints of character, so much that you're scarcely fit for human conversation, Jo. Who forgive the judge who gaols the Socialist?—the poor. The Socialist's disturbing the natural order, they say, he's envious. Who admire the state plug-uglies in their uniforms and lick the hand that snaps on the iron bracelet?—the poor. He's to protect us, you say,— your pocket-books, your safety-vaults, no doubt. Who tremble when they enter a private bank with portal twenty feet high made out of white marble, dug out, shipped and put up by workmen without a second pair of socks? Why, we do: the poor do. It's stupendous, we say, how rich he is! And if the banker should pass us on his way to his automobile, we respect the chauffeur's servile salute, and feel as if Jove had just walked that way. And our imagination opens out into innumerable white marble halls, hung with curtains, with bits of bronze on bits of marble, where tea is served on relatively infinitesimal tables to relatively minute ladies with neat hair. Our soul yearns over all that. Yes, it does; and your precious church, with its yawning vaults and thunderous doors, where you may walk, but may not talk or laugh, has given you since the cradle a holy respect for clinkers, the gold, the jewels, cash and plate, that it would take me years to clean out of your head. But here," cried Baruch, "in this country where you are technically all free, where you all vote and think yourselves political governors, where the land is free and you have no complications, if it weren't for your crazy bounties to protect what won't grow cheaply and your tariffs as high as the moon to protect the uneconomic industries of cheap capitalists, you should live in an earthly paradise: you shouldn't have to think of any other heaven. And what do we see? Beggars, tramps, thousands of workless in misery . . .

. . . Jo sat silent and doleful, perhaps touched by this discourse. Baruch thought he found it dull and tried to amuse him.

"But it isn't an economic relation at all, ours here, it's a connubial one. We're married to Chamberlain, or we're his concubines. He pets us, snarls, he sees to the general supplies and we get no pin-money at all: I am convinced that he looks at it as housekeeping. We can always eat, he says. He keeps Bovril in the cupboard and occasionally stands one or other of us to a meal. But I object to living in a harem, first, from natural jealousy, second, because I carefully surveyed myself in the glass this morning and I can certify I'm not an odalisque."

"You are right," said Joseph, "and my father is bothering me about it too. He's getting old now and he gets fretful. It's pretty thick."

"Thick? Yes, wait though, listen: what a man! This morning he wrote to his mother. He showed me the letter, being proud of his naturally eloquent style: 'Dear Mother,—As I write to you from a foreign land, I look out of the window at the bay leaves and think—' 'Bay leaves?' I said, looking at the fig tree. He was really hurt. 'What does it matter?' he says; 'she would like to think I was looking at bay leaves: there was a bay tree in the garden at home.' 'But,' I said, 'what foreign land are you speaking of? Isn't your mother English and you too?' 'Certainly,' he said, quite nettled, for he is proud of his phrases, 'but it seems a foreign land to her: she thinks there are hundreds of blacks running round the streets.' Oh, I had to laugh: he is a human after all, although such a dumbbell. To improve my opinion of his learning, he offers me an old copy of *Les Chouans*. 'You read French,' he says loud, to that the paper-carter waiting in the hall can hear, 'you might like to look at this,' he says: 'what does it mean, "Les Chouans," some sort of natives, isn't it?' 'Mr. Chamberlain,' said I, 'let's be vulgar —and frank. Before the mind some matters, before letters, let's start with bread, reversing St. John by a simple process of the oesophagus. When are you going to let us have the dough, the specie, the shekels? We'll take it in any currency or form, bullion, Treasury Bills, Argentine bonds, George III. pennies, new mint, anything but I O U's or tram-tickets. . . . Otherwise, Chamberlain,' I said to him, without making any bones about it, 'we'll strike and we'll put up a notice outside saying why, and then good-bye to your buyer and the bank'll come down on you.' I wouldn't, of course; but we certainly should have struck before. At any rate, next Saturday, the 20th inst., you, Mr. J. Baguenault, will get one month's arrears."

"Go on!" said Joseph, flushing.

"Yes, does that make a difference?" Baruch smiled with satisfaction, and related the incident again in different terms, with varying illustrations and pithy comparisons. . . .

Joseph opened his mouth once or twice, like a fish taking in air, as reflections of words came into his mind and involuntarily contracted the muscles of speech, but by now he had no ideas at all. He felt that there must be holes in any of the traditional remarks he usually brought out and he said nothing. Baruch had come to a stop. Joseph recalled himself with a tremor and said:

"Oh, really, it's awfully decent of you: thanks. I never know what to start with, when I ought to talk to a fellow: I always say the wrong thing."

"Come down to tin-tacks; that's the right thing. It's natural to me, for I am a Jew: we are realists."

Joseph smiled to hear the familiar phrase "for I am a Jew." It meant that Baruch had entered an intimate train of thought. Joseph looked down at his algebra book, and shyly showed the examples, hoping that Baruch would do them for him. But Baruch explained the problem for him, choosing his words simply, glancing up quickly through Joseph's glasses on which the sun shone brightly, to see if he understood the reasoning, patting his arm, threshing out fine seeds of thought from the golden harvest in his head, till his head presently overflowed again, and he sat chin-deep in a flood of exegesis which bewitched the pupil, his eyes, voice and body mobile with the love, wit and understanding of his nature.

"Grasp this and this, and you have invaded the whole question. More than that, you are on the road for the capital city, you can take the kingdom, you border on all that is known in science. Not so much is known, don't think it, that you can't make your way. The body of science is full of holes, ragged and clear-obscure like a moonlit ghost; but it is there, even if in the moonlight, even if a phantom of a shape that has been. If you make a stab at it, you'll find the stuff it's made of."

Joseph laughed. "You put things in such a way, nothing is serious to you, but then you have the brains; nobody ever thought me smart. Everything is really hard for me."

"Joseph, this is so simple. Here, you have a simple 4—four you have known since you were a baby and counted four fingers, four connie-agates, four sails in the bay; even savages of the most primitive sort have a word for 4. But that is their ultimate, and you, you can count to 10,000 and more with ease. You can multiply, divide, take the square root and calculate prime numbers! Why, your world, by that fact, is infinitely more complex, has many more dimensions. You understand already, without knowing you understand, thousands of relations that savages can't. But take 4, a simple thing, a final thing. You can begin to philosophise about 4—thus, there are four right angles all the same to a square, never more nor less. Fortresses and palaces, railway lines, skyscrapers, are built through confidence in that principle. Look, doesn't printing consist of ems and ens, simple measures? Then, with +

and —, there you have a very important idea. A man talks. 'I like this, I don't like that, Rembrandt is a great artist, Velasquez is a rotten painter, El Greco puts one eyebrow higher than the other, Boucher represents the corruption of the court, Boudin paints the light that is on sea and land.' Don't be alarmed, that is only + and —; he makes a song about it, but that is all it is: that is aesthetic criticism, for the most part. If you read the paper, you see (and you get bored with it), 'France has so many submarines, England has less, Germany has armed forces disguised as sporting clubs, Switzerland is swollen with the world's gold deposits, Russia is spending millions on foreign propaganda,' and whether they'll go to war or not, with whom, for what, where, when, it's only a question of plus or minus, guns, wheat, bars of gold, soldiers, markets. Thus: 'the French loan went up to-day'— that's plus a few votes given to the Conservative Party in a by-election; 'the Prime Minister is expected to appear in the birthday honours'— that's plus a lordship and minus a party; 'riot in Austria'—that's bread plus three groschen. Even in the crimes, when you read, for example, 'woman kills man who jilts her,' you should only read it as 'woman minus a regular income, gentleman minus his mortgages.' My ambition has sometimes been to issue a newspaper like that, but it would be suppressed; the professions, the whores, judges, journalists, usurers, kings and commons would be putting a tailor-made halter round my short neck. If the clouds should roll away from poor hearts there'd be too sudden a change to suit the gentry. Pray don't think mathematics is a mystery, Jo, it's the bunk that's obscure."

Joseph, surprised, gay, much agitated by the oddities of the young man, stubbornly fought out each problem, confusing and disentangling in turn mathematical conventions, stumbling over the conjugation of an exact idea of multiplicity with an unknown, mystified, but suddenly breaking open the rock so that understanding gushed out and watered earth barren and virgin. For a moment his eyes were opened, a pure stream broke through into the light, a new diagenetic principle began to work and he became aware of science, dimly, palely, because the light passed still through the clerestories of superstition; but it was as a ray of sunlight he had once seen crash through a memorial window in the village church, when he had wandered there with Michael, as a little boy, showing up a middle-aged mystery and the rusty black of devout kneeling women, a light even to the blind.

Baruch left Joseph to post a letter to an uncle in America. Joseph lay on his back in the sun and fell into a pleasant doze. He heard the rustle of papers being folded and went back with the workers to his workshop, blinded and irrational with the heat. The sun motes hopped about relentlessly all the afternoon, and it was true that his mind was a disk, as they often show to students in the University. The presses clanked a crazy refrain, "Chirk-chank-cho, Chirk-chank-cho, Chirk!" in a sort of mechanical lockjaw Choctaw chinwag in which they conversed among themselves all the afternoon. Graham, a commercial traveller, new to the business, whom Chamberlain had taken on as a freak, that week, brought in the copy for a handbill:

University Extension Courses.
A Course of FIVE LECTURES will be given on
LIGHT
by Professor A. MUELLER in the Physics Lecture
Theatre at the University, Camperdown.
Single lecture, 1s. Course, 4s.

and so forth.

Baruch called Joseph over.

"Like to go myself; would you go, Jo?"

"It's too much, and I wouldn't understand."

"Tom Winter sometimes gets tickets sent down to Communist Hall. I'll see if I can get a couple from him or the Folliots. The first lecture you can get deadhead tickets to attract a crowd. They reckon they get for the course a fifth of the first crowd."

Joseph sighed. He knew that Baruch would try to drag him to the lot, that this invitation to the first lecture was a trap. He was so tired and lectures were so dry; he would try to find some way of crying off before the evening. It was best. He looked at himself between his hands. The sole of one boot was attached by a hairpin, the worn knees of the trousers showed the colour of his pale skin when he sat down. His hat was an old one of his cousin's. The rest of his attire fell in with these items and produced a sort of harmonious costume, the uniform of misery. The children of Fisherman's Bay shouted after him, "Joey, Jo, Jo, 'Ullo, Jo," when he went past in the evenings. He knew what this song meant; it meant, "You are rubbish thrown out by men, and we are allowed to play with you, no one even has a salvage interest in you." The Clown of the Universe had produced a man in his image. The accumulated misery, shame, hunger and ignorance of centuries straddled the path as he advanced against the evening sun, and they shrieked with laughter to see his hat getting taller in the new lamplight and his coat more uncouth as his shadow fell backwards towards them. He was a stranger. It was marked in his face, which, of a dingy pallor, by some effect of skin or reflection appeared with the masterly distinction of an etched face, it was grotesque but more real, more human than the high-nosed, red-skinned, clapper-voiced, mussel-mouthed faces around him. It shone by the quality of its pain, incongruity and isolation. In certain men the flesh is as expressive of emotion as the eyes and voice. The flesh is most responsive to passion; it shows then how thin is the garment the blood puts on, and shines with a white lucent glare in a moment of agony.

Thinking of his debts at home, his clothes and the children, his face now took on this pallor of excitement, which Baruch remarked:

"Baguenault, you remind me of some one come of an old family: you have the colour of a race worn thin."

"I have."

"You mean, the human family is old?"

"No, my cousin Michael Baguenault told me some long tale, that my father and his had French ancestors. In France they were Huguenots and were persecuted there. Some fled to England, some to Ireland; those in Ireland became Catholics because they remained in the south and were very poor. My father says the story is not true, the tables of genealogy show that the last of the French family in Ireland died in 1808, and since then there is a complete blank. It doesn't make any difference, not to me; but Uncle Ben, Michael's father, spends a good part of his time trying to work it out because he says there must be still estates in France belonging to the old family. Uncle Ben found out that his wife is descended from an illegitimate daughter of Charles II, and he has the tree hanging on the door of his clothes-closet. My aunt pretends to hate it, but she shows it to you in secret. That beats me; don't you think it's childish?"

"Charles II has been an unconscionably long time dying, that's a fact," answered Baruch, but he looked at Joseph eagerly. "Wonderful," he thought, "antiquity is in the blood of the Jews and in his, that is why I am drawn to him. He is the concentration of the troubles the family has known: his mother's ageing womb and the long-memoried germ made this masterpiece in her late born."

III

Reflections of Joseph in shop-windows.

. . .A flush of joy went over the workshop; they looked at the office where the money was being counted. Presently, Chamberlain came round and paid them all. Each one felt against his thigh the little wad of paper, the weight of the loose coins, and at the end of the afternoon they were whistling and chaffing. Joseph walked up Pitt Street with Baruch, to find some little place to eat. Baruch was talking politics, but Joseph noticed how splendidly the shop-windows were lighted, how richly dressed in crumpled silk and polished ashwood. There was an inlaid tortoiseshell cigarette-case that he stopped and stared at dully, for the pleasure of looking at expensive things while he had money in his pocket. Baruch came unquietly alongside and peered at the objects in the window without interest. There were things Joseph had never noticed before, or had not noticed for years, he thought, "gossamer" shirts for the heat, blue and buff silk underwear with pleated waists. There were suits with satin revers "For the Evening Wedding," "For the Afternoon Wedding," "For the Evening Reception." He examined with surprise the styles of waistcoats, corded, white, black, satin, brocade, piqué.

"That's absurd, isn't it?" he said severely to Baruch, pointing to a waistcoat with revers of satin.

They both halted before the readymade tailors to compare the cut and patterns of the £2, 2s. suits; there were others at £2, 17s. 6d. "made-to-order with two fittings." Joseph looked out of the corner of his eye at the crowd passing him and studied the styles of suit worn by other small men; for instance, a sac suit rather neatly cut at the waist. A blonde girl in an organdie blouse and high heels tapped along beside the sac suit neatly cut at the waist. And shoes, with a small foot; he could look well in a rather classy pointed toe: as to the heels, perhaps they could raise them a little. There were hats, "merino-felt" and "pure hare felt"; but he knew a man in a hat factory who would get him one at cost price. That would come after. Oh, to spend it all in one splurge and turn out the next morning, fresh, clean, neat, a three days' wonder for the boat; a gag for the mouths of the little skipping girls. That was the rub, in fact; they would only laugh again to see him trying to conceal himself; Jo, for the boat, was that seedy dwarf that he now saw walking with him through the window-mirrors.

Baruch kept on talking, glancing quickly to see what kept Jo's attention straying: he once, even, with kind courtesy, dragged Jo to a shop-window and said:

"That's what I could do with, a badger brush with a silver handle: they never wear out. And look at that razor with the tortoiseshell handle: wouldn't we be the beaux of Lachlan Place?"

He then rapidly took Joseph from the window and plunged into his political discourse again. And Joseph, from long habit, said:

"Yes, yes, of course I do, you bet, too right," and made affirmative noises when the cadence of the voice required it. He quizzed the crowd. What harum-scarums they were, the skinamalink office-boys, making their fingers squeak on the glass, hurrying home to mother's Irish stew. A father with two little children all looked in at a fine drawing-board stretched with white paper; above were snapshot Kodaks, decorated with cherry ribbons. As Jo's step unconsciously lagged, Baruch hurried him on. There were old men by themselves carefully comparing the prices of shoes in half-closed shoe-shops; there was a huge "boot-emporium" for the populace, decorated with hideous cartoons in green and red, of tramps with red noses and their toes out of their shoes, and women in laced boots with bursting breasts and big behinds.

"I'll get a pair of socks," said Joseph, seeing a man with an open case at the corner of a side-street, "and to-morrow I'll get a pair of shoes."

"Let's get them here." Baruch stopped in the middle of a period and pushed him hastily forward.

"Are they good value, do you think, for a shilling?" asked Joseph.

"Yes, yes, at that price, they're all the same. You know what you're getting, don't you? They can't rob you at that price, it's an advertisement of quality, that price. There you are, take that pair." He hurried him on, and Joseph for a minute paid attention to Baruch's remarks, while the paper bag swished in his pocket.

Splendid were the silver shops, with their iron grilles half-up already. Grotesque but beautiful baskets in silver, receptacles of all sorts whose use he could not imagine, all decorated with scrolls, flourishes, chrysanthemums, cherubs, all punched out and pressed in, chased, embossed and pierced; fruit-stands, with lace doyleys and wax fruits, etched drinking glasses and champagne glasses, goblets, carafes, great silver dishes, heaps of fruit-knives with mother-of-pearl handles; signet-rings, mourning-rings, wedding-rings, diamond rings, studs, necklaces, magnificent opals like fire and milk lying on white satin pads, Arabian bangles for the girls. Inside the lights shone brilliantly on the cases, the polished wood counter, the purple velvet necks decorated with pearl necklaces, and the numerous mirrors. A small old white-headed man was there, noting the people who stopped outside, and a dandy in glazed collar and lacquered hair kept passing out and in of a swinging glass door with trays.

"What do you think he gets for that job?" asked Joseph.

"Oh, he's probably the son: you have to be introduced, and you learn the trade," responded Baruch in a breath.

"And pearl-handed revolvers," said Joseph in surprise.

"Yes, they exist outside the novelettes," smiled Baruch.

Joseph was embarrassed to see a young couple hesitating before a bedding shop, brilliantly lighted, where an automatic demonstrator was showing the advantages of a pillow containing a fine spring. How can they look and not blush? he said to himself, in his modesty. In fact, the young man brusquely took the arm of the lingering girl and moved on. Joseph breathed more freely. There in a chemist's shop was boricated vaseline, the sort he preferred, and a lotion for the hands, guaranteed to whiten them. His own had been very white, but now they were always dirty. There was a double tooth-paste guaranteed to whiten even difficult teeth, but he had no need of that, for his own teeth were beautiful. Weighing what he needed and did not need, he felt how round and complex was his personality. He almost felt the ebb and flow in the markets, the jostling in the streets, the polishing of counters by elbows. Supply and demand—Or what was Baruch saying about supply and demand? Something, but never mind, he'll tell it again some other day. There were pearl-pills for virility, with a diagram of the male organism showing a red line from the brain to the small of the back, and there were very odd rubber things, perhaps for women, perhaps for childbirth. Those things were the drawback with getting a wife, of course. He did not like these things, and they went on. At last Baruch gave up.

"You're window-shopping, Joseph; it's the most satisfying and least expensive. You've never done it before. Strange is the influence of Marx on character."

"How do you mean?"

"Come along in and have an ice-cream soda," replied Baruch, and they went into one of the numerous Italian fruit-shops, attractive with their glass windows full of glass shelves and fruit, cool drinks, ice-creams, sundaes, frosteds and what not. They each had a peach-melba: Baruch was a sweet-tooth, Joseph had not remembered that peach-melbas were so good. Afterwards, Baruch walked more slowly and attentively discussed every window Jo looked at. "Look at the nightie in pink silk: that whole outfit costs more than we could save in a year. Don't you wonder how the girls do it? Or the boys." In the other window were babies' clothes. Two hardy girls passed and tittered.

"Oh, you naughty boys," said one; and the other, "No, silly, they're two young fathers out shopping." The girls disappeared into the crowd. The boys blushed a little, laughed and went on.

They reached the less-frequented regions, they turned out of the shopping districts down by Paddy's Market and the Technical High School. Most of the shops were closed. Three young men with hats in their hands played leap-frog outside a closed bar. A pool of blood on the pavement, with several clots, made them look around: opposite were two streets in which were houses of ill-fame—a fight between bucks, a girl having a baby, a bleeding nose? They walked on, the light gradually becoming less, crossing and recrossing the road, dodging the little traffic. They were fatigued now. Baruch had walked for some minutes without talking, looking very pale, limping slightly. They stopped to breathe outside a lolly-shop brightly lighted, in which were purple, mauve and red boxes of chocolates with gilt filigree paper. Going with one of those under your arm to a red-plush parlour, a daguerreotyped aunt in a red-plush frame, to a girl: looking at the boxes Joseph had an affection for all girls. A doorman smoking his pipe, with a thick lined face, looked through the boys as they passed heavily. His red-braided coat was open down to the stomach, he slumped on his seat, and his polished big boots were unlaced; his wife played solitaire, through the machine-lace curtains, on a red fringed tablecloth. A well-dressed girl came up with them and passed them; she hesitated, looked at Joseph and walked on a few steps ahead, the high heels tapping impatiently, marking time. She turned down a side street; who knows? They have to earn their living. How did she know Joseph had just been paid? A broken ostrich-feather, pale blue and grey, lay on the pavement under an open window on the second floor; in the window was a pink blind drawn, on which a woman's head-dress darkly moved. They passed a lighted entrance, with polished handle, varnished door, and two whitened steps. Baruch was silent. Who knows? thought

Joseph. This is my city, where I was born and bred, I cannot be lost here, nothing can happen to me. I am Joseph Baguenault of Fisherman's Bay. I know the stones, the turnings; I know where the Markets are, there to the right and behind.

The lights were on dimly to light a little the interior dusk and still to admit what remained of the daylight; the street was not yet that covered way which is endless and mysterious at night, but the city had become warm, hospitable, a city of hearths and yellow-silk lighted interiors; spoons clapped on soup-plates, spoons clanked in cups, sugar-basins revolved. An old man out walking with a cane looked friendlily at the two boys, with the friendliness of a Biblical comment, "Look, what you are experiencing the prophets experienced in their adolescence two thousand years ago." He went stooping on. I am young, thinks Jo. This is what the old man intended him to think. The street-lights were switched on and glowed warmly in a slight thick dusk, as if to prove conclusively that the day had knocked off work and gone home. Near an old garden, he noticed how the trees had taken on an inhuman air with something wild in them, as lions have, sitting unreconciled in the back of their cages licking their paws, in the zoo. He heard again the tapping behind him of the nocturnal prostitute just beginning her beat: fresh, odorous, with shining curls and a big bow on her neck and frilled elbows, pretty, dainty. He smiled unconsciously as she tapped with vanity past him. More soft steps and, rubbersoled, came the lamplighter who had just got through the district of gas-lamps. Tea was preparing everywhere; night had begun.

"I am hungry," said Joseph.

Two old dowdy women huddling to each other, both thin, beaked, satin-hatted, and hatpin-eyed, passed him and looked approvingly at him because he was shabby, dull and modest. Joseph, too, felt comforted; his life had been passed amongst old shabby women. They would do him no harm; they would make tea for him.

IV

Baruch at home.

. . . Baruch lived in a room on the fourth floor back, in a side street in Woolloomooloo Flat, not far from the old public school. His window commanded the Inner Domain, the Art Gallery, the spires of St.

Mary's Cathedral and the Elizabeth Street skyline. On the right hand, as he looked from his window, were the wharves of the German, Dutch, Norwegian and Cape lines. In the backyard was a wood-and-coal shed covered with creepers, pumpkins, old tires, kites'-tails, buckets and old scrubbing-brushes. There was a clothes-line across the yard, on a clothes-prop, and upon the line the tenants' garments, washed by the woman on the ground-floor, appeared in regular succession throughout the week. There was in the house a bachelor Government clerk and Government medical officer, a school-teacher with his wife and two children, a navvy, a bartender, a junior draughtsman in the Lands Department, and a widow with a young child. The house backing on to theirs was only three storeys high. A cheap chop-suey restaurant occupied the ground-floor, its private assembly rooms the first floor, while the rooms above were for sleeping and for letting out. A couple of ladders reached from the windows of these upper floors to the roofs of lean-to sheds and outhouses. This house was usually very quiet, although lights appeared at the windows at all hours of the night. On Saturdays and Sundays the whole neighbourhood swarmed with children, and everybody was out of doors with sleeves rolled up. Tiny living-rooms with Japanese screens, fans and bead curtains, and reeking of bugs and kerosene, with bric-à-brac, vases, wilting flowers and countless rags and papers, sent out their heat and animal odours and old dust at seven in the evening when the hot day had gone down into the violet twilight, a deceitfully shady moment promising cool, but bringing in the torrid night. Everywhere couples lounged about, the waists encircled, the lips together; henna Titians, peroxide blondes, and uncoloured women faded beneath their hair still rich and young; women blowzy and painted, worn and tired, with crow's-feet and unequal powder, fanned their bursting bosoms or their empty sacks of blouses, as they slumped in rickety easy-chairs at their doors.

The doors opened directly into the sleeping and living-rooms and alone admitted air. Little boys argued outside the windows, shrieking and punching.

"My mother is not a whore."

"She is! Why isn't she?"

"No, Willy's mother isn't; she always has the same blokes, and she has only three."

"Yes, and I know who they are; a thin little bloke with freckles and . . ."

"Shut up or I'll gi' y' a lift under the lug."

The onlookers whooped during the set-to that followed. Some father or mother, full of ire, separated their darling from the heap of wriggling boys. There were protests, but the boys trailed off, their passions suddenly cooled, and ready in a quarter of an hour or so to begin all over again, apropos of the weather, a cricket hero, or Deadwood Dick. The lamps were lighted. The dwellings on the borders of the hot asphalted pavement were holes in which moved dimly a world of heaving bosoms, gasping mouths, fanning arms. There were visible black-socked feet and bare feet in slippers, bare arms starting upwards from a bush of black hair at the armpit; locks "straight as candles" hung wet and tangled, hairy men's breasts gaped in the vees of open workshirts. The oil-lamps or gas-jets lighted corsets and stockings carelessly thrown on beds, discoloured with sweat and dirt. The rancid breeze blew in from the wharves with the smell of weeds grown on the piles, beer from the saloons, rotten vegetables from the garbage-tins. There came the clanking of winches at ships' sides, and the fitful songs of men at the waterfront. The last cries of children came from the old streets by the Plunkett Street school or from the other side, where they were dashing up into the rank grass of the Domain to wrestle, smother their giggles, lie on their backs, tell inane tales, sing parodies of songs, and contemplate the high southern constellations through the sensuous summer evening.

The neighbourhood is interesting. One Sunday morning an irritable Italian chased a compatriot through Baruch's backyard with an axe, during a slight difference over Angelina, wife of the first. Sometimes coloured boxers, cheerfully dressed, paraded past with belles of the neighbourhood, and there was a stream of girls, Australian and Italian, large, bright-coloured, buxom, with high heels and transparent blouses. Opposite Baruch's back window, poor Chinese, sailors and loafers could be seen paying attention to females in the chop-suey gambling and lodging-house.

The morning sun rose clear over the wharves, and the evening sky, with its head dark and its scarves of colour, looked like an Italian woman with an orange in her hand.

There was scarcely any furniture in Baruch's room, but on the small pine table were papers for drawing, and inks. There he sat early in the evening, breathing seriously over some small black-and-white design, the margin scribbled with faces, legends and monograms. But it was just as likely that he would be miserably stretched out on his bed in his outdoor clothes. The rarity of his bursts of energy, due to his thin purse and bad food, seemed to syllabicate the sentence of a hopeless fate. He had a wide and wandering vision which showed him all kinds of miseries more than physical, the self-deception of vanity unapplauded, drudgery unrewarded, the mind which for recompense kneels to the tintinnabulating priesthood, the symbolist, sick and sunless for ever, the tempestuous who leap from brink to brink and the thin ambitious who wrench their hearts out to put one idea on foot in their lifetime, and those who are for ever in the green-sickness of an unrequited love or desire, and those who work out new-fangled systems to detect fate in her workings, those who are swollen with pride and those who creep in their dejection. He was so wretched to see these people swarming around him, with all these evils added to their burden of poverty, that he often fell into a fever, and this idea was with him, day and night, that he was obliged to relieve them in some way. But he hardly knew in what way. He lived by choice among the sordid southern lives of the native and immigrant poor to get himself impregnated with this fever so that it would never leave him. He suffered at all this misery, but he suffered less in the heart of it, because he thought he was nearer to understanding it and to solving it. He knew by heart the foetid rooms, eyes opening on littered streets, heavy wombs, market-gardeners' carts trailing a cabbage smell, moustaches washed in beer, working-men's tramcars rattling out to brown dusty suburbs, Alexandria, Redfern, Waterloo, pawnshop windows advertising their unredeemed pledges, grimy hands, sweat, unfolded papers relating the latest murder, wrinkles, hands with swollen veins, and eyes thick with the circular lucubrations of the dulled mind trying to escape.

There seemed to him to gleam above all this a city as on an adamant island, where the erudite lived and put the world to shame, told the truth to princes, and wrote tracts to enlighten the slaves. It is true, of course, that they write them to enlighten the poor, but they are usually sold at prices ranging from 10s. 6d. to £2, 2s., and the poor are too pig-headed to buy them.

But he doubted his own future. He described himself as "without malice, without cruelty, without pride and therefore without ambition": he was the pattern of inexplicable insuccess. . . .

V

A strange narrative; a new love.

"Let's go now," said Catherine, when the washing-up was finished, to Joseph. The two old people were sleeping. The Bay was full of rowing-boats, people in light clothes walked all over the roads, green Vaucluse, with its white palace and rich bungalows, sparkled beside the blue water.

"It's a lovely day," said Catherine. "We'll take the boat in. I want you to come and visit Baruch with me: we'll have tea somewhere in town. I want to go on the spree a bit; I'm going into an asylum to-morrow. You'll think I'm crazy, perhaps, but it's the best thing for me, the way I feel."

"An asylum? What for?"

"I want to rest, and I can only rest where people are allowed to be queer. You wouldn't understand how upset I am over Michael: I'm supposed to be without much family affection. But I want you to understand. You're not a bad fellow, Jo, and you take people at their own estimation, that's why you have faithful friends: there's no spite in you. But those others, half of them are stuffed with spleen, spite or gall. Every one in the asylum pities the insanity of the others. And they teach handicrafts there. They are kind people, the insane, easy to live amongst, easy to humour, and if cranky, no worse than plain men."

"Oh, I couldn't. But can any one get in?"

"No, I have a friend; a doctor who will certify me unbalanced. And I am."

"Do it if you want to. I don't think it crazy; you know best what you want. I'll come and see you."

When they reached Baruch's bachelor room in Woolloomooloo, they found him absorbed in books. He seemed annoyed to see them; then he sprang up.

"Catherine, I'm delighted to see you. How do you feel?"

"Rotten, thanks."

"You must; did any one know Michael so well as you?"

"No, I don't think so; I am sure not."

"Do you know why he died?"

"For want of breath."

He gave her a shocked glance. . . .

There was a silence. Baruch fingered the pages of his book, reading a line or two. Catherine turned towards him impetuously.

"Would you be interested to hear the private history of Michael?"

"Very much."

"I warn you it is strange and long."

"All the better; most lives are stale and short."

"He was Mother's illegitimate son, and knew it quite early. Our money came partly from his father, an eccentric surveyor, mathematician and astrologer."

"Whose mind was so much in the stars that he didn't know what he was doing when he walked amongst men."

"Yes, Michael arrived in one of those off moments. He was intended to go to the University because Mother had a romantic feeling about him, the bastard son of an eccentric man, quite evidently a genius. . . ."

"One of the great race of mahmzers."

"What? Well, Michael was emotional and sensual; he was first attracted to the Church, you probably can't imagine why in this country which doesn't exactly favour cloistral gloom and where every one thinks of the price of wool. His mind was lost in antique Celtic fogs: he drew designs in his odd hours, and had a very sweet imagination, *mitteleuropäische, Mittelalter*. He used to dream about colonies of angels and vast buildings whose columns had scaly winged feet. He told me every morning when he waked what he dreamed. I used to lie back, shut my eyes and see it too. He collected prints of Dürer and mediaeval artists, but he didn't like anything modern. He bought a wooden replica of a peasant Christ found in the Tyrol, a most grotesque thing, to have in his bedroom, which he had painted white. But it wasn't to pray, it was the grotesquerie, the bizarre monastic flavour, a shock in a suburban bungalow. He met a girl in the Bay called Mae Graham, a teaser, and he could not tear himself away from her even when she married. I imagine he committed adultery with her. He met Withers before that, and Withers liked to tote him around; he was the same then as now.

"He would always go out walking with me to tell me his dreams. He insisted on having a photograph of me, and said he walked with me in dreams. He left it at some friends."

She looked at Joseph.

"I broke the frame the other night by accident and put it in a drawer. I did not think it was of any use."

"You were very close to each other?" said Baruch.

Catherine was silent for a while. Her powerful tragic sense changed the small room, even in their eyes, to a theatre. Baruch remembered her scenes as if he had seen them stereoscopically. And this, hardly believing, he called Catherine's narrative.

CATHERINE'S NARRATIVE

"We were hearts united—before the war.

"Before the war. But I thought it was finished when he returned from the war, until a holiday we spent in the country. Once we went to Tuggerah Lakes during a vacation. We used to walk along the beach about seven miles to Norah Head where the lighthouse is, and back, over the soggy sand. The mouth of the lakes is always filling up. There is a sand-bank in the centre of the entrance lake, the tide runs out fast through thick mud channels on either side. It is very treacherous at the ebb. The sand-banks, too, at the mouth of the lakes often drop off sheer into the water. The water is like an aquarium underneath, and you can see the fish ten to twenty feet down.

"Behind the bungalow is low dense scrub, eucalypts, bottle-brushes, she-oaks, and in the backyard a tree with large white trumpet flowers of the nightshade family, I don't know the name. In the bush we sat every day before lunch and tea and Michael read me his poems. The place is damp, mournful, magnificently lac-coloured morning and evening.

"One day we rowed to the island, which is covered with trees and dripping with damp. We got out, tied the boat to a stump, and went in amongst the trees one behind the other. Michael walked in front, because I can't bear to have any one behind me—so I could not see his face. We continued to walk along over the leafy mud. It was quiet except for the ring-necked doves roocoocooing right up in the tree-tops and some curlews on the opposite shore—they have a dismal human cry.

"I said nothing. I was thinking about the meeting I was organising out at Double Bay. Laverty, the local secretary, was rather rocky and indifferent because I was a girl. Michael kept on walking in front of me. The island became silent except for the squelching mud. Michael's dark raincoat, gawky saunter and black hair seemed to stretch out into the undergrowth. He pointed out things with a bit of stick, without speaking, but he kept on, starting to speak on some subject which he was revolving in his head, without ever making anything but a coughing sound, as if he had changed his mind and started off on a new tack. A sea-fog had drifted in; the rolling vapour fell on the island. We plodded along aimlessly in the wet, cloaked in our ideas—it got darkish, blobs of water dropped from the foliage to the earth. I began to think about Michael, that if he walked long enough he would miss the path and walk off the island into the water, struggle in the mud four feet thick, be drowned and so end his unhappy, useless life. I wished he would. He was so dark and cold, like the moon; I felt the fire in me by contrast. If I had had a true brother, I thought, I would have had a companion; he always failed me. I thought, I will never get anywhere while he is a drag on me. He spoke to me,

" 'Do you think it is auspicious that my dearest friend is the paralytic, Kol Blount? What do you think of that?'

" 'I think it's a mistake,' said I.

" 'If Blount could walk, he would despise me to-morrow. No one, you all think, could have a true affection for me.'

" 'Every one is loved,' said I.

" 'Even Blount and even me. But they flatter themselves. If he were free he would leave them all. He is a better man than all.'

" 'He is a brilliant man, but whether he's better than any one of us —it's difficult to prove. He gains by his immobility. You overrate him. I prefer an active man as a companion.'

" 'Even you despise me. It's strange, isn't it? For a long time I endeavoured to be human. What is the solitude of a man? Not that he is a unit, but that he is a fraction. In my solitude, as a boy, I migrated people to the sky, peopled the dark spaces with bodies. I talked to the stones and the sea, the stones in the house answered me. I spoke familiarly to the furniture in my room and everywhere in nature and in the building materials of the city, in cast nails and puddles of lime, and underfoot, I saw a movement, a breathing, upwrenching, freeings and unhappy motion: I felt the trees had the souls of men prisoned, nature was full of gagged voices. Isn't Kol exactly like that?'

" 'Yes, I understand now.'

" 'No. I lay on my back watching a shining, futile ant fussing through green thickets of grass and climbing gigantic stalks to surmount them, instead of going round the roots—immense energy for nothing; next day he died and was tugged back to the ant-hill to be eaten. But the grass thicket and the ant-hill themselves were alive, creaking tremendously in my ears; I never heard, except in a storm, such a roaring in the air. There is a blasting like that in the uneasy silence of Kol's sick-room.'

" 'Is that it?'

" 'No; there is more. I went at night in the Inner Domain where it overlooks Garden Island. The tramps were there rolled in their caves, their fires were extinguished, and they were like dead leaves, or bad fruit fallen out of the trees. No, they were shadowy emanations from the ground, abortions. They were not alive, but the trees were alive. Awfully they began to move and bend over me; they crowded together in their congregations and unholy intercourse began. I was as invisible to their senses as their speech inaudible to my outward ear.

" 'When the wind comes off the Bay, as it often does at night-fall, when a scurrying and rushing of feet, a series of flurries and cat's paws comes off the hills, then they burst their cataleptic dream, with what horrible memories and unspeakable ideas drunk up out of the earth with the dead encysted in its flesh, I do not know, but I was always afraid at that hour. Yet the trees were more alive than the men. Woe to the man who has the soul of a tree: such I am!

" 'At last I could no more persuade myself I was human. I ran out into the country at night, on to the fire-scorched and blackened hills, where splintered boles and spaded burrows of little animals trip one up at every step. There are snakes in the long grass. I passed by sleeping farms and orchards where the roosting hens clucked and the dog shook his chains and barked. I looked for a stray sundowner or homegoer late at night on the road, a man going early to work to hoe the turnips, put in the potatoes or pluck the hairy caterpillars off the grape-vines, or a country boy coming home late from a country dance, overcoat on shoulder, drunk and whistling; but none I ever found, or if I found them they passed by with only a word.

" 'I thought I might fall in with a beggar or a thief, either is a human relationship, but I met no one. In the street, in the evening, the women only looked at me over their shoulders and trotted on. What is the mark that puts every one on their guard? A child sees me and looks at me solemnly and reflectively: "Look, Mamma, look at the funny man!" But there's really nothing funny about me, is there?'

" 'Nothing at all,' I said without looking at him. As you know, though, he had an absorbed, fanatic look, with his thin cheeks and eyes too close together. In Naples they would have said he had the evil eye.

" 'There is something,' continued Michael. 'What? I am a man: I can't see that deformity, it is not physical. Yes, my forehead is dark and my cheeks sunk in with the many nights when even sleep forsakes my bed, but there are thousands like me, in the crowds of workmen and students going to work in the early boats every morning, with every cast of forlornity.

" 'Do you remember the summer I was seventeen, I went into the country for the holidays and came back the next day, without saying why? I came to a town and drove down by pony-trap from the station. Oh, the radiant bush with eucalypt leaves and the stench of undergrowth exuding aromatic oils, the red tracks winding down the hills towards cabbage-tree palms, through cycads, blue sarsaparilla vines and boronia plants, their juices bubbling in the hot air. We came towards the water. Newly-varnished rowing-boats were drawn up in rows against the stone pier; no one was there but me. I was whistling with pleasure. There was a hut verandahed, and roofed with blinding unpainted corrugated iron, hot, red and silver under the hill. That was the place I had come to stay in. A woman with moon-white hair and yellow face approached with a rake along a row of worm-eaten cabbages, barefooted; she had no teeth. After her, in rags, came two children, yellow as wax. She grins, "Do you want cabbages? I'll have to arst my bruvvernlaw." She sends her husband to her brother-in-law's hut: for they have only one pair of trousers between them. They find out what I have come for; they stare. It is a mistake. "But you can stay," she says obligingly, "ten shilluns a week." The floor is only made in one room and stacked with fowls' excrement: as I come out by the backdoor, I see the brother-in-law having his bath, quite naked, in a tub under a water-spout. "We wash 'ere," says the woman. "No, thanks," I say. They all stare after me with lugubrious, disappointed faces. "I jest killed a chicken," says the husband; "you better pay for it, all the same." I paid for it. When I came home, I looked at the day's paper: there was the same advertisement. I never knew what went wrong, but I know that where I was mixed up in a thing something would be wrong.'

" 'That's funny, not tragic,' I said, and laughed."

—"I suppose there are people who can't stand any sort of rebuff or shock, but it's outside my world," said Baruch. "However, what happened then?"

—"Michael began to get more excited. He said:

" '. . . I resolved to become less human, then I should not miss people so much. I called up the brutish spirit of solitude, saying, "Put all sound out of my ears, drive me out with pricks and salt to walk the streets at night, let me wound bitterly my only and dearest friend, start with affectation at his simple words, suffer slight from his unintended innuendoes, give me a dry sharp voice, so that I will be entirely alone. Aggravate and embitter my sorrow with every expedient at your service, and you will not do enough. Your torments are weak compared with those I can invent for myself. Yesterday my cousin Joseph looked at me and laughed in my face. I walked three hours in a fever wishing I had screwed his neck. I saw nothing for three hours but the blood running out of his nostrils. You would never lose my soul as I can lose it, old bit of rubbish that you are. Get out of this, take yourself off, hoppygo devil, with your stage effects, trumpets and storms, you dumb jackanapes with two ideas and a black coat perched on your back, quite devoid of subtlety."

" 'But so perverse in everything; out of the vice into which I wished to sink, a new life came up into my nostrils. The world imagines that virtue and courage are honourable, because it benefits thereby, but for the possessor and doer they are vile error and sin; they destroy his humanity. The giver-up, the sacrificial agent, the atoner, the ascetic of the body will hereafter have no more restraint in his imagination. His desires flourish as their denial is pressed down; what they lack in satisfaction, they put forth in the fruit of understanding and sensibility. Then when they have fitted him to understand it, they destroy his virtue and make him the subtlest connoisseur of his own destruction.

" 'I thought my heart would burst my body, it so strained at the chain and wished to augment itself: I burned inwardly and my life flowed three times as fast, so that I could not see any motion in the world, except things blowing in high winds.

" 'This was what I thought, but this was the perversity—I saw Catherine through a new lens, and thus I am mocked: my destiny is stronger towards unreality than life.'

"Michael was silent for a while, and I thought: Who is this Catherine?"

—"Who was Catherine?" said Baruch.

—"You are serious and sympathetic," said Catherine; "I will tell you what followed."

—"He said: 'Why is there so much darkness in the world that even the sun can only illuminate a small part of our day, at noon? There is dewy darkness in the forenoon and dry radiant shadows at midday and dusk pregnant with imaginatory forms in the evening, but all through the day, thus, the kingdom of dark remains and lies in a guet-apens for the time it shall reign. Also in the mind there are very few things which are bright and clear, but the greater part of our day is spent in internal dark—and what of the inenarrable night sessions of dreams? If you dig in the earth, it is dark within, despite the gold and fire contained there. If you penetrate beyond the diffusing envelope of air, the heavens are black; if you even look into the heart of a tree, darkness seems to rush forth as you cleave the bark; thus man goes upon his way peering. The greatest occasions of life are made mysteries, such as birth, love and the adoration of God—the womb, dark and without air, the earth, the same; light is but a temporary star in our existence. Birth strikes the eyeball and says "Let there be light!" I often wonder what makes a child come forth for something which he knows nothing of: does he see a sudden flash of light in prenatal night, and hunger and desire it thereafter? Surely darkness is the condition of man, and light is all he thirsts after, for the Kingdom of Heaven is said to be all light, and it takes a very austere and not a fortified mind even to conceive of Hell without *light.*

" 'So a candle is a lovely thing, so I am ravished when I look at the starry way, and limpid Jupiter in the early evening; and also your eyes, Catherine, in their exceptional lucency, and your form, which is all darkness and white, the eternal contrast and composition of the world.'

"I was terrified. I said: 'Michael, hush! What are you saying?'

"He said: 'It is not permitted, in this part of the world, to a brother to love his sister. He may grow up with her and become familiar with her ways, and her thoughts, and the way she speaks, but he may not love her except coldly and indifferently: he may not love her as any stranger whom she accidentally meets outside may love her. The reasons for this prohibition, unnatural and cruel, which brings it about that brothers often hate their sisters, are among those nameless mysteries and darknesses I was speaking about.

" 'Whereas, as I was born unnatural, I have come to love my sister as myself, for you are myself, but everything appears in you with a greater perfection, and all that is dark and light in you is the very reflection of my own thoughts, my mind and my desires. A man cannot love himself, but all men do, and so there is no satisfaction in the world, for we must clasp another body, informed by another spirit to ourselves.

" 'But I love you not for myself, but for you. I cannot explain why in this or that way of speaking, and why in your expressions and glances there is such exquisite pain, such sudden revelations, as if I discovered every hour a new beauty in your face which is so familiar. But so it is, and so I am in love with you; not you, but that which is like you in me. I am lost because part of me is sundered from me for ever.

" 'You look at me in horror, fear and speculation, but your unquenchable beauty reflected in me, your sun, my moon, move in accord; you cannot hate me. Your silver eyeballs gleam, your silver brow and the lightnings of your aspect. Put your face in your hands. Because you are not beauty, you are terror, you are destiny, and what is destiny but death, and what else are you? If I ever kissed you, what would I have under my lips but the very substance and moment of death and dissolution?

" 'I have no meaning in ordinary life, and this is what releases me from being silent about my love, and it is what makes me love, perhaps, the image of myself: it is a hunger and lust for death at root.'

"He said this to me while walking slowly in endless circles round the island. He stopped once or twice and looked at me, and then turned round again and walked on, almost indifferently, as if he spoke about something impersonal. I did not know what to answer. He did not want any answer.

"We rowed to the house. We only spoke on that subject once again in our lives, that was the other night at Kol Blount's house, and then, by allusion. I endured it for a few months and I almost believed what he said: I lived in a sort of amazement, so that the sun did not have the same colour. Then I changed. I met a lot of people: my own world emerged. Michael went away from home, and when he came back and joined our circle I saw he was running after Marion. He knew her abroad."

Catherine was silent.

Baruch unwillingly stirred himself and remarked, "Then it was Marion!"

"No, it was I."

"How did you feel? You must have felt strange."

"Didn't you understand? I loved Michael: I have always loved him. I tried to make plans to go to some other country where they would not know we were related, but all these fantasies went up in smoke; besides, Michael would never have done it. It would have made the thing too real to him, he only wanted to play with the idea."

"Faithless to each other, you all are," said Baruch abruptly. "You can't believe in a sincere passion. All crazy and all seeking outlandish vagaries to distinguish you, a true oddity seems a disgrace to you. You bark like tykes when a true nonesuch arrives among your eccentricities.

I must say, I'm moved by your tale, and I don't think his feelings misplaced either; he could have found no one but you and Blount amongst all his friends."

"How lovely you are, Baruch!"

He looked in the glass, pulling a whimsical face.

"Nobody can think so. What a face!"

"You know I mean in nature."

"An insult, then."

But he fell silent, moved his chair and looked out of the window. Presently his eyes fell back to his book and he kept stealing glances at it.

"Excuse me," said Baruch presently, seeing his two guests sitting still side by side, not willing to move, "I can't get that tale out of my head. It's really so peculiar."

"I'm going," said Joseph, seeing Baruch absorbed.

Catherine did not move.

"I'm not; this is my last night amongst rational people."

Baruch turned his chair round and looked at her.

"I thought you were going into the asylum voluntarily?"

Catherine began to cry.

"I'm ridiculous," she said, "don't take any notice of me, but I'm wretched. I don't know what I want, and I don't really want to go into the asylum, but it's the only place where I have a home when I'm cranky and cracked. If I were always in touch with a person like you, with a golden sanity like yours, I wouldn't think of such things." . . .

They talked for a long time about odds and ends, while they felt the blood rushing through their hearts to a new measure. They talked automatically and disjointedly and unnecessarily, so that the conversation would soon drop and a silence would come when they could look at each other with full glances, questioning and responsive, understanding, hesitating. They grew more corpulent spiritually, they felt stronger, they grew to their full height. Innocent fancies filled them, they had a temptation to speak with a familiar simplicity which made them smile to themselves. They lived thus for several hours.

"I feel better," said Catherine soon. "I wish I had not arranged to go to Forestville, but now I must. I am going to help with the instruction in the workshops."

"Don't go," said Baruch.

"You won't be here long, Baruch. I can't antagonise them, I must have a haven to go to, when you are not here any more and I am upset."

"Do I really make so much difference?"

"Of course."

He touched her hand. She got up and put on her hat.

"Well, I am going home. I am tired out, and I have to pack a little bag, not much. I must see Mother, for I have told her quite a different story, that I am instructor at the asylum. Thanks very much. Good-night!"

He came downstairs with her, and at the door made a stiff European bow.

THE
BEAUTIES
AND FURIES

The Beauties and Furies was published in 1936. Elvira, an English-woman in her thirties, has left her dull but devoted husband, Paul, and come to live in a Paris hotel with Oliver Fenton, a Socialist scholar, several years her junior.

In the first excerpt Elvira rediscovers her attractions as a woman. In the second, she has found that she is pregnant. Blanche D'Anizy, a cabaret artist whom Elvira has picked up in a café, has offered her the services of an abortionist. Here Elvira, reviewing her options as a wife, mistress and mother-to-be, finds none of them satisfactory for realizing herself.

I

It was Wednesday. All the morning Elvira was wayward, languid, idle, untouchable: she looked youthful when she was so. She teased Oliver and refused to say good-bye to him when he went out to be shaved. Then she looked out of the window at him in the street and laughed but would not wave. She took a handful of chocolates and a handker-chief to the bed, and lay down wondering what Oliver was thinking about her, and whether her husband Paul would write to her or come for her. She closed her eyes and ran her fingers many times through her hair slowly until it began to crackle, thinking disconnectedly. Then she put her hands behind her head and began to think of the past night, addled memories of the theatre, *Faust* at the Opéra which she had not liked although they had a box to themselves, because she had been hungry. Afterwards Oliver, eager, leaned towards her asking, "Well? well? Now what did you think of it?"

"I didn't like it: it was so artificial with the old-fashioned scenery, she was so clumsy with the jewels."

He had been so hurt and angry. She laughed to think of it: that young man angry with her. She thought of the street-lights, dresses, the splendid ceilings when they promenaded in the intervals, the taxi whirling home, Oliver's white shirt, her pale-blue silk dress, which although dowdy had not looked worse than most there: it was not a dress-night, and the suburban women were in. She saw Oliver's agate eyes in their clear whites smiling at her.

Then she thought of the days before, the winds blowing, the fire roaring in the chimney, the snow, Oliver when he began to appear so often unannounced, the circle of her husband's men friends around her, idle scraps of her bitter conversations with Paul, about nothing in particular, Paul away and Oliver holding her hand, the postman bringing her Oliver's letters, the last hurried foggy morning with the luggage all bundled up in the taxi, the train, the snow.

Then everything was dark, she was very tired and was soon wrapped in a warm half-slumber, wherein she dreamed of nothing, but seemed to be suspended, a full-blooded great body in a dark scene where an obscure tower or veiled monument took the centre of a vast colourless plain. She opened her eyes placidly for a few moments, imagining she had heard the door click; then she closed them, and obscure images hopped into her mind's eye. She saw a rod with two headless snakes emerging from a dusky ivory egg, jagged lightning issuing from the great letter O, flame coming from a periwinkle's shell, a lake at the end of a row of dark clipped trees, a sea-lion creeping slowly towards her with melancholy head, a mushroom turning into a silver pheasant, a long stretch of yellow and black strand with the fringed sea invading it on one side and the black coarse grass on the other. She saw two cranes drinking from a soaring fountain, an hour-glass in the form of two swans embracing two eggs, a snake swallowing a blindworm twice wrapped round a bundle of wheat, a headless tree growing out of a thousand-fibred root like a peacock's-tail, a white hand balancing an empty retort, and many dull images impossible to recognise.

She got up, walked languidly to the dressing-table, undressed and made poses before the long mirror. Then she walked slowly, with a childish swagger, to the bathroom, turned on the water, and lay naked on the bed till the bath filled. She spent a long time in the bath, massaging herself, washing herself over and over with love for her soft skin, watched herself floating in the green water, like a strange sensuous water-animal, and got out to get her hand-glass so that she could see how she looked to strange eyes. She examined her head, neck and breast, grimaced to see how she looked when she was crying. She got out of the bath with reluctance, letting the water run slowly off her limbs, held up her arms in the warm air to see how slowly they dried, put her hands beneath her breasts and so carried them, glad to feel their weight, into the bedroom. She folded her hands round her waist, passed them round her thighs and looked at the profile of her belly. She glanced sideways at her olive shoulder and kissed it. She kissed her arms, tried to reach her breasts with her mouth, but could not. Then she threw herself across her bed, and with her arms raised above her head, imagined an old ivory female idol, old ivory sucking human children, she imagined children clustering over her like grapes, curtaining her. She suddenly felt naked, and getting up, put on her mandarin gown. She wandered about the room, giving her body hundreds of small attentions, using ear and nose syringes, sponges, files, scissors, chamois leather, swan's-down puffs, sticks of orange-wood, creams, powders, and the rouge that Oliver had brought her home. She rarely used rouges, but now that she had several of different kinds and a pot of dark powder for the eyes, she tried them on different parts of her naked body, and almost thoughtlessly began to move, lifting her arms, advancing and retreating. After one or two steps, she made an impatient face and began to dress. When she had put on her thin silk stockings, she stood before the mirror, admiring her legs and wondering if she would buy the new short stockings. Then she finally put on her dress, a close-fitting one of French blue, low cut, which she had almost never worn, because in London it seemed too low to suit her. She drew the belt tighter, polished her nails and divided her hair in the middle of her head so that it fell in equal curls on each side. She thought, "I never noticed how well this dress suits me: silly what prejudices you get! At the same time, a woman with a pretty figure who wears high-throated dresses—and occasionally a low neck, they see how white her skin is!—to be desired! H'm, of course it is every woman's duty: instinct, that's why you do it without thinking. A pretty woman probably has more instincts: made for it, made to succeed as a woman." She looked towards the door and started violently. Oliver was sitting on the valise in the entry looking at her.

"How long have you been there?"

"Since before you had your bath."

She blushed faintly and asked him to wait while she put on some powder. She kept him waiting for some time and then came forward into the dark room, with her self-absorbed smile. Oliver thought he had never noticed how thick the languorous graces clustered round her, robing her shoulders and thighs, nor how eloquent of dark enclosed beauty her body.

She loved him: she had learned to love him. His ardent eyes were fixed on her face; she looked away slowly. He turned her face to him and looked on the tide at its full, dark, lustrous, and full of internal music. He felt, if he ventured forth on it, it would bear him without storm or whirlpool, and he would finally reach the white thread of the distant shore. . . .

II

He began to tell her about his day's work in the Archives.

"Aren't you neearly finished, Oliver? Perhaps we should return to England now and try to settle down. I'd like you to get a position. You see, I've almost decided to keep the infant."

He tapped on the table with his pencil, his eyes lowered. She said:

"I've never felt so well in my life as now: I know now what was wrong with me. I was always so wretched and futile: now I feel wholesome, like new bread. That was what was wrong with me. I must keep my child, Oliver. It's Fate. It's ours. It's the fruit of our adventure. It was meant to be so."

He raised his eyes from his tapping, his eyes quiet.

"Very well, dear. Then I'll get ready and we'll go back and I'll look for a job. Just give me a month more, will you? I can get something impressive ready by then, I think. I must make a good impression if I have to ask the professors to recommend me straight away. I'll think it out. If you want me to do that, I'll do it. I'll put myself in your hands. You know my principle, I'll try anything once, and no growling, eh?"

She looked at him dubiously. He nodded at her.

"Of course, if we could put it off, just for a few months, it would give me a better chance to get something: we know we love each other, we know we can have children: we're both young. That's all we need to know. I want to see you in our home first, Elvira."

She looked at him steadily, the father and enemy of the child.

She said: "Of course, if you feel like that, and you think it would make a bad impression on your friends, I'll go home and stay with Paul till it's all over. He'll shelter me."

Oliver's eyes were lowered as he traced earnestly on the table.

"I have been a student: I'm relatively fond of the little nippers, but not like you are, Elvira. It doesn't mean the same to me. I can wait a bit, and I think we would be happier if we did."

She suddenly began to cry softly, so that the tears just stood in her eyes.

"You don't want my child; you don't want it."

He shook his head to himself, and called the waiter for the bill. He helped her on with her coat and they went out, unnoticed by Blanche, deep in her emotions with her lover. Outside on the pavement, in the fine evening, holding to his arm, she looked at his well-set profile, his fatigued, deep eyes, and thought of the evenings at home, when Paul was at his meetings, that she had seen him thus, looking melancholy into the fire. She said low: "It's degrading to be a woman, to have to bother about what people think, not to be able to provide for your child, to be dependent on men. If I'd kept on being secretary in that hospital, I should have been free, I should have had my job: now, he's taken me out of it, I've become a plaything; I'm no good. I can't even have my own child when I want it: it has to wait on circumstances. Do you think I like to pretend to be your wife when I'm not?"

Oliver walked along pressing her arm and shaking his head.

She said, "Oh, I feel so bitter when I think that, even though I give up my old life of wifehood, there is no freedom for me, a middle-class woman without a profession. They should give me a street-walker's card. I regret it, I regret it," she said violently. "I made a mistake to listen to you. I'm five years older: I can't start out afresh with a young man. I've done that already with Paul. I want something else now. It was only the need of a child driving me on, and now—I can't have it. Oh, I hate society, I hate the burdens it places on women."

"Yes, it isn't fair: women are not really free," said Oliver.

"The real thought of the middle-class woman," complained Elvira, "is the problem of economic freedom and sexual freedom: they can't be attained at the same time. We are not free. The slave of the kitchen and bedroom. Even if you have a maid you're supposed to be thinking about the cooking and linen. It ought to be done by people who make a job of it and leave the women with a good education free."

"There are plenty of women in laboratories, and in business, now."

"I've always been idle and useless," mourned Elvira. "It's true, I could have gone on to do something. I came first in things often at school. I got my B.A. What good did it do? I was born that way. Other women would have gone on and made a career. When Paul came along, I wanted him to love me but I didn't want to marry: I wanted to be myself, not a wife, with children. I wanted to do something creative: something—perhaps writing. I didn't want just to turn into a bad incubator. I didn't want to marry him, I just wanted to live platonically with him. But he wouldn't. It gave me a shock: I thought it was so gross of him. Afterwards, of course, I felt differently. I was a bad wife to him.

Yes, I was. Everything I have ever done was bad and inefficient. I never had anything out of life that I should have had. I'm pretty, and I didn't have a good time. I'm intelligent, and I never did anything. I married, and I didn't even have a proper home with children. I ran away with a lover, and I'm miserable. And it's all my doing." She was crying: Oliver felt the tears on his hand now. "I am good for nothing," she said in a lamentable tone. "I might as well commit suicide. You wouldn't miss me after a month. Paul doesn't miss me now. Sara is going to keep house for him."

"Elvira, I can't bear to hear you talk like that. You don't mean it. You know that Paul loved you and I love you. And you have plenty of time to make a career and have children if you want them." He laughed, rousing her. "Cheer up; what's all this? You're depressed: it's the—child perhaps."

"I suppose so, and I've been thinking what to do: I don't know what to do. It's that that upsets me so much. I'd rather decide to do anything than be like this, between wind and water. Somehow, though, I always seem to get into a sort of jam where I have to decide something momentous, and it tortures me. I was happy when I knew about the baby, because it seemed to have decided something by itself. But then, I began to think about you and the money and it all started again. Like a toothache. You're lucky. You're creating something. It sounds easy to you. But I never found self-expression. Perhaps I could have been a musician. But I haven't got it. It's something."

"I love you. Doesn't that mean something to you?"

"Yes," doubtfully.

"It will work out all right in a little while, then. All those troubles you mentioned, even the disappointment in life you have, will disappear when our love grows and we settle down. We'll have a fine life together."

"I suppose so."

She scanned the faces and get-up of every mother with a child, thinking, 'I will be something like that.' She saw this evening that they were dusty, drawn, violently fatigued and acid faces: the children looked like blobs of flesh, their clothing rubbishy. "Oh, not for me," she thought, and a slight nausea began in her. She thought of her eight long quiet home-years since she married Paul, her polished floors, washed carpets, recovered chairs, her new bed-linen which felt like silk, her underclothing of silk and lawn all put away in piles, her curtains, silver dressing-table ware, vases, doyleys,

the olive, yellow and smoke-blue bedroom, the red and walnut dining-room, her work-basket with an olive silk bag. She thought of
her soaps and cleansing materials always in stock, and her dusters
neatly arranged, the coats hanging in their entry, the shawled trees
waving against the sky in summer, the Adam window on the stairs
through which she looked, whenever the stairs were untrafficked,
dreaming like a child, watching the birds fly up beyond the curve.
If she had a baby, she would have to have a home at least as large,
a nurse who would sleep with it in a separate room, and look after
the washing, the bottles. She could not have it in a hotel, with Oliver without a position. Her face suddenly grew firmer. She determined to go back to Paul, if he would have her, with the baby. It
would be different at home then, and Oliver—Oliver would become a patient loving friend, coming to see them, taking her for
walks. Sometimes she would go to his rooms, in memory of old
times. He might marry, on the rebound—but he would come back:
their friendship could not be broken that way. But if he married
she could not see him as before. "Women have enough troubles,"
she said to herself. "I wouldn't bother another married woman.
Even Blanche, I wouldn't take a man away from her. They know it
instinctively, besides: that's why they like me."

Oliver turned to her, smiling, patting her hand.

"Wool-gathering, Elvira? Dreams for the future?"

"I was just thinking," she drawled, "thinking about us, about everything."

They went to the pictures that night. There was a moving picture
of the well-worn prodigal wife pattern. Oliver wanted to leave half-way
through it, when the erring wife showed signs of returning to her
husband, but Elvira was absorbed. She came out elevated, convinced
by the coincidence. Oliver began his usual raillery: "Gee, why don't
they think up a new story? I believe they have three since the wild west
died, the sentimental hurdle-race, the repentant gold-digger, and his-
torical heroics."

They went to a café for coffee, as they couldn't get it at the hotel
at that time of night. Since they were at Montparnasse and it was late,
there were numbers of male and female prostitutes about. They sat
opposite one and began a fuddled conversation about these unfortunate
people, whether they began through hatred of work, or excessive sexual-
ity, or early incest.

"Exploited labour, that's how I look at them," said Oliver. "I never could go to them, any more than I could sweat a workman."

"It's all a formula," proposed Elvira. "You could exploit a woman in a house, making her wait on you and cook for you, turning her into an idiot with ideas about mouseholes and curtain-rods, while you wrote essays on labour-unions. It's just the same, I see no difference."

"You're right. Lord, how we adhere to our patterns! We gibber like marionettes in trite situations. All middle-class novels are about the trials of three, all upper-class novels about mass fornication, all revolutionary novels about a bad man turned good by a tractor. There's nothing new on earth—and how well you know it, life-sick child! What's the matter with you, Elvira? Isn't there anything that gives you hope?"

"Human nature's the same all over the world, if you aren't taken in by poinsettias in the tropics and rainbows in the north to think it's different."

After a silence, Oliver said: "In a way, you were happy at home, Elvira, weren't you? You slept and had grey-footed dreams. And yet why did you come to me? Did you love me?"

"I am a dead soul; life is too heavy for me to lift. I thought perhaps I just had to shrug it off as a snake shrugs off his old skin. Since I bore life in me I feel a will growing in me. But the will is the infant. When he is born, he will just leave me like an old skin. I shall be the same as before, limp, aimless. Why was I ever born? My mother fell down a trap-door in a cellar before I was born, and nearly miscarried. I wish she had. Then Paul would have found a simpler, more extrovert wife, and your student's life wouldn't have been spoiled. You could have had women who didn't ask for too much: you could have lived cheerfully your selfish men's lives. You hate responsibilities, and I am nothing but a responsibility. I ask for too much. None of you is as generous as he'd have to be with me."

Oliver looked down at her. "Dearest, you only lack something, that is all: you are pretty, a true woman, often witty and gay. You lack an aim. We'll give you one. You'll have your baby."

"Oh, I have no will," she murmured.

He did not ask her about her own affairs, and for a week she said nothing. But she was turning her disappointments over in her mind. Every night they walked out till late, and he discoursed about his essay, his discoveries in the Archives, and his plans when the essay was handed in. One evening she said nothing the whole evening, but he kept seeing her bitter, white, contained face under the lamps: another evening, she suddenly put her hand on his lips when they were a quarter of a mile from home, and said:

"Now, don't say a word until I tell you," and then had laughed, in childish hysteria.

The last evening she suddenly cried: "You talk all the time and never think of me. I'll go mad with your journeymen and rates of pay. What the devil does it mean to women? Then and now it's just the same, the world isn't made for them. Why don't we all kill ourselves? Amuse yourselves with ephebes. Men used to like ephebes: they still do. Look at the way you admire those schoolgirls with breasts just starting and cropped hair. A passion for women before they become women, that is, for boys. You were talking aloud all through dinner to attract the attention of that little schoolgirl who can't comb her hair properly. I don't know what to do with myself. Let me go home; don't follow me: let me go home."

Oliver took her arm, but she shook herself free, passionately.

"Don't dare follow me or I'll scream: you're not my husband, are you?" She planted Oliver on the descending pavement of the Boulevard Raspail. He sat on a seat and watched her little hunched back go striding furiously until it was lost to sight half a mile down. . . .

HOUSE
OF ALL
NATIONS

House of All Nations was written in 1938; it was reissued in America in 1966. Set in the Paris of the interwar period, it is a vast panoramic novel of the intrigues, swindles and manipulations of the world of international finance as carried out in the private bank of the Bertillon family.

In the passage that follows, Aristide Raccamond, a specialist in "private services" to the right people whose job at the bank is in jeopardy, earns his bread and butter the hard way by dining with Georg Haller, a one-time spinner from East Prussia who has made his fortune in dubious ways. And during the evening Raccamond's wife, Marianne, discovers there are easier ways to become wealthy than by writing plays.

I

SCENE FORTY-TWO: A STUFFED CARP

The old question came up, "Is it the fourth floor or the fifth?"

"Sometimes I think it's the third."

"Last time I'm sure it was the fourth. They're all like peas in a pod."

But they got out at the fifth and walked down to the fourth, as the little gilded lift did not work in reverse. All the pale gray paneling and coconut mats were the same and with the constant walking up and down, Marianne and Aristide had begun to forget even whether it was the Bagpur Tea Company, the Mouriscot Hydraulic Company, or the Assam Carpet Company which had its quite exotic offices opposite the Hallers' flat. But, tonight, as usual, it proved to be the Bagpur Tea Company. They rang, settling their papers and parcels, undoing their gloves, smiling confusedly at each other. There was an uneven, heavy step, a key was turned, a chain rattled. In the crack of the door now grew a pale lump face with iron-gray hair, brown eyes, and hairy warts. The pale purple mouth laid open like a stale knife incision was mute but unrebellious.

"Good evening, Anna."

The maid opened the door wide. She ruggedly seized their coats and one hat, covered the coat-tree with them and speedily lumbered down the dark wide hall to another door, where she said something coarsely, in a foreign language—Hungarian, no doubt. A mistress voice answered. She closed the door, came back, took the long-proffered hat from Mme. Raccamond and, ignoring the gloves, pushed open the door of the anteroom, looked at them like an impatient sheep dog.

"Oh, good evening, dear Mme. Raccamond. How delighted I am to see you and Mr. Raccamond! You look tired. Please excuse my husband for a moment. He is telephoning the newspapers to get the latest on the Briand crisis."

"Good evening, dear Mme. Haller. How pretty you look!"

"Do I? No, you're kind. You have such a pretty dress on, too, Mme. Raccamond. Very pretty!" The little dark plump woman touched Marianne's sleeve lightly, like an affectionate cat. "Such good taste. You look so young, too! But why" (whispering) "does he look so tired?" A nod of complicity. "Yes, they are very busy at the bank. Poor man. . . ." (Brightly) "You must not work so hard, Mr. Raccamond. Mme. Raccamond is quite worried about you. No business worries, now, I hope." An arch smile to Marianne. "Let us go into another room."

The ritual went on. Mr. Haller now appeared smiling at the intermediate door, little golden hands outstretched, little golden head thrown back in welcome, little paunch neat, tight, and muscular. "Well, Mr. Raccamond! How are you? And Mme. Raccamond?" At once Haller drew Aristide apart near the Indian silk striped curtains. "I was just telephoning Havas. They tell me . . ."

"Come away, Mme. Raccamond, let us go into the other room for a minute—I will show something—you know what" (whispering). "Mr. Haller doesn't like me to" (a little gay glance). "We will leave the men alone for a while" (softly). "Eh? Yes?"

"What lovely crystal!" Marianne cried.

Eagerly, softly, Mme. Haller: "Yes: do you like them? It is real. Hand-cut. Feel."

"Oh, how heavy!"

"Yes—see, see! Feel the edges. Hand-cut. Can you tell hand-cut, Mme. Raccamond? It is easy."

"Such a size. Like diamonds, like vases in pure diamond."

Her solid, feature-encrusted face thought, What a price! Eagerly, intently, Sophy Haller: "Yes: really, like a diamond. You are right. I keep these two here. Georg wants me to put them away. Don't you think it would be a shame?" (Whispering) "He wants me to put everything away. He says it isn't nice to display them."

Marianne looked at her, silent with a confusion of protests and amazes.

The men moved nearer the doorway, standing still in the bow of the large window which overlooked the Rue Madame and the Luxembourg Garden. "Tardieu will overreach himself," said Haller, invisible. "He's been to the dry cleaners too often. The super Bel-Ami of every great swindle in the country."

"Yes, but look at his relations: he has all the thoroughbreds in his stable. . . ."

Haller's manly, fine-woven voice, "Too many lawyers in the Chamber of Deputies: no one loves them."

Mme. Haller looked round, drew a little closer to Marianne. "Mme. Raccamond, do you know, I am weak. I like to look at these things. What harm is there in it? I think they're beautiful, don't you? Do you see any harm in it? I am so glad you agree with me."

"What are beautiful things for if not to make our lives beautiful?"

"How beautifully you put it, Mme. Raccamond." An estimating glance, a nod. "Yes. Look at this powder jar from Florence. See the glaze! Do you see it, Mme. Raccamond? Do you understand glaze? See the wreath of roses! All done by hand!"

"Ravishing, unique!" Marianne had a breathless moment. Mme. Haller looked at her in gratitude. The heaven-blue little jar was a museum piece. She said deprecatingly, with upward glance, "It is said it was made by Benvenuto Cellini."

"Really?" Doubt in the air.

"Of course, no one can guarantee—but they assured me—" (Oh, please say that it might have been made by Cellini.)

Marianne conceded, "It is a Cellini *design.*"

"Oh, yes? Do you know—do you *know* Cellini, Mme. Raccamond? Oh, I always felt you were so artistic." The little golden hand of Sophy Haller was laid on Marianne's green silk sleeve. "Mme. Raccamond! Should you like to see some other pieces of crystal? I have many, many pieces" (mysteriously) "but Mr. Haller likes to have them in the cupboard."

"Oh, I love beautiful things. Let me see them. Do."

Coaxingly, "Mme. Raccamond, I know you love beautiful things; I can see it. I knew it from the first. I said to Mr. Haller, 'Mme. Raccamond is very artistic.' That is a pretty dress, Mme. Raccamond. Where did you get it?"

"At the Galeries Lafayette."

"Oh, do you get your things there? They are nice, aren't they? And not dear. Now this I paid two thousand francs for." She exhibited with satisfaction the dowdy little creation which did not flatter her milkdrop form. "I know someone there," she whispered. She became self-conscious, blushed, and darted to the immense polished walnut cabinet which almost covered the wall at one end of the room. "There! Look, Mme. Raccamond—all that—" Standing on three shelves inside were several dozen pieces of crystal, jars, vases, plates; occasional diamond gleams darted from the stuffy dark of the shelves. Excitedly, looking behind her, and whispering, she opened a drawer very softly. "He would be angry with me! Look, look, Madame—"

She drew partially out of its nest a magnificent encrusted piece of linen, with drawn-thread spiderweb lace and lace insertions, a lifetime of enwoven headaches and blind eyes. Underneath, in the gloom of the deep drawer, appeared the fold of another and yet another. "Six of those," whispered Sophy. "A woman in China has been working for me alone all her life and now her daughter helps her." Her face fell, her eyes looked like two tears. "They have never been on the table, Mme. Raccamond. They have only been out in the light for examination, for renewing the tissue paper." She shook her head, a tiny shake such as would not break a drop of water. "Don't you think it is a pity?"

She became reckless, opened both doors and all the drawers, one after the other. A cascade of pleasure waited for Marianne's view. There were eleven fur coats of various skins and cuts, a pelisse of fifty skunk skins, a splendid sable which had never been worn but twice made over into the fashion, a cape of twenty-four silver foxes. Marianne had to blow the hairs, feel the skin, examine the dyeing, feel the silky, silky feel. She was beyond words. Never had she imagined a fur so fine and costly. She examined Mme. Haller as a desirous coquette examines a little burrowing, busy animal, all unconsciously showing the silver of its pelt in the sun.

Mme. Haller for the last few months, ever since she had known her, had worn to the bank a poorish bearskin, mangy under both arms, and an old felt hat. Marianne lost heart. She realized what she had missed in her striving, ambitious world, never caring for the things of the flesh, laughing at people who were annoyed by her coarseness, resolving to show them all, to make her way, competing with men on their own terms. The display went on. What for? She might become famous at fifty. But look back at the silver pelted years, the warm, odorous years, when her thighs were white and firm to bear great twilight furs, the russet years when her hair was black and sleek to show up diamonds, the milk-round years when, though she was hard-featured, the gold patine of youth shone dully when she laughed! At the bank Marianne had actually patronized Mme. Haller for her worn, mangy little "trotter." Here, she had fourteen slips, all hand-embroidered by a Hungarian girl, whom she had found in a village and sent abroad to learn the art. ("Her eyes were now going, poor girl. But she still sends me something year after year.") The slips had never been worn or washed; hand-drawn thread, hand embroidery, handmade lace, tulle inlets, a very herb garden and rockery in Madeira work. A bedspread, never used, embossed and drawn, a tea cloth too rich and fine to use, curtains for summer use, hand-filet, to go up this week. (It shows you never can tell, thought Marianne: a little body with apologetic manners, caressing, unassuming, in old clothes and dyed hair and this veritable Open Sesame at home. Ah, ah, the simplest people have the greatest secrets.)

Bokhara carpets, Turkestan, Daghestan rugs—silky ancient Persian carpets. "We use them on the floor because that is the best way to keep them. Look at the lead seals. Do you know how to tell a Persian carpet, Mme. Raccamond? Look here, you see the other side? Didn't you know how to tell a real Persian, Mme. Raccamond? No? How surprising! Mr. Haller doesn't want them out, but I say" (briskly, sharply) "there is no sense in our storing them. They might substitute them. Of course, they are insured." Carpets, curtains, door drapes, piano covers, silk shawls, Chinese mandarin robes. "We have no room for them: they must lie in the chests. We have five chests inside" (in awestruck tones, she made a step towards the door, recalled herself) "all full. Don't you think it's a shame? But they will always be worth something. They will never lose their value, even if gold were to lose its value. With these things the value cannot be lost because the workmanship is there, don't you see? Do you see, Mme. Raccamond? All value is in workmanship! You use these rugs, a generation, two generations, more: the shahs housed them for centuries and they are still good. You do not have to protect them from the sun. They did not fade in the Persian sun."

Old silver, two whole services. "This is all solid silver—feel it, Mme. Raccamond!—and can never be sold at less than the price of silver. Do you think silver will be remonetized in England? I don't think so, Mme.

Raccamond. What does Mr. Raccamond think? No, no, I don't think so. But there is the workmanship. Look." (Low) "It is very good. There was a gold service, ten pieces, but I would not buy it. It is a bad thing —a bad thing—" she whispered and looked round. "My husband—and my father was just the same—says we should never exhibit our wealth: it is bad taste and it arouses envy in the working people. Look here, Mme. Raccamond! Brussels lace, do you know Brussels lace? One day, my mother drove into town to buy some embroidery frames at the big shop. My father came past and recognized our carriage waiting outside the shop. He was on foot. He crossed the street and ordered the coachman to go home. We had to hire a coach to go home. "Why did you do that, Ernst?' my mother asked in the evening. 'It was most inconvenient.' 'It is wrong to exhibit wealth, it engenders envy,' my father said. You see! Quick, quick, come here, Mme. Raccamond: I mustn't show it to you, but come quick. This we picked up in Rome. They say it was made in the reign of Hadrian. What do you think?" A gold fruit dish; a plate of gilded silver, the rim designed in bas-relief with a wreath of dancing loves and ribands; an onyx sirup jar, mounted in gold filigree in which small cameos were encrusted; a ring that opened with a little shrine to the Madonna inside the jewel.

Marianne felt faint. "But these things are priceless! It's a sin to hide them away. What are they for?"

"Even in case of trouble, some museum overseas would buy a thing like that," softly and eagerly said the little lady. "You see, it's much more useful than money, really. Come." She shut all the doors. "Let us go and join the men. Look, do you think I am like my portrait, Mme. Raccamond? A friend of ours did it. He has always painted pictures for us. We are a regular customer. Your hair is pretty tonight, Madame."

They sat in their usual seats in the far corner of the great salon, with half the lights in the luster turned on. Haller discoursed upon alternating and direct currents. In a minute Mme. Haller would return with the usual Indian grass-linen cloth, the usual teaspoons, the usual hand-painted service, the usual pearl-handled fruit knives, the usual old silver sugar basin which they always must admire. Above Aristide the second portrait of Mme. Haller, in a ball dress and pearls, smiled its rosy mediocrity.

Above Marianne, who sat next to Aristide, but on the settee, hung the paintbox-bright but execrably mediocre oil painting of a peasant girl, resembling Mme. Haller. She wore a red kerchief, by a blue river, in meadow grass decorated with yellow flowers. On the other side of the marble mantelpiece, decorated with great empty crystal vases, empty of flowers, hung another of the court painter's pictures: a barn-yard with a peasant girl in a red blouse, strewing corn for chickens and a cock with a red comb. Between the Turkish drapes in the great windows was a portrait of a gypsy girl, her head in a red silk shawl.

"Mr. Raccamond—a glass of Cordial-Médoc is what you need. You always have it." He took it unresisting. Haller had gone back to his telephoning. Sophy, waiting for the servant, sat down and smiled pleasantly at them both.

Marianne sat wedged in by a little round solid oak table, battered by feet and tea trays and time. Aristide's large dark eyes, roundly throned in his starch-white cheeks, rolled fearfully about the room, Marianne thought; the hall empty except for one cheap hat-tree; the salon empty save for this table, settee, chair, and Mr. Haller's desk. And not misers. Fearful of the revolution. And in the rooms beyond, doubtless, their furniture stored as were their treasures in the walnut cabinet; nothing for show. Mme. Haller had told them the first time they came that "all their furniture was stored abroad, including most of the carpets and a piano."

Mme. Haller patted Marianne on the arm. "You two are still such lovers, aren't you?" Her girlish, protected laugh. "I never told you that we first wanted to have you because we saw you walking arm in arm in the Rue Lafayette one lunch hour. I said to Mr. Haller, 'Those two love each other,' and then we saw it was you—although we had not found out your name, then." She confided, with a glance towards Haller, "We do not want people who have troubles because it upsets us too much. We cannot help them and they disturb us. You know how it is? I had a very old friend who came to see us for years! I did not see her for some months and then when she came she told us she had lost her husband!" (Whispering) ". . . he ran away from her." A shocked expression. Marianne had that uncomfortable rustling that women have on this announcement. "With another woman! Poor woman. My dear. At first we liked to let her come because she was so unhappy and she seemed to have no new friends, but she did not get over it. She always wanted to talk about it; she used to be here for hours crying and making me so upset. At last, Mr. Haller said, 'You must send that woman away, Sophy. I know she is an old friend but she is upsetting our whole life: it is getting to the point where our whole life is devoted to her and we can't get her husband back.' So I stopped asking her. You have to keep yourself strong so that you can face your own troubles. This is our home. So we only invite cheerful, happy people who love each other, like you and Mr. Raccamond." She nodded rosily at them both.

Marianne, who had a horrible feeling of cold when she heard the first part of this speech, and who was less complimented by their choice of her than shocked by the idea that she would certainly lose their friendship if they found out that Aristide, for example, had an old mistress and a son by her and that Marianne's own nephew was little better than a thief and so forth, said, with perfect composure, "You are perfectly right, dear Madame: it is your refuge against the world!"

Mr. Haller, coming from the telephone with a list, called like an earnest father, "Sophy! Sophy! They will have further news at ten-thirty."

Aristide, who had been brooding, doubtless on the same subject, now asked eagerly, "What do they say?"

"There is no doubt the foreign loan market in England is dried up; they're lending nothing abroad, either in Berlin, London, or Paris! J. Henry Schröder have urged foreign loans as an aid to world business. I have no confidence in the pound myself."

"Would you sell it?"

Mme. Haller pressed the bell impatiently, after a frown from her husband. The door in the far corner wobbled with some independent sign of life and she called, "Anna! Anna, hurry up there!" and some sharp command in Hungarian.

The door was kicked open. Anna rushed lopsidedly into the room with plates, cruets, a great oval dish of chicken livers and eggs chopped up and arranged in the shape and size of half a hen, a biscuit barrel with dry biscuits, a glass of rusks, a plate of round breads, and a glass of celery. Marianne knew what all these things were before they were brought to the table, for the dinner at the Hallers was a ritual. Mme. Haller began to arrange these things on the table and to set around the plates. Haller said sharply in German, "Sophy! You have forgotten the liqueurs. We must have them first." He looked consolingly at his guests, said in French, "Mme. Raccamond would like a liqueur. You will have a liqueur, Mme. Raccamond: we have yellow and green chartreuse."

The time was long past when Marianne or Aristide would have fought off liqueurs *before* meat at the Hallers'. Aristide was already a little pale. The ordeal of the meal had to be gone through, themselves fighting off the rich, relentless, noble food as best they could.

"Yes, thank you, Mr. Haller."

Once they had attempted to have the wine set before them, before the liqueurs, but the Hallers had been so wretched at this topsy-turvy order, and so sure that the taste of the expensive food was spoiled that the Raccamonds had never had the heart to fight the fight again. Mme. Haller had tripped off smiling and twinkling with the knowledge of good things to come. Now she returned with three bottles, green, yellow chartreuse, Cointreau.

"I know," she whispered, smiling to Mme. Raccamond, "Mme. Raccamond will have a little Cointreau. Ladies prefer Cointreau." Sharply, she reproved Georg, "You know that, Georg; I've told you ten times."

He said in German, placid, eying the food, "Softly, softly. This is very good, Sophy! I don't get dinners like this. Perhaps Mme. Raccamond prefers the yellow chartreuse."

"No, the Cointreau is older, it is more mature. And it goes better with chicken liver."

Georg bowed to his wife's superior wisdom and explained, "The Cointreau has been eleven years in our cellar. It is sure to have a wonderful taste. We have not opened it before tonight."

Sophy was pouring the fragrant transparent oily liquor into their little glasses. "Taste it, Madame. Eleven years," she said with awe. "Do you know that, Madame; that if you put wine into a cellar it is better for the keeping and the longer you keep it, the better it is? We have been buying them for years. They become very valuable after they have been kept. Do you know that? Take a little Cointreau, Mme. Raccamond. Drink it up, Mr. Raccamond. Oh, you must take more than that."

They were plying their forks and knives as fast as they could, drinking the liqueur, raining compliments on her, for that was the sweetest thing in the world to her. All day she prepared one of these dinners and dreamed about the compliments she would get in the evening when the "friends" came.

"Is it good, Madame dear? If I only hear you say it is good, then I am rewarded."

"It is wonderful," said Marianne, good soul, for the twentieth time; "no one can make it as you do." This was true, besides. "It's inexpressibly delicious." Actually, Marianne was hungry. They always fasted on the days they were to go to the Hallers'. As soon as they arrived, about seven in the evening, after a little preliminary chatter, this prodigious gorging began and went on for an hour and a half.

"There, it's delicious, you hear that, Georg! You don't pay me such nice compliments."

"I do indeed, Sophy. It is wonderful tonight; never have you made it better."

"Oh, Mme. Raccamond! Do you hear that? I have got a nice husband, haven't I? He is still a cavalier." She repented of this coquetry and immediately coaxed, "And does Mr. Raccamond pay you compliments, too? I am sure he does. Mr. Raccamond is *very gallant.* Are you a good cook, Madame? Oh, I am sure you are. I will ask your husband: he will let the cat out of the bag. Don't be afraid, dear Madame, whatever he says, I am sure you are a good cook. You are so intelligent." Her eyes searched Marianne's face and her expression became that unconsciously cunning one of a pretty woman flattering a plain one. "A little more Cointreau! How is it? Do you notice the difference in flavor?" Unaccountably her expression was suddenly dubious. "Do you really notice the difference?" She said sternly, "You know it is much better than the ordinary Cointreau you get in restaurants." She shook her head severely. "Georg and I never eat in restaurants. You don't know what you're eating. Mme. Raccamond, would you and your husband eat in restaurants?" As Marianne and Aristide ate in restaurants every day of their lives, Marianne was forced to say that they did —in good restaurants, of course. "Good restaurants!" Sophy looked too polite to say what she really thought.

To turn the tide, Marianne murmured, "This Cointreau is far, far better than anything I have tasted before."

Sophy shone, "You hear, Georg? You hear that?"

Georg emerged from his third helping of chicken liver and egg to beam gratefully on them both. "Sophy, perhaps they prefer benedictine. I think it goes better with chicken liver myself. It is a question of taste, of course. If Mr. Raccamond, Mme. Raccamond prefers Cointreau—but that is a ladies' drink—"

"Ann! Anna! Benedictine! Benedictine, fool," she added in Hungarian.

"Perhaps we have enough," reconsidered Haller, in German.

Sharply Sophy replied, "We must give our guests a choice, Georg. What are you thinking of? Anna, do you hear me? Hurry."

Anna, who was standing in the door, as if stunned, half-bumpkin, half-menace, turned in her rapid flipflop and bundled out. Mme. Haller had to go and presently came back with the benedictine, round, bright, smiling as the bottle itself.

"You see, the seal is unbroken. Fresh from the cellar . . . eleven years old. Anna" (she looked at the door and lowered her voice, even though Anna did not understand French) "does not understand anything about wines. She would serve the wine with the chicken liver if I let her. She objects to them, I *think,* and she pretends not to know which ones I mean." Her voice went still lower: "Anna's very bizarre. She objects to us having guests. She thinks we use too much light." Marianne involuntarily looked at the luster. It was a handsome affair and Marianne could see that the history of it would soon be on the boards again. It was a beautiful piece of wrought brass, just the same; they had found it, finally, in Rouen.

"Oh, Mme. Raccamond! Look at her, Georg! Mr. Raccamond, look at your wife!" Sophy pointed in despair at her empty plate. "You don't like it, Mme. Raccamond—oh, I'm going to cry." Marianne protested that, on the contrary, it was so much better than anything ever got in the restaurants of Paris that she was ashamed of her eagerness for it and was intentionally holding herself in; and, as a reward for this speech, found herself with another helping. Aristide was very pale by this time, but still a natural pallor, and not that horrible green to which he would advance before the feast was through.

Already the smell of the liqueurs and the great helpings of chicken livers had gone to their heads. Happily, little Mr. Haller lay back in his armchair, looking at his little liqueur glass. "We don't get this every day. She doesn't make it for me," teasing Sophy. "You must excuse me, Mme. Raccamond: I haven't eaten since five o'clock this afternoon. Sophy wouldn't let me eat."

"Georg! Some bread, Mr. Raccamond."

"Mr. Raccamond does not take bread, Sophy, don't you remember?"

"This bread wouldn't harm you, Mr. Raccamond: it is very good for you." Haller began to explain, taking a large piece of the roll and holding it up for inspection. "See, how it is baked! See the fine crust! You don't get that anywhere else in Paris. We looked all over Paris till we found this bakery. The trouble with most bakers is that they are dishonest and they use synthetic yeast. I insisted on examining their kitchens myself till I found one that uses real yeast."

"Did you know that, Mme. Raccamond?" Sophy asked accusingly, for she now suspected Marianne of entirely neglecting her husband's health. "Most of the bakers use paraffin in their cakes!" Her voice fell to the most shocked tone she had at her disposal. "Real yeast takes longer to raise but it is better for the digestion. Did you ever ask your baker what yeast he uses, Mr. Raccamond?"

"No," said Aristide. The little round couple were horrified, protestant, although they had eagerly awaited this answer.

"No! No! Oh, Mr. Raccamond; perhaps that is what gives you indigestion! They are so dishonest. It makes me so angry," cried the lady.

"Sophy, you forget that Mr. Raccamond does not suffer from indigestion; it is overweight he suffers from."

"Never mind." She was hot: "Yeast is not so fattening as paraffin. Mme. Raccamond," her voice was now a trumpet call, "do you ever buy pastry in a street pastry cook's?"

"Yes," faltered Marianne, for she very much relished little cakes in the afternoon, "yes, I do quite often. There is a very good pastry cook near me; very good." They were pleasurably scandalized.

"Mme. Raccamond!" High, and then low, "Mme. Raccamond, it is really dangerous. Do you know we never" (very low) "buy any cakes in a pastry cook's. I make Anna cook everything here and the fine cakes I make myself. I get the butter, flour, everything specially. One day I was walking with Mr. Haller and I saw a little cake in a nice-looking pastry cook's just near here, so I bought it, although he told me not to, and brought it home. She looked such a nice, honest woman. And I was sick all night. I ate it and after I had to go to bed. We sent for the doctor! He said there was something chemical in the cake that upset my digestion." She finished with a slight hysteria, "They're all dishonest, Mme. Raccamond."

Marianne said humbly, "This is very good bread! Where did you get it, did you say?"

At this the Hallers exchanged significant glances, smiled a little beside their noses, and Mme. Haller began with embarrassment, as if in the presence of vulgarians who asked questions that no one should ever ask. "Well, we looked all over Paris, you see it took us months. And one day—"

"A little place, down near the Marais," said the husband.

"Near the Marais," Sophy chimed in, gratefully. "Just a little place. I go there myself."

"Eat more chicken liver, Mr. Raccamond," recommended Georg at this point, the good host, taking up the great silver spoon. Unresisting, Aristide, the ameba, let him heap the plate. Aristide knew quite well what was to follow and he allowed his appetite to be carried out on a stretcher, with a mortal wound, at a first encounter like this. Marianne's strained glance reconnoitered his chubby chops. Would he hold out?

"You are not eating, Mme. Raccamond! Georg! Don't you see that Mme. Raccamond has finished all her Cointreau?"

At any rate, the burning, too-old or badly housed Cointreau made her throat and palate insensitive for the time being and she was somewhat prepared to shove down something of another dish. It was an endurance test.

Mme. Haller pressed the bell. Mr. Haller cheerfully wiped his mouth and remarked to Aristide who was sitting back, fat pale palms on fat gray knees, his round large soft mouth slightly open, that he thought the chemical fog lately tested at Lincelles, as a defense against air attacks, infinitely more valuable than the poison-gas drill, and that at the first sign of war they would, of course, pack up their few things and fly to America. Aristide was able to reply that he thought poison-gas drill very salutary and could not understand the action of the radicals in opposing it as it was most particularly to their advantage to know what to do: the rich, who co-operated, for example, would either not be in Paris for poison-gas attacks or would have their own gas cellars.

Anna pressed open the door and looked in with her habitual affronted unease. Mr. Haller slipped off pleasantly into a political discussion with his guests and the lady of the house excused herself to attend to a dish, with a good many nods, becks, and wreathed smiles, with a little self-conscious trotting step and a little coy smirk to Mme. Raccamond, at the door, which, they knew, indicated that the stuffed carp would be the next thing on the menu.

Anna, clearing away, gave the two visitors unfriendly, surmising, lowering looks, as if they were intruders who had been brought forcibly into the house from the entry, under police guard and upon whom she would presently have the pleasure of closing the front door and bolting it. She was about fifty-five years of age, of middle height, loosely built round the middle, with a sallow, impasted face, graying thick hair, a sloppy gait, and a manner which suggested mute rebellious and resentful submission. When they saw her, each of Mme. Haller's friends got frightened and counseled her mistress to send her away quickly. Not until the Raccamonds had come four or five times did Anna's manner relax towards them, for example, and then they had the impression that they were only admitted for inspection and were closely guarded all the time she was in the room. By this time she had once said "Good evening" to Aristide and she would even consider Aristide front on, for a minute, without embarrassment. As for Marianne, she got a cataloguing glance when she arrived with a new blouse, pair of gloves or bag, but never a glance of recognition or an answer from this savage creature.

Haller had been an engineer and he exposed his view to Raccamond, at this moment. "This is what I think, Mr. Raccamond, that in calculating political chances, we have to do the same as when we are putting up a bridge or a skyscraper: we have to ask ourselves, not only, 'Do the individual parts of our scheme fit together'; not only, 'Will they stand up on paper'; but, 'What invisible forces have they to withstand, what stresses and strains, what winds, traffic on holidays and at eight in the morning, the nature of the erosion, the type of subsoil': you see? To build a politic, Mr. Raccamond, we don't want a man of any particular party so much as a fine architect. I regard it as a problem in society physics, social geology, social climate. New countries develop new formulae to suit their conditions. Without fantastically evalued sites would the skyscraper ever have developed even in Manhattan? One had to have the conditions of overvalued real estate in Manhattan to produce the skyscraper, after that the traffic problem, the bridges, et cetera, et cetera. Now, no doubt in Russia they have their own unique conditions, no doubt, they are producing their own characteristic solution. We should here. I am not one for imposing a cut-and-dried solution. No. I am willing to consider the Russian experiment on its own data." He formed an ogival arch with his hands, let his clear, serious, blue gaze begin digging an answer from the mountain of China clay which was Raccamond's face.

"Yes, yes," Aristide's voice from its well, "but where is that architect? We cannot always have the best in the world: we are not Americans with their dollars. We are only looking for someone to keep the bridge in repair. Skyscrapers are not for us, any more than Le Corbusier houses. We have not that money yet. Some day, when our stock market is like the American—but even then we are not in the same position. There is the fear of war. Why should we build to give targets for German planes?"

Haller, with hands still poised, had the air of an engineer, working out his own style by using someone else as a sketching block. "New models are always possible." He laughed: his stomach was in a state of happy digestion. "For instance, there was the old Brooklyn Bridge, one of the wonders of the world when it was put up, the work of genius of the Roeblings, but now it is no longer useful for modern transport, although it is charming to the eye. How do we know the Third Republic, pleasant enough to look at, can't be superseded by a better model? Why can't there be a Fourth Republic? Naturally, it is to the interest of people who have invested in the old model, not to change." He stopped smiling. "If you want to know what I really think, Mr. Raccamond, I have been reading his works for five years and I have formed my own opinion, no man will live longer in the mind of man when the history of today is screened down, than Lenin!"

"Lenin!" they both cried out.

"An *arriviste* of genius," said Marianne with her sure touch for agreeable commonplaces.

"I can't agree with that," stoutly held Aristide. "Why do you say that?" (*Mon Dieu,* and the man is rich enough . . . it shows they get fantastic and whimsical when they get idle, these ex-capitalists.)

Haller replied, "Because he's got the engineering view of society. Look how he organized production in a wasted, undeveloped, antiquated society like Russia's! What man has done so much elsewhere in so short a time?"

"What has he done?" asked Raccamond, meanwhile. "What do we know? Everything we hear from Russia is propaganda, prepared in Leningrad. A friend of mine who was in Russia, on business, said that everything is impossible. His suitcase was stolen at the railway station. He went through with a party and they were supposed to go through according to schedule, parks, factories, all the routine. But he said to himself, 'Just the same, I want to see for myself.' So he pretended to misread the schedule and stayed behind a day. When he came down to breakfast the next morning after the party had left, all the good food had vanished. There was nothing but black bread and stewed tea, as the peasants drink! Stage dressing! And the hotel was full of bugs. And he said the people in the streets are in rags! His heart bled for them, and I assure you, Mr. Haller, that he is not a particularly philanthropic man. I don't think we should base our ideas upon what the press agencies hand out, Mr. Haller. The venality of the press, we know. And in a one-voice country. With a pinch of salt, at least. Then don't forget, the Russians are a very backward people: they don't know how badly off they are. It's easy to fool them. Things are better! Yes, indeed. I should like to see it first, with my own eyes."

The liqueurs working in their stomachs and the conversation, the interest aroused by the introduction of Lenin, one of their favorite topics, and their apparent victory, also habitual, made them begin to wonder when the next dish was coming. Sure enough, the door opened at the psychological moment and Mme. Haller trotted in, jolly, bearing a larger dish, on which was a huge stuffed jellied and nobly decorated carp, the *pièce de résistance* of the Haller feast, a dish Mme. Haller invariably spent the previous twenty-four hours preparing. Behind her, Anna was perilously toting red-bordered Sèvres plates, silver, a little crystal dish with extra pieces of roe, jelly, and stuffing, and a small dish of macaroons.

"There!" said Sophy, with a blush of triumph at them all, especially at Mr. Raccamond whose eyes opened and who quite openly licked his lips.

"Did you do it all yourself?" Marianne exerted herself to please, as her own eyes were pleased. It was the most delectable of dishes and Mme. Haller's masterpiece. She knew that Mme. Haller only made it when Aristide and she came to dinner. Some strange feminine instinct prompted Mme. Haller to feed that great mountain of flesh till his eyes popped. She passed the fish out more sparingly. It was very good. With less ceremony than before they downed the helpings of carp and Mme. Haller pressed them less to convert the good great delicate fish into Raccamond meat, for it was a particular delight of Georg's and she knew he would go foraging, at night, after the Raccamonds had left, in the kitchen, hoping for some remnants. Nevertheless, one way and another, with their exclamations of pleasure, with Haller pressing and she herself pressing, from habit, they got through the carp and several glasses of chartreuse each and there was no time for talking at all, except for asking occasionally, "Is it good, is it really good?" and exclaiming almost with tears in her eyes, "Oh, I am so glad! If it pleases you, I am most happy." But, strange thing, the tears were there as much for the vanishing of the carp which had taken so much labor, thought and love and delicacy and experience and money, and for the vanishing of all the dreams and desires of praise that had grown up round it in its brief afterlife, and for the astonishing end to which so much hard work was directed. Nevertheless, she was not wholly conscious of this last feeling: it would have been unworthy of a good hostess. Strangely enough, there was something displeasing to her, embittering almost, in seeing those two good, fat Raccamonds engulf her tender, kingly fish, surrounded by so much perfumed shining jelly and dressed in so many little sprigs, and bits of lemon, and olives and fancy bits of gelatine. This time she had really surpassed herself and there was not an ounce of the fish left. Leaning back a little, she therefore comforted herself with liqueur ("I mustn't take very much, my head turns, I haven't a strong head like you, Mme. Raccamond") and presently the slight shadow had disappeared. She had the pleasure of hearing the great blubber of voracious male, Raccamond, whose appetite attracted her dreadfully, almost sexually, say, "You are the best cook I ever knew or heard of, Mme. Haller. Isn't she, Marianne?"

"Oh, wonderful, wonderful, I wish I could cook like that."

"Oh, is it really good, then?"

They both cried out, "It is the best carp we ever tasted." Haller looked at them with a smile between gratitude and derision.

"You fatten me, really," Aristide shook a playful finger at her, ludicrous gesture in his solemn demeanor. Marianne, breathing a little hard to cover up that absurd gesture, rushed in, "Yes, you go to too much trouble for such poor folks as us: it is a shame, Mme. Haller. You ought not to."

The little thing's face clouded. "Oh!" She looked quickly at both of them. "You don't like it! Is it bad? Oh, how dreadful!"

"No, no, no." The boulder of Sisyphus to roll up all over again! But they came to it with willing, if exhausted shoulders again. "No, it's a delightful, wonderful fish." Aristide looked at her with a husbandly, tender admonition. "Only, we don't want you to go to such preparations for simple people like us. Why, it is fit for the President of the Republic."

"Simple people! Oh, how can you say that? You are people with such good taste. If you praise a thing I know it's really good. Then the carp is really good?"

"Yes, yes, indeed."

"Then I'm satisfied."

Mr. Haller was still picking bits of roe and jelly out of the second dish. Impulsively, gratefully, she leaned forward and helped Aristide to another piece of roe, one of the last titbits she had been reserving for Georg's night hunting. "There, eat that! It's nothing, not a feather-weight."

"Oh, no, I beg you."

"Not if you like it! If you don't eat it, I'll know you don't like it."

Aristide ate. His ears had flushed. He helped it down with a half-glass of chartreuse, not quite knowing any more what it was, only that it was an alcoholic drink which whipped his gastric juices into action.

"I am a bear on principle, you see, Mr. Raccamond," said Haller courteously, harking back to another part of their conversation, "because money is limited on the bear side: shares can only go to zero. But on the bull side the theory is that it can go to infinity simply because we can go on adding up. That is why, on general principles, the bulls are always wrong because there is no mechanical factor to limit their dreams. Ignorant people, with a limited knowledge of how money is made, like to bull. But money is really only made through bear operations, through put and calls, and through arbitrage, protected to a limited extent, through stop-loss orders, although they are unsatisfactory. You have to let money out on a checkrein."

"Unless you're in a pool," said Aristide, for this was his dream.

"I'm talking of the independent money-maker." Haller shook his head.

Marianne was talking aside to Sophy, rash because the carp was finished to the last crumb of the roe. "How did you learn to be such a wonderful cook? Did you learn it at home?"

She lifted her little dimpled hands in the air, delighted. "Oh, no, no, no, no. I knew nothing. When I married—Georg, I was eighteen! I knew—less than that," a tiny piece of fingernail. "My mother never let my sister or me into the kitchens. When I got married, a favorite uncle of mine wrote to say he would come and visit me and see what a good housewife I was. He loved jellied carp and I decided to make one for him. I got a big book, I went down to the market myself, and bought a very big carp. I've no idea what it cost me! Do you remember, Georg? Well, that was thirty years ago. Could you believe we have been married thirty-one years? The book said, 'Savonnez bien!' so I scrubbed it with a scrubbing brush and soap. When my uncle came I put it before him and told him I had done it all myself. He put one piece in his mouth, for it looked beautiful with jelly and everything, just like it did, tonight—and you said it was good tonight, didn't you?—and spat it out. Oh, my dear Mme. Raccamond, oh, my poor Mme. Raccamond, I burst out crying. 'What's there in it?' he said. 'Stuffed with soap?' Well, Georg, you have eaten all the fish."

She rang the bell while she gazed round at them, pink. "I am very happy tonight: you liked it." Georg looked at her, content, and then went back to his dispute with Raccamond. Sophy whispered, "Never mind, he left his estate to my sister and me, just the same; he was childless and loved us very much."

Marianne saw in the Hallers the sump of a large childless family.

Sophy nodded at her. "Your son is doing well at Oxford, of course? It is so charming." She nodded to her, congratulating her. "Anna! Hurry up!" (The rest in Hungarian.) "Try a little more Cordial-Médoc, Mme. Raccamond. We laid in a big stock just after the war, for Mr. Haller was sure there would be another war within fifteen years!" The Cordial-Médoc, like the other drinks, had sharpened and lost its original flavor by bad cellarage but they both cried out they were all excellent, superlative.

"Dear Madame," Mme. Haller again said, "I prefer to eat in my own lares and penates. Restaurants cheat you."

"Sophy! You ought to see what Anna is doing!"

She answered sharply in German, "Georg! Why do you always order me about?"

"A hostess," he laid down, as if repeating some basic assumption of physics, "should always make her guests' comfort her first care."

"Excuse me," she said to them both, blushing. She went and stood behind Georg. "Georg, you are naughty this evening. You command. You order." She laughed girlishly, still the nineteen-year-old bride, conserved, put her hands a minute on his shoulders. "Naughty, disagreeable Georg."

"Go," said Georg, gently. She tripped off at once. "Yes," continued Georg, in contented repletion, "Russia will one of these days be the most modern state in Europe and in perhaps twenty-five to fifty years will be better off than America. Look at the anarchy that reigns in America!"

Mrs. Haller came in with a deep fruit dish in which large half-peaches swam. Behind her, Anna, bearing a dish deeper and smaller, full of whipped cream; nuts and nutcrackers and sugar. She returned to the kitchen and brought back a plate of cakes, while Sophy nipped out and returned with a bag of chocolates and a jar of honey. "Georg, come and eat."

Georg had been looking through his engineering textbooks to illustrate some point to Aristide and now came back slowly, with his eager, sunny, blond face turned to him. "If the government has the foresight to form a trade pact with Russia, France will ride the storm in the next few years. Russia is making herself felt. France was boycotted for years after the French Revolution: statesmen all fulminated against her and those who supported her were treated as ragamuffins and tatterdemalion intellects, but it became impossible to neglect her. You see!"

"And she, of course," said Aristide nastily, "needs an outlet for grain.

She'll ruin the little grain producer in this country." He himself reaped a few bushels yearly on a little place down south.

"Mme. Raccamond, will you help your husband to peaches and cream?" asked Sophy. Marianne did so, putting only one peach on his plate. This caused a frightful outcry from both the hosts and Aristide's plate was heaped with peaches and cream, which his doctor had told him not to touch. "Just a little . . . it won't hurt you!" Sophy nodded confidentially, "This is better than you get anywhere in Paris; a man brings it in specially for me twice a week from the country. Just taste it, Mme. Raccamond. There! Eh?"

"No system can support compound interest," said Georg. "I will show you a little calculation of my own. Do you read propositions in algebra easily?"

"How would we run the state without it?" demanded Aristide, whose dream was to insure his old age by a great quantity of War loan, Treasury bonds, and so on. "Why, colonial expansion has only been possible on compound interest. My customers wouldn't buy stocks or bonds if they didn't expect compound interest on their money. Money can't lie sterile, Mr. Haller."

"Eat, eat, Mr. Raccamond; you are eating nothing." He ate obediently, saying between mouthfuls, "I know it's a burden on the mortgagee, but that is the only way you can encourage people to save and to hold property. Mortgages and rent are really a sort of compound interest on your saving and foresightedness."

"Georg, don't talk to Mr. Raccamond: he wants to eat. Look at him, his plate is empty. Help him to some cream, Georg. You see, Mme. Raccamond, these are tinned peaches, but I only get the very best. They are the Australian brand, Yanco . . . do you know it? There is only one place where you can get it. You don't know?" She bit her lip, almost irritated: the Raccamonds were really no connoisseurs. She felt it her duty to save Mme. Raccamond from poisoning Raccamond by inches. "Mme. Raccamond, I'll go and get the tin."

"Sophy! There's no need to do that."

"Georg, don't speak so sharply; you don't understand that they don't know the brand!" All this in German. She hurried out. At the door: "And after, some tea, some coffee? Yes? A little tea with wine in it, surely."

They were glad to see her go, being anxious to plunge back into the interest discussion again. Marianne especially, who was slowly accumulating an income from bonds, was heart and soul for interest.

"Interest is sound arithmetically, but unsound and revolution-producing politically," Haller set out, placing a little slip of paper with algebraic symbols on it, between the peaches and the chocolates. "Interest is unsound financially and revolutions are necessary to purify the financial system; revolutions lead to a revival, the dead weight of indebtedness is thrown off: repudiation is necessary to liquidation and this to optimism and new hope. Nothing arouses hate for the ruling classes like excessive taxes and an excessive burden of internal debt. Lenin saw this. He acted as a cathartic; the ruling classes in Russia had stuffed themselves to bursting on interest. You see, the financial papers enable the people to see the Fat People eating."

"You mean the financiers?"

"Yes, I call them the Fat People. Now, human nature teaches us, we know by instinct, that there is something wrong when five per cent of the people stuff and ninety-five per cent have almost nothing to eat and no money to put into interest-bearing bonds at all."

Aristide said cloudily, "Perhaps, there are thieves, my dear friend, amongst the rich, but what about the sound bourgeoisie to which you and I belong? The sound bourgeoisie—the workers don't realize this —are hard-working, intelligent, saving, modest, liberal, the only good people. The best intelligences are found amongst them, the highest positions in the State. The workers live from hand to mouth. If they ever seized the State, it would be a fearful thing: the State would live from hand to mouth."

Marianne nearly nodded her head off at this and looked positively Chinese with grasping and avarice. Not that the Chinese are grasping —this is just the way she looked. "We go out on the road on Sunday in our little car which we have just been able to afford, out of our savings. We can hardly get along the roads with working-class people in cars too. Secondhand cars. God knows they can't afford them. And there they go racing past us, jeering at us, using up oil, destroying the roads, risking human life, not only their own lives—they can do that, with pleasure, but ours too. They have no idea of economy. I shudder at the thought of the money that must be poured out in Russia: every sou is gone. No wonder the country is breaking down. It's a detestable thing. It's because they were a nation of animals and personally I don't blame them so much as the old aristocrats. They were very charming people in themselves, but they didn't improve the country and now they have to pay for it: a nation of animals and pack mules have got hold of their estates and their factories. When the landed people and the capitalists get back it will take them twenty years to repair the country."

"You are wrong, Mme. Raccamond," said Haller, in his deliberate manner, intending no offense though. "A backward economy eventually proves more economic than an excessively hurriedly modern one. Do you know thread at all, Mr. Raccamond? Look at the thread in this shirt, it is made of six strands; it won't wear out in forty years, probably. I was getting some very fine thread from a place in Lille, but only a little of it, some years ago. Finally, I went to see the man, thinking I would buy the place and improve it, make a big business out of it. I found him in a side street and his machine a tiny old-fashioned thing, more like a bedstead than a modern filature. I sat down on the floor with him and he told me, his brother went into business, put up a modern spinning factory, and has been bankrupted because of the constant need for modern improvements in machinery. The buyers demand it. Then the slack time comes, he is left with it on his hands, weeds grow in the courtyards, dust falls from the walls; in five years when business picks up, industry has got far ahead of him. He has used up all his capital, he owes everything to the bank, and he has nothing to start with again.

"Meanwhile new competitors are starting from scratch with the latest thing in machines. You see the waste? America, for example, has spent all this time, labor, money, lives, has seen bankruptcies and suicides, to learn how to build modern buildings; and England has now only to take over the latest designs and profit from American experience, without bleeding for it herself. The expense of experimentation is enormous and I assure you, Mr. Raccamond, that thousands of profitable, time-saving inventions are throttled in their cradles, even in America, to save money. Now Russia was saved all the elementary struggles of machine capitalism. She is that much to the good. She can start right off now, with her first tractor factory the same as the best tractor factories in Germany or America. She need count nothing for depreciation. But in an old-fashioned economy, like England's, the profit lasts only a short time. The preservation of antiquated styles by tariffs and loss of trade by old patterns eventually disable the country. It cannot be done artificially. Only in the revolutionary way. And Lenin saw that, too. He was a great economist!"

"That is very well for men of our cultivation," protested Aristide, with a blank expression, "but workers cannot understand these things. We have had a university education. I once tried to read Marx and found it quite impossible. I didn't understand even the first page. How can workers then?"

"That is a comfort to me," Marianne peaceably put in, lapping up her peaches. "Even if the Reds continue to govern in Moscow, which I don't believe, it will take them fifty years to acquire any culture, a hundred and fifty years to produce a Velasquez, longer than that to produce an El Greco."

Mme. Haller returned with the opened peach tin which she had rescued from the garbage box. She was flushed. "You see, Mme. Raccamond! This is it. You will recognize it by the label? It's a pretty label, isn't it?"

"They are the very best," Georg explained. "You see, they get so much sun, they are unusually luscious. Otherwise we would not eat tinned things at all. The ordinary brands are unhealthy. You don't eat tinned things, do you, Mme. Raccamond?"

Marianne's eyes brightened at a recollection, "Yes, we do . . . not much. But we do get a simply marvelous *pâté de foie gras* from the Dordogne, the best I ever tasted; it is made by a little firm down there. Do you like it, Mme. Haller? I would get you a tin."

The Hallers were pale with astonishment. After a moment, Mme. Haller managed to say, in a stricken voice, "Mme. Raccamond! You know—" (very low) "how they are made, *pâtés de foies gras?*"

"Why, yes."

Almost tonelessly, she questioned, "You know they are made from" (a shocked look) "the diseased livers of overfed geese?"

"Of course."

The two couples exchanged glances of complete incomprehension. Almost stonily, Mme. Haller said, "No, no, we never eat them. We could not eat them."

What was so particularly shocking to them in the sluggish livers of lazy, overfed geese? But Mme. Haller had managed to convey a feeling of cannibalism. Briskly, Haller broke the spell, "Some wine, Mme. Raccamond? Do you like Burgundy or Bordeaux, red or white?"

"Oh, Burgundy, thank you . . . red." A pleased look, "I didn't know you had wine." She began to think, after so much liqueur, ugh! but I need a tonic.

"Tell Anna, some Burgundy, Sophy."

"I'll get it myself. And Mme. Raccamond, did you taste the butter? I must show you the box we get it in. We get it specially from a place near Mulhouse. It is sent up every month."

Yes, and now it is rancid, thought Marianne. "Really, I used *beurre d'Isigny,*" she said with confidence, mentioning the best domestic butter in Paris.

"*Beurre d'Isigny!* Oh, Mme. Raccamond, do you buy it from the butterman like that? But you know that they *mix* it! You get nothing *pure*. You must get it yourself from the producer. You don't know what you're getting."

Marianne flushed. "We don't use very much . . . we eat out most of the time." She dared him to go back to the ground of restaurants. He eyed her for a moment and turned courteously to her husband.

"The reason I have built up a reserve of goods as well as gold is that gold itself is sterile and the holding of it sterilizes not only money-making capacity but even the mental faculties all round. It stultifies its holder. You see, even me—Mr. Raccamond. I was able to retire at forty-five and what have I done the last ten years? Nothing. When the depression came I realized that not only was the world sterile, through overproduction, but I was sterile. I want to go back to my home town and become a doctor. I regret that five years ago I did not start my medical course, but there is still time. I think I will do that. I fear the sterilization of gold. I hold it in so many places, England, Switzerland, Canada, for example, that even traveling has no pleasure for me any more. I am afraid to disturb my gold reserve. You see, how it is with me? Do you understand, Mr. Raccamond? And so the only thing for me to do is to go back to earning with my bare hands! . . . Do you remember when you were a student, Raccamond? I was happy when I was a student. I was a prize student. I thought I would be building machines all my life. . . . You know, we are lazy, Mr. Raccamond. The government should force us all to do some vulgar labor, like weeding gutters, or cleaning sewers, for a month every year: it would act as a purgative for our laziness . . . Yes, indeed, Mme. Raccamond, we have to be forced. Working people too must be forced; if things go well in Russia, they will have to be pressed to do the dirty jobs, they will have to be pressed to obey hygienic regulations! I had some peasant girls once who would not bind their hair in handkerchiefs to save their hair from the looms. I had to be very strict with them. . . . I would not mind going to a new developing country myself, say, like Australia or Palestine and showing the people how to work."

Sophy returned with the butter box and behind her, Anna, carrying a plate of sausage and a bottle of red wine.

Aristide was spilled in his chair, his mouth half open, his eyes bulging and his pendulous cheeks some pale shade between French blue and mauve. When the wine was poured for him, although his head was reeling, he grasped the glass and drained it, hoping to combat the nightmare indigestion that had already set in. He looked with bitter astonishment at Haller, breathing freely, cheerfully, cutting up the sausage, which (of course) came from a special, though nameless, shop, brought specially in a basket by Anna, the only shop in Paris free from bacteria, poison, and pollution, according to both the Hallers. Anna, at the door, surveyed them a minute. She knew, of course, very well, what they came for, the two black pigs: they came to snuffle and grub in her master's dishes.

"A little port wine?" asked Sophy, and getting out a special glass, put the purple-mantled port, not a particularly good one, by Aristide's plate. He pushed it away a centimeter, "No, please." But with the usual protestations, he drank.

"If Hitler or some demagogue like that insisted on everyone going to a labor camp for a month a year," said Haller, "even I would say there was some good in him. But he's a weak fellow."

Aristide shook his head: he had quite lost the thread of the conversation; he blurted out feebly, "You, Mr. Haller, pay your own debts. Where would the sausage maker, the bread baker be otherwise? You wouldn't get your butter from Mullhouse."

Haller laughed and ate a big piece of sausage with relish, "Yes, but if it were a question of paying them compound interest for ever on a sausage, if I had to mortgage my bread to them as well and keep on paying through the nose, I would run away and remain solvent and honorable in another country where such fantastic practices didn't exist. I would even run away to Russia. . . ." He raised his eyebrows, looked seriously at them. "The little harmless bourgeois, with little homes, haven't been touched. They respect them. I would keep my money abroad. . . . Take America," he went on, not remarking that Aristide was past taking anything, "in America the increment of wealth is three per cent per annum, the increment of population one per cent, but the Government gives four per cent which is more than reason allows, and most people casually expect to reap six to ten per cent on their money—in the stock market even more. All that should be purged from the system, industry should lose that dead weight, the common people should have all that shifted off their bread and cheese. . . . We take laxatives, Mr. Raccamond; the system should, too."

"There would be no confidence," Aristide said slowly, with a death rattle in his voice, a choke which made Marianne blanch, "if such things were said publicly."

"Aristide," cried his wife, "what's the matter?"

"Oh, what's the matter, Mr. Raccamond?"

"Air—a little air . . . I'm faint."

"Oh, dear. (Georg, you hear!) Air. Open the window."

Georg got up and went to the window, with precise haste. Aristide rose and hung trembling to the arm of his chair. Marianne darted anxious looks round, wondering if he would have the courage to go outside the room. But their tiny hostess was struggling on the other side, already heaving him towards the window. "Oh, Mme. Raccamond, your husband . . . help him, look!" At the window, Aristide collapsed into the window seat. Georg stood by him and spoke to him in murmurs. The curtains flung themselves out into the room again and again as the blessed zephyr blew in. The two women retired once more to the sofa and sat talking, Sophy commiserating with Marianne. Poor Mr. Raccamond worked so hard. These rich clients were so exacting: the market turned for a day and plop, down they came on the customers' man. The men had left the room.

Pale, but himself, Aristide now returned, took his place, and Georg, relieved and content, sat opposite him. "Sophy, is the tea ready? Mr. Raccamond needs some tea."

She pressed the bell. Meanwhile the clock had been going round and round and Aristide, with drops on his brow, had watched that dreadful minute hand dragging itself with malevolent slowness to the half-hour, to the hour. They had now been here gorging two hours and ten minutes, and it was by no means finished. What a man goes through to keep customers! And this one, too, who sometimes passed a hundred shares in a month, and who paid himself ten times ten per cent interest by getting the Raccamonds to dinner and pumping Aristide about the bank, about the market, about Bertillon's position in the market, about Alphendéry's relation to him, about the great goldbugs who had their bonds with Bertillon and about a thousand other things, upon whose details he fed in his long idle hours of the day and night. But Aristide knew that engineer or no, mathematician or no, one of these days Haller might require a "private service," some transferring of bonds, or gold, and that it was just possible he would get it for himself. . . . He looked at the little rubicund blond gnome with his mountains of gold and despised him; him, once a leading spinner of East Prussia, now a frog in a giant bell jar predicting the political weather!

"The tea, Sophy! The tea."

"I suppose she has gone to sleep. When I went into the kitchen, she was singing and she would not answer me."

"Then go out yourself, Sophy." (In German) "Don't show yourself so incompetent in the management of a servant." She trotted out.

The door opened. "The tea!" said Sophy cheerfully, ushering in Anna with a tray on which stood handsome glasses full of a transparent orange liquid. "Now, Mr. Raccamond, you will feel better. You need a little stimulation."

"Put a little more wine into it than usual, Sophy. Mr. Raccamond is tired, he needs it."

The tea became the color of blood.

"Moderation," said Haller, "is a wise use of liberty, a wise limitation of plenitude. There must be a redistribution of goods."

"Some of these chocolates with your tea, Mr. Raccamond; they are the best chocolates in the world and come from Switzerland. Lindt and Sprüngli. It is amusing that when I was at school in Switzerland," said Mrs. Haller, "I was told to be most careful not to acquire the Swiss *'li'* for *'lein'* and once when they asked me what chocolates I had bought (they were very careful of our diet), I said Lindt and Sprünglein."

"Ha, ha," said Georg. "Well, Mr. Raccamond, moderation is a thing financiers won't hear of and so we have revolution, their own fault. They can't be moderate, and so neither can the ninety-five per cent disinherited. It is inevitable."

Marianne said tartly, "There have been a lot of revolutions already and no one is satisfied."

Sedately Haller shook his head, as he put another macaroon on Aristide's plate (he assumed that as Aristide was no longer suffocated, he could eat again). "No, where the redistribution goes only from five to ten per cent of the people, that is not a revolution. You see, Russia is the only revolution that concerned ninety-five per cent of the people. That's why they like it."

"But the worst elements are on top," cried Marianne, in real distress. "Look at *L'Humanité!* Look at the way they criticize the theater and literature. 'The impact of dialectics.' Bah! How can they use such barbarous words!"

Haller pleasantly sipped his wine-filled tea, "Ah, my dear lady, they are not trying to please us . . . no! They will do away with us. Entirely. They don't need us! A shoemaker, Madame, can make shoes: he doesn't need our executive ability at all. It's sad, but it's true." He laughed sunnily. "I would love to go to Palestine, for instance, and knock some sense into their heads."

"Whose heads?"

"The workers' heads . . . teach them how to work."

Aristide said, "Would they listen to you; they're obstinate brutes."

Sophy fluttered gaily, "Oh, we had a communist and an unemployed man up here to talk with us, at dinner, on two separate occasions; we know just how they think."

Georg flushed, looked extremely flattered, boyish. "Yes, I quite agree with the communist, a most intelligent man and not a bit grateful for the dinner, you know."

Faintly Marianne asked, "What was he? The secretary of the party or something?"

"No, just a tramman Georg found down at the sheds. He wrote a letter to our paper about it."

"What paper is that?"

"The *Frankfurter Zeitung*. It is the only liberal paper. It is the best paper in the world. We read it every day. The literary criticisms, my dear Mme. Raccamond: you would be delighted to read them. So very refined, modern, too."

Georg, on the point of revealing his naked soul, said to Raccamond, "Why do you work for Bertillon, Mr. Raccamond? It is (don't laugh at the old-fashioned phrase), it is rather sordid, isn't it? Why don't you free yourself and—better yourself. You are the slave of great capital, aren't you?"

Aristide looked displeased at this admonishment. "I hope to get on, you know. A partnership—"

"Aristide?"

"With some house or other—later on. That is not so bad. A private bank, you know, is the needle's eye to influence in finance, in Paris."

"Yes, but does that satisfy you, Mr. Raccamond? You seem to have such a cultivated view," said Sophy, regretfully.

"Oh, yes. I was born for finance," Aristide said. What a curious look Marianne gave him!

"Give Mr. Raccamond a leetle more sausage with his tea," urged Sophy. At this moment Anna came triumphantly in, as if she knew Aristide's state—and who would not, seeing his complexion and bulging eyes and sweating chops?—and more tea was forced on him, as well as a splendid Doyenne de Comice pear, specially bought for him, "because he needed fresh fruit for his digestion." There was a hailstorm of protestations and inquiries, refusals and moral suasions. Sophy won. Suddenly, Georg said, two hours and forty minutes too late, "Sophy, you know it is not polite to press anything on people. They know what they want." She looked guilty and desisted.

When they got out into the quiet street and found it past midnight, they felt as if a battle had been lost and won. "Never again, Marianne," said Aristide choking. "I feel as if I will die. I can't do it again . . . I am suffocating."

Marianne bit her lip. "When I asked you to go and get my handkerchief, didn't you understand I wanted to give you a chance to go out in the hall? Instead, you passed me yours."

"I didn't know, Marianne; please forgive me. It was kind of you."

"You should have refused."

"Oh, I tried . . . didn't you see that? But they are terrible; they are ogres. Marianne, we will never go there again. He comes to Bertillon's for quotations and places his order in Cleat, Placket, and Company, and I don't believe any amount of listening to his nonsense will make him realize that it's unethical."

"They must be fabulously rich, just the same," sighed Marianne.

"Yes, you are right, unfortunately. Well, it won't be until next month. They only ask us once a month."

"They are our friends, and true friends. Friends are true in the measure that they appreciate our moneymaking ability and financial staying power. Mme. Haller asked me to go shopping with her and I will. She will be useful to me."

Aristide looked at her curiously and after an inspection said, "How can she possibly be useful to you? You don't need anything, that I know of."

"I may," Marianne declared. "Aristide, I have been chasing a ghost light: physical goods are power. I am going in for moneymaking, flat. I've sold my play in London, but there's nothing in it. I'll go in for big moneymaking, naked business, and when I'm through I'll have enough material to write a real play, something in the Bernstein line."

Aristide looked at her with admiration. "Marianne, you have a man's brain. You never swerve. Whatever you want you will get. I wish I was as resolute as you."

"Why, so you are, my dear."

He shook his head faintly, then seeing her glance, smiled and nodded in acquiescence, "In my own way. We are well matched, Marianne. I will always be glad we married. Where should I have been without you?"

She was cheerful, resolute. "Still in the arms of Lucienne, I suppose."

"Ah, I don't know, I don't know. I had outgrown that."

She smiled to herself in the dark. "Do you feel better now, Aristide?"

"Yes."

"Our son, Aristide, is very like his mother; I see Lucienne in his eyes and brows; his mouth is like yours." There was a silence. "There is a sort of spiritual bloom over his face, which is like Lucienne's," she continued.

"I don't think so," he murmured half-heartedly.

"Ah, yes. She is very brave to let us educate him and have him come home to us."

Aristide said bitterly, "She is poor. She could not expect me to give her your money."

"A mother will do a lot for a son," Marianne said cheerfully.

Aristide looked at her in unconcealed surprise, "You are so strong, Marianne . . . you have an incredible strength of soul."

"Ah!" She smiled with intense secret gratification.

"Lucienne," he murmured, "never had your breadth of vision, Marianne. She was kind, she is good, she is a woman, but it is impossible for her to think with the moral vigor that you have. Nor have I," he ended with faint, instinctive malice, well hidden.

Marianne frowned, and they fell silent, until she changed the subject, to her advantage. "There's no subject so rich in ideas as Money." Aristide grunted. "I'm thinking," went on Marianne tenderly, with a richer tone than she usually used, "that money is a very pure thing in its way; that's why the Hallers have such curious habits. They have nothing more to do, they do not even need more money—they have enough for avarice. Now they are looking for the absolute. They caught that from their gold bars. It is an absolute. People have such a delicate love for money that if you speak jealously of it or of those who own it, all the dirt falls back on you: people take you for a miserable, poor-spirited person." She laughed richly. "I could almost love money, I should like to wash my hands in gold coins. I should feel like a princess. No, it is not sterile. No, water seems sterile, too." Aristide grunted. "I will, some day!" Marianne murmured with energy.

"Will what?"

"Will wash my hands in gold coin."

He laughed a little, looked sideways at her. A curl of her wiry black hair had escaped and softened her round, firm features. "I love you, Marianne."

FOR
LOVE
ALONE

For Love Alone was written in 1944. The story begins in Sydney, Australia, and moves to England as Teresa Hawkins breaks away from her family to follow her night school teacher, Jonathan Crow, to London where he has gone to continue his studies. Teresa gets a job as secretary to James Quick, a businessman. As she discovers Jonathan's emotional impoverishment she becomes aware of her own possibilities for passion. She marries Quick; but it is not until she has had an affair with another man, Harry Girton, that she is able to free herself from the sexual strictures of her upbringing and realize fully her gift for loving.

The first three excerpts give us the Hawkins family: Teresa and her sister, Kitty, as they get ready for their cousin Malfi's wedding; the brothers, Lance and Leo; and Andrew Hawkins, the father, in whom some readers will find the forerunner of Harry Pollit in *The Man Who Loved Children* (1940). In the fourth excerpt we see the deprivation and poverty which have formed Jonathan Crow. In the fifth, Teresa has come to visit Crow in his room in London where he is spied upon by his landlady, Bagshawe, and makes casual love to the rooming-house maid, Lucy. The last two excerpts are about the early days of Teresa's marriage, her brief affair with Harry, and her return to Quick.

I

SEA PEOPLE

In the part of the world Teresa came from, winter is in July, spring brides marry in September, and Christmas is consummated with roast beef, suckling pig, and brandy-laced plum pudding at 100 degrees in the shade, near the tall pine tree loaded with gifts and tinsel as in the old country, and old carols have rung out all through the night.

This island continent lies in the water hemisphere. On the eastern coast, the neighbouring nation is Chile, though it is far, far east,

Valparaiso being more than six thousand miles away in a straight line; her northern neighbours are those of the Timor Sea, the Yellow Sea; to the south is that cold, stormy sea full of earthwide rollers, which stretches from there without land, south to the Pole.

The other world—the old world, the land hemisphere—is far above her as it is shown on maps drawn upside-down by old-world cartographers. From that world and particularly from a scarcely noticeable island up toward the North Pole the people came, all by steam; or their parents, all by sail. And there they live round the many thousand miles of seaboard, hugging the water and the coastal rim. Inside, over the Blue Mountains, are the plains heavy with wheat, then the endless dust, and after outcrops of silver, opal, and gold, Sahara, the salt-crusted bed of a prehistoric sea, and leafless mountain ranges. There is nothing in the interior; so people look toward the water, and above to the fixed stars and constellations which first guided men there.

Overhead, the other part of the Milky Way, with its great stars and nebulae, spouts thick as cow's milk from the udder, from side to side, broader and whiter than in the north; in the centre the curdle of the Coalsack, that black hole through which they look out into space. The skies are sub-tropical, crusted with suns and spirals, as if a reflection of the crowded Pacific Ocean, with its reefs, atolls, and archipelagos.

It is a fruitful island of the sea-world, a great Ithaca, there parched and stony and here trodden by flocks and curly-headed bulls and heavy with thick-set grain. To this race can be put the famous question, "Oh, Australian, have you just come from the harbour? Is your ship in the roadstead? Men of what nation put you down—for I am sure you did not get here on foot?"

THE ISLAND CONTINENT

BROWN SEAWEED AND OLD FISH NETS

Naked, except for a white towel rolled into a loincloth, he stood in the doorway, laughing and shouting, a tall man with powerful chest and thick hair of pale burning gold and a skin still pale under many summers' tan. He seemed to thrust back the walls with his muscular arms; thick tufts of red hair stood out from his armpits. The air was full of the stench of brown seaweed and old fish nets. Through the window you could see the water of the bay and the sand specked with flotsam and scalloped with yellow foam, left by the last wave. The man, Andrew Hawkins, though straight and muscular, was covered with flaccid yellow-white flesh and his waist and abdomen were too broad and full. He had a broad throat and chest and from them came a clear tenor voice.

". . . she was sitting on the ground nursing her black baby, and she herself was black as a hat, with a strong, supple oily skin, finer than white women's skins: her heavy breasts were naked, she was not ashamed of that, but with natural modesty, which is in even the most primitive of women, she covered her legs with a piece of cloth lying on the ground and tittered behind her hand exactly like one of you—" he was saying to the two women sitting at the table. "Then she said something to her husband and he, a thin spindle-shanked fellow, translated for me, grinning from ear to ear: she asked how it was possible for a man to have such beautiful white feet as mine."

He looked down at his long blond feet and the two women looked from their sewing quickly at his feet, as if to confirm the story.

"I have always been admired for my beautiful white skin," said the golden-haired man, reminiscently. "Women love it in a man, it surprises them to see him so much fairer in colour than they are. Especially the darkies," and he looked frankly at Kitty Hawkins, who was a nut-brown brunette with drooping back hair. "But not only the dark ones," he went on softly. He kept on coaxing.

"I have been much loved; I didn't always know it—I was always such an idealist. When girls and, yes, even women older than myself, wanted to come and talk to me, I thought it was a thing of the brain. One poor girl, Paula Brown, wrote to me for years, discussing things. I never dreamed that it was not an interest in speculative thought. I used to tell her all my dreams and longings. I could have married a rich girl. In the Movement there was a quiet, pale girl called Annie Milson. Her father, though I didn't think about it at the time, was Commissioner for Railways and was quite the capitalist. They had properties all around here, dairy-farms down the south coast. I could have been a wealthy man if I had become Milson's son-in-law, and I believe he would have been delighted. He seemed to approve of me. I spent the afternoon at their Lindfield house two or three times—and spent the afternoon talking to Milson! I never suspected the girl liked me. I believe she loved the good-looking, sincere young idealist—but I had no interest in earthly things at the time and I never suspected it. Poor Annie! She used to send me books. Yes, I believe I was loved by many women but I was so pure that I had no temptations. 'My mind to me a kingdom was.' I suppose, now, when I look back, that I was a mystery to them, poor girls, such a handsome young man, who didn't dance, didn't take them to the theatre, and worried only about the social organism."

He laughed, his brilliant oval blue eyes, their whites slightly blood-shot, looking gaily at the two girls. He sighed, "I didn't know that I was a handsome lad.I didn't know then what a woman, a married woman, said to me much later, a fine, motherly soul she was, Mrs. Kurzon, but she said it with a sigh, 'Mr. Hawkins, how many women have wanted to put their hands in your wonderful hair?' She said it with a twinkle but she said it with longing too; and then she asked me if she could, laughing all the time and sweetly too, in a womanly sweet way. I let her, and she plunged them in and took them out with a sigh of gratification, 'Oh, Mr. Hawkins, how wonderful it is!' And how many women have told me it was a shame to waste such hair on a man, they would give anything to have it."

One of the girls, the younger one, who was blond, looked up at the marvellous hair of the man.

Andrew Hawkins ran his hand through it, feeling it himself. A thought seemed to strike him; he brought down his hand and looked at the back, then the palm. It was a large, pale, muscular hand, an artisan's hand, hairless, diseased-looking because streaked and spotted with fresh cement. "Not a bad hand either," he said. He had something on the tip of his tongue but couldn't get it out, he went on about his legs instead, "Poor Mrs. Slops said I had legs like a 'dook.' And I have seen 'dooks,' at that, and not half so well-calved, I'll take my affidavit. But do you know, Kit," he said, lowering his voice, and his eyes darkening with modesty or wonder. "You see this hand, my good right hand, do you see it, Kit?"

Kitty laughed in her throat, a troubled, sunny laugh, "I've felt it, too, in my time."

He said mysteriously, lowering his voice again, "Women have kissed this hand." They both turned and looked at him, startled. "Yes, Kit, yes, you disbeliever," he said, turning to the younger girl. "Teresa won't believe me perhaps, for she doesn't want to love me, but women, several women have kissed this hand. Do you know how women kiss men's hands? They take it in both their hands, and kiss it first on the back, and then each finger separately, and they hate to let go." He burst out suddenly into a rough ringing laugh. "You would not believe that has happened—not once, but several times—to your Andrew!"

"Handy Andy," said Teresa, in her soft, unresonant voice. She did not glance up but went on sewing. Each of the girls had before her on the table the wide sleeve of a summer dress; it was a greyish lavender voile sprinkled with pink roses and they were sewing roses made of the material in rows along the sleeves. "Ah, you think you know a lot about love," went on Andrew, coming into the room, and throwing himself full length on the old settee that stood underneath the window that looked upon the beach. "Yes, Trees is always moaning about love, but you don't know, Trees, that love is warmth, heat. The sun is love and love also is fleshly, in this best sense that a beautiful woman gladdens the heart of man and a handsome man brightens the eyes of the ladies. One blessed circle, perpetual emotion." He laughed. "Many women have loved your Andrew, but not you two frozen women." He continued teasing, waiting for an answer,

> "Orpheus with his lute made T'rees
> And the mountain tops that freeze,
> Bow themselves when he did sing:"

"We will never be finished," said Teresa.

"And there are the beans to do, I must do them," said Kitty, throwing the long sleeve on the table. "When they're done, I'll call to you and you put away the sewing. You must have some lunch, the wedding breakfast won't be till late."

"Beauty," mused Andrew, looking at them. "What a strange thing that I didn't have lovely daughters, I who worship beauty so much! Yes, Fate plays strange tricks, especially on her favourites. My dream as a lad was to find a stunning mate, and different from most youths, I dreamed of the time when I would have beautiful little women around me. How proud I was in prospect! But of course," he said confidingly to Teresa, "I knew nothing of a thing more sacred than beauty—human love. My dear Margaret attracted me by her truth-loving face, serious, almost stern—as sea-biscuit! ha-ha—but soft, womanly dark eyes, like Kitty's. I don't know where you got your face of a little tramp, Trees, a ragamuffin. If I had had three beautiful bouncing maidens like old Harkness! I saw the three of them coming down an alley in their rose garden last Saturday and I went up and pretended I couldn't see them, I said, 'Where are the Harknesses? Here I see nothing but prize roses!' They burst out laughing and Mina, she has a silvery, rippling laugh, said, 'Oh, Mr. Hawkins, how very nice!' "

"Do you mean that fat one?" asked Teresa, spitefully.

"Ah, jocund, rubious, nods and becks and wreathed smiles," said Andrew, writhing on the settee in ecstasy, a broad smile on his face. "I peered in among the roses and then I pretended to see them and I said, 'I was looking for Mina, Teen and Violet, but all I see are the Three Graces!' "

"You should be ashamed," said Teresa, morosely.

"That just shows you don't understand the world and your Andrew," he retorted comfortably, leaning back and flexing and stretching his legs. "The girls were delighted! They went off into happy peals of golden laughter, like peals of bells. Mrs. Harkness came running up and said, 'What have you been saying to my girls, Mr. Hawkins? I must know the joke too.' We all laughed again. Mrs. Harkness—I wish you could meet her—is a wonderful woman, motherly, but full of womanly charm and grace too. In her forties, plump, round, but not ungraceful, the hearthside Grace. And she too told me how beautiful my hair is. They can't help it, the desire to run their fingers through it is almost irresistible."

"Did she kiss your hand? Mrs. Harkness, I mean," enquired Teresa in a low voice.

Hawkins looked at her sharply, "Don't jest at things that are sacred to me, Teresa. I have suffered much through love and when you come to know human love, instead of self-love—"

"The beans are done," called Kitty. Teresa gathered up her sewing.

"If you ever love! For I verily believe that inward and outward beauty strike one chord."

"You do," said the girl, "do you? Well, I don't. How simple that would be."

"An ugly face is usually the dried crust of a turbid, ugly soul. I personally," he said in a low, vibrant voice, "cannot stand ugliness, Trees. I worship beauty," he said, throwing his limbs about in a frenzy of enthusiasm, "and all my life I have served her, truth and beauty."

Teresa took the worn damask cloth out of the sideboard drawer and set five places.

"I want to be loved in my own home," said Hawkins, contemplating his long legs and speaking in a fine drawn silken murmur. "Sometimes I close my eyes and imagine what this place would be like if it were a Palace of Love! All your ideas of decorating the walls with fifteenth-century designs, peepholes, twisted vines, naked-bottomed fat and in-decent infants on the ceiling—that's dry, meaningless, dull work, but if this house were peopled with our love, murmurous with all the undertones, unspoken understanding of united affection—a-ah!" He opened his beautiful blue eyes and looked across at her, "And yet, in a way, you're like my dear Margaret, but without her loving nature. How tender she was! I was her whole life, I and you babies. She knew that I had something precious in my head, like the whale with amber-gris—"

"A sick whale has ambergris," said Teresa: "A whale that's half rotting while it swims is the sort they go after, because they hope it has ambergris in its head. And you know how they bring in every soapy thing from the beach, everything that's greasy and pale, for ambergris."

"And she was modest," said the beautiful man, joining his hands and looking down at them. "She had a curious thing she used to say, 'Andrew, how did a mouse like me get a man like you?' What charm there is in a modest woman! If you could learn that, Teresa, you would have charm for men, for they can forgive a lot in a woman who is truly devoted to them. What do we look for in women—understanding! In the rough and tumble of man's world, the law of the jungle is often the only law observed, but in the peace and sanctity of the man's home, he feels the love that is close to angels! A pretty face, a lovely form, cannot give that—or not those alone. No, it is because he knows he is loved. . . . Don't forget, Kitty, to clean my boots," he said, sitting up. "I'm going into town this afternoon."

"On the same boat with us?"

"No, later. And ask Trees if she sewed the buttons on my white shirt. Trees! Buttons—shirt?"

"Well, you could have gone to Malfi's wedding, you're going into town," objected Teresa, bringing in a vase of flowers.

"Ha—I don't approve of that hocus-pocus. You know that, Teresa. Love alone unites adult humans."

"We're not illegitimate," Teresa grinned.

He had risen to his feet and half turned to the window; now he partly turned to her, and she could see the flush on his face and neck. "Teresa," he said gently, "your mother and I were united by a great love, by a passion higher than earthly thoughts, and I should have kept to my principles, and she too was willing to live with me, bound only by the ties of our affection, but—I had already rescued her from the tyranny of that hard old man and we were too young and weak, we could not harden ourselves to hurt her mother's feelings as well."

The young girl went on smiling unpleasantly, "And if you loved someone else?"

The man looked out over the beach and bay for a moment and the girl flushed, thinking she had gone too far. He said, sotto voce, "My girl, since you bring it up, I am in love again, with a young woman, a woman of thirty, a—" His voice dropped. He came towards her, seized her arms and looked into her face without bending, "A wonderful, proud, fine-looking woman, pure in soul. My whole life is wrapping itself around her, so I'm glad you brought it up for you will understand later on—"

She angrily shook her arms free, "Don't touch me, I don't like it."

He sighed and turned his shoulder to her, "This is no way to treat men, men don't like an unbending woman."

"I am unbending."

"You will be sorry for it."

"You ordered us never to kiss or coax or put our arms around you or one another."

"A coaxing woman, a lying, wheedling woman is so abhorrent to men," he said. "I have seen a woman sitting on a man's lap, trying to coax things out of him, isn't that shameful to you? I hope it is. I was firm on that one point and your mother agreed with me. *She* never flattered in hope of gain, she never once lied—never once in our whole married life, Trees. Think of your dear mother if temptation ever comes your way—although you will never be tempted to lie, I know, but the other little things in women, the petty, wretched things, the great flaws in female character—flightiness—" He paused and forced himself to go on with a grimace, "flirtatiousness—though," he continued, looking round at her with a broad smile, *"that* is not likely to be your weakness, nor Kit's. If, I say, you should ever be tempted to tricks like that, thinking to please some man, remember that they detest those tricks and see through them. They know they are traps, mean little chicane to bend them to woman's purpose. I was at Random's the other day. He let his little daughter climb over him and beg him for something he had refused. He gave in. It was a humiliating sight for me, and for the man. I could see her years later, because she is pretty, a warped, dishonest little creature, only thinking of making men do things for her."

"Have you ever seen me coax or kiss?" asked Teresa, indignantly. "Have I ever begged for a single thing?"

"No," he said, "and in a way it's a pity, for you have no attraction for a man as you are now, and it might be better if you knew how to lure men." He smiled at her, "Why can't you be like me, Trees? I am

known everywhere for my smile. I have melted the hearts of my enemies with my smile. You know Random Senior, the man who did me
that great injury—we used to pass in the street, afterwards, every
morning on the way to work. I always smiled and offered him my hand.
After a month or so, he couldn't bear it. He used to go round by a back
way, to avoid me, he couldn't bear the smile of the honest man. If you
would smile more, men would look at you. Men have their burdens.
How delightful it is to see a dear little woman, happy and smiling, eager
to hear them, delighted to cheer them. No one can say why a woman's
bright face and intelligent eye mean so much to a man. Of course, the
sexes are made to attract each other," he said with an indulgent laugh,
"don't think I'm so innocent as I seem, Teresa, but sex has its delicious
aspects. Sex—what a convenient dispensation—yes, sex," he said,
changing his tone and coming close to her, ardently, intently, "I am
not one to inveigh against sex! You don't know the meaning, the beauty
of that word, Teresa, to a loving man. On the other side of the barrier
of sex is all the splendour of internal life, a garden full of roses, if you
can try to understand my meaning, sweet-scented, fountains playing,
the bluebird flying there and nesting there. There are temptations
there but the man sure of himself and who knows himself can resist
them and direct his steps into the perfumed, sunny, lovely paths of sex.
Oh!" he cried, his fine voice breaking, "who can tell these things to
another, especially to you, Trees? You are too cold, you have never
responded to me, and my soul, yes, I will use that word, had such great
need of understanding! I saw right away that Kitty, my dear girl, was
a woman's woman, a womanly little girl, pretty, humble, sweet, but in
you I saw myself and I determined to lead you out of all the temptations
of your sex, for there are many—many of which you are not aware—"

"There is simply nothing of which I am not aware," said the girl.

"You don't know what you are saying," he said tenderly.

Her face became convulsed with anger. "How stupid you are," she
cried and rushed out, upstairs, into the breezy part of the house. All
the doors were open. Her room at the back of the house, painted Nile
green, was an inviting cell, almost bare, neat, cool. She rushed in, flung
herself on her bed, and stared upwards at the ceiling, mad with anger.
In a short time, however, she cooled down, and thought once more that
she would cover the walls, the ceiling, yes, the walls of the corridor, the
walls of all the house, with designs. She got up and began to draw fresh
designs on a large piece of white paper stretched by drawing pins on
her table. She had combined all sorts of strange things in it; patriotic

things, the fantastic heads of prize merino rams, with their thick, parting, curly, silky wool and their double-curved corrugated horns, spikes of desert wheat, strange forms of xerophytic plants, pelicans, albatrosses, sea-eagles, passion-flowers, the wild things she most admired. She forgot all about her dress, which she had to wear at the wedding that afternoon, and which was not yet finished. She came downstairs reluctantly when Kitty called her.

Andrew, viewing her solemnly from the end of the table where he unfolded his worn damask serviette over his bulging naked belly, laughed and chanted as he banged his soup-spoon on the table, "Ants in her pants and bats in her belfry." Teresa turned pale, half-rose from the table, looking at Andrew, and cried, "You offend my honour! I would kill anyone who offends my honour." There was an instant of surprise, then a low, long laugh, rolling from one end of the table to the other. Andrew began it, Lance with his hollow laugh, Leo with his merry one, Kitty's cackles joined in. It was far from spiteful, healthy, they had a character there in the simmering Teresa; she never paused for reflection, she rose just the same in defence of her "honour."

"Your honour," said Lance, her elder brother, low and sneering. He was a tall, pale, blond lad, chaste and impure.

"A woman's honour means something else from what you imagine," said her father, laughing secretively.

"A woman can have honour," declared Leo, a dark, rosy boy. He turned serious in honour of his admired sister.

Lance muttered.

"You would not kill, you would not take human life," said the handsome man, the family god, sitting at the head of the table. "Don't say such things, Teresa."

"Honour is more sacred than life," said Teresa sombrely. Andrew said abruptly, "What's the delay? Where's dinner?" Kitty brought in the soup.

No more was said, and they fell to in a gloomy, angry silence. The unappeased young girl, relentless, ferocious, was able to stir them all. They suddenly felt discontented, saw the smallness of their lives and wondered how to strike out into new ways of living. She did not know this: she brooded, considering her enemies under her brows and made plans to escape. She reconsidered the conversation; she had not said the right thing, but exploded into speech in the usual way. Her father meanwhile had been thinking it over. She supped her soup and without looking up, declared to him, "I am formed, on the moral side. You're ignoble. You can't understand me. Henceforth, everything between us is a misunderstanding. You have accepted compromise, you revel in it. Not me. I will never compromise."

Lance and Andrew, from laughing up their sleeves, came out into the open and burst into joyous roars of laughter. Leo considered her seriously, from above his soup-spoon. Kitty looked from one to the other. Teresa sat up, with a stiff face and a stiff tongue, too, and tried to crush them with a glance. She buried her mouth in another spoonful of soup. Several of them threw themselves back against their chairs and laughed loudly; but the laugh was short.

"Eat your soup and don't be a fool," said Andrew.

Teresa flushed, hesitated, but said nothing. Andrew said, "She dares to say her own father is contemptible, her brothers and sister."

Teresa looked ashamed. Hawkins pursued the subject. "Mooning and moaning to herself and it's evident what it's about—no one is good enough for her. She hates everything. I love everything. I love everyone. My one prayer, and I pray, though to no vulgar god, is for love."

"You disgust me," said Teresa, lifting her head and looking at him.

He began to laugh, "Look at her! Pale, haggard, a regular witch. She looks like a beggar. Who would want her! What pride! Pride in rags! Plain Jane on the high horse! When she is an old maid, she'll still be proud, and noble. No one else will count!"

The nineteen-year-old said calmly, "I told you I would kill you if you insult me. I will do it with my bare hands. I am not so cowardly as to strike with anything. I know where to press though—I will kill you, father." With terror, the table had become silent, only Kitty murmured, "Terry! Don't be silly!"

The father turned pale and looked angrily at her.

"You don't believe me," said the girl, "but you should, it's for your own good. Base coward, hitting your children when they're small, insulting them when they're big and saying you're their father. Base coward—to think," she said, suddenly rising, with an exalted expression, staring at him and at them all, "I have to live in the house with such a brutal lot, teasing, torturing, making small. I know what to do —keep your yellow blood, I'll go away, you'll never see me again and you can laugh and titter to your heart's content, look over your shoulders at people, snigger and smirk. Do it, but let me live! I'll go this afternoon and after the wedding, I'll never come back."

The answer to this was a terrifying roar from the father, who knew how to crush these hysterias, and the subdued, frightened girl sank into her place. Presently, she burst into tears, threw herself on the table and shook with sobs. "When we are all suffering so much," she cried through her hair and folded arms, "you torture us."

"Meanwhile," said the beautiful man quietly, "you are letting Kitty do all the work."

She rose and went ashamedly to work.

"Dry your eyes," whispered Kitty hastily, "or you'll look terrible when you go out." "I have suffered too much," said Teresa, "I have suffered too much." But the storm was over.

Meanwhile, Hawkins sat on the stone seat in the wild front garden, whistling. They came down, their hands still red from washing dishes. He saw them running for the boat, burst into laughter, then suddenly, "How wonderful is marriage—the Song of Songs . . . makes the women leap like roes . . ."

THE COUNTLESS FLAMING EYES OF THE FLESH

The girls looked so strangely different, tearing round the bay, that their father, who was quite proud of their talents, doubled up with laughter as he stood at the gate shouting good-bye and they could hear his ha-ha-ha pursuing them. Everyone that they had known for years turned out and stood up to see them pass, fishermen, shopkeepers, as well as school children and visitors to the bay.

Kitty, with her neat brown dress, wore brown walking shoes and a turned-up brown sailor hat. Teresa's remarkable robe flared and floated on the ground and had medieval sleeves, narrow at the shoulder and eighteen inches wide at the wrist; the roses were affixed round this opening. She had high-heeled slippers and an immense palette-shaped hat in champagne colour. Their straight cropped hair, brown and blond, tossed wildly round their sunburnt faces, unpowdered and unrouged; sweat poured down their cheeks.

The day Malfi March was married, it was hot, past one hundred degrees in the shade at two and growing hotter. It was a brassy and livid day, come after a year of drought and fierce summer, at the end of February. The air was thick with dust, the smoke of bushfires drifted along the hills and the red glare and combs of flame could be seen even at midday.

The ferry trip to Circular Quay took nearly an hour. The girls sat outside and stared at the water.

"Your dress simply shrieks at mine," Kitty said.

Teresa looked down at herself complacently and said, "Not at all."

She went on thinking about married women and old maids. Even the frowsiest, most ridiculous old maid on the boat, trying to shoulder her way into the inner circle of scandalmongers, getting in her drop of poison, just to show that she knew what was what, was yet more innocent looking than even a young married woman. They, of course, hushed their voices when such a person butted her way in. She might talk coarsely and laugh at smut but they saw to it that she missed the choicest things; and of course, when they talked about childbed and breast-feeding, she had to sit with downcast eyes, ashamed. As for the secret lore that they passed round, about their husbands, she could never know that. The unmarried were foolish, round-eyed, even in old age with a round-cheeked look (or was that just her Aunt Di?) and even when withered, with pursed lips as if about to swallow a large juicy tropical fruit. That was the way they looked when they talked about the sexes! Poor wretches! Teresa would never endure the shame of being unmarried; but she would never take what her cousins were taking either, some schoolfellow gone into long pants. Teresa gave Kitty a dissatisfied look. She was dreaming away there, with her fine shortsighted eyes, wearing that dress that ruined her lovely nut-brown skin. If she didn't change, she would never get married.

Kitty looked at Teresa.

"We're gadding lately, aren't we? Tina's engagement and now Malfi!" She had a fresh laugh, delicious, disquieted.

"They're all getting married, it seems."

"Except us—and Anne, and Anne's been a bridesmaid three times," said Kitty. "That was unlucky."

Teresa was silent, thinking, "And they never even asked Kitty once. It's a shame, they ought to give her a chance." She stole a glance at her sister, thinking, "She ought to have someone to dress her."

"Maids of honour often marry the best man," said Kitty. "I suppose it gives them the idea."

The step between being an unattached girl and getting married is so enormous, thought Teresa, how does anyone get over it? How is it done? Not by kindness. What about Malfi? She always had chances, though she was ill-tempered and now she is marrying young Bedloe, though at the engagement party she stumbled over his high boot with an oath, "Take your bloody legs out of my way," and he answered nothing, just looked, fair and flushed and timid and loving. Incomprehensible. Her first fiancé, Alec, was there, holding her thin arm, kissing one of her sharp shoulder-blades standing out above the low-backed evening dress. "Oh, leave me alone, can't you!" Malfi cried, pulling away gracelessly, standing round-shouldered and with a sly, angry, trapped expression. She was no longer pretty, her seventeen-year-old bloom gone, but the suburban boys milled round her; she was never at home alone. Malfi wasn't satisfied, though she had led a golden youth, thought Teresa, had everything and never had to work. Teresa saw in a sketchy way in her mind's eye the faces of the boys and girls who went to work with her on the ferry. As the burning sun bored into her and the reflections from the water dazzled her, she saw insistently, with the countless flaming eyes of her flesh, the inner life of these unfortunate women and girls, her acquaintance, a miserable mass writhing with desire and shame, grovelling before men, silent about the stew in which they boiled and bubbled, discontented, browbeaten, flouted, ridiculous and getting uglier each year.

Tina Hawkins, their cousin, a husky-voiced, long-legged brunette, had her engagement party in January, a cool day for summer and they had both gone out to the cottage at Roseville, to see the man, Tom Swann, to see how Tina took it. It was a blowy, sandy day. Tina, with thick dark brows and large eyes, was sullen, or timid— which? They helped to carry out tables into the back garden and there, shifting his feet, near a privet hedge was a starved little man with stiff black hair; "What do you say his name is?" "Tom Swann." She'll be Mrs. Swann then, from Hawkins to Swann; not a bad exchange. "It's a black Swann," said Aunt Bea, who had already nine times offered the joke, "Her goose is a Swann." Each girl met the groom-to-be, Tom, and to each he was very kind and modest, saying, "I'm your new cousin. How are you, cousin? Call me Tom." Later Tina sat with him and Anne at one table, while the others looked at them; Tina, who knew what they were thinking, was awkward, flushed and dropped her eyes. He was counterman at a sandwich-shop where she worked.

It might have been Tina's engagement that made Malfi March send her wedding invitations out so soon. Harry Bedloe was another of those small, underfed men. Teresa suffered for herself and for the other girls; each year now counted against them; nineteen, and has she a boyfriend? Twenty, and does she like anyone particularly? Twenty-one, now she has the key of the door; she ought to be looking round! Twenty-two already! Twenty-three and not engaged yet? Twenty-four and not even a nibble? I'll never be one of those women on the boat, thought Teresa, never fail, never fail like Kitty, never fail like Malfi, never live the life of shame.

"Will you wear white when you get married?" asked Kitty. Teresa had never thought of getting married, however. Now, with a start, she saw herself in front of a staring crowd, with pressing bosoms and shoulders and staring, glad eyes. Some faceless, memberless heavy shadow stood somewhere near, keeping her company, a man yet unborn in her life.

"Would you wear orange-blossom, a veil and all that?" continued Kitty. "I don't like brides to wear a coat and skirt, although I suppose it's more practical."

This was a burning question in their circle. If a girl wore a long satin gown, she had to have bridesmaids. Then came the questions, How many, whom to ask without heartburnings and without financial hurt, and how to have a pretty wedding without impudent display. Teresa thought over all these arguments without coming to any decision; at last, she said,

"Well, I'd have a bouquet of red rosebuds."

"Then you couldn't wear white satin, Terry," concluded Kitty.

"No," mused Teresa. After a pause she said, "Yellow satin would be marvellous, wouldn't it, and you know, stiff heavy yellow lace."

"For a wedding dress! What could you use it for, after?"

"Yes, you'd just have to keep it."

"Or for an evening dress."

"No, you know how they always giggle—she turned up in her wedding dress dyed."

"I'd have something you could make over," said Kitty virtuously. "I think it's a silly waste when you need the money for other things."

"You would look wonderful in eggshell satin, with old lace," continued Teresa, looking her up and down, "with your dark skin and eyes."

Her sister smiled and meditated.

"When you get married, I'll give you fifty things," Teresa said. "Fifty, don't forget."

"Will you really?"

The girls were silent for a while, until Kitty, stirring and sighing, said, "Don't you think we ought to go in out of the heat? My dress is sticking to me."

"I'm spouting rivers," said Teresa, "but I like it."

She admitted that they could go to the covered end of the boat; there might be a faint movement of air there. They looked out at the glare, wondering if there would be any change that day. There was no wind, but the sky was an immense workshop of wind where they saw pipes, bottles and horns of vapours, spindles, inexplicable flares, tongues of steam, falls of purple and orange. It was a day without white light; at this hour the birds sang no more and even the cicadas skirled drowsily. The ferry scarcely broke the oil eddies and the soot, instead of drowning, merely scudded off over the slippery waves. Middle-aged people slept in the cabins. The voices of schoolboys going to a boat race came down from the upper deck. A Portuguese deck hand who knew the Hawkins boys, Leo and Lance, stood in the gangway and looked at the sisters. When they glanced his way, he nodded gravely and his dull, long dark eyes gleamed. The water had a ruby light in the path of the sun, the milky waves sent out by the ferry hissed round the thickly weeded shore. The deck hand looked over the water but at last said nonchalantly, with a quick look at Kitty, "Are you Leo's sister, too?"

"Yes, Mr. Manoel."

Manoel looked out at the water again, slowly turned, looked aft and went inside. He stopped, however, when half in, and lounging against the upright, said to Kitty, "See you were Leo's sister anywhere."

His severe face creased, caved in and was polluted by a black laughing mouth, revealing several decayed stumps. He nodded to them and dawdled round the outside deck aft. The girls were flattered. Even plump business men put a hand to the gangplank when it happened to slue under Manoel's hand. The schoolboys came home bragging when old Joe Manoel favoured them with a joke. He would not allow the girls or the business men to call him Joe, however; he was Mr. Manoel and would only answer if so addressed. He lived in the bay and owned two small cabins in a forgotten alley under the cliff. He had a wife, an old mother, and children, and when it was rumoured that he cuddled with the bay's only wild girl, genteel married ladies who had melted at his agreeably sinister smile, doubted and hesitated. Could nice Mr. Manoel do such a thing? Only the other day he had helped them with a parcel, or a valise. Kitty said, "When I went into the cabin, Gladys was sitting on the engineer's bench."

"She always sits near the men."

"Do you think he really kisses her?"

"Oh, no; that's slander. She lives in his street, that's all," said Teresa.

Gladys was fifteen. She ruffled the women and to young girls this Venus was taboo. She was a large, square-faced, ragged hoyden who knew all the boys, the fishermen and the deck hands. She tumbled about with them, not caring how she showed her legs, that was the story. Andrew Hawkins said, "We must not judge, she lost her mother when she was a little thing, just like you children." The sisters still had confused notions of what her life could be. Teresa imagined that she slept in the boat sheds at night, near the fishermen who were waiting for an early start, amongst their old clothes, bottles, tackle and wading-boots. Kitty had seen two schoolboys in a cave on the beach, rolling, riding each other, giggling and shouting, "Gladys, Gladys." She was puzzled by this obscure revelation. Teresa, seeing the wild girl rush shouting down the streets with boys and go bathing with them in lonely parts of the harbour, hearing that she had the freedom of all the sheds and boats, had a pang of jealousy. Girls wanted to take the road, but how could they, how could they? She would have liked to ask Gladys certain things.

They picked up their parcels, gloves, and bags and moved towards the sheltered back end of the double-ended ferry. Teresa held up her long skirt with casual elegance in one hand. They rounded the corner and came to a breathless stop. Gladys was sitting down, while the deck hand, bending over her, had his arm plunged down her back, up to his armpit. The girls stared. The deck hand began to withdraw his arm, they saw his hand bulging under the cloth on her loose breast. He squeezed the breast, gave the girls a look and withdrew his knotted claw. He shambled off to the other side, settling his dirty cap on his head. Gladys sprang to her feet and hurried after him, tossing her hair. The sisters looked at each other, looked about uncertainly, and sat down in the place.

"That was funny," said Teresa.

"Yes," breathed Kitty. After a few minutes, her curiosity unloosed her stiff tongue and she timidly asked, "What do you think he was feeling right down her back like that for?"

"I don't know."

After another silence, Kitty pondered.

"Why do all the men and boys like that tomboy? She's so dirty, and so awful."

"You mean her figure? Yes, I know."

"Not that, but the way she behaves. She's so rough."

"They don't all."

"Well, Mr. Manoel—"

"You wouldn't want him to kiss you?"

Kitty burst out laughing, and blushed, "Oh, no." But she began to ponder again and said almost in a whisper,

"But he's married!"

"I know."

"But he has no right, then—"

"He has a right."

"A married man?"

"If he loves her."

"But he's married."

"If he loves her," said Teresa.

Kitty looked at her in astonishment, "Love?"

"It's love," said Teresa.

"What do you know about it?"

"I know."

Kitty looked at her fascinated and for a moment, suspicious, but at her sister's expression, red face, grey eyes turned black with anger, she smiled slightly, and murmured,

"Oh, of course, you know everything."

Teresa, flattered, said nothing more and cooled off.

When the ferry docked, a few boys with private school caps stood jostling near the gangplank on which Mr. Manoel rested his hand and then, in a spurt, they all leaped, the boys, Gladys, some more boys, over the thinning lane of water; and after them came the rope, the gangplank, and the two sisters walked off followed by the other citizens. . . .

II

LANCE WITH HIS HEAD IN HIS HAND

. . . The room! She literally jumped across the threshold and stood panting with pleasure near the middle of the room. Then with a silent, shivering, childish laugh, she closed the door, quickly and softly. She stripped off the bathing suit, which she hung out the window to get completely dry and felt her flesh, cold as marble in the warm air. She shivered again with excitement and went to kneel at the uncurtained window looking out on the back road, the road into the camp and the hill. This hill was half a hill. On the other side it fell straight into the sea, part of South Head; the open sea was not more than two or three hundred feet away from where she stood. She envisioned it tonight, a water floor out to the horizon, with a passage strewn with moonrushes and barely breaking at the base of the cliffs.

"Oh, God, how wonderful, how wonderful!" She muttered half-intelligible exclamations which were little more than cries of ecstasy as she stood in the window. If someone was crouching among the rocks on the hill, he could see her, but otherwise she was safe here. She leaned over the sill, her round arms and full breasts resting on the woodwork. Her flesh was a strange shade in that light, like the underside of water beasts. Or like— She began to think like what. She did not care if she never went to bed; the night stretched before her. "I know every hour of the night," she said joyfully and repeated it. It seemed to her that she knew more of the night and of life than they all did down there; hunched Kitty, cheesy Lance, girl-mad Leo, slow Andrew Hawkins, entombed in their lives. She heard footfalls in the Bay, far off—people going home—voices, a pair of lovers perhaps, climbing higher up on the cliffs. The footsteps of anyone going home late to the camp, the permanent staff, going by the paved road, could be heard long before he came in sight and so too in the blind road underneath the house.

She was free till sunrise. She was there, night after night, dreaming hotly and without thinking of any human beings. Her long walks at night through the Bay, in which she had discovered all the lost alleys, vacant lots and lonely cottages, her meditation over the poor lovers from the city, her voluptuous swimming and rolling by herself in the deep grass of the garden and her long waking nights were part of the life of profound pleasure she had made for herself, unknown to them. She was able to feel active creation going on around her in the rocks and hills, where the mystery of lust took place; and in herself, where all was yet only the night of the senses and wild dreams, the work of passion was going on.

She had a vague picture of her future in her mind. Along the cliffs on a starlit night, very dark, strolled two figures enlaced, the girl's hair, curled as snail-shells, falling back over the man's shoulders, but alive of itself, as she leaned against him walking and all was alive, the revolute leaves, the binding roots. This she conceived happened in passion, a strange walking in harmony, blood in the trees. The playful taps and squeezes, wrestling and shrieking which Leo had with the girls was not what she expected and she did not think of this as love. She thought, dimly, that even Leo when he sat on the beach at Maroubra with his girl, made some such picture; a turbulent, maddening, but almost silent passion, a sensual understanding without end.

She abandoned herself and began to think, leaning on the window sill. In a fissure in a cliff left by a crumbled dike, a spout of air blew up new foam and spray, blue and white diamonds in the moon, and in between the surges the ashy sky filled the crack with invisible little stars. Hundreds of feet beneath, the sea bursting its skin began to gush up against the receding tide; with trumpet sounds, wild elephants rose in a herd from the surf and charged the cliffs; the ground trembled, water hissed in the cracks.

The full moon shone fiercely on the full-bellied sea. A woman who had known everything, men's love and been deserted, who had the vision of a life of endless work and who felt seedy, despairing, felt a bud growing on its stalk in her body, was thirsty; in her great thirst she drank up the ocean and was drowned. She floated on it now in a wooden shell, over her a white cloth and over all the blazing funeral of the sky, the moon turning its back, sullen, calloused.

What the moon saw. The beaches, the shrubbery on the hills, the tongues of fire, the white and dark of bodies rolling together in snaky unions. Anne—Malfi, "Don't think too badly of me!"—herself! She sighed, shivered and drew in. All the girls dimly knew that the hole-in-a-corner marriages and frantic petting parties of the suburbs were not love and therefore they had these ashamed looks; they lost their girlish laughter the day they became engaged, but those who did not get a man were worse off. There was a glass pane in the breast of each girl; there every other girl could see the rat gnawing at her, the fear of being on the shelf. Beside the solitary girl, three hooded madmen walk, desire, fear, ridicule. "I won't suffer," she said aloud, turning to the room to witness. "They won't put it upon me." She thought, a girl who's twenty-seven is lost. Who marries a woman of thirty-five to get children? She's slightly ridiculous to marry at that age. Look at Aunt Maggie, everyone laughed. Take Queenie, few marry at fifteen. Say eighteen, eighteen to thirty; twelve years, whereas men have eighteen to—any time at all, fifty at least, well, forty-eight, they can have children at forty-eight. They can marry then; thirty years. A woman is a hunter without a forest. There is a short open season and a long closed season, then she must have a gun-license, signed and sealed by the state. There are game laws, she is a poacher, and in the closed season she must poach to live. A poor man, a serf say, clears himself a bit of land, but it's the lord's land. As soon as it's cleared, he grows a crop on it, but it isn't his crop, only partly, or perhaps not at all, it isn't in his name; and then there must be documents, legalities, he must swear eternal fealty to someone. A woman is obliged to produce her full quota on a little frontage of time; a man goes at it leisurely and he has allotments in other counties too. Yes, we're pressed for time. We haven't time to get educated, have a career, for the crop must be produced before it's autumn. There are northern countries where the whole budding, leafing, and fruiting take place in three months. A farmer said, "What do they bother to put out leaves for, when they must go in so soon?" We put out leaves and flowers in such a brief summer and if it is a bad summer? We must do it all ourselves, too, just like wild animals in the bush. Australian savages arrange all that for their women, they don't have women going wanting, but we do. Girls are northern summers, three months long; men are tropical summers. But then there are the savage women, and the Italian, Spanish women—do they have as short a time? The women of ancient Greece, the Romans, so corrupt and so libertine, but happy no doubt—there might be other women. It isn't necessary—Malfi, Anne, Ray, Ellie, Kitty—me! But they won't even rebel, they're afraid. They're afraid to squander their few years. The long night of spinsterhood will come down. What's to be done? But one thing is sure, I won't do it, they won't get me.

How about the boys, too, Lance and Leo? They were different, but they were pressed too; nothing that was, suited them. If nothing that is, suits people, why do they all take it lying down? Because they have so little time, no money—but is that enough excuse?

Standing upright at the window, thinking, thinking, feeling rage at her floundering and weakness, and at seeing all the issues blocked, she thought of how cocksure she had been at school. Awkward, easily faced down, of course, but confident about the future. The things she wanted existed. At school she first had news of them, she knew they existed; what went on round her was hoaxing and smooth-faced hypocrisy. Venus and Adonis, the Rape of Lucrece, Troilus and Cressida were reprinted for three hundred years; St. Anthony was tempted in the way you would expect; Dido, though a queen, was abandoned like a servant-girl and went mad with love and grief, like the girl in the boat outside. This was the truth, not the daily simpering on the boat and the putting away in hope chests; but where was one girl who thought so, besides herself? Was there one who would not be afraid if she told them the secret, the real life? Since school, she had ravaged libraries, disembowelled hundreds of books, ranged through literature since the earliest recorded frenzies of the world and had eaten into her few years with this boundless love of love, this insensate thirst for the truth above passion, alive in their home itself, in her brothers and sister, but neglected, denied, and useless; obnoxious in school, workshop, street.

Teresa knew all the disorderly loves of Ovid, the cruel luxury of Petronius, the exorbitance of Aretino, the meaning of the witches' Sabbaths, the experiments of Sade, the unimaginable horrors of the Inquisition, the bestiality in the Bible, the bitter jokes of Aristophanes and what the sex-psychologists had written. At each thing she read, she thought, yes, it's true, or no, it's false, and she persevered with satisfaction and joy, illuminated because her world existed and was recognized by men. But why not by women? She found nothing in the few works of women she could find that was what they must have felt. By comparison, history, with its lies to discourage the precocious, and even the inspired speculative stuff, meant nothing. But it was either rigmarole or raving, whereas the poets and playwrights spoke the language she knew, and the satirists and moralists wrote down with stern and marvellous precision all that she knew in herself but kept hidden from family and friends.

In her bare room, ravished, trembling with ecstasy, blooming with a profound joy in this true, this hidden life, night after night, year after year, she reasoned with herself about the sensual life for which she was fitted. She smelled, heard, saw, guessed faster, longed more than others, it seemed to her. She listened to what they brought out with a galling politeness, because what she had to say she could not tell them. It was not so that life was and they were either liars or stupid. At the same time, how queer that she understood what was going on in their minds so well! For it seemed to her that they were all moved by the same passion, in different intensities.

The newspapers made it appear so. Even the most sedate and crusty newspapers recounted at length, in divorce suits, what happened on worn divans in broken-down old office buildings, they all laughed together over those unlucky paramours who had been followed and caught in degrading positions, the schoolchildren gulped down the stories of bathing parties in the bushy reaches, mad cohabitations in the little bays, dives where sailors and black men went, miserable loves of all kinds, the naked dancing in the sweltering Christmas days and the nights of pale sand. Love panted in and out of their young nostrils, and the adolescents dreaming of these orgies, maddened by the tropical sun and these dissolute splendours of the insolent flesh, spent their nights in a bath of streaming sweat and burning blood.

A faint breeze had risen, rather damp. A mosquito sang windily. "What have I done yet?" said Teresa to herself. She had had a dream the night before. This dream made her realize her age and she felt the shame of being unmarried. She had given the breast to her child, she dreamed, a small dark-haired baby. Everything was as clear as life, the nuzzling, sucking, and the touch of the child's spread hand. She was a woman, she was nineteen. Funny that at fourteen she had felt quite old! Her life was dull and away from men. Where would she get a husband?

She made a fretful gesture and accidentally pushed the bathing suit off the window sill into the yard. She pulled on a sweater and skirt and went downstairs.

There was no light in the back as she passed between the boys' rooms to the kitchen. Leo's room looked out on the grass slope and Lance's on the small alley by the neighbour's house. The moon had passed over, the kitchen was dark, only the yard shone. She went out into the yard, picked up her suit, hung it over the sawhorse and sniffed around for a while in the toolshed, fresh with sawdust. When she came in, Lance was at the old ice chest, near the back door, munching and pulling out bits of food.

"It stinks in here," he said cheerfully.

"You stink in there," responded Tess.

"Good job I like sour milk, there always is plenty," continued her brother, holding up a bottle towards the lighted yard.

"Sour milk is good for pigs and goats," observed Teresa, coming into the kitchen and lounging against the table. Lance hid a furtive smile in his long cheeks.

"What were you doing out there?"

"Getting my bathing suit, it fell out the window."

He thoughtfully munched for a while, standing side on and giving her meaningless glances; then he grinned to himself. "You pushed it out."

"What for? Don't be silly."

"You're lying."

"What!" She sprang forward.

Lance turned round and smirked, "You're a liar. You threw it out." It was the signal for battle. Teresa felt the blood rush to her head. Lance was the only one who dared to give her the lie.

"You're a liar," repeated Lance lusciously, waiting. She flung herself upon him, pounding his chest, his long neck, and his head.

"Hey, hey!" said Lance, turning his head from side to side. She panted. He could see, even in the gloom, the dark flush over her face and neck.

"Don't you dare say that."

"You're a liar," he panted.

As if delighted, though puffing and writhing in her grasp, he merely fended off her clumsy blows, his face now stark and serious. Teresa punched his face on each cheek and temple and grasped his hair. Suddenly he groaned and staggered away from her. "You got my boil."

She stood back, dark with anger, furious with him, heaving and ready to rush in again and beat him. He staggered down the hall, moaning, holding his hand to his head. "Oh, my boil."

She looked after him contemptuously; he was always a coward. It did not occur to her that he had not hit her.

She saw him in the ghastly hall light. Blood trickled from his temple, two threads reached his neck. Fists clenched, astride and full of fight, the girl watched him go towards his bedroom. Kitty was halfway down the stairs, asking him questions, getting no answer. She clattered down the rest of the way, ran in after him. She came into the kitchen for water and put on the light. "What were you doing?"

Teresa frowned at her and muttered, "He called me a liar."

Kitty said nothing to that. She went in again and said to Lance, as she bathed him, "How did it happen?"

Lance said, "The fool! I called her a liar for a joke, just because it gets her goat." Teresa choked. She stood in the kitchen door and shouted, "That's no joke, it's no joke. You knew what you were saying."

Kitty said reproachfully, "You knew he was joking."

"It wasn't a joke! I'll kill anyone for that," shouted Teresa. "I'll kill him if he says it."

Lance, satisfied, said nothing, only moaned as Kitty washed him.

"Poor Lance," said Kitty, looking at her sideways.

"I'll smash him to pieces for that," said the girl. "He knows it, too."

Lance groaned. Teresa went away furious. He had said it with a grin and kept grinning right through. That was a knife in her gall. She knew that out of malice he enjoyed the fight. She moved off sulkily. When she got up to her room, she sat down on the little sewing box and thought about it, clenching her fists and grinding her teeth. She would kill anyone for that! She would kill for honour. A scene flew up in her mind in which she killed in hot blood, for honour and was glad of it, saw the spilt blood spreading. Ha-ha, that paid him off! For twenty minutes she sat there, her breath coming quickly and then her other thoughts began to creep in. She flung herself on her bed. Downstairs she heard the noises of the house as Kitty put things away and she heard her father beginning to lock up, leaving the door unbarred for Leo. Presently he came upstairs. He saw her open door and looked in. "You hit Lance?"

"Yes." Her temper rose again.

"You hurt him, you know, Terry."

"Let him look out."

Andrew Hawkins said quietly, "Good night, Terry," and went away towards his room. Terry felt rather flat. He called out, "Early to bed, early to rise."

"Yes," she muttered, "yes."

Her father called from his room, "Terry? You get Leo up?"

"Yes," she answered impatiently.

His door shut. She heard him wind his clock. This time she left her door open.

LEO WAS LOST IN ROARING SLUMBER

Leo was lost in roaring slumber by now. The others could be heard getting into bed. Teresa put the clock face where she could see it from the bed, then undressed, and throwing herself on the bed, gradually tweaked the mosquito-nets out of the bed top and let them fall round her like a veil. A train shrieked far off in the hills across the harbour; she had never found out where the train was, for it looked as if there was nothing there but wild bush. At the same moment, she heard a faint *boom!* The ocean was stirring again. *Boom!* Yes, at the foot of the cliffs, it was beginning again. The first sounds had come several hours before, a faint boom, washing the silent bay. In the clear still weather, with the hordes of fish and the filming of the sky, this irregular humming meant a disturbance approaching.

"Change of moon, change of weather!" There was a splash in the bay. The swell had now caught the low water and the beach hissed. Teresa went on with her more serious meditations.

She ought to run away. The only reason she did not run away was that she had not the courage. How could she teach little children when she herself knew nothing about life? She thought of the day she had signed up with the Education Department. They were all there, high-school girls of seventeen, most of her classmates. There was nothing much else for them to do and they were going to teach until they got married. The grey-headed man there had asked her if she wanted her pension money subtracted as for retirement at sixty or sixty-five. She burst out laughing. Then she saw her best friend, Viola, saying "Sixty-five," because they subtracted less each week. Viola was a chubby blonde, secretly engaged. She saw Viola at sixty-five! Then she looked round timidly, with a flush, at the man who was watching her sternly.

"Don't you intend to stay in the Department? We don't want to train women who intend to marry or take up some other profession."

"Put sixty, then." It was five years less, at any rate.

"You are not thinking of getting married?" said the man.

"No." She heard Viola denying it too.

They all walked out together, fourteen or fifteen of them, "young giggling girls," as Aunt Bea called them, who had been in high school together and who now were caught, herded into teaching until, sup-posedly, they fell off from old age, desiccated virgins. Teresa, fright-ened and horrified, had made up her mind at that moment to leave teaching, but at the time the training course was her only chance to get some higher education. But at home what rejoicing! They thought of her as fixed for life—no bother about unemployment. At school they had expected her to do better, but she was a poor student and not of the stuff that takes University Bursaries. She never could sit up at night to study. If she sat up, she dreamed, her head and body nodding with carnal intoxication. At one time, encouraged by some teachers, she had dreamed of the great universities of the old world. She knew it was only a vague wish of the teachers who had liked her and who had mistaken her intense rummaging in libraries for scholarship.

But now! Now, in the schoolroom, ignorant still, unhappy, choked with dirt and dust, with the noises of the playground which she herself had only just left, having for comrades the very same fat-waisted, thin-haired women and bowed, unhappy men that as children they had always jeered at, those very wretched slaves of a headmaster and an inspector that the children in their wicked perspicacity led by the nose in a life of misery; knowing that she was one of them, and obliged to go on like them with coarsening face and voice; something, it seemed to her, from which all ordinary human beings fled, and which, in her circle, was only associated with one phrase, "an old maid of a school-ma'am"—now she was on the treadmill. The other teachers hated the work too.

As soon as she caught sight of the school buildings in the morning, their dirty yellow, and heard the bell, the shrieks, the boots rushing across the asphalt; as soon as she smelled that thick oily and dusty scent which school buildings alone give out, human grease and neglected corners, old varnish and urinals in the heat, the little oils from lunches in paper and boot polish, old stuffs ironed at home with the soap still in them, the dirty heads; that huge, fat, sickening smell that poured down the street, on every side, and seeped from outside into the purer dust of the closed schoolroom—as soon as she saw it and smelled it, that illness to which she was condemned for life, until she was sixty, when a woman is not a woman, she began to float in her misery, not to walk. She forgot her feet and yielded herself to a kind of delirium of horror. Yet she did not have to do what the other teachers did, that is, go to the headmaster's room and sign on. She did not have to line her class up with the other classes; and her class alone did not have to stand in the sun, salute the flag, and sing "God Save the King." She laughed when she thought why. It was because she had the unclassified children, called Special Class by the teachers and Dope's Class by the children. The sight of the Dope's Class or Mad Class, eleven poor creatures, two deaf and dumb, some lame, some twitching, and all with long school reputations as madmen or idiots, standing there and yet straggling while standing, was the only pleasant sight in the whole school. Some were high, some low, some goggling, and some dignified, some amused because they were marked out and some oppressed. The sight of them the first morning behind the other classes had caused great merriment, disorder, and excitement. The king and the flag got no attention; everyone turned round. The teachers themselves had had strange feelings—shame and embarrassment; they had been shocked. Now the eleven lined up in a little asphalt patch of their own, near the flower beds. It was not the eleven poor children that Teresa disliked; they were more affectionate, interesting, and tractable than the ordinary children who conformed, and were sly, prosy, or smug. It was rather the school system and the idea of being in jail, for she kept thinking to herself, "Why, I have never been out of school, I have never learned anything and never will!" Even more than this, she was afraid of drying up there, being forgotten by the world and dying in the chalk-dust.

Running away was not such an easy thing. If she ran away, she forfeited her bond and lost her wages and her family lost her wages. For the past two months, during the long summer vacation just ended, she had been studying shorthand and typing at night, but she had yet a month to finish the shortest course available; the other consideration which ought to have stopped her did not. She owed something to the state official who ran the special classes. He had picked her out for this relatively soft job and had talked to her of the Sorbonne, Berlin, London, where he himself had gone; his fatal words, Europe, Jena, Weimar, the Black Forest, stuck in her mind with old scenes accompanying them, just as if she had already been there and seen them. She must see them; they were part of an old heritage. But how?

It was simple enough. It was for this that she was studying at night. "There is office work all over the world." She saw the significance of the maps of the British Empire showing the world strung on a chain of pink, all the pink was Britain's. In every one of those pink patches, no matter what the colour or kind of men there, nor the customs of the native women, she could get a job, she was a citizen there. There were advertisements in the Sydney papers for typists to go to Nauru, Cocos, Shanghai, British Columbia, and these could be just jumping-off places.

She had mentioned nothing of all this to anyone in the family, to frighten them. She was bringing them thirty-five shillings weekly and could have given more. They hoped she would when her pay was raised. Only once to Leo had she hinted at it, "When I go overseas—"

"When? Are you going?"

"When I get the money."

"It's a good idea."

"Why don't you go and get a job in San Francisco, Leo?"

"Yes," said Leo restlessly, looking with a vague yearning out to sea.

"Yes, do. Yes, do." She had begged and argued with him. "Home-keeping youths have ever homely wits."

Goodnaturedly, Leo laughed and tried to please her by talking about it from time to time. But now Leo was at work—at present, out of work —a lockout; and he wanted to get married.

"Get married!" said Teresa aloud, violently, and sat up, thrusting her legs down the folds of netting. At the same time she reflected that she must leave the school as soon as she had finished the next month's training at shorthand. She would go to the Department and tell them she could not stay, she would pay them back the bond in instalments. She would pay them back, go to the university at night, and sail away, or sail away first. She looked at the clock: eleven-thirty. She was surprised to see an ugly ring round the moon already and cloud materializing as she looked.

Bad weather! The sea was noisier, increasing gradually. By morning it would be surging round the path; they would have to go to work by the back road. "Who can does, who can't teaches!" She could not make up her mind when to run away. Should she leave home now?

She had to go down to Leo at midnight. In the meantime, to forget the gnawing thoughts about school, she reviewed some of her favourite private movies. They were mostly from old legends she had read somewhere. The first one was by her entitled, "The Cruel Huntsman." Through a thicket in the wild wood, a pale girl with flying hair darted a length in front of a supernatural black horse, its lips drawn back as if snarling. On its back, dressed in black armour, without a face except for the black visor, sat a giant huntsman, and yelling, at the sides of the foam-flecked stallion, ran his hellhounds, black and black-splashed white. The hunt raged through the thicket, leaving trembling and torn boughs dashed about, was heard farther off and reappeared in the opposite direction, in the middle distance, in sunlight. (The girl was a tormented shade and in life, said the legend, was a coquette.) This was the mildest and most sentimental of her movies, an hors d'ocuvre. The others followed fast. There were halls of veined marble, strewn with purple, red, and white, with golden goblets and splendid male and female slaves to bring in the food; there were scenes of taverns, taken from Breughel, and in cathedrals; a Hogmanay party in the Highlands with the bursting of a great haggis, and the guests fallen down in a flood of pease pudding, small birds, giblets, and tripes. There were insatiable Bluebeards in some gloomy northern castle, surrounded by pale bright hosts of condemned women; monsters in sea-caves, horrible bargainings, butcheries, black masses, Sabbaths haunted by flying corpses and old wives' gatherings in hidden valleys; routs of black horses, drawings and quarterings, impalements; cannibalism from Grimm, brothels from Shakespeare. All this gave her unutterable pleasure. She believed all these things existed from time to time, if they were not daily occurrences, and it was to reach some circle, some understandings in touch with these pleasures that she felt she had to break the iron circle of the home and work; for she knew these things were not thin black shapes of fantasy, but were real. It was a country from which she, a born citizen, was exiled. She struggled towards it.

She heard eight bells from two ships in the bay a few moments before she indolently got up to go downstairs. How happy she felt at this moment! Without these orgies, she would have had nothing to look forward to. In a reasonable way, her trip overseas, the halls of learning, were part of this grand life that she lived without restraint in the caves, taverns, woods, colonnades, and eel pools of antiquity and the night. Smiling to herself, she went downstairs slowly, feeling the dust and the grain of the splintered wood with her bare toes. With this liberty of head and mind went a kind of vigorous discontent which was pushing her out into the world faster and faster. She felt at this hour strong, energetic, beautiful, full of the gaiety of the invincible, untried young girl who has not yet gone to work. She was a girl for any man, geared for a long night of love. She always knew at this hour of the night that if she met any man now he would fall in love with her, such was her serene power. But at that right hour, a girl was at home, in her eyeless room.

For a moment, the house seemed chill. It was a poor fate to climb the stairs and claim that single bed, those bare neat walls, that little pile of sensible clothes and those pencil marks in a notebook. She sighed and went on downstairs. When? How long? How could she bear it? Tomorrow, again she would begin to wait for the next day. What could happen to her, taking the ferry, talking in the teachers' room? Would the sky fall if she simply walked out? She had never done a single brave thing in her life, defying the rules; just obeyed, gone to school, paid in her money.

She walked into Leo's room. The lower panes of the window were stippled over so that passers-by on the overlooking street could not see in. Hawkins had made Leo's bed himself, saying it was something like a sea-hammock and would harden Leo. On a wooden frame some old sacks were arranged, thick and firm, and on this a small, hard mattress laid. If Leo did not sleep so deep and so long, Hawkins opined, he would not walk in his sleep. He told Leo, in the daytime, that he could conquer this weakness by will power. Hawkins was much ashamed of this defect in his son and felt it might be taken as a sign of a defect in his heredity. Teresa's voiced opinion was that Leo walked because he wanted to marry, the same thing that made Lance stay up senselessly at night, and Kitty weep. The house was haunted by legends of sleep-walking. Every relative who came there had something to say about it, the men to the men, the women to the women. There were sleep-walkers who had been seen on roofs, travelling on drain pipes, dancing on chimney pots. They returned safely to their beds unless spoken to, when they lost their balance, their wits or their lives. It seemed that a woman having a sleep-walking son placed a tub of water at the foot of the stairs and went to bed, easy in mind. She heard a howl and rushed out to find her son dead of his footbath. Leo might get into some trouble; and so one of the watchwords of the house was, "Last to bed, get up Leo." Hawkins had another, simpler theory about Leo's weakness, that it was due to a small physical irritation and the brother or sister waking him had to see that this was attended to.

Lance was not fond of his brother and detested this duty, though he was the one who usually came in late; and Kitty had to rise early, so it was Teresa who went down to him as a rule. Leo was hard to waken; he never really waked. Though he would get up, do what he was told, walk, drink, go outside, he did it all in his sleep. He got up rosy and tousled, muttering and laughing. Sometimes he would hit out. Sometimes he snapped and when scolded would answer, but however his sentences started off, they always ended incoherently.

Teresa tonight helped the big boy up and led him flaring and staring wildly to the kitchen, to the yard, and back into bed, where he rolled suddenly over on his side, with his eyes shut. He often snored while standing up, loud, sudden, peremptory snorts, and snored at the moment of rolling into bed. Sometimes he fell sideways across the bed and seemed unable to move further, so that she had to drag him in, tugging at his heavy muscular limbs, fighting with him for the bedclothes in which he was entangled. Many times he fell into her arms, leaned on her neck, her shoulder, stood like an apple-cheeked country drunk with his head against her cheek while he slept. The fragrant moist heat of his brown body came to her nostrils in gusts from his open nightshirt, sliding off his smooth chest; in summer he slept naked. His nakedness was nothing to her; she did not even think of him as a man. He was only her brother, her own flesh. It was pleasant, friendly, to help the adorable boy, staggering with his eyes shut and often a silly smile on his mouth; or the brown eyes peering as if wickedly in the slits of the weighted lids, his hair ragged, a glimpse of the square white teeth as he answered with his comical mad babble. She remembered the funny things he said, to ask him afterwards,

"Last night, you said, 'Oh, gemme, gemme, down on the Lawny'— what did that mean?"

"I never did," he would grin at her sideways.

"And you said, 'The lights were down at four o'clock.' "

He grinned and shook his head. He was proud of her, he did not know why.

She was staggering about there with Leo for fully half an hour tonight. She heard the single bell ring from the ships while she was still in the lower passage. Presently she came up to bed. The house was shut and locked now, Leo could not get out, no one could get in. It was night, lingering, drowsy, real night.

She was in her room again with the door shut and suddenly she threw herself on her knees at the side of the bed, where the nets and sheets were tumbled. Into her hands she whispered, "Let me find a lover soon, let me get a lover soon, I must, I must, I beg, I beg." She was willing it, not praying. She believed firmly in the power of will to alter things and force things to an end. Cheerful, she got up and jumped into bed, as if she had heard a promise. She did not sleep yet; she was too tired for her legends but she tossed convulsively. She thought, "Oh, I'll never be able to sleep." The girls in the Botanic Gardens last Saturday had all given their remedies for sleeplessness; one said, "Breathe deeply." She tried that and it woke her up. Another said, "Take hot milk." There wasn't enough milk for everyone to be having glasses of milk. Teresa said, "Read an abstruse page, it's infallible." But the other girls, one a young doctor, one a social worker, said reading kept them awake. She tossed and turned. She listened to the sea, thought of it rolling in, and herself began to roll, like a ship at sea, moving quite ignorantly as women move with their lovers. "A storm far out at sea, coming in," she muttered. "Love, learning, bread—myself—all three, I will get."

A crying was ringing in the air when the girl started up. The moon was down, and a pallor and a cool air creeping in. She remembered she too had been calling for help, "Mother! Mother!" Now she heard faint noises downstairs. She jumped out, pushing the stifling mosquito nets aside and stole out in her nightdress. She could smell strong tea, so she knew Leo was going out with the men. She came quietly downstairs and stood in the kitchen door.

Leo turned from the stove with his smoke-blackened billy-can in his hand, "What ya doin'?"

III

THIS EMBARKATION FOR LIFE

. . .Jonathan, for the first time in his life, was almost alone. His life until now, and he was twenty-three, had been spent in class. His class comrades now were working or were looking for work every day. A few were married and joining small suburban circles of the respectably ambitious. This embarkation for life of his friends made him feel old for the first time. It was true he was on his own, not a prize student, not someone to be watched for in the next examination results, not someone who might pick off one of the plums of next year. He had to render his accounts. He was just a poor man who had made up his packet and was trudging off to sell himself, reduced once more to his original situation and talents, with a poor and jealous family and that drawback to success which is a thin, hungry face, with brown avid eyes, the stealth of the evil eye. He was not insensible to his own looks; when he faced himself in the bathroom glass in the morning, shaving, he studied and meditated upon this starvation face, that single leaf of flesh which had been given to him to write his own history upon.

Meeting Teresa Hawkins in her proper role, as a sad and hungry-looking girl, without family or prospects, he felt at ease; they might give each other a few hours of shelter from the raw climate of life; but if she was going to expect anything else? "Well," he thought, "she will soon find out, I'll teach her too, the bleak truth. The hungry cannot feed the hungry, they merely march near them in the struggle for survival, they shudder together merely in some night-refuge, but out of the night-refuge, next morning, they are wolves. Man the wolf of man and woman. What the devil, I've got to start somewhere. Who am I to be picking and choosing? Who am I?" Very depressed, in that state of indifference to life which borders on horror, he went through the dark streets, looking dully at the customary sights; fruiterers and pastrycooks' windows that he had pasted his nose against, stationers' windows full of exercise books, very tempting to him at high school, the open doors of men's outfitters and haberdashers, that he had never entered, and the bootshop of thrown-out specials where some "Blucher boots," the class mark of the very poor child and man, were marked at seven and sixpence.

He had trained himself from earliest childhood to stoicism and had no daydreams; nor did he dream at night of what he could not have. What he could not buy, it was unmanly to desire. In the course of years he had reduced himself to a miserliness of mental life out of this sense of honour and revolt. If he desired or dreamed, he struck himself a mental blow; it was not *thus*, wanting like the weaklings, that the ambitious reached the moral and material heights; he had wanted to wear a hair shirt at one time, but where to get a hair shirt? That too, he saw, was a luxury for him and so was a weak fantasy which he quickly suppressed.

But tonight, in the paroxysm of horror that the sight of Teresa's joy had given him, . . . he saw his barenness. He not only wanted nothing but he had nothing. By God! They had taken him at his word. He had forgotten how to want. What sterility! What meanness! Loving is giving; they gave me nothing and I have nothing to give, so I cannot love. Is that it? O Lord, they have taught me not to want, only to work with my bare hands and in the sweat of my brow. *J'accuse!* A fire was lighted in him. All right, he said to himself, all right, from this out, from today, I am alone and all the others are scrambling for the largesse, I will teach myself to want and to take. Let's see what I *want.*

I want a woman. I want a new suit with chalk stripes, cuffs, and a high waist, the shoulders padded, breast pockets, shoes, socks, blue, red. I want dinner, and for dinner what? And after dinner, the movies—I'm a rotten wanter yet. I want to be with those who can want and who are crass enough to know no self-denial, who all their lives have wanted and are satisfying themselves now . . .

I want, I want, he said to himself, let that be me from now on. . . .

IV

PORT OF REGISTRY: LONDON

MODERN IS AS MODERN DOES

. . .They turned into Malet Street and walked along side by side without a word. At his gate, Johnny hesitated, expecting her to say good night. She felt as if she would burst, almost threw herself into his arms, to get the momentary comfort of his arms and breast. But she saw him standing there like a stone, his arms straight at his side; Jonathan resignedly walked to the gate, put his hand on it. "Well, Tess, here we are. Night-night."

She could not force a good night. He looked at her curiously, with a faint smile. She turned to go but after taking a step, came back just as he was pushing open the gate. She began speaking hurriedly, in a low tone, "Jonathan, let me come back for a while, inside for a while, only a few minutes."

"What to do?" said Jonathan insultingly, throwing back his head.

"Not to do anything, to be there a moment."

He turned stiffly and walked up to the door without saying a word. Afraid and ashamed, she stood at the gate watching him. He put the key in the lock, looked over his shoulder, opened the door, went inside and stood there, then he beckoned stiffly. After apparently wrestling with herself, she came up the path and stairs with uneven steps and stood outside the door. He pointed the way to his room without a word. She stood inside the door with a flushed face, then blustered, "Johnny, I'm going."

"Why?"

"You don't want me."

"I do," he said in a hard tone. "I want you very much."

She looked frightened.

"Come in," he said with rough good-humour. "After all, I didn't give you tea, that's what you need perhaps, it's been a long evening. Then I'll set you on your way."

"I didn't come back for tea," she said, slowly pulling off her gloves, but she was hungry.

He pushed her inside his door, took off his hat and muffler, pulled down the wall-bed and threw her things on it.

"I'm pretty sleepy," he said, "so I might as well air it a bit before I go to bed. The maid used to do it but old Bagshawe started to make a row about her coming here in the evening, said damned suggestive things that no doubt she chews over in her lecherous old mind, and so now I do it myself." She sat down by the fire in a low seat. He filled the kettle with fresh water, put it on, all the time casting glances at her, while she looked downwards, with shame, at the mat. He smiled wryly. "Well, feeling better?"

"I impose on you, you have troubles of your own."

"Nothing that will break or bend me. I'm not like you, sufficient unto the day is my motto, but you look before and after and pine for what is not." He knelt by her to light the gas. "Eh? Isn't that it?"

"I don't know why I'm like this," she said, still looking down with shame. "I've practised self-control ever since I was a child, never let on, never let them know what was the matter with me, that was my ideal. It just passed from me. It doesn't work any more."

"You're a masochist," he said. "Your whole history shows that, that girl on the boat, everything. You enjoy seeing yourself suffer, you see, you don't want others to share the spectacle with you, all the Christian martyrs under one hat—" he looked up, smiled, "one blond thatch. Isn't that it? Put it to yourself."

"No, it isn't."

He laughed. She went on thoughtfully, "I never meant anyone to get the better of me, get through my armour so to speak. I couldn't work it. You did."

"What do I do?" he asked gently, still kneeling by her feet.

"It isn't your doing. It's my fault. I don't know what's the matter with me."

"Don't you?"

"Beg pardon?"

"Don't you know what's the matter with you?" He looked into her face with such a strange, hard, gay expression that she felt the painful fire corkscrew through her from her knees where he knelt to her head. She looked warily at him. He veiled his eyes, got up to get the things out of the cupboard and said thickly, "What's the matter with all of us? We haven't what we need, the sweets of the world go to property and privilege."

"I don't want those things."

"If you had them would you be in the hole you're in now?"

She looked up with sudden pride. "What hole?"

"Where you are," he said vaguely. "At Quick's beck and call, working all day for a man who can sack you at the end of the week. You'll be looking for work perhaps next week. But you," he snarled, turning and looking hard at her, "now you see a lot of good in Quick. You're credulous, you believe in the boss. What's that but masochism? This masochism of yours is just a way of making spiritual capital out of your weakness. You're helpless, but you don't see it. So you go on putting yourself at the mercy of one person after another. It all comes from your inability to move freely. You're pinned down. If you don't like your job you must stick to it—"

"But I do like it—"

"If you don't like London you must live here, if you don't like me, you must stick to me—"

"I've changed jobs and countries."

"But not me," he said, smiling.

"No," she said very low.

"I'd rather you changed me too, I can give you nothing."

"I know, Johnny." Her voice broke. "Johnny, you have given me everything."

He laughed slyly up at her from where he crouched holding the toasting fork. "Not everything, surely, Tess."

"You gave me something to live for, a purpose, it was for you I came here, without you I might never have come. I would have failed."

"You must have had an empty life," he said with contempt.

"Empty? No, full! A burning full life, I had, while I was saving—"

"Hold on," he said easily, "hold on, there's your imagination again. You see, you're different from me, you still expect to get something from men." She recoiled and he went on steadily, with a grim smile, "But I don't expect to get anything from man or woman. I know better now. There's no rainbow for me. I want love as much as the next fellow, but it's out, and so I'm beginning to give up worrying about it. You won't face it as I do. That's why you are upset like you said just now."

"Face what?" said Teresa with horror.

"Face doing without love, facing doing without a man, you won't do that."

"Of course not."

"Why not?" he asked in an impudent, boyish voice. "It's been done. Women haven't the courage to face it, they've got to fill their lives with emotion as a house with knickknacks. There are old maids, plenty of 'em—but it isn't from choice." He laughed bitterly. "Take a leaf out of my book, tell yourself there's no such thing as love and forget it."

"Never," said Teresa.

He grinned and turned round to her. "So, you've made up your mind not to be different. You want to be a cave woman, slave of the bedroom and kitchen, just like the rest. I'm surprised at you, I thought you were a modern woman."

"Are you a modern man?"

"Modern is as modern does. I do modern."

"What do you do that's so modern?"

"This!"

"*This?*" She pointed at the room, at the bookcase.

He pointed to the bed, laughing recklessly.

"You sleep your life away?"

He burst out laughing again. "If you like." He filled a plate with toast, and handed her some. "Drink your tea now and then trot off, so that I can get my forty winks. Besides, I'm expecting someone."

"So late?"

"Only Lucy. She's coming in to see that things are fixed for the night. She likes to when the old Bagshawe won't see her. She even said she wanted to read some of my books, to pull herself up by her bootstraps. Touching, isn't it? She might be jealous."

Teresa laughed, "But does she still live with you?"

"Eh?"

"In the house."

"Oh, I thought you meant she lived *with* me."

"Don't be ridiculous!"

He said belligerently, "Why would it be—is that snobbery?"

"Of course not."

He relaxed. "A good thing—in every way." He told anecdotes, the gossip he had heard. She yawned. "Bagshawe told someone," he said, "I don't know why, one of my friends, the old devil, that she listened at the door and heard us in bed together, the maid and me."

"Oh, Jonathan! Why don't you leave?"

"Why? It amuses me. It gave me a clue. She stays in there next door and her lecherous old imagination weaves fantasies round me. Comic, isn't it—me! But that landladies always hanker after their student lodgers, that's an old story. She's a vicious old body. She has a dog. She told me the dog had syphilis because it had had relations with some prostitute she had as a maid once. She tried to indicate, I half imagine, that Lucy was no better than she should be."

Teresa opened her eyes wide, petrified with astonishment. Then she gave a shriek of laughter. "Oh, that's killing! Do you think she's quite sane?" she asked.

"Quite sane," said Jonathan drily. "She just hankers after my bed, that's all."

Teresa wrung her hands. "You have to put up with dreadful things, why don't you leave?"

"Gossip can't touch me," he said coldly, "and in the meantime she pays for her fantasies—I mean, she lets me have the room cheap. I suppose there's a touch of senility in it, senile decay. I don't give a darn, I never think of it," he shrugged his shoulders. "But don't make too much of it, it doesn't touch me. But I've got one thing to say for them —they give free rein to their fantasies." He smiled askance at her, grimly.

"You must be glad to get away from here, down to the country, twice a week."

"Oh, those country girls are just clean pals." He put the cups and saucers together in a basket at the end of the room, and meditated aloud. "I'm not serious in all I say, but I suppose in a way I ought to live with one of them, it would keep me out of jams. But, you can bring a horse to the brink but cannot make him drink." He flung back his head and laughed. She saw the double whorls of hair on his head, the ducks' tails.

He came back towards her, dropping his tone. "As for that, you know, I'm getting afraid of Lucy, I think she likes me too much. That's the trouble of the near-cohabitation of a house like this. She comes in at all hours and she is free to do so, of course," he looked away, "and old Bagshawe knows my habits. If I have a girl to my room, even you," he smiled, "though they know it's not serious—I've told them so, to keep them quiet—there's a cold wave for a day afterwards. Then I have to be sweet to them, butter them up, you know. I even kissed Lucy, once, after you had been here, just to keep the house running on its tracks, you know, nothing to it!"

"Of course not," she said. "I never thought for a moment—" He picked up one of her gloves, fingering it. "Pretty, what colour do you call that?" he asked, teasing.

"What colour? Wine. What other colour would you call it?"

He flung it down. "Wine, women, but no song. Oh, by the way, Tamar is coming this way, I've just had a letter from her, she expects to get here by September. I had a note from Elaine too, but," he smiled wryly, "I'm afraid Elaine has given me up as a bad job. A nice girl, too!"

"Are you going to marry Tamar, Johnny, is that it?" she asked. He crumpled down on the rug, close to her, half-reclining and looking at her with half-closed eyes. All she could see were his long black lashes. He glanced at her legs. A laugh blurted out. "Marry Tamar! No fear! I stick, my dear, to the pure intellectual life. Tamar has been engaged for two years, so I suppose I don't even count in her young life. At any rate, with her, life is physical." He saw the tears in her eyes. He said gently, "Physical love, to a girl like you, is impossible, isn't it?"

She was tired of answering him. She looked at him thoughtfully.

"Well," he continued, plucking at the mat, "I suppose I'm a freak!

I must be, but I'll stick to it. If it be so, let it be so. Amen, says Jonathan Crow." He laughed thoughtfully. "I see voluptuous females on the street, with the requisite superfluous adipose tissue, the sort nature made to seduce men, who are always taken by profit, a bonus, you know—" He laughed and shot her a brilliant glance. "I'm a man like the rest, it would take no effort to seduce me, I'm no monster of chastity, quite the opposite. There's a girl down the country, in one of my classes, who, funny kid, said she'd teach me about life, introduce me to it, just as if she had a shake-hand acquaintance with it, initiate me—" He laughed heartily. "Would you like to see her photo?" He got up, pulled out a drawer and brought across a bundle of photographs, out of which he took three. He showed himself, lying down under a tree, his head in a girl's lap. "Not bad of me really, eh?"

"No, very good."

"She's just a youngster." He pointed to the girl in whose lap he was lying. "There's another kid, she's engaged, a bonza little blonde, she came up to London two or three times and I had her here and I thought my number was up—I'm not totally insensible, you see—but she would have none of me, she was wearing some fellow's ring, labelled for life, there's the eternal harem for you, like all the ones you really want," he said with bitter regret. He raised his eyes. "I assure you, Tess, I'm a man like the others, if you like." He ground his teeth, his curious habit. "I'm not as I try to make out. That's just self-preservation. But the two or three women I've wanted, the sweet kernel of the carnal—" he laughed, a soft, troubling tone—"those two or three darlings fashioned by insensately prolific nature, with more than usual relish, to receive man's heat and give heat and carry man's seed and make more for the next generation of men to desire—they were already some other fellow's, and as for the seed—that crazy yearning you have to perpetuate yourself in some woman, purely instinctive, against all common sense, but so real, I'm mad I know, but they give it to you. There never was one of them that wasn't burning with love, I felt it myself. Your plain-faced, skinny girls, without the profit of nature, as I call it," he grinned at her, "they're standoffish, and it's a dispensation of nature as I see it. The French say instinct is never wrong, so I was told by a French girl." He smiled a wolfish smile as he plucked at the mat. "I felt the radiant attraction, but—it wasn't to be. Our system was made for the misfits, the ugly women, who get one man and hold on to him like grim death," he said viciously. After a silence, he resumed, with a quiet laugh. "No, really, I have had hard luck, and after the dear little blonde I determined to pay nature in her own coin, bad coin. Very well, says I, Dame Nature, if I can't have what I want, I'll have none, I won't beget myself on a hangdog woman that *will* have me. That's my motto, let 'em shrivel. I won't have one of my sort. Youth at the prow and pleasure at the helm or no boat ride at all! And, provided that kind of girl does not turn up again, I'm sticking to it. I suffer like the deuce, I'm on the rack, at least sometimes." He turned over on his belly, looked up at her through his lashes and went back to scratching at the carpet. "But I'll get over it. What's wrong with that, eh? Don't you do the same? Why should I put up with a misfit, one of those?" he flashed a plaintive glance at her and lowered his eyes again. "When I've been cheated, I cheat back. Eh? What do you say?"

She was silent.

"What I suffer from unrequited and unsatisfied love," he said with a deep groan as if he had just been wounded newly, "I'll keep for my own record. Night-thoughts. Pleasant, eh? The price of decency. What do you think?"

"I suppose so," said the girl. She was terribly pale and her eyes glittered. "But, Johnny, do you want to know what I think?"

"What do you think?" He looked up with a pleasant smile. "To get women to say what they think is something."

"I think that any love affair with any poor woman who loves you— even like this Lucy—"

"That's got an invidious sound—'this Lucy!' "

"Lucy, or the girl in the class who wanted to initiate you," she shuddered. "Not Bagshawe, of course, she's vicious—but anything decent is better than to suffer as you do. I hate chastity. It is torture, invented to make us suffer, and I don't know why. The people who invented it do not suffer themselves. It is for us, the young. I hate it and them, they are hypocrites. When I think of you suffering, Jonathan—" she said and then stopped. Then she said, "It was a bad idea invented late in history and not adhered to much or by many people, but by the poor and helpless. And it is a mistake wherever it is. Look at us. Think of our age! We were strong, we used to be. I used to be strong. We ought to be thinking of our futures and on the first great creative lap of our lives we are smashed, pinched in by this, I don't know why. You don't seem to be able to get out of it. I can't. But a man can, easier. I think you're holding to an old monastic ideal, you have too many ideals. Your idea that the student must be chaste or must only take the best is monastic, it's an adolescent ideal. Why should you wait for the best and die in the meantime?"

"You mean be satisfied with carnality! Is that your solution?"

She pursued, "The student, all of us, should know about life, and what life is about. As to your feeling about Dame Nature and your possible children—I think those are the feelings of a student, who doesn't know much about life yet." She paused as she saw his darkening face, but went on bravely, "Almost the feelings of an invalid, like the ideas of a world by someone in jail so long he doesn't remember the world. When you toss about in bed, thinking of the pretty little blonde, that is a dim memory of the world, all your other ideas are jail ideas. There are lots of women in the world. Why don't you go and get one of them? There must be plenty of women who would appeal to you, the sort that makes you happy. In some way, they have managed to give you ideas of hundreds of years ago. Monks used to give up their lives for an ideal woman, the Virgin Mary. It's nearly the same with you. Don't suffer, Johnny, I don't care. Love someone. Anything is better than that."

"Why should you care?" he said slowly.

"I don't."

"Would you take anyone?"

"No, I'm different."

"You see."

"I can love."

"So you advise me to make love—that is, to go to bed with, the first girl who will have me."

"Why not?" she said mournfully.

"I will try it," he said briskly, getting up, and standing above her with foggy eyes. She looked up and saw the expression, like hate, in them. She got up. "Well, I must go, it is terribly late."

"Yes, it's terribly late and you must go. Poor Lucy—I forgot her! She's still sitting in the kitchen waiting for me."

"You ought to tell her to go to bed."

"I will. Don't forget she's sweet on me," said Jonathan with a coquettish glance. "She's like you." He paused. "Well, maybe I'll take your advice one of these days." He came to the door with her, saying softly, "Well, is it all right now? Did you get what you came for?"

"Yes, thank you."

He opened the door, and she hesitated, expecting him in his soft mood to kiss her. He did not, looking her straight in the face, expecting her really to kiss him. She waved her hand and went down the steps.

He started to shut the door, gave an irritated laugh under his breath, watched her curiously, just the same. He muttered to himself, "She wants me but I've got her trimmed, it's an interesting little case in psychology, by Jove! She'll come out with it some day." When he crossed the hall he saw the maid's head and long, lumpy body coming through the back door. She stopped at the muttering, looked back curiously but went on. She went into the room before him, with a composed face.

"What's the idea?" said she. "Keeping me waiting up till all hours of the night."

"You'll have to give me some advice, Lucy," he said. "I don't know how to get rid of her."

"Tell her not to come back."

"That's pretty hard, isn't it?"

"Too hard for you, I suppose."

He laughed. "Now you'd better hurry up and clear out, Bags will be back soon."

At this moment they heard the key in the front door. Jonathan quickly switched off his light, and they both stood breathing softly until the landlady's door shut. Then Jonathan pushed the maid out of his room softly; she had meanwhile taken off her shoes in the dark. She crept upstairs with tears of fatigue in her eyes. She avoided the stairs that creaked and thought angrily on the ways of young men. She was fond of Jonathan, but she knew he was weak, he went with the tide. "I know what I am," she muttered to herself, on the top landing. "Yes, I know what I am, all right."

V

DOWN THE FLOWERING LANES

There are bad A.B.'s who make good officers and unruly innovating army subalterns who are born to be generals: Teresa was a girl who had no fitness for girlhood and its limitations but was apt as a woman as soon as she shared a roof with a man. She felt no difficulty, no need for adjustment, but at once understood her husband; all her study of love fitted her for marriage. She adapted herself so quickly to the easy connubial life that she was puzzled to know where the stumbling-block had been at first, why had she not married years before? She was conscious of two desires, to accomplish her Testament, which had now become the "Triumph of Life," and to get to understand and love men, from whom she had been wrongly, feloniously separated for so long. For Jonathan Crow, that useless husk from which the whole kernel of passionate suffering had been expelled, she had not even a thought. From the day she went with Quick, she did not give Crow another thought; and at this moment, strange as it may seem, she did not even wonder about Quick's nature nor feel surprise at his behaviour. She said only, "You never made me suffer, you never made me hunger for you, you gave me no pain, you did not set any value on yourself," and in his complete surrender, his passionate, greedy love and the recital of all he had undergone before he met her, she found rest.

She was too formed by adversity and too firm and ambitious by nature to take pleasure in her marital union alone. It was scarcely Quick who had done it, but fate, and though her only concept of fate was that she was mysteriously in tune with some inaudible, continuous single note in the universe, it was impossible to think even for a moment of how she had met Quick and of his influence on her life, without thinking involuntarily of fate. "If this is not fate, it is what is called fate." She felt towards Quick as must have felt those old-time girls educated in a convent and brought out in a fortnight to marry an unknown husband.

They had taken a flat in a renovated building at No. 10, Crane Court, Fleet Street, near Chancery Lane. There was a large window looking upon the alley, or court, but most of the light was cut away by a printers' building opposite and the rest was filtered sickly through the fogs of soot and the cloud on weekdays. On most Saturday afternoons, as soon as the chimneys stopped smoking, the sky appeared and the Sundays in Fleet Street were quiet, cool, sunny, with a marine sky and a salt wind.

Quick had led a very dull life in London, spending most evenings walking about the streets, and as he was naturally a genial, loving, unsuspicious, and gay man, exuberant in company, of which he was fond to the point of vice, he now set about making friends, eager to introduce his sweetheart to them, and to expand into life again, like a robust plant. He had acquired a few habits during his bachelor life, small and insignificant, like the twiddling of his fingers and a quiet talking to himself of which he now had to break himself, and the breaking of these habits he found hardest of all.

His new life, too, was not without its hurts and scars. About two weeks after his settling in with Teresa, he had been obliged to leave her at home for about two hours one evening. He did this with great repugnance and was desolated with fear and misgivings during those two hours. When he came back, Teresa had been reading a novel by Proust which he had given her, surprised that she had never read Proust, who was then the fad of all up-to-date metropolitans of whatever profession. They threw themselves on the bed to talk and here, in the half-light, in unchecked intimacy, Teresa began to tell him about herself, what her feelings really were in this honeymoon and how she felt now that she had the whip and check-rein in her hands—he went cold, so cold, that she felt the warmth dying out of his breast; he lay like a dying man. She realized her mistake, with a pinching of the heart, and at once abandoned the thought of telling him the truth about her love. There were a thousand sides to it, it was pervasive, strong, intellectual, and physical, but he only wanted "a woman's love," the intensely passionate, ideal, romantic love of famous love affairs. She now threw herself into a frenzy of endearment, tried to charm him, went back on her own words in an engaging way with a thousand embraces, kisses and touches, such as she had never given him, but which flowered from her, from the depths of her long desire; but for the first half-hour he merely said in a weary voice, "Yes, yes, I know," or "Let me alone, Tess, it's quite all right, there's nothing wrong, only let me be," and so on; but at length the warmth returned to him and he turned over and slept. When he awakened, he was more cheerful but still serious and it was a week or ten days before she felt that he was beginning to forget the blow in the dark which she had given him.

She resigned herself now to playing a part with him, because she loved him, and in order to give him happiness. She felt the fatigue of life, believing like so many young women that she had found out the truth, which was that man and woman cannot be true companions for each other. But she did not wish to confide in a woman. What woman knew more than she did? She did not think that a child, or years of union, would alter her silence. She thought that each day would be a step farther into the labyrinth of concealment and loving mendacity. And why all this? Because she had wished to speak about the steps which had led her from Jonathan to Quick, steps which were taken quietly every day for months. "But," she thought, "I belong to the race which is not allowed to reason. *Love is blind* is the dictum, whereas, with me at least, Love sees everything. Like insanity, it sees everything; like insanity, it must not reveal its thoughts."

She was like a cornered animal before which, miraculously, an escape through rich quiet flowering country is opened; she fled away down the flowering lanes of Quick's life, and had not yet stopped to reconnoitre or to see and admire the plain. Quick could not see himself, for this, as an escape, and as for the rest—marriage was not new to him and it was part of a plan of action, while for her, involving a different kind of knowledge, a status, new embarrassments and regrets, each part of her new state merited thought and dissection. It was because it had come upon her so suddenly, without forethought or discussion, that she was restless too, wanting to find out what she had come into, like an unexpected heir of estates in distant lands. His first pleasure is to go abroad and be shown every acre, barn and hayrick of the new estate. . . .

Quick, who believed Teresa to be brave, independent and passionate, expected nothing from her but affection. He had tasted and anticipated this joy, almost unknown to women, of introducing a young, pure, ardent but naive mate to the world of social life, action and ideas. He said, "You are fitted for more than me, other men will love you and I will be prouder of their love than you, because I will understand it. Don't think I'm a coward, you are free, I will share you with another man who is worthy of you." This he kept on expressing in the excess of his love. He naturally supposed that the life he offered her would not eventually satisfy her, idea-hungry, ambitious and energetic. He imagined with horror and pity the life she had led up to now, especially the heart-rending struggle for the affection of a cold, vicious man, and he thought of her as streaming with gratitude and delight, sensual pleasure and visions of the future, and knew only this with certainty, that for the time being she would be glad to rest in him. She said in answer to all this, "He giveth his beloved sleep." He loved her with the sentiment of his own generosity, he loved her because she was strange, thin, pale, hot-tempered and a dreamer, because he fancied other men had neglected her as they, with their small hearts, neglected the ugly waitresses and old waiter of the unfortunate manner. He told all this to Teresa, too, adding, "It's true we are all beefsteaks to a Bengal tiger, but why do men prefer in women the fat and tender cutlet? Cannibalism dies hard. Your inestimable friend, Mr. Crow, for instance—"

"Oh, don't mention him!"

He chuckled, "—objected that you were too thin. For this stringy sultan, they must be round, fat and pink-cheeked. However, he has a theory also to cover his choice of hungry waitresses and tubercular servant-girls, he is the necessary supplement to their income. Wages are pitched so low that they must whore, says our friend. So he is there. The dear little strikebreaker."

But Teresa never mentioned Crow's name and did not want to hear of him. James mentioned him every day, insulting him and destroying his arguments, still carrying on with him, in absence, an argument that he, Quick, had long ago won. Then Teresa discovered that James was seeing Jonathan about once a week, and that Johnny was putting out feelers for a job. Jonathan had proposed himself as their dinner guest, in Crane Court, and was rather surprised to be turned down. "You could not see him, Teresa?"

"No."

"Never again, eh?"

But Teresa had no interest in these attacks on extinct Jonathan Crow. Her chief anxiety was to live from day to day. She still felt that she might only have a few months to live. Some would have said that she was unable to bear the burden of happiness. But was it happiness? Quick told her that it would take years to undo the work of that flint-hearted, evil-handed young man, who, for him, saw herself a Lucy —unloved, sinful if she put on lipstick and repugnant if she did not— nowhere able to escape the rebukes of Mr. Crow; this was how he, in his perverted desire to crush all women, had moulded her. *"Evidently a man of small sexual powers,"* said James, "and afraid of the empire of sexual love, to boot, he yet tried to get women in with him in every possible way, by his letters, lectures, and lamentations, but woe to those who believed him. He did call them, they did come, and what a panic he was in!"

"I shall never understand Johnny Crow," said Teresa. "I can only ask, *why?"*

"You cannot understand the weak," said her lover. "He is not conscious of having done wrong, he did all he did to survive. That is the supreme argument with the weak. They think all mankind should do them homage because they survive. Can you understand that?"

"No!"

Quick looked at her cold face and changed the subject. "I will not think the time lost if I spend many years at your feet building up what Jonathan Crow broke down!"

She was embarrassed by this devotion of the man whose idea of heaven was the rapture of married love. She respected him for his loyalty, which she understood because she too was loyal, but all her life she had expected to give passion and never thought of its being given to her. She had wished for the night of the senses but not anticipated a devotion of every day and night. Quick laughed at her, calling her his "Hard-luck Annie," but he had no idea of how his constantly proffered love, sympathy, and help troubled her; she was used to thinking for herself.

It was as if a modest young man had been made king and woke each morning to find loyal subjects singing his praises outside his window. Most young women are surprised to find themselves with a lover at all, the oblique remarks and casual slurs of relatives, the naked domestic drama and hate of parent and child, lead them to the belief that love does not exist, that it is a flare-up between the sexes, a fever, or a nugget which must be capitalized as soon as found. They are brought up with the idea that their cousins and aunts do what is next-door to blackmail, robbery, and a confidence trick to get married at all. They secretly agree with the Jonathan Crows that they are failures, freaks, if they don't. They love, but they are taught that their love is ridiculous, old-fashioned, unseemly, and inopportune, an obstacle to their life-game, an actual menace to their family society and to the lives of their children to be, for "show a man you love him and he runs in the other direction." This was her aunts' timid belief. A poor woman has only one property, her body; passion destroys all relations and liquidates property. So that open love is a serious stain on her character even if she is as pure as the Virgin. The poets killed Paolo and Francesca, Romeo and Juliet, for such lovers are dangerous. Teresa had never noticed this, but she was not surprised that Crow turned her down. What surprised her was that there was not only James Quick but another breed of men who loved women who loved. She saw at the same time that her horrible disease, her love, which she had covered up for years, was admired by this kind of man; instead of being loathed, insulted and sent to her death, she was adored.

She changed at once. She did not revel in the physical pleasures of marriage, but her secret life became more intense. She was like a scientist who has had many failures and who, once he succeeds, thinks that all his previous researches were not wasted; he regrets his dullness and the fumbling of the mind which is more like the fumbling of instinct, and yet he is proud of the blind sight that led him to this. She began to think that she could master men. She wanted to penetrate and influence men, to use them, even without aim, merely for variable and seductive power. Why the false lore of society? To prevent happiness. If human beings really expected happiness they would put up with no tyrannies and no baseness; each would fight for his right to happiness. This phrase startled her, she had heard it before. It was she who, corrupted and hopeless, had told Francine that woman had no natural right to happiness. She saw now that she was the cheated one and that Francine was right. Woman, as well as man, had the right to happiness. Only it was necessary to know how to answer the grim, enslaving philosophy of the schools.

The nauseating ideas of the slick magazines, the chit-chat of every foolish woman were, in a way, right as she was in every way wrong. Woman had a power to achieve happiness as well—but in what way? Only by having the right to love. In the old days, the girls were married without love, for property, and nowadays they were forced to marry, of themselves, without knowing love, for wages. It was easy to see how upsetting it would be if women began to love freely where love came to them. An abyss would open in the principal shopping street of every town. But Teresa did not worry about her sisters, and she was so ungrateful as not to worry even about James Quick. Her hunger had made her insatiable, and she was not content, as he thought she would be, with what he told her, she was not at all satisfied with the end of physical craving; she wanted to try men.

VI

"TODAY PUT ON PERFECTION"

. . .She stood at the window and looked into the flagged yard. The sun was higher, it no longer shone down there, the flags were shadowy. She was glad that he had gone out, now she felt something—the first feeling of all. She was in a strange state of ecstasy, she seemed to float upright, like a pillar of smoke or flesh perhaps, some little way above the pavement. Down below flowed a great slaty river, smooth but covered with twisted threads of water, swollen with its great flow and directly under the window was an immense dusk-white flower with drooping petals, surrounded by green and living leaves. This extraordinary flower, alive though shadowy, and living not as material things are, but with the genius of life, the interior breath of living things, after moving uncertainly like a raft began to float downstream to the left.

In a few moments, it was a hundred yards away, and much smaller. She lifted her eyes and noted the houses, the back fences, the details of roofs and a large tree behind a shed, the things in a lean-to near the fence, on the other side of the yard, old and not unsightly outhouses in the yard itself, and she heard a single note of a human voice floating somewhere at the bottom of the stairs. "Time is already floating away," she thought, smiling peculiarly. She was astonished at her feeling of wanting nothing.

"Today put on perfection and a woman's name" she repeated several times, and still as if dreaming moved away from the window and put her things together. She was withdrawn into an inner room of herself and here she found the oracle of her life, this secret deity which is usually sealed from us. This oracle was now perfectly visible in a room with a large barred window but otherwise not unlike this one, and to this oracle she said, "I only have to do what is supposed to be wrong and I have a happiness that is hardly credible. It exists. Who could believe it? Why is it that just this, this sure happiness, this perfect, absolute joy, is the thing surrounded with 'thou-shalt-not'? I seem to be in a stockade—outside, the shindy is going on, mumbo jumbo, voodoo; here am I face to face and lip to lip with a living god." She was unable to think out the reason for the taboo; she saw no malice there, but a true insanity. "We are primitive men; we taboo what we desire and need. How did the denying of love come to be associated with the idea of morality?" Lifted high, the mind was, now, by a great surge (of the pale crested black water? Or was she voyaging by air?). She continued in a fit of absence, the black river before her. The world, it seemed, silent around, and clasping her hands ecstatically together, she thought, "Chastity? But I never was chaste till now, and as for transitory passions—this is. Even when my mind closes forever, this absolute love must somehow go on . . ."

She finished packing their things in a pleasant solitude and then heard his steps on the stairs. They met again like a bridal pair, then once before they went down, put down their bags at the door, and held each other in a passion in which their bodies evaporated.

"We are made of smoke," said Teresa, panting. "Like those genies in bottles in the Arabian Nights." . . .

I AM THINKING I AM FREE

. . .She turned and looked out of the train. Perhaps there is balm in
Gilead! Perhaps this will never cease. Perhaps this cry-woe and *mea
culpa* story, the sadness of the world, the misery of existence is a lie,
some abracadabra that for an unguessable reason, though there's certainly something sinister in it, is wished on us—but by whom?

Can I doubt my own senses? Great love exists, mad, fervent, self-
sacrificing love exists, and perfect passion exists; how many other things
exist then that merely sound like dreams and songs to us, things denied
to us when children and now, when grown, foregone? All things
desired, are they possible, are they already in existence? Do we only
have to find them and take them, not each and each, but all—are they
there for all? Because if this thing is here for me, no one, a miserable
creature after all, a vain, thin thing, a wretched thing, if I, sinner and
talentless, can have it then all pleasures, all desires should be for all—
weak, struggling, mean, and drab, for us all, the hungry and the dispos-
sessed, the ugly, the dying of limitless pain, the people left behind—
it must be! Yes, it must be! Yes, we will have it, all passion, all delight."
And suddenly as a strange thought it came to her, that she had reached
the gates of the world of Girton and Quick and that it was towards
Girton and Quick she was only now journeying, and in a direction
unguessed by them; and it was towards them and in this undreamed
direction that she had been travelling all her life, and would travel,
farther, without them; and with her she felt many thousands of shadows, pressing along with her, storming forwards, but quietly and eagerly, though blindly. She even heard the rushing and jostling of their
patched and washed clothes and the flapping of their street-worn shoes,
their paper-stuffed soles. She began to blush deeply, deeper than ever
before, into her entrails and into the brain, her heart thickened with
shame and at the same moment, life itself seemed to choke her. She
suddenly understood that there was something beyond misery, and that
at present she had merely fought through that bristling black and sterile
plain of misery and that beyond was the real world, red, gold, green,
white, in which the youth of the world would be passed; it was from
the womb of time she was fighting her way and the first day lay before
her. This was beyond the "Seventh House"—and when she understood
this, that there was something on the citied plain for all of them, the
thousands like thin famished fire that wavered and throve around her,

pressing on, she knew why she continued restless and why the men, having so much in the hollow of their hands, kept on striving. At this moment sprang up in her for them, an inarticulate emotion of excitement quite beyond anything she had ever felt. All on this fabulous railway journey seemed divine, easy and clear, as if she had a passport to paradise.

Quick met her at the station. As soon as he saw her, he came running fast, his swarthy form flying through the crowds, people making way for him, his eyes beaming, his face convulsed, as if he would cry. He seized her like a man seizing a hat that has been bowling away and carried her off, like a sand-whirl carrying off a rag. He put her down and kissed her face all over, and in the taxi held fast with both hands, bending down with his head in her waist. She felt a tear drop on her hand. She was confused by this hurricane. He began to cover her with kisses. She was paralyzed and without emotion.

But she did not know where she stood, any more than if a high tide had rushed in and swamped the road where she used to walk. What relation had she to Quick, to Girton, to the men who surrounded her, to all men? What was her fate? Here where she stood no old wives' tale and no mother's sad sneer, no father's admonition reached.

Was love freebooting? But stalwart, excellent, full of glory and generous, also, were all the freebooters. She was one of them. But she suffered already from the intensity of her husband's passion, she sensed that in it was doubt, fear, and much suffering. She lay quietly in his arms while he told of his lonely days since she had gone away, she was moved by it but she could only bring herself to say, "I missed you very much, so much."

This was sufficient; he became joyful and he began to picture their home-coming a few moments off, their evenings, their home life, and their whole future life, exactly as she had done. But now overwhelmed by his storm, and out of an apposite modesty and shame, she could not bring herself to say anything of what she had thought. A silence fell. He said suddenly, "And did you like Oxford?"—for she had sent him a postcard saying she had spent a few hours in Oxford with Harry Girton.

"Oh, yes, but you know so."

"And was Harry with you? Did he look after you? Show you round? Did he go on with you?"

She answered all the questions and a sort of anger rose against Quick that he was pushing her to the wall in this way. She wanted to keep the two men separate in her mind forever, without intrigue; they were hers, they had nothing to do with each other. But Quick continued that he had heard from Harry, who was coming over tomorrow to say good-bye. He looked at her with genial attention as he said it, watching her impassive face in the light that came into the cab from the scarce shop-windows and street lamps. At these words she remembered her relation to Harry and she turned to Quick and embraced him with warmth and assurance, without the naive and awkward shyness which had irritated him a little in the first days.

"I love you very much and never anyone else," she said. After the episode of the first days when she felt her life would be a secret from him, she had felt lonely, unkind, and oppressed by him, who, however, said he would die for her. Now, with a secret that would perhaps kill his love, she felt able to give to him freely, unforced; she had lost nothing and would never have anything to regret. She thought, "How miserable I would have been if I had had to go on for years, wondering whether I should love another man! But now I know, this is the only love, but not the first and not the last. I will know how to make myself a life apart. If James robbed me, I would dislike him for my empty heart, but as I know how to cultivate my heart and mind in secret, now, I can only love him for giving himself to me."

She was smiling as she thought this again, and he said, "Why do you smile like that?"

"I am thinking I am free." . . .

LETTY FOX: HER LUCK

Written in 1946, *Letty Fox* is the story of a young girl growing up in New York City in the thirties and forties. Her father has left the family to live openly with his mistress, Persia. Her mother, Mathilde, now lives with her three daughters: Letty, Jacky and a much younger child, Andrea. On the periphery are various relatives and friends: Letty's maternal grandmother Morgan; Dora, her aunt by marriage, who at one time lived out of wedlock with Letty's uncle; and Pauline, a Frenchwoman whom the Foxes met during the years they spent in Paris.

In the first excerpt Letty is seventeen and still in school. At this time she has her first experience with Clays Manning, a British journalist and one of many lovers to come. In the second, a teen-age friend of Andrea's gives birth to an illegitimate child in the Fox house. The event has an impact on the women in the household, including Letty, who is losing her current lover, Cornelis de Groot, and has begun to fear that her luck is running out.

ON MY OWN

I

. . . I wrote to Clays (whom, for fun, I called Sir Clays, he was the parfit knight),

My darling *Sir* Clays,
. . . We had a debate in economics on the legality and ethics of the sit-down strike, and I was on the affirmative; that is to say, they are both legal and ethical. As you predicted some time ago, oh, seer (by courtesy of Marx), the wave of strikes is hitting the United States, and the workers all over are becoming more and more labor-conscious, and realizing that they have rights too, and are setting out to get them. Labor is marching on and growing very fast, despite the opposition of the typical bourgeois "mistaken liberals" who claim that sit-downs will lead to Fascism, be-

cause the middleclass will be *aroused* by this "destruction of property rights" (ha, ha, ha!). This feeling is echoed by my dear Republican history teachers, who point out with sadistic pleasure the rise of a group of all of 50 vigilantes, as if every new thing in history, as if every new force of progress and democracy (yes, in our supposedly free land) had not always been attacked by the forces of reaction. Our teacher said that the vigilantes are a national institution. This must embrace a very small scope of the nation and even if it were true, who encouraged the vigilantes, dear lady! who started them? My Eco-teacher is Trotsky-ite, not mistaken, but a real one! It's too much to always give them the break and call them Trotsky-mistakenites. She infilters the duckiest notions into the class; as the class is special, and supposedly for the bright girls, they have taken care to include very few members of the real working class in it (we have plenty here), so that the snug, comfortable brats are all too willing to receive the bad idea. The working-class girls may not have had all that leisure to read Marx (they generally have to wash the floors in between times), but oh, boy, they know what is so and what isn't, when it comes to the wage scale, ticklish proposition, for example. I have the biggest arguments, and go up afterwards and discuss Marx (I know nothing of him, as you state, but she knows still less), and so life goes on. . . .

My darling Clays, I am not sighing and pining for you. This is an unusual love letter. I would, though, if I had the time, so don't take offense. I can't see you pining for me, either, but I hope you do. You have more experience than me in pining—I know your record—so I hope you pine somewhat from mere habit. What a shame that I can't tell everyone! But what fun, too. I love to look at all those simpering brats and think —oh, baloney, what do you know about that thing they pronounce in the movies LERV? I'm getting sticky, my boy, and I move on.

I am taking Art-ah-Art. We have been studying, in one week, what should take at least a year. We are now supposed to be able to identify romanesque, byzantine, babylonian, greek, gothic, renaissance, neo-classical, and such forms of architecture—the truth, we cannot. Also, now we are going to Painting. I like this better. I have to make special reports on Leonardo da Vinci and Jan van Eyck—that's all. I know you'll laugh at me, but "it's the custom of the town." I am taking J. van E. because I saw the *Adoration of the Lamb* myself, with mine own eyes, and she doesn't usually have reports on him. She reminds me of a person who builds a house without foundations; because he is the true founder of the Dutch school. Of course, I'm dying to take El Greco, but she said I had enough.

I am going crazy. The Y.C.L. is being reorganized (again)—I approve of the idea that communists should be human beings; that in their relations with others they should be tolerant and broadminded; that they should do as the world does because they can thus convince more people of the efficacy of another world (not the preacher's, the Marxist's)—but I am sick and tired of the idea that people join the League, not to be told anything about communist theory, or to be trained in any way for the struggle later on, or to make them better Party members when they grow up. Oh, no! You must not scare them by doing anything but having meaningless discussions. You must forget that you were a communist and make the League a "mass organization" with NO PURPOSE (essential)! with little or no chance for Marxist education, and with the already established leaders remaining the already established leaders; the Leadership—God Bless 'em, over the water! Still 'n all, I am trying to educate myself—I should love, love to go to France, Spain, England—with you —learn something—how little a girl knows. When we see men conforming, how worse than bad! For we are supposed to regard men as the tigers, the outlaws, the "beloved bandits"; but, actually, are they? Very few mavericks, in my experience. But the theory still goes, among these (soon-to-be) horned heads, that the maverick, the leader is what women admire and choose, in order to carry forward the best of the species, or something of that sort; actually most of my classmates, female, have their eye out for the willingest, not the best. It's a tattle-tale gray world, my masters. Well, there'll be no sense in sexual theories until women start telling their minds; and, of course, until they have some; that'll be when they abolish the ads, for all the kids I know get their ideas from the ads; but even at that, what they choose men for ain't at all what the boys think. But don't start asking me why I choose you. You know why! I couldn't resist you. That's terrible. I don't want to think about it.

I am coaxing Mother into giving me, for my birthday, the collected works of a gentleman of the Bourgeoisie known to fame as Lenin. Then, maybe I can start catching up on you. (This IS a hint.)

You will probably think I am just a loony kid gone intellectual, but I just felt like writing to you. You are the only one to whom I can tell my whole life. What a pleasure that is, what a relief! Don't let me down. I am giving myself away. Every book on etiquette, not to mention on *How to Attract Men*, tells you to do the opposite. Meanwhile, I am listening to the dances from Prince Igor; my taste is crazy, but it and you make me feel freer and less nervous than I have in months and months—and years. I think I grew up fast. Jacky is still at the idolized-professor-of-English stage. His name is Peter "Varnish"! Poor kid! She thinks men are gods.

Yours
LETTY-SCHLAGOBERS
(easy to whip into shape).

Clays wrote back, among other things:

I'll throw you out if you say *all over* which is German, instead of *everywhere* . . . and a friend of mine (in the Foreign Office, so many of them are; it's the old school tie operating) explained the Nazis to me this way: "It's you communists that brought it on, it's the reaction." Don't ask me, dear Letty, why I go to see him. Gilbert (that's him) always knows when war is going to be declared; and it always arrives on time. I don't even need Marxism when I know Gilbert. I don't make any inferences.

Lovingly, Clays.

P.S. Why *Sir* Clays? Do you think that a handkerchief and a tourney were love? That was adventure! This, that *we* have, is LOVE.

We spoke of our marriage, but we waited for the double divorce, which Jean, his wife, the crime writer had not managed to get. This was not malice. We had asked ourselves if we ought to wait so long. While we were asking this, a letter came from the wife, saying that she expected us all to be free very soon, as her parents were paying for a Mexican divorce and she was even then in Mexico City. I could hardly believe it. It was like hearing that Europe was free. Do these things really happen? Underneath the excitement and joy, I had felt down in the mouth—marriage was really too hazardous these days, I sometimes thought, and I thought of poor Mother. . . .

Now came the letters and papers from Clays's ex-wife. What joy! But she warned him his marriage would not be legal in New York or in England. She had no money to come to New York State to get a proper divorce. The present trip had been paid for by her family, who were very angry with Clays. They had always had great hopes for their beautiful daughter, expected her to make a career in the movies, or with some rich man.

Clays's residence was both Washington and New York, mine New York; but I was under-age.

"Be careful of bigamy," wrote his ex-wife.

"A figamy for bigamy," said Clays.

I cried. My mother and father were very anxious indeed. Aunt Dora who came in, of course, having a great nose for smut and trouble, said, "I suspect her motives," meaning those of the ex-wife.

"No, no," said Clays; "she's a fine woman."

"Go and live with her then," I sobbed.

"Must I live with every wonderful woman?" asked Clays.

At this moment, Clays received a message that he must be ready to leave for Spain at any moment. Since he had decided to go there he had got himself a job as special correspondent, and "they expected things to break at any moment."

Clays now plunged, and asked, Would my mother and I come to France, and wait for him; or would we risk the separation? I did not like this idea, though Mother did. He would have to be on the spot (Madrid or any designated place) for ever so long, and there was, after all, only a faint likelihood of trips to France or England. Once there, our movements would be uncertain; for all his friends in embassies, foreign offices, and points to windward and leeward of the world, couldn't assure us, or him, papers when they were wanted. And all because he was an avowed radical!

My mother was in the dumps. She was in no mood to go and sit in cannon mouths, or under the red flag or under the skull and crossbones (for that's what it all seemed to her). She was sick of ill-starred immatrimonies. A stormy time! I said, "What is all the trouble about? We'll live together and I'll go over unmarried and go to the Sorbonne while waiting for him."

This was the first time I felt an overwhelming desire for him. I had thought of marriage and knew what it was, naturally, but at the thought of losing him I felt something different, a jealous fire. Then, he had made his promise to me before so many people, and before my family; he could not let me down. This publicity has a wonderful effect, in itself causes passion. This is age-old, just an auxiliary to true passion—but how powerful! I never thought of his defrauding me, though others did, and said so. I felt that sureness that Persia must have felt all the time. Marriage bonds and guarantees mean little when you feel that. No sooner did I feel this, than I forgot all the innumerable not-impossible-she's and he's that might cross our paths, and fell into the Great Illusion; which was that Clays alone would suit me and I must have him at any cost. I stormed, turned into a shrew. "I must and will go with Clays to *Ultima Thule*," I said.

Jacky thought this was splendid, and began to take my side. (She now regarded me as a party girl.) Clays said, "In little more than a year you'll be eighteen, and legally a woman then. What I'm saying is queer, but not underhand, because it's for your mother to hear. We can't pretend we're in the nineteenth century. If I live with you, I'll marry you. We'll be bound. But I won't promise to marry you, if you don't live with me; not because I have other intentions now, but because I know the world, men, women, and myself. If you live with some other man, you'll marry him; and I'll be in Madrid, but out of your life; and the same with me. This is the truth about passion, though you don't know it, Letty, and, probably, Mrs. Fox doesn't like to admit it. I wouldn't say such things normally, but our whole lives are being decided here and now, and we'd better be clean about it."

"This is impossible," said my mother; "I'm not a prude, but I don't care for such speaking in front of my daughter."

"There are old standbys," said Clays, not unkindly, but in his superior way, "which don't help us at all."

"Whatever I say, no one will listen; everyone will do just what suits them," said Mathilde.

"Very well, then; it's left to you and me," said Clays to me. "We will go out to talk this over. I am sorry to cause you any anxiety," he continued to my mother; "but as you are unable to come to any decision, we must do it ourselves. We will see Letty's father."

"I am left to myself in a moment like this," said Mathilde.

My sister Jacky came forward, a flush flooding her pale, serious, but fleshy face; her eyes flashed. She took Clays's hand, not mine, though she looked at me friendly, and she said, in German (from Heine's poem *Der Asra*),

> And the slave said: I am called
> Mohamet; I am from Yemen
> And my family are those of Asra
> Who love, and die of love.

He held her plump, white, and rather pretty hand too long, patting it. Then he came away, saying, as he jammed on his journalist's hat, "She's going to be sweet, too, Letty. One of the bemused. Of course she'll be unhappy, I should think. Depends on the lucky chap!"

"Why? There's a chance she'll go to Paris and study art. That's all she wants, and the Great Lover!"

"Not much! Not much at all! Is she strong? Not any trouble?"

"She fancies she has. But that's only dreaming. She's always reading old stories where women always had tuberculosis."

"Yes, but that long neck—and her complexion—white and quite lovely; transparent, waxy, clear as possible—"

"You must now forget other women, your Steepleship!"

"I can't forget them. But I won't betray them, or you. I'll get you some Parma violets—I adore them, don't you?"

"No; but they will do."

"How saucy!"

"I'm not going to be meek with my husband."

"Your husband—now, that's just what we've got to talk about!"

We went to a Stewart's Cafeteria near Fourteenth Street. This was a stolen trip and Clays had to be back in Washington. Could I go with him? He could put me up, perhaps; he didn't know. I had never spent a night away from home at the famous "girl friend's," and knew that my father would not forgive this, either. He gave me every liberty, but would despise this kind of trickery.

"Well," said Clays, "then I must come to you, but can you arrange a night away somewhere; for don't you see, once we are—man and wife, to be frank—they'll allow you to go with me, to France, anywhere; and it isn't exactly rape."

"It's screwy," I said, hesitating, wanting, after all, a wedding with parents in their frills, and champagne cocktails at that Longchamps near City Hall.

"I've got to run," said he. "Look, Hebe, I'll send you a telegram and you fix up that girl friend, for you know I'll have to be in and out like this, and if we can get married, I'll fix up the boat ride; and if not, you must come after me, but we won't be separated. Fate weel naut zeparate zem. Gracious," he said, in that lovely way he must have got from a charming, foolish mother, "I must fly." And he flew.

Ten days later came the telegram. I got it just before school, cut classes, and rushed off to buy myself a wedding dress. I used one of Grandmother's accounts, for I had nothing left of the $150 (I had lent a lot to Clays and Father had refused to give me any more); I bought an ochre chiffon, with some colored satin ribbons wound round the waist, and rushed home to bathe.

I spent an hour brushing my hair and looking anxiously at the short white wool coat I had to wear with the dress. I never was one for doing things in advance, and had not one thing ready. I told Mother simply that Clays was coming, and perhaps would marry me that afternoon.

Clays jumped off one of the first cars at the station and came striding toward me with that forked, humped, and undulating gait of the very tall. I was dumb with my feelings; no doubt even my color went. I stood quite still. He flooded me; the dam broke; I trembled all over.

"A cab!" said he.

We got in, and I still had not said a word. He looked at the string of beads.

"Nice," said he; "the old boy was decent—let me off. I told him I had hooked a beauteous New York society girl. You look lovely in that faeces color. I'm so excited. Isn't this all preposterous? As soon as we get a ha'penny between us, promise me you'll always have a faeces-colored dress. But I forgot, we're going to live on the hop, rather, aren't we? Not even time for a toothbrush between plane and machine-gun shots—have to learn to do like the blacks you know; they have wonderful teeth; rub them on a bit of fiber when they do anything; they chew up caterpillars, I think. Worth it, to have their teeth—I mean the Aruntas. And we'll have to learn to manage like birds you know, wipe our beaks on fences."

I said nothing.

"What's wrong? You're supposed to repent at leisure, after you're married. Good God! You're not starting to repent now? You've got the entire future of the world to repent in. Your child and grandchild and great-great—they can all hear the story of how you ran off, to your cost, with that preposterous Clays Manning; but now, now is too soon, my darling."

I laughed now, "I'm coming out of it. Too much excitement. Are we going to get married? This is my wedding dress, Clays."

"Oh, charming," he said, flurried. "Well, we're going to run off, my dear, if you want it; but we must tell Pappy and Mammy, odd as it all sounds. My divorce has not come through yet, and we haven't time, and I've got to go—you'll have to trust a Briton—"

"You know, now we have the united front—"

"Yes!"

"Politically, I mean."

"Even with George III? With The Man with the Umbrella?" Saying this, he stopped the taxi at an address in Bleecker Street, before an old tenement, newly brick-faced and made up into high-priced flats for artists. I had been here once or twice to visit friends in college.

"Let's go in here," he said.

He had a key, and we got into a flat on the ground floor, with one very large living room, and a series of three closets in a dark passageway, run up out of thin partition board. Curtains were hung here and there; everything was old, and covered with scaling paint. There was a name on the door, one I knew and respected, a writer who was now in Spain.

"He sublet this to Joe," said Clays, mentioning another well-known character, "and Joe is in the country at present, staying at Jake's. Jake and his wife are in Hollywood and cannot sublet on account of bad times, so they gave him the place free just to keep it up, and I can have this place for week ends free, until Joe finds a sublease, or himself returns."

"This is new," said I.

"Yes; I told him my predicament; ours. And now all we have to do is go and lay down terms of surrender to the previous generation."

"Or present them with a *fait accompli*," said I.

"We'll visit Mamma," said he; "no representation without rights. I'll brush up first."

After brushing up, he bought me wine gloves and red roses, and some carnations for Mamma. We telephoned her from the bar where we had drinks and spoke to Pauline, who was with her, giving sage advice about me. Clays bought a bouquet for Pauline. He kept me firmly in one hand, and all these flowers in the other arm as we reached the house. I was quite small to "His Steepleship!" I found myself within the old doorway with a tumult of feelings. A discreet old gentleman who lived in the house, and was always going out to affairs or concerts, passed us and smiled. I heard my father's voice. He had come from work, too.

Clays was very gay with all, and quite chattily discussed his matrimonial tangles. It was "preposterous." He might not be out of them for a year—longer. He would be away; "I lead a risky life. You may think of her as the airman's bride. You give her in me a love which she may never have again; and you may have the pleasure of seeing her a beautiful widow of seventeen or eighteen. Perhaps I shall hop this mortal twig in short order. I may say I consider it quite proper."

They argued it up and down. It was naturally hard for even the most liberal of the four (Dora Morgan was there still) to agree to free love. Finally, Clays took me out to walk and to eat.

"End of the second chukker," said Clays, "and no score yet."

"Oh, Clays, why did you start all this? It's just a mess."

"Then what's your idea?"

"Let's run away, now. Not go back."

"My own decision, Hebe. But I want you to be sure. I had visions of you making up your vacillations too late and following me, on the spur of the moment, all round Spain; while I, obedient to the whims of Mars, chasing the canards of Rumpus, left you far behind. I saw you sleeping alone under the Spanish stars, and I, not alone, but in caravans, trains, coaches, motorbuses, inns, water cellars, barns, ditches, ruts and caves, attics, and hiding under beds, kissing the wormeaten boards and flagstones in lieu of Letty; and tempted by those black eyes and those high pouting busts—"

"Clays!"

"You must be inured to the truth."

"What makes you think I'd do all that for you?"

"My ex-wife would have done it. She was that sort. She's quite a grand girl; but of course, you're better, so you would have."

This cast a gloom over me. I didn't think I would have, but on the instant became persuaded. I murmured, "What you are is such an olio of romance and rococo sentiment, pathos and vaudeville, that really I must believe in my knowledge of human nature to take you at your word, Clays. Don't kid me, I'm going to cry again any minute"; and I declared I was ready to throw myself into the land of fire for him. Let him just get the passport. He became hotter and hotter, interspersing his declarations with regrets for wasted time, gladness that I was born no later (for then I would have been much too young for him), and making allusions, so raw, to the night coming, that I felt something like sharp knives in me. He kept referring to my virginity, and to how little I knew (for all my supposed, but innocent wildness) of life and love; and how exalted and at the same time sordid and bad love could be, till I felt more than drunk.

"I'm tired, worn out, Clays. I must go home."

"All right. Here's a cab. Home, James!"

In the taxi he squeezed my hand and said, "How you love me! It's wonderful! You've really got me!"

This made me angry. He seemed stupid and animal. But I felt so sick that I was determined to bring things to a finish, so that I should know where I stood, both with him and with other men, always afterwards; "so that they cannot tease me," I thought to myself. I had nothing to wear to bed; but so suddenly to bare myself to a stranger did not upset me, for I was in a coarse, glum mood, and hardly counted him. His eyes were glued to me, and I saw myself as he must see me, a stumpy, young female, whose legs came out like columns from my white shirt. We got into bed, and I threw myself into his arms quickly. It was just as if I had done it every night of my life.

What a surprise! We rolled there, smoking and uneasy for some time, when Clays, with shocking calm, told me that his excessive love had made him impotent and that we would have to get up and sit talking for awhile. I was abashed. I sat with downcast eyes, blushing. Suddenly it occurred to me that I must telephone my parents. He looked after me anxiously. I told my parents I had gone out dancing. At once, he brought me back to bed and, taking my hand, showed me where to put it; and then he declared that he had been up five nights in succession, with only three hours' sleep a night, and had been beating up the town to get his papers for Spain, and anxious about his divorce and me; and that all this had an effect even on a young, strong man in love; I must forgive him. Many were the apologies he made, but in a manly tone; and laying his head on my breast, he went to sleep. We got up at seven in the morning, hungry, disquieted, and worn out.

Clays was supposed to return that day to Washington, but said he would risk another night. His friends in the office would stall for time and let him know immediately if he was wanted.

From the café where we breakfasted, I rang Mother again, and found that Pauline had stayed the whole night with her. It was Pauline who came on the phone and told me I had better come home at once with "the man" and see them.

When we got there, it was ten-thirty in the morning. Mother was asleep, having been put to bed by Pauline; Jacky was home from school, but Andrea, my little sister, had been packed off to Grandmother Morgan's with Dora Morgan, till the scandal should have been mopped up.

Pauline was delighted to see us; "So you spent the night with him, naughty girl! You thought you would pull a fast one, wicked child! Well, darling, I am really your friend, and you must rely on me. But Mother, naturally, is horribly upset. You cannot understand that, you are only a naughty child. But he is the one to blame," and so on.

Pauline's remains of a French accent made all this sound quaint and cheering.

At the noise, my mother rose and lumbered out of her room, in her amazing way, bringing a thundery atmosphere with her. As she stood in the doorway and surveyed the scene, I felt once more her grand stage power. As soon as she was with us, her bad temper poured into all of us. We stood dumb before her.

"Well," faltered Pauline, "go on, Mathilde; you said you would be nice to them. Besides, frankly, it makes little difference what you are to them. It is all over."

"Come here," said Mathilde to me, taking no notice of the other two; "you can't expect me to be very pleased to see you! I suppose you knew I should be very worried all night? And I suppose you know you should have asked my permission to do so crazy a stunt, before going off? Instead, you notified me this morning that it is a *fait accompli;* and, of course, I can do nothing about it. And then, you're here without giving me any of the information that I, as a mother, or even as a guardian—for the name of mother doesn't seem to have any more influence with you than the name of wife with your father—"

My mother lost her way for a moment and stared at me with her lustrous, morbid eyes. Then she recollected her role, which must have been rehearsed in her mind in the long hours of the night; or long before, perhaps.

She continued with so much talent that it merely had seemed a dramatic pause, "It has not been an easy or pleasant time for me, all this folly of yours, Letty; and I have had no comfort from you at any time, for you are quite selfish! And, knowing what you do about my troubles, it does seem to me that you should have made some kind of an effort, even if it cost you a little discomfort, to keep me as free from outside worry as I can be. By that, I don't mean that you should have done this thing secretly, but you should have taken me into your full confidence before doing anything so unexpected, unusual, and—irreparable. You have subjected yourself, you will subject yourself, I know quite well—to all kinds of inconveniences and perhaps dangers, which you cannot possibly foresee; and which he, no doubt, did not trouble to point out to you, though he has been a married man, and knows all about it. I do not like you to marry a man of this experience and way of life. He cannot give you any kind of comfort; he cannot even marry you!"

My mother turned her eyes to Clays, for I was standing my ground, though consulting my boot tops more than my mother, with my eyes. I felt myself a very little, guilty girl. My mother's echoing voice continued harshly, "You have given up school for the week; that, I presume, is unimportant from your point of view?"

"I am going back to school. Clays said I must study and graduate."

"Oh! Clays will allow you to continue school. That's very pleasant to know."

"*Ah, mon Dieu!*" I cried passionately, in French, so that Pauline would be all for my side: "*Elle me dit ceci; c'est tout ce qu'elle a à dire; et toute la nuit l'autre murmurait, Je t'aime à la folie, je bois ton corps, j'aurai tout de toi, je t'avalerai jusqu'au sang; des mots fous, voltigeants; de la passion, toute la nuit.* He loves me and she does not love me, that is all. What else am I to think?"

"Yes, you are both suffering now," said Pauline, rapidly, in French.

"It's a fine day in my life, and she brings rain, cold, dust," I cried. But Clays and Pauline intervened and brought us together, somewhat. Also, even I knew that Mother was weak and helpless; that this dramatic scene which she had gradually evolved had nothing behind it. All her strength went into these strange characterizations or impersonations. She had nothing left for life. She could not stand up to anyone; and, as she gloomily said at the end of the discussion, "What does it matter what I say? I wonder you came back here. You always get away with everything, Letty!"

Clays and I now found it proper to vanish. It was not till I got outside the house that I suddenly heard Grandmother Fox's voice ghostly whispering in my ears, "Much ado about nothing, as Shakespeare the great dramatist said."

I mentioned this to Clays, to tease. I felt injured; but really, his failure was a thing I would not have told for the world.

"You are lucky," said Clays; "you can still turn me down if you like."

"My goodness! That's not the kind of thing you can explain to your mother. I am sunk, just as I am."

I went back to the Bleecker Street flat to read, listen to the radio, until Clays should come back with our dinner. I could not bear to touch the flat: the bed lay in disorder.

Clays came in with what was required for the occasion: cold fowl, wine, fruit and flowers.

"I am no poet," he said, "but I thought up something for you and I present you with the sole poetry of my life:

I, the thirst, thou the wine!"

"Is that all?" I burst out, laughing.

"Well, I could enlarge on it; I could say:

I, the thirst and the cup;
You, the wine and the riot."

"It would be better if I said that to you; the cup, that's Letty."

"Well, at times like this, we think for each other."

Well, I thought, this is really my wedding. But it was not so. We were just in bed, and he had just begun to fulfill some of his promises to me when the telephone gave one of those long, signal rings and he was obliged to answer it, being not only a journalist, an electric spark jumping when the line was vitalized, but also A.W.O.L.

"My darling," he said tearfully, signaling to me from the telephone.

I heard his abrupt tone change. He became interested, he agreed. He laughed, "It's damn inconvenient; but I'll be there, if it will really be only half an hour." Then a laugh; "I was not sleeping alone. You hit it. See what I do for you."

With this, he turned from the phone and began a fraudulent lament, "My darling little Letty, I know it's simply preposterous, but will it be all right if I leave you here for half an hour? Well, it will take an hour, all told, and I'll race back, but I've got a chance to see this particular chap—it's Blank, of all people. He's leaving town for Paris, and he'll hardly see anyone. It's been arranged for me by a frightfully good pal. They found out I was away and he managed this, to screen me; and it is a scoop anyhow. Not only this chap, but the paper would be frightfully miffed if I let them down."

I lay still, choking with rage.

"That's right," said he, kissing me, "now take a little snooze, while Papa nips out. I'll be back before you know it. There's my darling darling—Gracious, I must fly!"

He nipped out, after dressing rapidly, with a good many winks, nods, and blown kisses, all of which I received with eyes of rage and scorn. I lay still in bed, thinking everything over. Was a young girl ever treated like this, I said. Spasms of fear and pain tortured me. Was he fooling me? Was he a pervert of some sort? Was I really ugly? Perhaps I did not attract anyone! What should I do? Dress and go home, tell the humiliating story, and be received back as an unfortunate? Cut my throat? Run away? Pretend I had quarreled with Clays? But—"my reputation"! I said to myself. If I had been a stray of the streets, he would have treated me differently. The business would be over long ago. Does he doubt my virtue? Is he afraid? What is it?

This lasted a long time apparently, for when I got up it was near morning and Clays had not yet come back. He would never come back, I now fancied. Perhaps he was a lunatic. I suppose I was not the only woman who wondered this on her wedding day, or just before it. Who knows? He is a stranger!

But Clays returned, apparently as fresh as a daisy, about seven in the morning. He had dropped in at a Turkish bath for a couple of hours, for a pick-me-up. "So far I've cheated you of your rights," he said, nonchalantly. "I thought of you all the time. Blank was quite talkative; gave me three hours, not one; and even made jokes and laughed at mine. I'd never heard that he was amusing. He takes himself very seriously. He doesn't know the world—at least the newspapermen—look upon him as a mountebank and a crook. Isn't it the truth? All great men! Even embezzlers and cutthroats."

He lay down while talking to me, stretched his arms out, then round his head. His face was merry, drawn, dark, his eyes bright. He yawned, shut his eyes and was suddenly asleep. I threw myself into a chair, but in a few minutes went out into the long room. "Was ever woman in this manner wooed? Was ever woman in this manner won?" I asked myself, as I stumped up and down. No, I am sure not. This outrage was for me alone. Yes, I must be uncommonly unattractive, repulsive even. I smelled of dull girlhood, simply. But to attract him, must I get first another man? And to get the other man, another man before him; and so on, *ad infinitum?*

With a thousand different starts and pieces of luck such as I had assuredly had in my life, I had got myself into a thousand jams and traps quite unique. Yes, there are women who look for trouble—that's called, *taking a chance;* and there are the children of the poor; and there is the suicide squad to which my mother belonged, hell-bent for misery; but I was a happy-go-lucky, confident, credulous, and even magnificent girl in my own way. I could not work the whole thing out. What was wrong? Fate threw everything at me—I had a better time than Mother, Jacky, or Andrea. The separation of my parents had turned out to be a Christmas tree for me, so that I had twice the chances most girls of my sort have; and now? Why, I even hooked a man like Clays Manning —and now look! Asleep on my non-nuptial couch, dead to the world, and—don't mention the rest!

Well, I thought, perhaps it's all a warning. I am still quite young and can learn. It was pitiable.

Another telephone call summoned him from his sleep back to Washington; this might have been foreseen. He had only just time to dress, catch the train, and hug me crushingly, kissing me all over the neck and face, telling me I must never breathe a word of our accident (he called it) to anyone; he would grab a holiday in a few days, and we would go away somewhere. He promised it to me if it was the last thing he did on this earth. He promised also to cable his father in England to try to get some money, so that he could, perhaps, expedite divorce matters.

"For we are going to be married soon, and it's forever and ever," said he; "you're a wonderful girl, the best in the world."

With a lot more of this, which I wanted to hear, and which gratified me somewhat, he jumped into the train. He had given me some money, which I took, of course, and I took a taxi home. But in the taxi I burst into tears. I was sobbing when I got out, when I came into the hall, and could not stop for an hour.

I just threw myself on my old bed and lay face downwards crying.

My mother came softly behind me, and said: "What is it? What can I do? Letty, I'm your mother. Tell me everything, poor child. You're my daughter. You can trust me. I'll help you."

But I could only tell her that Clays was coming to take me on a honeymoon, and she could not see anything to cry at in that. At last I could see by her remarks that she supposed the experience with Clays had unnerved me, and I left it at that. . . .

II

. . . To tell the truth, I was feeling old. Everyone I went with was too old. There were girls ready for marriage and married younger than I; many younger than I had children. Even my smallest sister, Andrea, now thirteen, was as precocious as all the youngsters of both sexes, at this time. The boys she knew swaggered down the streets, tossing their clipped, slicked hair like dogs or cocks, and many of them at the ages of fourteen and fifteen were going about with that smooth, sly, sweet air of the successful libertine.

They all knew more than I had known at that age. I felt my infant endeavors to be corrupt, ludicrous. Besides, Andrea, a girly girl, had been boy-mad since eight; in fact, she knew the soft men, the seduceable, at four. She had quite a correspondence with her boys. She had never had anything else in her shallow, pretty head. As I heard her babble her confidences, and felt myself stiffen, my tolerant, easygoing laugh sounded positively like that of a plump maiden aunt.

My mother was now anxious about Andrea, who, during this summer, did what a lot of New York kids do, and stayed out all night, roaming the streets with boys and girls on the nights when it is too hot to sleep. Andrea and her crony Anita ("the two A's"), a girl of fifteen, were inseparables, often spending the night together at the home of one or the other. Anita's father was a war worker, gone to another city, and her elder sister, a good-looking girl and said to be a genius in precision work, was at a war plant in New Jersey: the mother meanwhile, worked in a five-and-ten. Mother did not like the Andersons, Anita's family, but could do nothing against Andrea's girlish devotion and was obliged to put up with their sleeping arrangements and with Anita herself. The plump, strong, high-colored Anita used pretty strong, cutting language and knew the seamy side of her worker's life; not only that, she insisted upon opening Andrea's eyes to the dangerous time in which she was growing up, "putting her wise," as she constantly said. She looked upon Mother and me as old women! Anita (whom I detested) was growing taller and plumper and had a magnificent skin that work and nights in the streets could not alter. She used either a thick layer of cosmetics to show that she was "in the groove," or no cosmetics at all, to triumph over the other girls with her natural looks. What she did, Andrea did. We could do nothing about this either. Naturally, the girls in the factory thought a lot about their appearance, nothing at all about the labor movement or the war; they wanted to be glamour girls, marry a rich feller; they made up, talked outright filth . . . , felt each other's breasts to see how far they still were from full womanhood, bragged about their good times, and exchanged addresses of transient hotels, little bars, and accommodating druggists. There was quite a lot of going together, sapphism that is, necessitated by their early awakened sex and the absence of men; but it wasn't rotten, as it had been amongst us at the aristocratic, progressive school; it was just the madness and headiness of poor youth which for a moment held the purse-strings and knew, sure enough, that this time would soon end. They were oppressed by the future, hurried forward into this riot by the worker's fear of the future and the girl's fear of men and of pregnancy. All their lives had to be pressed into this wartime, a shoddy contraption like the valises they brought for weekends, into which all kinds of shoddy finery had to be pressed.

It was a brief saturnalia and dangerous; but Andrea's was such a young spring, she had such a good home, that we never thought she would be in it at all, nor understand what Anita told her. She was with those girls when they came out of work, but she could never be one of them. Of course, Mother had her melancholy spells and blamed my father, Jacky in her absorption, and me, for leaving Andrea on her own. There were plenty of girls, twelve, thirteen, all over the country going out whoring, and plenty even younger than Andrea, who had made up their little call-houses, or went out boldly in children's socks and without girdles, with their childish obesity, to pull in young men from the services, at railroad stations, bus stations, parks and other public spots.

Mother was afraid now, on account of her dreaminess and her irregular hours, that my thirteen-year-old sister was meeting boys or men, and receiving love letters, and asked me what they should do. I said, "Have you looked in her purse?"

I looked in her purse and found some prescriptions from an out-of-town doctor.

"What are they for?"

"For headache," she said. "They're Anita's."

At the factory they used chemicals which gave the girls headaches. They had gags or respirators, but the girls still got headaches.

I took the prescriptions to David Bench, Luke Adams' buddy, and found that they were prescriptions for emmenagogues. But don't worry, said David Bench, who was the man who had helped me through my own trouble, pharmacists don't usually make them up in proper strength for young girls, who are usually scared about nothing. However, he came to visit us and see Andrea. Andrea, fraternally questioned by him and us, and bullied by Mother, and investigated by Father and Grandmother Morgan, still laughed at us and said, "Yes, it was not quite a headache powder," that she knew; but what it was, she didn't know. She thought it was some drug. The girls at work took drugs, some of them, and Anita was a bit of an addict; she didn't want her parents to see. Her mother spied on her, and so she had given it to Andrea to keep.

Mother and David Bench explained what the "headache powder" was for, to see if Andrea would change countenance, but she did not, merely laughed, and said, Perhaps the girl was frightened; she knew she had a boy friend and sometimes stayed with him overnight. In fact, said Andrea, at times this girl friend of hers was supposed to have stayed with Mother and Andrea in their Eighth Street flat.

"Oh, God," said Mother, "whatever will I say to the parents if they come? You mustn't land yourself in such lies, Andrea."

Andrea said she would not if she could help it, but all the girls helped each other, and it was the right thing to do. My mother worried endlessly about the immoral and lying life; and Papa said that Andrea must leave Anita and her crowd and Mother must keep her company at night. Thus Andrea stayed at home and scowled. She pretended to go to school, but we soon found, through inquiries from her teacher, that she had got herself a job not many streets away, where it was advertised on a loft building—

LIGHT WORK FOR WOMEN AND GIRLS, PLEASANT CONDITIONS,
GOOD LIGHTING, REST ROOMS,

and so on.

As was common, the too-young applicant had forged the necessary certificates. When caught, she said, "I am used to company; I can't stay home any more, Mother." And she went off again, quite pleased to be with the girls again and have her twenty-five dollars a week. She was still such a child at this time that she had not shaken off her pubescent embonpoint; yet she was half a woman. More than that, she showed signs of being a very large woman, a "Spanish beauty," as I said about myself, when her age. Mother wrung her hands, as mothers always appear to do, not able to resign herself to the idea of her daughter's growing up.

This went on for some time, during which I, of course, was too absorbed with Cornelis de Groot to pay any attention to anyone at home; and then Mother came to me again to say there was really something the matter with Andrea; she was again out at night, and made terrible scenes if threatened, saying she would run away and live in a flat with five or six girls she knew who had good times with men. I called for Andrea at work and saw Anita waiting there. There was something very strange about Anita, at any rate. When I brought my sister home, I observed in Mother's presence that Anita looked very peculiar for a young girl and Andrea at once said, Yes, she had had to leave work on account of a glandular disturbance. She would not see a doctor on account of the expense, but was going to get a job in the loft where Andrea worked; and when she had the money would look after her health. Anita had quarreled with her family, she said. Mother invited the girl to the house and had meanwhile arranged for a doctor to come; but it leaked out too early and not only did Anita make good her escape, but Andrea ran out and stayed away from home the entire afternoon and night, only coming home during the next afternoon. She had missed the day at work (where we had inquired) but was prepared to return, if we would stop persecuting her adored Anita. I went to see my father, who seemed to think we were a hen-coop making the feathers fly about nothing. He said, "You must not harass a child at this age; you must remember her sensitivity, and treat her with delicacy."

Cornelis de Groot was away two months during which I was able to visit my family, and it then became apparent to me, certainly, and to any woman at all, I should have thought, that our now constant visitor Anita was going to have a baby. I spoke to Andrea and told her I myself had been in a jam like that, and I told Mother the same, "You did not know, but it is true; let me handle this," and I muffled her laments so.

Andrea listened to my story with great interest and seemed to warm up to me, but she smiled at my idea and said Anita had had nothing to do with a man; she had no real boy friend. She had kissed a boy once; and could you get a baby from kissing a man? I felt I must be mistaken. However, I said, "But, Andrea, you know she does look funny, and you can't blame people for thinking such-and-such, and you ought to get her to go to a doctor just for our sake."

"She went to the doctor at work," said Andrea, "and he said it's just a combination of her age and the hard work, with some glandular disturbances like you said, but that she mustn't take anything, it wouldn't be safe."

Anita, too, when questioned, was so innocent and composed that the evidence of our senses was as nothing, and we were all defeated. She could not have a baby; her stories about her relations with men were childish. It was clear that she had not had to do with one: her corruption was only superficial.

Meanwhile, Cornelis returned, and when we met, on the first evening after my work, I, full of emotion and relief, and he, full of his trip away and the prospects for his advancement, and of kind words, though not of love (that was not his style), we went out together, as if to spend the night together, for that had been the way of it. But after dinner Cornelis refused to go to the theater, although I had bought the tickets, and said he had something to say to me, and I, although angered, because I had to pay for the tickets myself, stayed with him, in expectation. He then told me that I had broken our contract myself by becoming fond of him; as for himself, he had come to look on me as a comrade, friend, so we must never spend nights together again. He owed life and love already, he said, to the woman in London and his wife, and perhaps another woman whose affections he had engaged; he was an honorable man, and realized he was playing with fire. He would not lead me on and then let me down; better to stop now. I burst out crying. We were in a big café in the Village. There were dozens of people and I detested scenes, but I felt my heart was broken.

"Oh, how can you leave me, Cornelis? You mustn't leave me; I love you, Cornelis. It is too late for me."

"You'll get over it, dear, and you see I am justified; your attitude shows that."

This went on for about an hour, when he said abruptly, "I am going; come with me, if you like. I am very, very glad I broke tonight, before we went any farther."

As he was leaving, I got up and followed him, weeping. He went out, quite soldierly in bearing, and with a frightening composure. Even I, bowed, crying, well aware of their looks but unable to stop myself, had a flash of perception, "Is he very used to this scene? What a dangerous man! And I am in deep with him. I have nothing to live for now."

As he was getting his coat I broke out in a loud voice again, like a little girl, "Oh, Cornelis, you should have written this to me while you were away, and prepared me."

He said, "I am not so cruel. I tell my bad news in person."

I said, "Oh, Cornelis, this other woman; you met her while you were away just now. I'm not a woman. I'm only a girl; they're women, they can bear it better"; and by that I meant all of them, his wife included. His bearing was perfectly easy. He liked the attention he was attracting, and I thought, What a fool I am, putting the limelight on him, this way; this is how he gets his women; but I was too unwomaned to stop crying.

We went along the streets this way, he with his arm round my waist, wiping my tears away, but perfectly firm. He took me to my gate and there left me. I flung myself on his chest and kissed him, kissed him, and he held me, but remained chaste and cool as ever.

At the office the next day I could see they had heard part of my misfortune, and Charmian told me that that morning Cornelis had asked one of them for the address of another girl, "but, out of the office." I was grateful for this; I supposed he did it to spare me. To my surprise he waited for me after work in the evening as if nothing had happened, and when I made to pass by him, he said, "Letty, aren't we friends? It was only agreed that we should stop making love, but not that we should not be friends; why did you stick your chin out, Letty? We talked about it before; everything was fair and square. Why, I thought you were on the up and up."

"Well, so I am, Cornelis," I said, turning my face away and taking his arm; "let's go somewhere and have a drink; I'm just tired out; I'm worried about my little sister more than you."

During the next few months this strange man, this man dangerous to me, kept me company most days in the week, and was, as before, a generous friend; but his spending was a little less lavish and he told me, as man to man, about his needs for the women abroad. I could hardly swallow it, but did not want him to know that he had my number, so I grinned and bore it. Other times I roared at him like a fishwife—I trust not so much to his advantage as the first time. He would never visit my parents' house, but he opined that Anita was going to have a baby; she was a sly one and had got Andrea to stand by her. One day when we walked by her loft, and he saw the girls by accident, he said, "Well, apparently they can argue away anything; that kid's long gone."

One summer night, after twelve o'clock, when I was not sleeping, with the heat and mosquitoes, I had a telephone call from my mother who asked me to come over and help her with Andrea and Anita, "terrible trouble," said Mother. I found a taxi and got there in about half an hour. Andrea and Anita had gone to bed in the room used by them, before my mother's arrival. Andrea was asleep when she had come in, but Anita was lying there with bright eyes and pale face, which twitched occasionally. As Mother looked at her, she groaned. I now looked in. She was very bloated, and she put a hand on her belly, twisting toward the wall. Andrea said something in her sleep. "Wake her," I said to Mother; "this'll be a terrible shock to her," I continued. "Anita! You're having a baby, aren't you?"

"No, no. I ate some lobster and it was bad for me; just get me an aspirin."

Mother looked at me. I said, "Let's get the doctor at once—it's obvious—"

Mother said, "But she said, she says—she denies absolutely—"

I rang up a doctor I knew in the Village, a good-natured middle-aged man, and told him, "There's a young friend of ours here having a baby; she's a young girl and the pains are quite close together; please come at once."

"It must be," said my mother, suddenly collecting herself.

"Of course, it's a baby. How can you—?"

"Anita's mother or sister must come; I can't take the responsibility," said my mother, and went to the telephone. My sister had got up and was standing, sleepy and confused, in the middle of the floor, saying, "Is Anita sick?"

"Andrea, you're just a baby," said I. "Anita's having a baby too. We don't mind; it's wonderful—but you'll have to help, and don't be frightened."

"A baby," said my sister, looking pleased. She went to speak to Anita. She was already suffering, terribly. As soon as she could speak, however, she said, "It's not a baby; it's just something I ate."

I helped her next time she suffered, then she looked up at me with darkened eyes, and said, "I don't understand, but I'm feeling so bad, Letty."

"Every woman does—but it'll pass; it'll be bad again soon, but when you have the baby—"

"No, no; I'm not having a baby; it isn't a—"

She suffered. Andrea, in doubt, brought a chair to the bed and began to cry when next she heard the girl cry.

Fortunately for all, the labor was not long, but it was not till about four in the morning that the girl, in pain and confusion, suddenly cried out, "Mummy, Mummy! I'm frightened. I'm going to have a baby."

She was delivered about eight o'clock in the morning. I did not go to work that day, but sat with her; and all that day I did not once think of my own petty troubles, but thought of Andrea and her friend and would not let anyone bother them. As she had denied the baby to the end, I expected her to hate it; just the contrary. Anita was delighted with it, and looked at it in ecstasy. Andrea, ravished and with an expression both childish and maternal, looked beautiful, and I saw she was the handsomest of the three of us, or, perhaps, I thought with a pang, that is just innocence and love of maternity; and a hot, sad feeling went through me: I wish I were a mother too, I thought. Cornelis and all the men I had played round with seemed far away. This was the reality, and this was, truth to tell, what I, in my blind ignorant way, was fighting for, trying to make shift with one and all of them. But what chance has a smart, forward girl to be innocent or maternal? That's a dream.

Presently, I left Andrea to Mother and went back home. I felt converted, saved. It was hard to go back to the office next day. Presently, in my slipshod way, I had told them all, and was back in my old intrigues. Such is life! But what a life! I hated it.

Anita refused to tell the name of the father, though I fancy Andrea knew it by now. Andrea only admitted, after we had brought up all the science, medicine, probabilities and the like, that there had been a father. But she pretended it was no one they knew—as if she really thought that possible. She had the extraordinary naïveté to say that "sometimes in the subway men do things to you," and this little boy was the result of a pinch, or a gliding finger!

The Andersons refused to have anything to do with their daughter. They were very poor and glad enough, no doubt, to see Anita fallen into a middle-class family and one so shiftless, nonchalant as to receive her. My mother could think of nothing better than to get money from my father for the baby and mother; and complained that at her time of life she was saddled with a newborn child; but to tell the truth, she was very pleasant for once, and being essentially a vigorous woman, she seemed delighted to have someone to work for. She cleaned the apartment from top to bottom and even reproached Jacky and me for not having given her the present joy that Anita had provided. This state of things could not go on. Anita declared that she would go back to work at once.

"I was never so bored in my life as when I was lying on my back," she said; and in ten days she was up, walking about painfully, and making plans for going back to the factory. "I can't live without friends and some fun. Do you think I could live at home?"

I wondered if her boy, the father of the child, was not at work; and whether she did not miss him. No man telephoned and she would never give us any indication about him. Mother said, "But don't you want a father for your child? Don't you want to get married? Think of this beautiful baby boy without someone to look after him!"

Andrea at once said, "I'll look after him when Anita is at work."

"You mustn't count upon me," said Mother, ignoring Andrea. "The best thing is to count upon the father for support, for you can't pay for a nurse."

"No, I won't tell him about the baby."

This was actually the first time she had mentioned the father so much as to say even "him." Andrea said, "We want the baby." Anita continued firmly, standing up straight, plump, and more voluptuous than ever, "He is mine; if it hadn't been for me, he wouldn't be here. I don't want anyone to share him."

She was nursing the child as she spoke, bosom naked, her breasts full of milk, like two white gourds. Andrea stared at her with admiration, with violent desire. When the baby had finished and fallen asleep, she took the child from Anita and sat on the edge of her cot with it. We went on trying to persuade the young mother to start a suit against the father. Mother turned round, I saw her blush deeply; I turned too and saw that my little sister had unbuttoned her blouse and was pressing a small nipple between the sleeping baby's lips. The baby gave a suck or two.

"Andrea!" I thought my mother looked quite giddy. Andrea started and put the baby away from her.

"Someone's got to work for him," continued my mother mechanically.

"I'll work for him," cried Andrea, "I don't want him to go away."

She spent hours with him, crooning over his bed when he was asleep, prophesying his moods, delicate, fussy and accurate. She sang all the time she was with him, spoke to him, told him her affairs. He smiled at her first, that was a great event; she called me on the telephone at the office to tell me about it.

Meanwhile, Aunt Phyllis had heard about the whole thing and had interested a friend of hers, a lawyer, in the affair. This lawyer at once

set about persuading everyone to start a paternity suit against the father
and himself underwent the expense of tracking down and locating the
young man. He turned out to be a very young man, handsome, disagreeable, spoiled by many affairs, but only a poor factory worker and living
meanly in one room. He denied all knowledge of the affair. We had
all grown sick of the idea and Anita firmly refused to prosecute. It was
done for her by others at first. When she went to look for work, she
found it the same day because of the war shortages. She called the baby
Alex (and this was the father's name, it turned out), Alex Anderson.
She could not be brought to see that this was odd.

"I'm a young girl," she said placidly; "I'll get married later on. Not
now. Wait till he gets a bit bigger."

I was very curious about this independence, greater than any I had
had; and I pressed her, when she was quite well and I saw how cool
she was.

"Why didn't you tell us? You weren't afraid of us."

"No. But it was embarrassing; I didn't want to talk about it."

"But how could you let it go on like that? A baby is a real thing; it
has to be prepared for."

"I know, I just let it go on, day after day; that was the way it
happened. I didn't want to think."

"But—the father, Anita—"

"It was a love affair; I thought he meant it; and when he didn't
answer my letters and told me on the phone that it must have been
someone else—when there never was anyone else—I didn't have the
heart. I didn't write or phone any more."

"You don't want to marry him?"

"No, not now. He didn't mean it. It was a shock to me."

Anita was now a grand, calm, splendid woman with a great rose-flush,
with large, thoughtful eyes. She ate a lot, laughing and taking things
easy, and when home from work loved to lounge in a wrapper and
slippers. Queer it was to see her so, turned into the plump, sensual
slattern. When she went out on her Friday nights (she took them off
just like any other working girl, just as if she had no baby in the house),
she dressed up in dazzling bad taste, in sequins and black satin, with
velvet roses in her hair, and high heels; and a brilliant, sordid, shrewd
flash came into her eyes, while her looks became sensual and quick,
antagonistic, and almost wild. I have seen plenty of girls with that look
tear a dance floor to pieces. I wilted before her myself, though keeping
my looks well in hand, and felt myself weak before the woman in her.

Andrea worshiped and imitated as before, but neither could now be called a bobby-soxer. They were the true sisters. They lived a secret life of their own in our midst.

The family went on in the same old way after this scandal and I began to see that was what the family and society were for—to scatter during bombshells and then calmly cultivate the back yard. Even the individual lives much on that plan. Letty next door to a fancy-girl; Jacky gone off into the blue beyond after an old philosopher; Andrea doting on an illegitimate baby; and the Family plodded along as if nothing had happened.

When next Cornelis went off, on one of his long commissions, I was left to consider my situation; twenty-four or nearly, unmarried, no lovers to speak of, nothing but debts and no family. The family had closed round Andrea, almost excluding Jacky and me. I was just at this point when I thought of taking a new and better apartment. The old place was getting on my nerves, and, finally, was the scene of so much bad luck that I had to get out of it.

A LITTLE
TEA,
A LITTLE
CHAT

A Little Tea, A Little Chat was written in 1948. Like *House of All Nations,* the theme is one of money and property, although here the scene is New York City.

The hero, Robert Grant, is a cotton merchant with investments in a variety of ventures. Among these are a collection of women whose common interest is getting what they can from Robbie. In the passage that follows, Grant is overheard by his son, Gilbert, and his long-suffering secretary as he wheels and deals with his women on the telephone.

I

. . . He reached his father's offices much before he expected. The offices were on the ground floor, small, gloomy, sparely furnished but paneled in wood, and with a family air because the real living place of two old people, Grant and his secretary, who had been associated with him for twenty-five years. Miss Robbins was nearly fifty. Gilbert had known her for twenty years. For twelve years she had been his mother, sending him to boarding schools, meeting him at stations, counting his laundry, attending to all his wants, privately handing him a little change, finding places for him to stay in the holidays (quite often with Grant's favorites of the day), and sending letters to him. She had done it all without selfishness, as part of the duty of a good employee. She wrote for Grant the letters that no one else was allowed to see, and kept his accounts. Her low pay, common sense, and firmness of character had prevented her from ever loving him, ever admiring him; but she spoke about him to no one. She had conceived, also, no maternal feelings toward Gilbert, and she still believed that Mrs. Grant was as Grant described her to others, "—an angel, a wonderful wife and mother, a sweet, pure woman, an angel."

The light fell through a high, dirty window on Miss Robbins' yellow hair, which was piled high in the then fashion. Her hat with roses and her blue suède gloves lay on a steel filing cabinet in the corner. A dusty ray lighted up the blonde fur on her tweed coat with a dogtooth check. A lizardskin bag stood against the wall. Gilbert saw all this—a woman and kind—blonde woman. He smiled at Miss Robbins and pointed to the inner room.

"You'll have to wait a bit while the fit's on him," said Miss Robbins, and pointed to a chair. Grant was talking in the inner room, his voice hurried, clear, singing. The door stood open. He leaned against his desk with his back to Miss Robbins' office.

Gilbert sat down in the sunlight behind Miss Robbins. She turned about to say something, saw his shining hair and face, shook her head, and went back to her typing. From where he sat, Gilbert could not be seen by his father. Miss Robbins paused a moment over her typewriter before she went on with her letters. Her thoughts were a calm argument, "Gilbert is entirely a man now, let him know everything that comes his way." It had often come to her since Gilbert was eighteen that the youth was grown and could take care of himself, but she had continued to look after him. A moment ago it had come to her, but this time, with the force of the physical presence, that Gilbert was a man, and of an age that women marry. She knew what his new pleasantness meant, she knew him so well.

Grant talked continuously, urgently, into the phone, and at first Gilbert heard nothing, thinking once more automatically, Then she came away from the door and came toward me—what happened then? —there's a blank there—and after, I stood still a moment; I went toward her and put my hands—The incident unrolled itself before him, fixed forever in attitudes, unexpected sentences, silences, and the beauty of many absences. The past day and the present clung to each other. He thought, Then she put out her hand to the lamp—And one of those pauses came: what then? What then? He knew what came after. At this moment, he tried to shake off the enchantment and listened to his father's voice, which was saying, "Yes, darling, I am back in New York. I left about those muskrats that Goodwin had warehoused on a wrong certificate. Don't know the business. I'm very sorry, sweetie, couldn't get you the lambskins, got held up, all sold. I hardly had time to pack, go there, come back. Only a grip—well, you know, sweetie, I never take a train without having you to tea and a little chat, I don't like to be separated—"

To whom was he speaking, Gilbert thought, Livy or Mrs. Kent? Not his mother? The incident began again of itself in his head. "Then she came away from the door—" in the same words, the same vision. He forced himself to listen to his father's voice irritably asking the telephone girl for a number. . . . Then she put out her hand to the lamp. "You are so late," she said—He listened to his father, "My dear Barb, and now I hear from a third party there is a div—a private matter, and I know nothing of it. . . . From the Goodwins. . . . You told them two months ago, but not me. . . . But, sweetie, you told me you were busy all the time, I didn't see how I could get in touch with you, I thought you were trying to shake me. . . . But at four o'clock, Barb, darling, I met you and you told me nothing. Two hours later I hear this news and it was a terrible shock to me. . . . I'm very, very sorry, darling, but I couldn't get to Saratoga and besides you were very cold to me. . . . I have been very busy all the summer and needed consolation and—I'm sorry about the bank, darling, but I dropped fifteen thousand dollars last week, Sam did, I mean, and those muskrats were no good and Goodwin is head over heels in sheepskins, no good. I paid out five thousand dollars and there was the lawyer too. . . . I want to see you this afternoon and you must tell me all about it; it's not fair to leave me in the dark. . . . I'm not scared, sweetie. What can they say, I was your friend? That's no dishonor, is that wrong, I helped you when you were down and out—bah! those fellas have nothing on—I am not taking a run-out powder—I must see you, Barb; you're not fair to me. . . . Some hocus-pocus. I know you're not to blame; at the White Bar, darling, and don't bring Paula, I want to speak to you alone. I'm sure you are worried, darling—I'll see that there's money in the bank, Barb, tomorrow—good-bye, then—oh!"

It was evident that the woman kept plaguing him, for he went on, "You shouldn't have got an overdraft, I didn't make a deposit this month because—I know it's the fifteenth of the month—and Christmas coming—I'm twenty thousand behind at the moment! You remember that deal with that bloody Percival? Goodwin's mistake with the muskrats looks like it's going to be a big mistake, cost me four or five thousand at the beginning and now—and he's quarreled with his brother, who can get him in the jug if he wants to and I'm telling him, don't have any family quarrels, the family is made to stick together; and such fights cost money. Those are the fights I hate, darling, where love is involved—" He listened; proceeded in a languorous listening voice, "You must get another lawyer besides Walker—I don't like that fella —I know you're operating on a narrow margin, I am too, you know my expenses and how hard it is for me to get exchange through, but I'll look through my accounts tonight and try to give you a check tomorrow

—I know you can't fight it without money—of course, fight it, that's my advice—fight it—get another lawyer, not Walker, he looks like a shyster—I'll be at Manetti's—by myself—don't worry about blondes, sweetie, I got one blonde on my hands, that's trouble—I don't mean that—of course, reverse the charges—good-bye, yes, I'll give you a check—good-bye—yes, I'll send you the gloves—good-bye—I know your lawyer's in Florida, reverse the charges—good-bye, sweetie!"

There was silence for a moment, in the friendly green-painted room, then Gilbert heard his father giving a telephone number. The sun streamed in. . . . Gilbert thought, I said, "Do you really like this tie?" and she came nearer and—He heard his father saying, "Wright's Agency? Miss Wright? Livy darling, when do you get in? How are you, darling? I miss you, sweetie! I wanted to go to Philadelphia right away after your sweet call the other night. I feel just the same about you, Livy. I met the right woman. You're the woman for me. . . . Never mind about the oasis. You'll be glad to be here, so will I. I couldn't be too busy—we'll make the wires hum—on Sunday? I had no one with me, I swear, Livy. If you heard a woman's voice, it was a cut-in. I'm very tired, pooped-out, no interest in women, but you. . . . I would lie to you, Livy, otherwise I'd feel like a schoolboy, but this time no need to. I lie when I have to, but this time, not. You know I don't say I don't like women when I don't have to. I'm a terrible liar but not to you. Well, Philadelphia doesn't give me a pickup; nowhere to go and no beautiful woman—I mean, except the one I have with me. Or perhaps it's the effect you have on me. . . . Barbara?"

His voice changed and went lower, "Bloody 'ooman—is there of course, got back from Saratoga only to plague me. She's getting a divorce. I heard some ugly rumors. I'm glad you brought it up. Livy, I must see my lawyer this evening. I'll meet you at ten o'clock at the White? I told you all that was through and now, by heavens, I have the proof. She thought she had me round her little finger, and now when she's lost me, she gets a divorce—I'll tell you. I gave you a true account of all that. Now she thinks she has me where she wants me. But let's forget her. Don't ever want to see the bloody 'ooman again. She went through my pockets and did me no good. Never loved me. She's not even dangerous any more. I'm easing her out—and she knows it and I think she's pulling something—Not me, sweetie. . . . Not now. . . . She was on the phone just now asking for some money. . . . I only heard yesterday that she's got into a mess and trying to drag me into it—though she can't, I'm pure, I swear it—wouldn't bathe in a mud-died pool—I swear it—and this morning, she knows I know it—and she coolly asks me to pay into her bank account two thousand dollars to pay her lawyer—No sense and no manners, eh? . . . On the phone this morning, asking for money for her divorce! She took me for a ride. No sense and no manners and she's looking washed out too. Eh? . . ."

At the word "check" Miss Robbins had paused in her typing and written the words, "Mrs. Downs—check; at Manetti's tonight" in her notebook. Grant had gone into his gallopade, marking the end of a phone call, "I miss you, sweetie, you liven things up. Well, I can be quiet too. With the right woman—no, not cocktails. Not taking cocktails, not good for me, too. I like Sue, but too staid, eh? A bit old-fashioned, you're very modern, like me. You're like me; that's it, you're like me. Everyone here is anxious to see you. Told them all, that's the woman I should have known years ago. Gilbert thinks a lot of you. Boy has a lot of character, go by his opinion. He told me, 'Dad, that's the kind of woman who would understand you and put you straight.' Bit of a mentor with me. Means very well. Honest boy. He thinks a lot of your ability, too. Like me, he likes a fine woman. You're beautiful, too. I better watch my step. Better watch myself! Dangerous 'ooman—but you like me, sweetie? Don't you? Only a little? Don't believe it. Can't credit it. I know better. Made for each other, that's the word. Well—"

He listened and continued with immense bravura—"I always said, 'Livy, all I want is a woman'; and now it looks like I got her! Looking for her, I got into those messes, that's all. . . . Eh? That blonde cow? Don't laugh at me, Livy. I've been hurt too much by that blonde. Besides, that was so long ago I forgot her. She's through. She's not a nice woman, not like you. . . . Doesn't care for me, personally, always thinking of going through my pockets. . . . Do you know what she just asked me? Not to forget to keep the Coca-Cola bottles. . . . And she used to take the half-empty liquor bottles out of my closet so her girl friend could give parties when she was broke. . . . She takes trading-stamps, yes. She's a one-way girlie. Didn't remember my birthday. Well, wants too much, selfish. No way to get a man. Well—don't let's talk about her. . . . Gilbert will meet you five-thirty at the Ritz and I'll see you at ten at Manetti's; right?"

He did not put down the telephone but asked for another number and almost immediately said, "Miss Holloway, please? Hello, Katie! Yes, I'm in New York. Got in last night. Philadelphia is all right—"

Gilbert started and looked apprehensively at Miss Robbins, who, however, went on with her typing.

Gilbert's father chattered away, "When do I see you, sweetie, for a little tea, a little chat? I want to ask your advice about something that's bothering me! We'll have tea tomorrow sometime? My boy's here and I'm not altogether free. I'll be alone for a while tomorrow and I want cheering up. Had a bad time in Philadelphia, bloody 'ooman let me down. I want to see you, sweetie. . . . I mean it. Well, I got to be careful: your family might get the wrong impression. Like your mother, very fine woman. Never forget the dinner she made me. Wonderful cook. Can you cook like that? You have to if you want to get married some day. I can't tonight, dearie. Tired out with traveling. Train was late, didn't sleep all night, wishing I had asked you to meet me. Then I got here, lots of trouble, big surprises, big blows, blows below the belt, unpleasant things, quite a shock, that bloody blonde 'ooman, I told you. Thought she had me round her finger like a piece of string. Made a mistake for once. Tomorrow, four, at my place. The Pickwick—my housekeeper's there. I want to give you a little business for your store. Bring me ten pairs of nylons at two dollars. . . . But you can get them for me at two dollars, like last time, eh? Want them for my business friends' wives. Christmas coming, they all got their mouths hanging wide open. Surprising how you can get a hundred dollars' worth of business with a two-dollar pair of stockings. . . . The wives are cheaper than the husbands, my sweetie; take ten dollars apiece to buy a Christmas present for their husbands! . . . Don't say that, sweetie; we understand each other, we're friends—no, we're comrades. I'm a liar sometimes but I tell you when I am, and never to you. Why should I? I like you too much. I respect you. I rely on you, Katie, don't forget, ten pairs. Bye-bye."

He at once asked for another number. Gilbert glanced in astonishment at the muscular busy back of Miss Robbins, who went on typing, when they heard quite clearly, "Is Miss Sapper there? Hello, Violetta! Hello, sweetie, well, when you are free are you going to come and cheer me up, have tea, a little chat? I had a big shock, hit below the belt, and want to take your advice. A woman hurt me. I had a lot of shocks lately and I've been out of town and couldn't see you. There was no oasis in my desert; now I found you and I have an oasis. My wife hasn't any backbone, can't look out for herself, and is no good to me. But I have to go to Boston just the same. I regret it. Not like you. I'm very busy now, darling, tonight I've got to see a lawyer about getting rid of my business here—I want to settle down and have a good time with the right woman. Come to my place day after tomorrow. My housekeeper'll make us tea. Can't see you before, sweetie, because my son's here and I want him to have a good time. I respect him; want him to respect me. I don't mean the wrong thing. Wait till I get him settled out on the farm, then I'll see more of you. . . ."

Gilbert took out a vest-pocket notebook and wrote down Katie, Violetta (Miss Sapper). He had not finished when he heard his father speaking to another girl and he wrote within the next quarter-hour— Bernice, Janet, Helen.

Suddenly Robert Grant yelled savagely, "Miss Robbins!"

The woman with golden hair got up, went placidly toward the door. At the door, she turned and smiled at Gilbert. Grant said, "Someone there?"

"Gilbert!"

"Come in, come in, son."

The young man went in and sat down by his father's desk.

"You look well this morning, Gilbert."

"Wasn't that Mrs. Downs you were talking to before, Dad?"

The three old acquaintances looked at each other in silence for a long moment. Then Grant said, "Good God!"

He frowned, fiddled with the paperweight, began dictating, interrupted it to say quietly, "Well, son, it's no good pretending I'm a monk. I'm no angel and it clears the air if you know it."

"You don't know me, Dad. I—"

"Your mother's an angel, a perfect mother and wife, but I'm not good enough for her, that's all. And she never did me any good. Well —better go outside while I finish the letters, 'Dear Spatchwood, About the house on Owl Island, let him show me my signed order for the bronze bell.'—Flack will sign it, Miss Robbins."

He lowered at Miss Robbins and by the time he had finished his letters, was in a roaring temper. He yelled, "Get all those off before you go to lunch, don't delay."

Miss Robbins put her book down on her desk, sat and stared for a long while at the partition. Then she got up, put on her hat and coat. Grant looked at her through the glass, "Do those letters for me first, like a good woman."

"I think I need a little air, my head aches."

Grant looked at her queerly, and said in a low tone, "All right, all right—but get them off for me before three, like a good woman."

Miss Robbins said to Gilbert, "You don't know what he's like. I'd have resigned years ago, only that he's rarely here."

Gilbert looked genial, asked, "Is it new—with the women—?"

Miss Robbins let out a peal of laughter, and was restored to good humor, "It is time you knew your father: you don't know how he made your money nor how he wastes it. It's a shame how he wastes what we work so hard to make, that's all—but he would say it's his. I suppose it is."

Grant came to the door and looked at them suspiciously.

Miss Robbins went off to a cheap restaurant and Grant and Gilbert to "the Italian's." . . .

THE PEOPLE
WITH
THE DOGS

The People with the Dogs was written in 1952. It is set in New York City and the Catskill Mountains in the period just after World War II.

In the section called "Whitehouse," Edward Massine has come to the farmhouse, surrounded by once fertile but now decaying farmlands, where for generations the Massines have spent their summers. Margot, Edward's mistress of twelve years, is pressing him to marry her. But here, the wide and warm embrace of his loving if eccentric aunts, Oneida and Norah, of his in-laws like Lou, of old friends like Victor-Alexander, make it impossible for him to break away.

In the section called "Scratch Park," Edward has given up Margot. Feeling depressed and aimless, he goes to stay with old friends, Nell and Philip Christy, who run a boardinghouse in Harlem, in uptown New York. Philip is a one-time member of Tammany Hall who uses whiskey to soften the pain of political disillusion; Nell is his devoted elder sister. We see also the rich assembly of people who live in the boardinghouse.

The mellow tone of this novel sets it apart from Christina Stead's other works; this tone is reflected in the relationship between Philip and Nell, which is altogether different from the savage possession between Nellie and Tom in *Dark Places of the Heart (Cotter's England),* or the fantasies of Catherine and Michael in *Seven Poor Men of Sydney.*

WHITEHOUSE

I

It was midsummer. Their nights were long and cold on the mountainside. They went to bed early and slept without waking. All through the night in the sky were reefs of stars and shoals of cloud. In the early morning, the old trees rounding the gardens stood nearer to the house, looming in land-cloud. Towards sunrise, this land-cloud began to pour down the valley which widened away to the east. Cloud reeked out of all the mountain wall, poured towards the sun. In the garden, in each corner of the house, old pear trees choked by a great vine stood like bronze, with their rare leaves and pears in the first light. No one slept indoors, but on sleeping balconies, inclosed or open, which projected from all parts of the old house, upstairs and down. On the higher hill the farmer and his family woke first and drank their black coffee, the cows lowed mournfully, the old horses stamped and the dogs woke in the big house.

About five, the Abbot, a young Manchester terrier, began chirruping. He stood on the body of his owner, Flora, with his forepaws on the sill of the balcony, stared through the green rattan blind and trembled. He could see the farmer in the field, and Edward asleep on the next balcony. Musty, invisible on a third balcony, barked in reply. Massines began whispering to their dogs. At a quarter to six, the first trumpet, with a sweet airy tune, came from the watchtower of a summer camp in the neighborhood. Dingy, a Skye, was already out and flopping through the long grass. His mistress Norah was scouring pots in the kitchen. In the silence came the sound of a heavy car approaching. The car panted up the slope to the front of the house, doors slammed, all the dogs barked. The van skipped away, over the ruts, tussocks and stones. Flora got up, dressed, and they heard the Abbot scampering down the wooden stairs. He rushed through the screen door with a shout of triumph. He was silent for a time and then ran wolfishly through the long grass. There was now a noise of pails, a jingling of harness, shouting and swearing on the hill as van Kill the young farmer got ready to take his milk down to the highroad where it would be picked up. The thirsty cows lowed plaintively. The wife called from the cottage on the hill. The farmer kicked a can, jingled the harness, cursed: his two little boys imitated him and it came out quaint and harmless in their fresh, ragged voices. . . .

. . . Edward turned over, pulled the weather-beaten blankets and dogtorn quilts to his chin and closed his eyes. Another bugle spoke, the sunrise flushed the whole sky. Edward thought for some time. People had recognized him at the stops in the valley. With him in the bus yesterday was a factory girl coming to Haines Falls for three weeks. She was a strong broad-toothed bronze-haired young animal, ferocious but good, and she was exhausted by work. He had drawled out the names, Haines Falls, Saugerties, pointed out the things to her and said with pride, "I lived here all my life; this is my home." In France, in Cairo, in Rome, he had hated Whitehouse and thought of it as stifling his talents. In the deep sweet summer cold, sluggish and healthy, like a pool that never stagnates under pinewoods, healing, with this cloud on the orchard, the open air and the bear they said was still on the mountain, and the strong black-eyed women of the family up at dawn and active, people of a gaiety and love he had not met elsewhere, he thought; I am wrong, a modern restless nervous man: this is right, and what is wrong? I am wrong. He fell asleep again.

About six-thirty, Oneida woke on the large sleeping balcony facing north. Through the broken rattan blinds to the north she saw the sky mild and fair. Facing her, there was no blind nor sky, only the rising hill on which she saw, as in a painting, the horses, farmer's cottage, the hill beyond and to the right, the corner of an old plantation of pines, elms, birches. She heard the noises of the dogs outside with interest. They indicated to her how far the rising and housekeeping had proceeded. Some noisy birds in the pear tree behind her head troubled her. And then she knew what had been insistent in her last dreams, far off, continuous, a little dog barking, a nervous female dog quivering, wearing herself out. She knew it was Big Jenny's favorite dog. And why? She pondered, no, she can't be in heat, a danger to the dogs. Perhaps it is only Charlie, that poor Spitz tied up all his life at the Adamses' shack. She murmured to Lou asleep at her side, "That Spitz . . ."

"H'm, h'm?"

"That Charlie of the Adamses' is so neurotic with being tied up, he has no more sense than to bark at our dogs. If Madame X attacked him, the Adamses would be angry." She gently pulled the ears of the old French bull snorting away into her breasts and neck. She observed the farmers, without raising her head from the pillow, saw young van Kill the farmer coming down the slope, down the kitchen steps. He dropped out of sight and knocked at the kitchen door. Oneida remarked, "Lou, the farmers want to leave today. There is no water for the cows again. They are going to the Morgans' after all."

"Why doesn't he see Leander?"

"Leander saw the reservoir man. He went up and turned on the water, but the pipes are too small and those summer camps take all the water for the showers and kitchens."

Madame X barked sternly into Oneida's face, telling her to get up, while Musty teetered anxiously upon Oneida's legs, unwilling in his old age to leap to the floor for nothing. Lou stretched his broad white throat from his blue shirt and said, "Keep those dogs away from me. I dreamed I was reading a book written in a beautiful unknown language. I read a page and then turned it over. I read it all and I understood it too, page after page. When I waked up, I could almost remember it."

Madame X who had jumped to the floor, put her paws on the bed and sent her iron knelling in Lou's direction. Lou looked slyly at the dog, "LO K9 OBCT," said he.

Madame X barked angrily. Lou leaned over and kissed the smooth top of her head, "Hello sweetheart."

"Lou, get up, it's the wedding day."

Oneida, puffing, was now trying on a pair of rope-soled sandals. She wore her sleeping gear, faded blue cotton overalls, something the dogs could not harm. Her breasts stood out in this, full and heavy, but with her tousled hair, brown arms, freckles, small stature, with her pants torn and flapping at her ankles and the spoiled, clever grin on her face, she suggested a boy. When the dogs saw her sandals on, they stopped barking and ran to the door.

"Come on, poor babies," she shouted, tearing out a ribbon she had been trying impatiently to braid into her hair, "Mama will do iss way," and she suddenly raised her voice and repeated it babyishly, naughtily, "Mama . . ." with a laugh to herself, she opened the door and left it open. They scampered on the dusty worn wooden floor of the corridors and stairway. . . .

Lou, in the second movement of his Beethoven sonata, stopped the piano and listened. The catbird was in the pear tree outside the studio window. Every day, the bird, which began the morning by singing would listen for a while to Lou's practice, then would run over two or three times some little theme that interested him and, inspired by art and jealousy, would burst out with full throat and try to outstrip, outsing the music. At certain brilliant trilled passages he would stop again, listen; and once more song would pour out of him. He sat on a naked twig. Sometimes, overcome with effort, after nearly bursting his throat, he would fly off to a distant birch, sing there on the top branch and fly back, fly off to the dying top of the poplar by the barn door, give a splendid solo and fly back. Each year, this superb musician came back from his winterings, to the same pear tree, chased away all other birds from it. There were a few catbirds in this part of the hill, attracted by the overgrown slopes, water-courses, groves and thickets of laurel, but for singing and mocking, not one like this one. Lou played a bar over several times: the catbird, in the middle of a repetition, began to imitate it. Lou paused and listened, smiling, played it again for the bird.

Meanwhile, he heard skirmishing in the kitchen, which was distant the breadth of two sitting rooms and the length of a hall. He heard his wife's childishly severe, "Musty, Musty, stop it!" He sat back on the piano stool smiling faintly in a reverie. After the first bird awakened him, about three-thirty, he had fallen asleep for a while and awakened to hear the cedar waxwings stripping the fibers from the vine on the pear tree. Then the bugles, the cows, the clanking of the enamel coffeepot on the stove in the farmer's house, the empty milk cans, the mewing of Westfourth, the cat he loved, miserably mewing to be let in for breakfast; and Darly, that spry little dog, that jumped like a butterfly, singing for a mate. Surprising that after that he had not heard Big Jenny's loving contralto. Lou heard Oneida clattering and the answers of her sisters, Norah and Ollie. Far off up the slope from the long disused bowling green he heard the first notes of Vera Sarine's morning scales. The clock had not struck. Oneida was angry but not worried. Then nothing had happened to Big Jenny in the night. He heard Flora, full of love, say to her dog, "Abbot! Bad dog!"

Then came the mad race of the Abbot through the downstairs rooms. He knew everything that was happening. He had lived with this family since his childhood, been loved by Oneida's parents, known all her friends. Lou was hungry and thought, "Yes, but I must wait, of course, till the dogs have got through their breakfast." He started playing again. . . .

II

Edward with the cat in his arms, strolled round the house. He stopped under the low trees to let the cat scratch at the twigs. Westfourth purred and clung. When they came to a smooth path, Edward put him down carefully, saying, "No more scrapping, you old weather-beaten pug."

Westfourth walked up the stone coping and stretched himself out in all his majesty. Edward picked up a pair of shears and went into the raspberry patch. He started on the dead canes.

The patch, though not more than two yards square, was tossed and tormented where Lou, Oneida and various guests had been plucking and tearing at will, getting rid of the latest offshoots of the great wild hops vine, tearing away at its roots. Here, it crawled over the tool shed, through the grass, to throttle a thin small birch, through the rosebushes, tangling the canes. The vine fell from the roof and the porch and the tool shed and rose from the ground in thin runners and pencil-thick stems, and with warp and weft endeavored to trap all the plants and bushes in one coarse moss. Edward, for a few minutes, stripped and tore, ravished, unwound and wound, and then felt stealthily and thoughtfully for the climbing stems which ran down the main stems of other bushes and so followed them underground. When, led by these stems underground, he had cut and cleared a little space, Edward began to pull out the runners of the vine. The first were only threads rising from a tough cord; and below this cord was a thicker one from which it arose, deeper down; and the lowest one was the size of a ship's cable, and about a foot below ground. The stringy starved bushes were freed, stood apart with their miserable stems half naked.

He grubbed farther down, pulling out the strong and quick vine from the engaged roots of the bushes but even when these were horribly drawn out from the entrails of the garden, his fingers felt new and greater intricacies of thicker runners, deeper underground, to which these upper stems merely led down; and most of these systems of runners and stems had grown round each other or stones, or things lost in the earth for years. Edward made a hole and plunged his arm into the blood-warm earth to the elbow. Groping, he found old piping in a coil, a hammer, the tapering root of the nearest tree, a shoe sole. The root of the nearest tree was in the grip of the vine and feeling under this embrace, he found another tap of the vine, thick as a man's arm.

The vine aboveground was clambering at a distance of a hundred feet on the farm hand's old shed, now broken in, and farther off on a corner of the barn; and here in the raspberry patch, and towards the bowling green and on the wall of the summer house. The same vine, rising from these great arteries, issued from under the house at the pergola corner, at the corner where Lou's downstairs studio was, at the corner where the newly married couple would sleep tonight; climbed the walls on the other side to his own veranda, and reached out to the suffocated pear trees and through the pear trees to the pergola which it canopied, a heavy stuff which was breaking down its heavy worn beams and spreading beyond that to the first trees of the plantation where the sump water seeped through. Beyond that, it had begun upon the old trees which formed the screen above the sunken farm road, down all the half-acre to the road, the same great system and one vine; and this was more than the foundation of the garden, it was a dark communication of sinew forming the body of a great being. It held, embraced, but did not crush the ground, the house, and all there brought by dogs and men: bones, sheathed copper wire needed for watering the cows, old leather shoes hidden by a predecessor of the Abbot, a sadiron, and all the things lost by this fertile careless family, and all the things loved by this productive, abundant family for seventy years; the deep ineradicable cables plunging into the hill soil and sending up at great distances their wires and threads; and the whole family and house and barns and the home-acres, in the great throttling of the twining vine. It tore away easily, leaving all the growing roots there. In a few days, the injured roots completed their repairs and sent up a new line of roots and leaves and the work of monopoly went on.

Edward said, sitting back half-exhausted and half in anger, "Like what it does to me: the sloth that stretches back into my childhood and had its foot in my cradle."

Edward put his grubby fingers in his pocket and fingered the letter. That too stretched through the years and was suffocating, useless, and was like his life with the sisters, a love of old women. He sat down on the grass among the dry thorns and weeds and opened the letter.

DEAR EDWARD,

Perhaps you will read this letter days after you get it and, knowing you, I will wait two weeks for an answer. Please read my letter carefully. Please do not let it lie around for days and weeks or drop it on the dining-room table and forget it. Do you now, or at any other time, expect to marry me? If you do, please let me know, don't think that because the news is good, it can wait. And say so, write me a letter to say so, and don't be vague. And if not, please say so. There is no need for you to make any excuses. I have made more excuses for you than any man could make for himself. It is another man who is asking me to make some decision myself. I realize the fault is all mine. I have been very weak. I have let you go on and on, whistle our lives away. This man wants to marry me: but I can't make up my mind without giving you a chance. This man knows about you and he asks a very plain question: Are you going to marry him? I told him that it was all very unclear. That is why I write and break into your holiday.

Yours, as ever,
MARGOT

Edward was still alive in the life of the vine in the earth. All was still. The sky did not yet show any sign of the thunderstorm which comes almost every afternoon at this time of the year and pours down the escarpments and valleys with that curious steady hopping boom-boom. One tree in the strip, which stood between the big house and Leander's, began to dance slightly at the top, a few leaves wagging against the delicate sky.

Edward thought, this tree knows a wind is coming and yet nothing else is moving and no other tree is moving, and no leaf, just this branch. They live a life different from ours. They think. How wide the view was! He got up and walked on thoughtfully, but had no particular thought. He passed from the timothy field which was reddening now, across the hidden foot track which led to the front gate and through the laurel and wild rosebushes to the other wild grass patch in front of the house. The great vine had begun to crawl along the trees at the far side of this patch, which overhung the sunken road. This had once been a lawn. It was now a grass patch cut twice a summer by the farmer for the cows. It had not yet been cut and was knee-deep in coarse grasses and large broad-leafed weeds, with numerous potholes made by the dogs and concealed by the tufts, and with old beams, an immense pile of stone crumbling down from the terrace and covered by the vine, old wire, all kinds of building and garden trash, and in a stony half-moon, several stunted pines transplanted when mere green feathers from the pine patch by the weir which had never done well.

The farmer, van Kill, was coming up the road. Edward hopped into the wagon. At the barn, with the usual vociferation, they all got down and went into the barn for harness and implements. Edward followed him to the barn and, after a few friendly remarks, nodded towards the filthy straw, the unwashed flags of the barn, the choked guttering, all fly-infested. A drone of flies rose through the barn. Said Edward, "The girls are complaining about the flies in the kitchen."

The farmer went on collecting things and said at last, "You know there's no water coming down from the dam. I can't water the cows. How can I wash the barn? You want to get in that new piping."

"With what? Who can I get to put it in? Leander will look to it at the end of the summer, when he's finished with the houses in town."

"I can't wait till the end of the summer. That's why I'm going."

"This muck has been laying round for weeks," said Edward. The farmer said nothing, and drove off.

Edward went round the barn to look at the old car. At the prices now given for old bodies or even junk, he could find the money for a down payment on a new car. He decided to walk down to the village in the afternoon before or after the wedding and talk to the garage boys. Edward crossed in front of the farmer's house and came to the white railing fence. He unlocked the gate and crossed the dry cow-pad. . . .

. . . Edward came back and sat down on a seat which lay in the grass at the bottom of the Outcasts' hill. It was the remains of one of those bought for the cowpad. It had fallen on its back and the thick grass grew all round. All round Edward now was nothing but grass with thick bushes and trees in front along the cart track. He was out of sight. He heard a cow lowing. His heart was thumping and the caustic calm with which he had first read Margot's letter had passed away. His decision plunged from one extreme to the other: "He can't have her!" and "If she wants to go, let her!" He began all sorts of letters in his head, lofty, gay, poignant, rallying, and bitter. "And to think that a month hence it will be all over, I won't be in this torment: it will be settled one way or another. I must keep that in mind and it will help me to do the wise thing." He felt that a door was about to close on him; he didn't want to marry now: it was too late: he was used to his rambling freedom: he was afraid to be free and to pick on the first girl who came his way merely out of loneliness: he would be sure to pick the wrong girl again. "How many fellows came back from the war to a thing like this? Plenty I suppose." He lay looking at the midday sky and tried to think out his future. He fell asleep. When he awoke, it already seemed easier for him. He would forget about it for a day or two till things arranged themselves in their own way and the right things came cleancut to him. . . .

III

. . . In the kitchen Oneida, who was making coffee, saw the storm on the mountains and the dashing about of the near boughs; and worried about Big Jenny; yet exulted. She was unusually moved. It was true that she spent too much time with the dogs, so that nothing ever got finished and yet everything was finished, everything was in order. The wedding had come off to perfection and the day was not yet evening. She was not unhappy, as other women, such as Irene and Ollie, and she had no ambitions, she was not dissatisfied. Why? It was merely candor to say that it was because of her dear doggies. She was still a lonely child, hordes of friends had evaporated, from those that remained, like Victor-Alexander, this love had gone, the dogs had been her only friends. She did not care for furniture or clothes as such, only for affections: and what alone was faithful? But she hardly thought these things: she only thought them out in dogs as mothers think them out in children. She had her family, the farm, her town house, Victor-Alexander, Lou, Big Jenny, Edward of course, Thaïs and all such people; and the sweet close honeying ones who were her intimate life, her perpetual joys—her dogs. But she thought these things with her flesh because she was excited and upset with the tingling of her dispute with her old friend-enemy Victor-Alexander. He had said plainly today that she had wasted her life, since the day her own wedding had taken place at the well. She loved storms: her brain lived in them. Now she was obsessed with ideas of her life, the eating, drinking, wassailing, the barking, feeling and lingering love in thousands of images that tumbled through her brain—dogs leaping on and off her, racing down the garden, jumping at people who were not her, giving them cruelty while they gave her love, even the Abbot, going out of his senses when bells rang and cars came, but leaping round her. She was so united to them that when they tumbled down the stairway and surrounded some timorous visitor, it was herself tumbling down, greeting the visitor with a malicious gaiety, shaking hands; and when they jumped, pretended to bite and tear, it was their way of doing what she felt, a sort of hot, exasperated, unsatisfiable greeting.

"No one ever loved dogs as I do," she said to herself, "that's it and that's what they don't understand. And with such a great love . . ."

But a certain lost feeling came to her. It was a fact that the dogs did not understand her love, for a human being has so much more passion and devotion than they. Here she broke off and thought, "Lou is right; I must work."

The dogs would be frightened by this storm. But no doubt everyone was seeing to them. "I don't see how anyone can say that I have a bad nature. I don't like wild animals. A woodchuck clawed up my poor Picky—" tears came. "Victor-Alexander is against the dogs because they jump on his flowers—I know it's a substitute for children and, as I told him, his flowers are a substitute for every human responsibility. And at this he takes umbrage." She smiled and repeated maliciously exactly like Victor-Alexander, "I am obliged to take umbrage."

Edward sauntered into the kitchen. As he approached, thinking how she had quarreled with their old friend, a curious idea came that she had never loved any man but Lou and could not: that she lived sheltered from crude and bestial life, from passions, in short that she was very much like Victor-Alexander and that she owed this, after all, to Lou, himself, the family, Edward and most of all the dogs. When he came close to her, with a gentle expression, but without smiling, she turned to him, with a cup in her hand (she was trying to match cups and saucers, but none fitted).

"Don't you agree that persons who hate dogs are afraid, dogs are so clever, they know at once if there's something wrong under the surface."

Edward said, "Well, we all have something savage in our nature."

"Just what I think! Anyone is capable of anything: but especially when you know them. Dogs sense things we don't."

Edward laughed. "You are the only person I know that really has a cult of dogs but dogs don't understand adoration. They're always just greedy and blood-shedding."

"How true that is, Edward, how true that is! And you see we have idolized Victor-Alexander, made a lap-dog out of him."

Edward looked far away.

"It's midsummer but the leaves have changed already; whole patches are coppered. Lou just brought in some fall leaves from the road; at the bottom of the tall beech, they're red and yellow. You should hear what Lou is telling them about the party down at Dan's."

She said, "Edward, if I went away and left the dogs to Lou, he wouldn't even feed them." He laughed. She added, after a while, "I can live without them, never fear. But, Edward, without them at all in the world, the world would seem empty. You have to have something to take care of and love; and to have something love you unquestioningly."

"All people don't need that."

"I think it shows selfishness not to want love unquestioningly—like our star-gazer friend, like our star-gazer friend. Ho-ho!"

"Don't talk to me about love, Oneida. I can't bear the subject." . . .

IV

. . .Oneida and Edward sat long on the stone wall in the sunken garden. The stars were out over the house, the mountains and the trees and the grass were full of fireflies. The sky lightened. It was coming on to moonrise. At last, they went to bed, and were soon lying on their sleeping balconies in the western corner, separated only by a rattan blind.

The moon rose. "There is nothing to stop it," thought Edward involuntarily, in the New York style. The dogs began to bark. All over the valleys, a hundred degenerated and misshapen wolves, some with bulging eyes and snuffly flat noses, some with flap ears and some clipped, patched, blotched, streaked and flecked, some shaggy brown and some rusty black, some yellow-white, these twisted, dwarfed wolves' children like old dwarfs in courts, brought to light under irons and brought up in casks, so that no feature of theirs would resemble the human and yet they would be human, brought up to be vicious, foolish, coarse, snarling and flattering, richly fed and well combed, for the pleasure of kings, but at all times dressed in their master's insolence, and insolence their sole profession, a hundred court fools, hangmen and watchmen and kill-ers; so these hundred dogs, whether chained like poor Charlie or free like Madame X, furiously, unhappily in the dark gardens, stirred by an ancient passion, fear and awe beyond their feeble souls, barked at the moon, at the furtive shadows come alive, at the strangeness of a world born again at night, in which their poor minds, seduced and debauched, were stirred and so rankled. The wolf came back. Thus they barked, Edward and Oneida listening with beating hearts, to that great arrival in the world, the moon, the cold sun of night; and presently with their rattling and yelping, their leaping and racing, they got the moon in all their bewildered eyes while birds woke and fireflies swarmed and in waters things rose to the surface. The dogs let out a roar, and howled in unison and singly in the hills. Their masters heard them, were pleased, and slept. . . .

SCRATCH PARK

V

Edward began to arrange things in his room which had not been touched since his father's and mother's time; for in a day or two they had to be either boxed and carted down to the basement or to Oneida's, or be taken upstairs. He had little room upstairs. Among them he found a life-size mask in plaster, painted green-bronze. It was a mask of his friend, Philip Christy, Dr. Innings's optician who had a fashionable store on Madison Avenue near 57th Street and who lived with his old sister in a poor rooming house near 125th Street. Philip Christy made glasses for various Massines and charged them various prices according to their bank balances. He admired people in the measure that they were failures in life and had lost all ambitions. Those who succeeded or still struggled for position in the big town he regarded as comical sorts, unreasonable, mere jots of souls, something like animals or children. His grandly indifferent soul was gifted with the kind of penetration which is called cynical, satirical; in fact he was unscrupulously sharp and instant in his judgments. He saw what men and women did for a small, dreary, mediocre position in life and he mocked their miserable crimes, their petty venality, their inconspicuous success, the dreadful failure of the heart, which they tried to compensate by lechery (he was indifferent to lechery though a lecher): and out of indifference and a passionate attachment to all the wonderful early ways of the century, the Tammany Hall days, the dirty days when anyone could find his way out of anything, and the anarchist days, when anyone could hope his way out of anything, he liked large misdemeanor, generous crime. He showed this divine humor only to the nonchalant like Edward, or socialist theorists like Walt or (his beloved) the disabused, kind fixers like Al Burrows, or disgraced people and poor, the Third Avenue element, or unfortunate criminals.

Christy had no patience at all with the climbing and made-over suburban women spending black-market money and full of clumsy coquetry; to these he was rude and he overcharged them. Philip Christy, with a wealthy client, was a formidable creature; no one would have dared familiarity with him. The next moment, the client gone, he would go to the back room which was separated from the studio only by a little passage and a handsome heavy silk curtain, and he would call out some friend of his, Walt, Edward, who was keeping him company, or, more often than that, some deadbeat actor out of a job, defrocked priest, itinerant worker, wretch who had drunk himself out of a job, gangster in hiding—the naturally guilty scapegoats of the population, the hungry and the rats.

Some such humble friend would sit with Philip on the leather divan, a piece of furniture so well and deeply upholstered that it felt like satin. They would lounge against the fashionable cushions, and spread their broken shoes on the beautiful dun carpet. His own shoes were run down. When the shop downstairs warned him that a client was coming, he dismissed his friend, placed himself behind the desk and assumed the air of a society consultant. The glasses were always ready in time and, if they were still in the workshop behind, he had only to press a button, and his assistant would bring them to him. He rarely left his desk and if his courteous act of the moment asked for it, then he maneuvered skillfully so that his shoes never came into view.

He was not too poor to buy shoes: he did not care about them. Besides, he needed his money for other things; his friends, his pleasure and a little for the upkeep of the store and to take food home to be cooked by his sister. His pleasure was only one and it was simple. He drank enormous quantities of one brand of bonded rye whiskey and mostly lived upon it. He was fifty-seven and so robust had he been originally that in spite of his vice only in the last few years had he given up polishing the lenses himself. Even now he would go into the workshop and show some assistant how to polish: he had at one time an incredible precision.

He was short, with a singularly deep and broad chest, strong limbs, large face and large hands of beautiful cut and mobility. Edward's plaster mask, although carefully done, was by no great artist and, in any case, could not show the luminousness, proportion and expression of the face. Under a steep and broad forehead, were two large blue eyes, the flesh about them cut like gems. He had a large, fleshy, sensual nose, a long, well-opened but finely cut mouth which disappeared into light folds at the corners. His striking beauty was not only in the refinement of sensuality expressed in the lines but in the expression. His flesh could shine from within as a lantern; he was often masked by an expression of noble contempt, rage or indifference.

His remarks were not all humane. He was moved by no usual considerations. He did not say the polite thing and coaxing old age, pretty youth, simpering childhood, the benevolent, the public altruist did not move him: he would say, "This is a dishonest back-biting old woman;

he's flabby, he'll sell out for professor's pay; he's just a two-by-four fraud, a chameleon; how did you get ten thousand a year, George, if you're a socialist? They know you're not."

At the same time, he started, snarled, and would battle in his confident way with anyone who described an unfortunate as "poor, vulgar, mean, a self-made man, an auto-didact" in short, for any expression which indicated to him pertness in the speaker. He was large about vice and fraud. Strength, skill and low vice are levelers. Life-long soaks and drifters and ne'er-do-wells are likely to have a great humanity, wisdom; they are sages of a sort, on condition that they never reform. The reformed drunkard and wastrel is usually undependable and will corrupt for two cents.

In Edward's boredom, loneliness, aimlessness, when his family and old habits were repugnant to him, the mysterious pleasures of Philip's life, these pleasures, affections and lives which cost nothing, were worth nothing, and took place in an even stranger setting than that at Whitehouse, appealed to him. Here he was acceptable, as acceptable as in his family, but an unknown. He was not "that man Edward we have heard about all our lives." In that circle they spoke about no one. He did not know from what came his horror of his present condition. Oneida took it lightly. She had been startled to know that he had actually offered marriage to Margot and said she was indignant that Margot had turned him down. He was surprised to see that he did not care to take walks. He had lost his dog and he had no interest in the people he used to meet with their dogs. He no longer recognized them and they, since he was without his dog, and they had never looked into his face, did not recognize him. Once he had to explain, "I am the man who used to have the Scotty." He had all the appearance of the homeless bachelor who is looked at with patronizing good-will or concealed irritation by families.

He put the plaster mask of Christy on the table in the mess of things and sat down to look at it; though it was not it that he was looking at. He remembered how once his father and mother had rebuked him for being without ambition. To escape reproach, he had at that moment gone for a week to the rooming house kept by the Christys relatives of Mrs. Annichini in Harlem. They had not been surprised at his arrival; they gave him a room; and they had not been surprised when he left. It all seemed to them natural; and to Edward himself. And he had the joy of thinking that for once he did not know what his family was saying about him, nor did they know anything about him.

"I will do it," said Edward. . . .

•   •   •

In the morning he threw some things into a grip, took the L at 18th Street and got out at 125th Street, about twenty minutes later. The rooming house, which Christy called the "Flop," was a few minutes' walk from the station. It was about ten in the morning. Housewives were sweeping doorsteps, buying food in fish or meat stores, the sidewalks were dirty, busy. He felt very happy as he turned into the street which ended almost at the Triborough bridge. Garbage was thrown about on the sidewalks, coal was going down the chutes and children were hopping in the gutters. He felt a long way from his own home. It was a long time since he had been there and he hardly recognized the "Flop" at first. But his feet had a good memory: they led him to it. He saw that there were clean curtains in the first and second floors and that they had washed the windows of a second-floor room, his, he supposed. Christy's whippet, Lady, curled like a pool of molasses on a worn bit of coconut matting, at the door, getting the thin sun. She looked sick. Some bedroom mats lay across the entry with a carpet-beater beside them, and a mop stood against the banisters. He heard Nell Christy talking on the phone: so he put down his bag by the mop and went across the street to a small grocery store where he had bought things on other occasions when he had visited the Christys.

"Hello, Mrs. Narks."

The fresh-faced middle-aged woman looked at him curiously. He grinned. "I remember you from seven years ago. I'm going to stay with the Christys across the street."

"Plenty of people from downtown stay with her. They're old Harlem-ites."

"She used to live over near Mount Morris Park."

"It's all colored there now," said the woman.

"Sure," he said in his grudging, meditative tone. He went out slowly, lifting his finger to his hat. He deposited his goods in the entry and went to the A & P to get a duck. He did not like the A & P grocer to see that he had been elsewhere; he fancied he would be hurt. The clerks in the A & P were new: he was disappointed. He liked to astonish people pleasurably by remembering their names. At any rate, he listened and learned the names of the new clerks. After careful inspection, he bought the best of three ducks and went back to the Christys'. It was a short slum street ending in a patch of grass with a bench, which Christy called "Scratch Park." Homeless unemployed men sat there in the daytime, slept there at night until the nights began to freeze. A lame boy, in braces, laughed and shouted with a crowd of children who treated him without consideration. He was a bright lad with red cheeks and brown curls, the son of the man who sold coals in the cellar. When Edward crossed the street, two small boys, with a homemade truck, were standing in front of Nell Christy's door, knocking and shouting feebly, "Miss Christy!" In the truck were splinters of wood. Edward went in, saying he would call her.

"What's it for?"

"Miss Christy always buys our wood, mister."

"O.K. I'll tell her."

He went in along the passage and Miss Christy came out, with a broom, a duster tied round her neck and her old apron around her waist.

"Hello, Edward: I thought you'd come later: I thought you got up at noon."

"Shame, shame! What a greeting! You have callers."

She went out to the little boys and came back with her apron full of wood. The little boys went away seriously, talking, pulling their truck by a string. She said, "They bring me wood whenever they pick it up on the lot round here and I give them ten cents. They help their mother."

So saying, she led the way into the kitchen. This was a big room stretching the width of the house and taking up one half the depth. It looked out on a small back yard partly paved and partly earth in which were some rags of plants. Several chickens appeared behind wire netting at the back. The large-paned windows looked out there. There were four doors, one to the yard, one to the coal cellar, one to the corridor, and one, blocked up, led into the front room. A couch stood across this one, but the panes of glass of the door, masked by a curtain, looked into the front room. In a white-washed alcove stood a wood and coal stove, no longer used, and a large gas stove stood beside it. An old horsehair couch stood under the back windows. In the middle of the room was a battered wooden table, covered with an oil cloth, and flanked by several wooden chairs. There was a radio and a few old books. Edward put his provisions on the table.

"Oh, Edward, I bought a duck for lunch. I got it at the A & P. There were only four and this was the best. I'll wash my hands and put it on." He showed his duck and they joked about the two ducks. Nell said, "Sit on the couch while I get the duck ready. I sleep there usually. I like to sleep in the kitchen, I have a room upstairs but usually someone comes along to sleep in my room."

"Will I finish the stairs for you?"

"No—a girl comes tomorrow. You know, Flossie?"

"Is Flossie still around?"

She put the food away in the icebox, prepared the duck. He sat idly on the older couch under the inside window, not her bed. She put on the radio. The plastered walls of the kitchen were dingy. There were half curtains on both sets of windows. It was an icy day. He could see the street children down the passage, running round in ski-suits. When she had put the duck in the oven and told him he need not watch it, she went out, shutting the passage door. It was very quiet, much quieter than Edward's own house, which, though supported by stupendous oak beams, trembled with every truck and roared with the passage of the elevated. Nell was cleaning in the corridor. It was reasonably warm in the kitchen and there was nothing to distract the eye. Edward sighed, took off his coat, and rolled up his sleeves. He leaned back on the couch and listened to the radio. Presently, Nell came in, washed her hands and took out the vegetables. She was a bright-faced woman about sixty, with short white hair. She went on talking rather nervously about friends, lodgers, and made him feel as if he had been there already six months.

"Is that all there is to ducks?"

"Yes. What else do you want me to do?" she said anxiously.

He laughed, "I don't know. Will it be all right?"

"Yes. It's not a good duck, but they generally turn out all right."

"It's nice here. It's a real home."

"It's very ordinary here."

"I'm happy here anyway."

"There was a woman we knew a long time ago, a French woman. She came here once or twice when she was tired of being at home with her husband and mother-in-law. When she felt they were going to quarrel, she came away for a few days."

"Why did she go home again?"

Nell laughed, but went on, "There was an English woman used to come and stay here too. I understand why you come. She said she wanted to feel she was with people. She was an artist. She stayed three months once. I have her photograph somewhere."

Nell got out an old cardboard box and sat down on the couch but in the dumpy alert way of a woman who may have to answer the door at any moment. She held out the photographs in her swollen hands, sorting them out: she was now neither tense nor nervous. She showed Edward several photographs, some of which were faded and yellow. She

said, "That's the English woman—no, that's a model my brother
Norman used to have; she stayed with us, too." She showed a picture
of her brother with his wife and child and said, "I love that little girl."
Then she found another photograph and showed it to Edward, but she
said, "I don't know if that's a picture of Betty, the English woman, the
model, or myself. It is so faded."

It showed a handsome woman of thirty, with a broad forehead,
strong, well-modeled face, and body, dressed in a blouse and long skirt.

"It looks like you."

She considered it, then found another photograph.

"No, that's Elsie, the model; she stayed with us for months; I loved
that girl."

This was a woman in her late twenties, with a fine figure and strange
eyes, like split unshelled almonds.

"This one's blonde."

"Yes, that's Elsie. I was dark."

She gave him the old cardboard box, and said, "I understand what
you want; I understand it. Many people have come to us." She got up,
smoothing down her faded housedress.

"I must give Lady her lunch."

"She smells like distemper, Nell."

"I know, but Philip says she has a touch of the grippe. I don't think
she's well. He gave her a dose of whiskey. He says it cures anything.
It was all he had in the house last night. He didn't keep any for himself.
It shows how kind Philip is."

"Distemper with grippe is serious. Put her to bed."

"Would you send for the vet?"

"Yes."

"I'll ring him up. But I'll try to feed her first. She just turns her head
away."

He went with her to put the dog to bed in the warm cellar, near the
boiler; and meanwhile the roasting duck could be smelled all over the
house. She took Edward to see his room. It was a large, very high room,
on the second floor and looking on the street. There was a cot-bed
pushed against the wall, tall windows, and a big wooden partition with
a door in it. In the smaller room behind the partition was a cot and
a wash-basin.

"You can wash in there. If any of Philip's friends comes, we put him
in there. It's not a real room."

She was a small woman. She looked up at him with kind gravity.

"Since you said I must charge you, I am charging you a dollar a day while there's no one in the backroom. Can you pay that?"

At that end of the corridor was a tiny room, with one window, into which the cot-bed could scarcely fit. It was painted white, very clean. This was her brother's room. At the other end of the corridor was a larger, stuffy room with heavy furniture, tapestry curtains and a carpet. This was used several times a week, by Philip's lifelong friend, "Nan-Mann," now a woman of forty-five. Nell slept in various rooms in the house as they were unoccupied; at other times, in the kitchen.

They had their lunch together when the duck was cooked. Edward sat about while Nell cleaned up the kitchen and they then had coffee and listened to the radio. Nell had been up at six or five-thirty, was tired now. She sat in a corner of the cot, against a pillow, and they talked idly. Edward liked her and she had a generous nature, not simple, but dispassionate and fatigued. The brother and sister had been anarchists in their youth and had grown up in that moment when New York anarchists, as also the followers of Henry George, were founding their communities round New York. The hope and belief in American destiny felt by all people and especially immigrants and their children, in the beginning of the century, and just before it, had resulted, among other things, in the establishment of these idealists' communities where, it was hoped, purity of principle, absolute equality, freedom and free land, would abolish, reduce or sterilize human weakness and state iniquity. The ease with which Nell spoke of the most intimate things and of faraway things, her confidence in Edward, was part of the attitude of Philip towards the strange people in his back room, in his Madison Avenue shop.

Afterwards, he went round the house with her while she finished up. He did not help her but idled in each room while she amused him with accounts of the tenants in the single rooms. In the room above Edward was an engineer of German extraction who was now trying to get permission to visit a surviving relative in Germany. Otherwise, he had no friends but his brother, a mining engineer, who sometimes came in from Pennsylvania. No one ever visited his room. A few technical books, a bottle of ink and a scarf were alone visible of the engineer's belongings in this chill poor room.

"Lives of obscure men," said Edward, looking thoughtfully at the scarf, and the black-painted old dressing table on which a mirror stood.

"Yes, and would you like to see the other rooms, Edward?"

This room had once communicated with the back room. The large double doors were fastened and a bed stood against them. In the back room lived a middle-aged Jewish clerk who had parted from his wife over a religious question.

"He doesn't like to be disturbed. He reads the *New York Times* steadily and finishes it at night. He goes to sleep early. Of course, he must keep them, so he has not much money. He never goes out. He seems fond of his wife and boy and he's quite gentle. She comes every Friday, says he must go to religious services and he just says, Oh, no, no. Then he laughs, he asks after the boy, and sometimes he takes them to dinner. And then she asks him to think of the child's morals and go to Temple, but he laughs and says, Oh, no, no, I will not. It is surprising to hear such a mild man so firm."

The room was high, dark, and furnished with heavy curtains, a gold-framed landscape, an upholstered armchair. It had a Victorian look. At the head of the third flight of stairs was a small room over Philip's which was used by an old woman who came for a few weeks every few months "when she got tired of her family" and who paid for this very cheap room out of a pension. She had sons, daughters-in-law, and seven grandchildren. Said she, "Instead of quarreling like other mothers-in-law and grandmas, I come away when I am sick of them and the children get too much for me."

She took walks, read magazines, and sat in the kitchen with Nell; but Nell found her tiresome as she had got all her ideas out of magazines. But Nell called her "a strong old shoe."

There was a tin of cocoa, a rosary, a lavender silk hair net and a satchel with the old woman's change of clothes. The top floor front was occupied by a married couple with a child and at the back lived another couple, two Italians, father and son. At present, they were in trouble at work, having gone on a beer party and overslept for half a day. At the side was a small room occupied by Eugene, whom she also called "the Straw Boss." Eugene worked in the navy yard, and, in consideration of a reduction in rent, did the furnace for her.

About five, they came downstairs, for Nell had to do the shopping for dinner. She had Nan-Mann and Philip, as well as themselves. He went out with her. She showed him where she got the meat for the dog: it was the only butcher in the entire district, said she, who sold good chopped meat and not block scrapings. The people of the district naturally bought anywhere for themselves but the dog lovers came to this butcher. Edward suggested going to a pharmacy and getting some medicine for the dog. He believed she had a cold; she panted deplorably.

When they came back, the young wife who lived upstairs was just coming in with her baby. She was a thin girl, only nineteen, with an eighteen-months-old baby boy. With her was her friend with whom she passed most of the day, a twenty-year-old mother, with a queer black satin hat, a pale face and long black hair. They swayed the baby carriages and continued their daylong confidences. When they got into the kitchen, Nell told Edward about the wife as she got the vegetables ready. Her husband was twenty-two. He had been rejected for the army and could have got all sorts of jobs. But he knew nothing, could read and write very poorly and preferred doing odd jobs. He, at present, had a night watchman's job near Central Park. The night before there had been an attack on a night watchman in the district and today he had given up his job. He had stayed at home, gone and sat in "Scratch Park," taken a walk, to see what was over the bridge, drunk some beer, and now declared that he would wait a few weeks to find something that "really suited him." The young wife had another baby coming. At the end, Nell said that they had not paid their rent for a few weeks. They were Catholics and they were getting relief from their own church and from the Salvation Army. The young mother simply explained, "It is for the babies. What does it matter who they give it to? We have a right to milk for our babies." She saw no harm in having babies when so young and in her misery. "You're still young when they're grown up and they are soon able to earn and help you; we're all like a gang of kids together in the house."

Nell could not see where they would get the rent. At the same time, she would not put a pregnant girl on the street; and she must wait till they found another place. The young mother knew nothing about food, preserved the childish superstitions of slum children; her views about children were those held by her priest.

About six-thirty, Nan-Mann got home from work. She was chief accountant in a new and successful cheap bazaar in the Bronx. She was a short sturdy swart creature, in a black satin dress, a Robin Hood hat, a red sweater and an old sealskin coat. She had wiry hair and red cheeks.

She remembered Edward. She had the tough slangy local manner, the local obscenities, the curious American relative pronouns: *what-the-hell, why-the-hell, where-the-hell, who-the-hell, how-the-hell* were the only ones she used. She had a rich strong voice.

"Well, look who's here! What the hell are you doing here? I know you're Edward, but what the hell's your other name? How is the world treating you? Old Sanderson kept me late. I told the son of a bitch I had to get the hell out of there. It's the Christmas rush. What the hell do I care? I told him not to start slicing off my bonus. He said, Have a heart, I'm here till seven-thirty; I'll take you to dinner. The hell with it. I told him I was goin' fishin' tomorrow. I beat it. What the hell . . ."

She worked hard, was a competent, reliable worker for weeks or months at a time; then would stop work, would play poker, pinochle, bridge, go fishing, spend the days in bars, in male company. She was a boon companion for men. She had affairs with them, slept with them as casually as the brutal expeditive male. She was sentimental as he is. Her name was Nan Pockett. Philip called her "Mann-law Nan," Nan-Mann, therefore. She went upstairs to take off her coat and Nell set the table. She said in a quaint, affectionate way, "But in the morning, I always find her in Philip's room."

Philip was late. The two women, with Edward, sat down to eat some chops. Though they all thought Philip must be drinking, only Edward was anxious. Nell said tranquilly, "He despises chops! I suppose he knew." Nell washed the dishes and they sat round the oilcloth-covered table under the single electric light. They turned to a political discussion on the radio and then played cards, idly, timelessly.

The young man in the front room had come in long ago and had cooked for himself, on his "one lung burner." He was now practicing the flute, doing physical exercises and writing on a typewriter. He had not drawn the curtain on his side of the window and they could see him walking about, writing, bending, through their thin curtains. From time to time, Nan-Mann called out something to him and he replied, or not, as he pleased. Once he came to the window, pushed it open, and asked Nell in a begging style if she had any coffee going. He came in for some and retired to his room. He left the window open and carried on a conversation with them all. He told them that his girl was trying to help him reform and he had just typed out the list of twenty-five recommendations which she had given him in a penciled list at lunch hour. He worked in the Natural History Museum, making sets in which the stuffed animals appeared in their natural habitats and settings. There were a number of them at it. All his friends were from the Museum and his girl friend, Edith, worked upstairs in the library; she was a folklore expert. He showed them the list and they saw him pin it up on the door of his clothes closet. The recommendations were of a simple sort such as "Get up early," "Study some French for half an hour every evening," "Keep my clothes in good order," "Don't leave things lying about," "Don't grouse," "Save money each payday."

Nell said, "There are too many. You won't be able to do it all. Why don't you stick to three or four?"

He thought it a good idea but preferred to reform entirely and at once.

"I know it will be a slow job," he said, through the window. The heat of the kitchen entered his room which was large, faced the freezing street and was poorly heated. Presently, the front door was opened violently, held open, and something large bumped down the two steps which led into the passage. "It's Phil," said Nell, getting up slowly. Something large, a tire perhaps, rolled down the corridor, ran into the door, circled, fell. The old floor shook. Nan-Mann opened the door and at once there rolled past her a large circular object brown in color. It wobbled, fell. It was an immense round loaf of black bread.

"Oh, Philip, you're drunk," said Nell. He stood in the doorway, looking gigantic in spite of his lack of height, his large pale face sparkling, his eyes bloodshot. His fair and white hair fell over his forehead and his hat was on one side. He waved his hand but was unable to speak. He looked at the three of them with a flashing satirical grin. His face changed, but with his mouth still twisted, slightly open, he fell face forward on the floor, with his arms flung out. Nan-Mann went over and, putting her shoulder under his shoulder, started to heave him along. He was heavy. With difficulty, they got him to the couch where he lay.

"Will you put on some coffee?" said Edward.

"Coffee! He won't touch coffee for days now," said Nell.

The three of them sat round the table. Nell laughed sadly, "Poor Phil! We teased him. I was telling him the other day that he was so hungry as a growing boy that he stole the bread from all of us. When it came fresh to the kitchen he'd smell it no matter where he was and he'd come in and start to peel off the crust. He went on peeling until there was nothing left. Phil resented it, you see. The idea that he took the bread out of our mouths."

The loaf of bread lay on the floor. Nell looked at it for a while and then got up and picked it up in both arms, putting it on the table where Phil could see it when he got up.

"He'll lie there till morning; and then he'll want whiskey. And he gave it all to Lady. I never keep any. Perhaps the Straw Boss has some."

Later on, the Straw Boss came in to say the furnace was fixed for the night and to say good night. He himself brought down half a bottle of whiskey when he saw Philip asleep; but Nell rejected it. She took one glass for Philip in the morning and a spoonful for Lady. Edward declared that it was not good for the dog, but Nell shrugged amiably.

"You know he wants to give her whatever is most precious to him."

After sitting round four hours, they all went to bed. The fire was out, but they covered Philip with a blanket. Nell went up and slept in his room.

A new life began for Edward. He got up late, after the others had all gone to work. He went to bed at eleven or twelve, which was early for him. They had shut off the other room, partitioned from his, because "Billy the Priest" had come to sleep there. In the daytime, Billy went downtown with Philip and lived in the room behind the store. He was a defrocked priest against whom, declared Philip, "the Powerhouse" (the hierarchy and its officialdom) had committed every injustice. He could not get work because a priest does not know how to do anything.

Edward would hear the ex-priest breathing and moving behind the partition. A street lamp stood outside the window and lighted his room all night. Edward stayed for long intervals alone, at different times, and in the bare cold high room, night after night, he thought about himself. Sometimes in weariness he would think of the way Margot harassed him, nagging, seeming to hate; he thought of her need to spoil everything. It seemed to him that her black moods came out of nothing, especially when things were sailing along smoothly. She would become furious at their peace, say she did not intend to live like a Lotus-eater. These scenes made him unhappy so that he soon went back to thinking of the love they had had. Each night, without any other desire, he passed calmly into sleep in the midst of some vision or other of his former happiness with Margot. He was astonished at his lack of desire. This intense delicious life in visions gave him deep quiet sleep and his body was asleep all day. Nan-Mann, in her rough, ready and generous way, would have thought nothing of having him in her bed long ago, as he knew. He did not want to wake out of the repose in which he was sunk. His downtown life seemed months away and as if in another city.

Once or twice, he walked downtown with Nell. Every few weeks, her only pleasure would take hold of her, and she would go downtown, on foot, to look at various "opportunity shops," "white elephant stores." She would spend hours picking over the things in these repulsive bazaars, in which the clothes of the dead, old-fashioned styles, stuff from boxrooms is brought together; she would spend a few dollars and come home pleased with a blouse, a mirror for the bedroom, a picture. At home, she had a chest full of beautiful hand-embroidered linen and elegant collars, fichus, jabots, in lace, such as are not worn any more. She had done hand embroidery as a girl.

One day, they went on foot as far as 56th Street, and at the end of the trip back, they were both very tired. Edward invited Nell into a bar in 125th Street. They sat up at the bar, she tangled her small feet in their old cloth shoes round the legs of the stool, and she became confiding, girlish. Perhaps she was a little embarrassed. She began to tell him about her life, how Philip had gone to work at fourteen, how he had brought home money on the very first day and being suspicious she had followed him and found that he took money out of the cups of all the blind beggars on the streets. In those days, there were more than now. It had turned out that they were organized and that a collector came round twice a day to pick up their takings. Phil had preceded the collector, that was all. The same day he had his first drink of whiskey and it was the brand of whiskey he still drank.

Their father had come to America from Eastern Europe, but not because of oppression or persecution, or even out of the love of liberty. The grandfather had had a big business, town house, seven sons; and in the houses several young maid-servants, all got in with the object of keeping the boys at home. As each maid-servant became pregnant, she was given a passage to the United States, so that there would be no claims upon the family. No resentment was felt against the girls: on the contrary. One of the sons had fallen in love with such a servant and had followed her—or had eventually been won over by the idea of this country. Now, all the members of the family were in the country. She told Edward about her youth and many times spoke about Philip, whom she loved. She told him about all the people she had known as a girl, people who had long ago become famous, Emma Goldman and Alexander Berkman, many others. She did not see that type now. She knew people in other camps: artists, actors. They had all been youths together. Then, without transition, she said to him, lifting her head so that he looked straight into her large eyes, beautiful as Philip's:

"What is the use of it, Edward? What did I gain by having lived all that? I am an old woman. I never had a child. I never had time to have anyone. You can hardly say I lived, can you?". . .

VI

. . .Nan-Mann stayed away. Philip was absent. Edward lived in this silent house with the old sister for two days. Philip came home in two days having found money for some of his debts. He came home drunk, at about four in the afternoon, when Nell was preparing hashed meat for hamburgers and creamed onions as the vegetable. He came into the kitchen without hat or coat, his hair astray and his marvelously sculptured face lively, malicious. He tacked and veered. He seized his sister's hands.

"Come along, come with me, Nell the Belle: we'll call on everyone."

He was in that state of extreme excitement when he remembered telephone numbers, addresses, names long forgotten. He enumerated these, told what sort of receptions he would get, laughed at the bourgeois, the "Cozy-Murphys," the strait-laced. He came back to the word, the strait-laced. He insisted, pulled his sister away from the stove, peered into the dish of pearl onions and said, "You eat that and you think you are swallowing your tonsils."

He put his arms round her and waltzed round the kitchen with her.

"Ah, Nell the Belle, Nell the Belle, wait till my friends, the Cozy-Murphys, the strait-laced, see my sister Nell the Belle. They think I'm a souse. They can't say that about Nell the Belle! And then we'll take our dish of creamed onions with us. We'll tell them we eat our tonsils for dinner at the home of Nell the Belle. Nan-Mann and Nell the Belle. I'll tell them you're two gun molls. We're going to see Arnold Brown, that's it. He's got a gun moll; I'll take him my gun molls, Nell the Belle and Nan-Mann. Nell cooks tonsils and Nan gets the boys under the Mann Act."

Eventually, Nell, at first embarrassed, became irritated and shook him off but only with difficulty for he was mischievous and very strong. He found himself insulted by her coldness and to insult her, he seized Edward's arm and cried, with glints of merry fury, "Then you come, Edward. Ned the Fed you come, you're paunchy, you sleep too much, you think about that girl of yours that left you in the creamed onions. Come out with me: I'll take you to see some people you never saw. You need shaking up, Ned the Fed. Let's go and have a drink first, I'm dry. I'm dry. Ha-ha. Aren't you dry?"

Edward let himself be pulled out by Philip. They went to a bar near the L at 125th Street, a red-lighted, red-curtained, red-plush corner bar, and had a few drinks, and Philip, irresistible, dangerous, took him to other bars, all the places where he was known in the district. . . .

After this, Philip, more extraordinarily drunk than before, led Edward through a series of visits the chief purpose of which was to annoy strangers, upset meetings and alienate acquaintances. They burst in upon the meeting of a cell of socialist youth on Lower Third Avenue, not far from Edward's own home. They visited a meeting in a private home of communist free-thinkers (that is, they were free-thinkers in communist theory), in the Village. They blew in on a strange couple, a man and wife who were sitting moodily before an empty grate, eating *tortillas* and drinking beer. This man usually made seventy-five thousand dollars a year in Hollywood, and spent one hundred thousand dollars. At present he was "in the doghouse" for having supported a scene-shifters' strike. "Romantic red rash, you should have got over that when green," slobbered Philip. "There's nothing you can do about it," said the man downheartedly to his wife. "Pipe down, Phil, and have a drink," said his wife. "Suckers!" said Philip, but drank. At another time they called at a city club looking for and finding an old inventor in his late seventies who had supported the Haymarket martyrs many years before with all his money. "I called on you, Mac," stated Philip, "to tell you you're a god-damned sellout, I never saw you stumping the country for Sacco and Vanzetti: what are you, a socialist now? There aren't enough socialists to pass the buck. You always were too canny, too ca' canny!"

The old man frowned. "I'll show you to the door, Philip, since you can't find the way yourself." Philip laughed all over the writing room, dining room, staircase and front hall. "Don't commit yourself, Sandy, eh, don't commit yourself: I think I see a sail, eh?" shouted he yelling with laughter.

"I commit myself when I see the lifeboat," said "Sandy" gravely. Philip, now on the sidewalk, turned round, shook his great white fist at the man and the building. "Lousebitten creamskimmers! Malefactors of little gains! My price is higher than a million berries!" The old Scot turned inside with a calm expression. Philip chuckled. "Hard as nails! He's already got options in heaven and hell."

They visited a Trotskyist and Philip standing in the door shouted, "You're a self-seeker, a stoolie"; and to a writer who jogged along and had no opinions at all, "Grubstakes! Bread-and-butterfly! Potboiler! Sellout!"

"I haven't sold out," said the middle-aged, half-bald, agate-eyed grinning writer.

"Have you got whiskey? Because you've nothing to sell! He's a writer too: no idea, nothing to sell!" he said kindly, pointing to Edward. He grabbed the bottle of whiskey and said, "And no one has my price, no one has my price! Every man has his price but no one has got the price of Me!"

And so on and on. Philip, always drunker and drunker with his libations on the way, a bright demon in the doorway, a loathsome oaf on the couch, even rolling with fanciful leers upon the matting, the bare boards, repeated his jokes of earlier in the evening about Nell the Belle, Nan-Mann "that whore" as he now called her because she had been for days on a party, the creamed tonsils, the gun moll, the price of Man, and so on with memories of his mixed Tammany and anarchist youth, the characters he had hobnobbed with, schoolteachers, editors, judges, congressmen; and other personages now known to all New York, political figures, socialist, communist, Henry George adepts, anarchists of long ago.

They ended in a hall on the East Side, where anarchists, mostly poor Italian barbers, waiters, bootblacks, a few Spaniards and Hungarians, were listening to a play in Italian. Philip crashed to the floor in the corner of the hall. This enabled Edward to see the play, a gaseous *commedia dell' arte* jest with improvisations twenty minutes long. When the lights went up, Philip, who recognized many people there, was so badly considered and rebuked for the scandal of his condition and presence that he grew angry and pulling Edward by the sleeve, said, "Let's get out of this band of Pharisees, white supple-curs, downtrodden Philistines, revolutionists of the absolute, worth two cents, let's get out of here and get some clean air in a barroom." They got to another barroom; and shortly after this Edward was able to get Philip lifted into a taxi and take him home.

The kitchen was warm. Philip threw himself upon the couch and at once went to sleep. Nell's heavy figure as if crumbling, boneless, from fatigue, slumped in a chair at the table. She helped Edward with Philip and then had a cup of coffee with Edward. She told some stories of Philip's youth and Edward could see how she loved him.

He ventured, "You have sacrificed your life to him. He is almost your husband."

"He is not my husband. He is my dear, dear brother." She turned to Edward with a calmer face. "Do you think a life can be sacrificed if you give it to someone? I don't.". . .

VII

. . . Philip, after his one outburst, was staid, bored. He came home every evening about seven and the family played mild games of cards. Philip dealt and played at dazzling speed. The cards whizzed round and out faster than sight and all the time he wore his satisfied clever smile. He cheated consistently as a pastime but he could wipe the floor with them in any case, as he said. The cards flashed out like the spokes of a wheel. He scooped up the points, threw down the cards. Bored with his partners, suddenly a pattern of insulting courtesy, he rose courtly and went down to the basement where his dog Lady wheezed on Philip's own blankets, near the stove. Philip covered himself with his overcoat, up in his icy little room. His penetrating voice, with its sweetest accent reached them.

One evening he came up with the dog in his arms. "Lady's sick; my Lady's sick."

He brought her to the sofa and placed her there on her blanket, keeping one hand near her to warm her. She whimpered and presently tried to move; she licked his hand and stood up arching her thin flank. The smell of distemper was strong. Philip said, "Lady's elegant, isn't she? She's a maiden, a young maiden, she's very young yet. She's delicate yet. How graceful! You're my lady love, Lady, Lady." He put her back in her bed, with his smile. The others were playing cards. He looked at them with a wicked twist of the lips, watching them as if both fools: he followed the cards automatically with sharp glances. He called ironically to them, telling each play.

Nell laughed. "Philip can't bear anyone else to handle cards."

"You don't know how to play."

He lingered by the dog. The dog whimpered and licked his hand. He said, "Lady loves me, you see."

"Why not? I love you," said Nell.

"And it's just the same love. Love is all one; there is no difference," said Philip.

"A goldfish loves me," said Edward.

"Fish." Philip sat, with his eyes resting insolently some feet above them, curiously twisting his lips.

"I read isinglass comes from a fish; I never knew it before," said Nell.

"Now Nell knows that isinglass comes from a fish."

Presently, Philip got up and came to the table to deal the cards. He kept the sharp glance and twisted smile all the time; but as he dealt in legerdemain, a demoniac look of astuteness and pleasure came into his face. He won three games, then threw down the cards and got up without laughing, intensely, coldly, restlessly.

"Do you play much?" asked Edward.

"With Billy the Priest," he said with lazy insolence. He told the story all over again although he knew they knew it.

He sat about by the dog, with a lofty insolent stare. It happened that that evening, Nan-Mann came by to say hello. She had on a new fur coat and a new hat and wore her engagement ring. Philip saluted her with impudent commentaries but plunged at her, seized her by the strong wrist and took up the cards.

"Come on, play, Nan-Mann!"

"I can stand up to you," said Nan.

"Both cardsharps and sharks; it's a question of who can cheat the other oftener," said Nell.

"That's half our game. Look at him, look at that Buddha look!" said Nan. "Now he's at it."

He kept his Buddha look. She tossed the cards down and kept up her tough patter, laughing, crowing, bantering. He answered never a word, though sometimes he smiled faintly. The game went on till long after midnight. The others went up to bed, Nell saying, "See the lights, the gas and the stove are out!" . . .

The street lamp outside shone through the Venetian blind, on the ceiling; and he looked at the shadows for a while, thought again how Margot had offended him by saying, during a trial blackout during the war (the people opposite had been slow in putting out the lights), "See the lights on the ceiling? I don't suppose you ever sit by yourself and study effects, or think. You are just imaginative."

By imaginative, she meant "without imagination." She meant plots of suddenness, crime, adventure.

"I like analysis only and that's something you don't like," she had told him. Edward had never been able to get this grain of sand out of his hide. She despised his brains and soul. Really, they were not suited for each other. A man does not avoid a woman for twelve years for nothing. Habit speaks one way, instinct another.

Edward heard the front door open. It stayed open. He knew Nan-Mann was staying there that night in her old room. Therefore it was Philip going out for something. He liked to get the bulldog editions and take them to bed with him. Perhaps Edward dozed. Some time later, he heard Nell going down, to see if all was tight and safe. It was nearly morning. She closed the house door. She did not go upstairs again, and must have been resting on the kitchen sofa. He felt the morning, when the air and sounds have changed and the lights begin to penetrate the flesh. He slept again uneasily and was awakened by someone knocking at the house door, Nell's steps, exclamations, and Nell's cry, "Nan! Nan! Eugene!"

People went into the kitchen and Edward, putting on his winter coat, went downstairs. It was very cold. The Straw Boss, who had been sleeping near the furnace, because his room was cold, had just come up in his pyjamas. He was a tall rotund red-faced man. Nell was dressed in some nondescript grayish clothes and with her were two men, one a policeman. Lady, the whippet, in a very bad way, lay on her side on the blanket on the couch, gasping, her eyes turned up and her limbs stiffening.

Nell was very pale, as if breathless, trembling all over and when the policeman asked her something, only shook her head and looked at Lady. The Straw Boss said that about four o'clock in the morning, a man had been knocked down and injured by the trolley in 125th Street. The conductor saw it all and it wasn't his fault. The man had crossed the street when he turned, whistled, called and walked back across the road. At the last moment, he ran stooping in front of the trolley car. The stranger was a taxi driver. He had been parked there and half asleep. He saw a whippet just creeping along and only saw the man later. The whippet started to cross the road, then stood still trembling. The man whistled and called and the whippet got in front of the trolley car and dropped on its haunches. The man ran in front of the car and pushed the whippet off the tracks but was himself knocked down. The man had been taken to one of the nearby hospitals and the dog, apparently dying, taken to the sidewalk and left there. But someone had come along who had recognized the whippet as Lady; they supposed the man was Philip. He had no identification marks on him. He was unconscious, was being given oxygen and probably would not survive.

Nell stood up and said she would go in the taxi to the hospital. Edward waked Nan-Mann, who came down in her nightdress, a skirt and her fur coat and hat, ready to go.

The two women were away the whole day, and until late in the night. About two o'clock, they came home. Philip had just died. He had never regained consciousness. Nell said, "If it had not been for his great strength, the doctor said he would have died at once." After a moment she added in a firmer voice, "He had not been drinking. He had not taken any liquor all that evening and it was certain he had not drunk anything. He had gone out for the papers and the dog followed him."

When she asked they told her the molasses-colored whippet had died of pneumonia and was lying in the cellar in a box. She said, "If I could, I would bury Lady with him; he died for her, didn't he? And he said I loved him only as much as Lady; or she loved him as much as I did. It is the same. I would not mind if they buried me with Philip, would I? But they won't allow it. We will bury Lady in the back yard tomorrow."

This they did.

After Philip's funeral, Nell was resigned and did not seem to weep. She told people that the whippet followed him across the trolley tracks under the L and made him turn back and that he threw her free. She told them what the doctor had said, and the nurses too. He never recovered consciousness, but he was fighting in the dark for eighteen hours: he would never have lasted so long but for his great strength; they had rarely seen such a strong man for his age. She went with Nan-Mann, the Straw Boss and Edward to the local movie, a very poor one where they had Bingo every night; and Nan won a set of teacups which she gave to Nell. The Straw Boss took them to a Chinese place afterwards, and coming back, Edward bought frankfurters to eat at home. They talked a little, Nan told them what was going on in her boss's business, how she had gone fishing last summer with Big Boy Al Burrows and spoke of her "daughter and son" still meaning the grown daughter of the man she was to marry and the girl's fiancé. Nell was interested, laughed; but she did not move about very much. After three days Nan left; and the Straw Boss, of course, went to work every day. But one morning, when Edward came down to the kitchen for his breakfast, which he took with Nell about nine-thirty, he found Nell stretched on the couch, with a rug over her.

"There's coffee there, Edward."

"Anything wrong, Nell?"

"I'm going to die," she said composedly.

"For crying out loud!" He was frightened and went to her. "What's wrong?"

"I'm going to lie here until I die. . . . I don't want to live any more."

"Don't talk like that, Nell. Get up and have some breakfast with me. Come on, dear."

"I made up my mind, Edward."

He got down on his knees beside the couch and took her hands which were crossed over the blanket in a restful position. He began pleading. "Come on, Nell. Get up. It's the effect of the terrible shock. You don't feel like that. That's not for you. You're not that kind of person."

"You don't know me. We don't know each other."

"That's true."

"You'll excuse my saying that. It's cruel."

He made his coffee, hoping she would have some; and drank it sitting beside her. He laughed, held her hands, creased, with old stiff skin, as if both were blistered, ruined by strong cleaning fluids, and dirty water, he unfolded them. He kissed them, rubbed her feet, brushed her hair.

"I did this for my mother."

"I never had a son."

Her disinterested frank eyes looked at him continuously, she had no bitterness or melancholy. He said, "You don't think you can die by just lying down on the sofa, do you?"

He kept it up in the same commiserating strain, never smiling or wounding. She said several times, "I'm not going to eat or drink. You must die that way."

He did some shopping for the house; and did his work. When he came downstairs, in the afternoon, she was weeping and turned her back to him. He telephoned Nan. When he saw Nan from his window, he came down and told her about Nell. Nan went out with him to a bar. They had drinks and telephoned several people, Nell's sister, and some very old friends, comrades of Nell's and Philip's youth. The sister however refused to come to the house, saying, "It's Nell's fault that Philip died. She let him drink and he died drunk. I told her so. I told her she'd never see my child again. I won't have a child visit such a house."

Nan wished her the worst of fates and destinations through the telephone and came out raging, "It's that so-and-so's fault that Nell's in this condition." They brought home some things for dinner and ate in front of her. Then they piled the things in the sink and sat at the table playing cards just as before Philip's death. Nell lay quietly on her back but did not speak.

At about eight, two old friends arrived, Mr. Atkins, who had been Philip's best friend, though separated from him later by differences of political opinion; and another old friend, Mrs. Morrisey, a strong squat woman of fifty, with graying hair but fine brown eyes. Mr. Atkins was a printer and Mrs. Morrisey a pharmacist, who was district leader in Borough Park. They had been anarchists in their early youth, had long ago changed politics, but remained quarreling friends with Philip. He usually called them turncoats, rats, political mongrels and so forth; and exalted the golden age in the beginning of the century. Nevertheless they were like a good many ex-anarchists, humane; at any rate they would be able to talk to Nell in her own terms, thought Nan. But after greeting her and hearing what she had to say, the two friends merely sat down and played cards with Nan and Edward as if everything were in order. Edward became angry. His heart thumped away and at last he asked the two visitors if they were not going to reason with Nell. This was at a moment when they were not playing but were sitting, scarcely saying a word. Mrs. Morrisey's eyes were softly and lustfully shining; her thoughts were far away. Mr. Atkins had been having a discussion with Nan about the Third Party question. Edward spoke to the woman pharmacist twice before she heard him. She was dressed all in dingy black with a string of white beads and a new hat. She was fat, her figure crumbling, but she had a certain beauty in her present mood. She roused herself and spoke slowly, detaching her thoughts with some difficulty from the other object.

"Don't you think that Nell's right—to do what she likes? Is there someone in the house who cares for her? Life and death is the same. We do not owe anything to society; it depends, eh? We can do what suits us best; it is the best thing for all. Even if not, what use is it to the individual? Have you a right over Nell? If she wants to die, she has good reasons for it. You have to live with a reason for living, or what's the sense?"

"The living and the dead are just the same," said Nell.

Nan turned her chair round.

"Oh, have a heart, Nell. You're giving us all the heeby-jeebies. Think of us. We lost Philip and now we must lose you? Get up now. Once you get off that couch, you know you won't lie down again. What the hell, baby, according to your own argument, if the living are the same as the dead, then you're the same now as you would be, so get up and live. If it's the same. We love you, we care for you. You'll break our hearts if you die before our eyes. Are we to sit here all that time until you pass away? You'll make us murderers. People would call us murderers. They'd say we should have sent you to a hospital, forcible feeding, that horrible stuff. You can bet we won't, lovely Nell dear, but for

Pete's sake, take up your bed and walk. What do you want to make it so tough on us for?"

"You loved Philip, you said. The same as me, all love is the same. And you don't want to die. But I do. There isn't anything to talk about."

"Ah sweetheart, ah god damn it, Nell, you don't know what you're saying; would Philip have lain down to die for you?"

"He died for Lady. Why not for me?"

There was a pause. Nell said more nervously, even feverishly, "Philip believed, well, when we were youngsters, we knew, all of us, all things and people were equal, dogs, girls, gangsters, bums, republicans, reds —friends and enemies. He only couldn't stand sneaks and climbers. They were a bit lower than the rest. My brother Philip once had a man implicated in that Murder Incorporated gang behind his curtain for three weeks. He fed him himself and played cards with him half the night. He had a leper there, a man with a huge face; it made you sick to look at him. He wasn't afraid of the gangsters and then they called him Doc. I asked him about the leper, because it's contagious, and he was angry at me. Doesn't it give you goose flesh? I asked Phil. They're just the same as you or me, what's the matter with you? Do you give me goose flesh, he said? He looked at me with contempt. He's still looking at me with contempt. No one is better than anyone. Only Philip could feel that."

They had some beer and icebox cookies brought by Mrs. Morrisey, chiefly for herself, it seemed; and they went about eleven o'clock. Edward was left alone with Nell. He sat quietly near her reading a book until she said she wanted to sleep and then he put out the light and went upstairs. He believed she would get up in the night and eat. In the morning he found on the table the dishes used by the Straw Boss. He said "Good morning" to Nell but she did not answer though he knew she was awake. He ate his breakfast and piled the dishes with the Straw Boss's in the sink. Nothing had been done in the kitchen for two or three days. She turned again and asked how his work was going.

"Slower and slower."

"You'll make something of it. You found something to do, while with us," she said. She was flushed now, her hair untidy and her eyes bright. Her lips were cracked, she gasped occasionally and drew heavy breaths. She said, "Bring your work to the kitchen; it helps to pass the time. What day is it, Edward?"

He brought his work and began to type out the notes he had made before. He left the kitchen door open and the house door, so that fresh air from the snowy street would come in and purify the air. The sink was filled with dirty water and there was garbage on the floor. Nell asked him once suddenly whether they had buried Lady. This startled him, since she had been there at the burial in the back yard. Later she said, "Whenever Philip came in, he came into the kitchen to see if everything was out. I seem to hear him often, you know. I hear his footsteps, and his voice when the door opens. I suppose it will go away soon. I am listening for his voice all the time and at times I am sure I hear it."

"Yes, those hallucinations are very strong."

"Yes, you can hardly believe it is a hallucination. It is like some sort of reality. I suppose there are other ones than the one we know. It seems to me so strange that we think we know the reality, the only one there is."

"Yes, it's questionable, isn't it?"

"Supposing what they say is true: that looked at one way, Philip and all the others are still alive. I don't mean the afterlife, I mean the present life, the fourth dimension. I read that there are other dimensions. We only know three, but there are others, about eight. So there can be another reality."

"Yes, yes, there can, there is."

"So it is true that we are alive and dead at the same time: the living and the dead are the same. And Philip and I are both living and dead at the same time."

"Yes, yes, Nell dear."

He had turned to her very attentively. She sighed and said she was very thirsty, that was the chief thing.

"I'm afraid I'm getting funny, I don't want to be funny in my mind. I feel different now. I feel happy in a way. Before to me the dead were dead; now I just feel as if the same earth covered with small plants, as I see it, is stretching far, very far away; and quite near me there is a grave. But all around it and as far as you can see is the same earth we tread."

"That's very beautiful, Nell. That's so touching; that's very true, dear Nell."

He went and sat beside her again taking her hands as before and kissing her forehead. "You see, you are feverish; you are very thirsty. Let me get you some cool water, just a drop. It would make you clearer in your mind."

"No, no; I am going to die."

She turned her back and tried to go to sleep. He went back to his work. When the Straw Boss came in the evening, the young naturalist came in and asked if he could eat with them. It was lonely for him in there. The three young men sat round their meal, cooked by the Straw Boss, and talked of anything, at first quietly, and then louder. They presently got out the cards and played for some time. Then they all went out for a drink. At the bar, they discussed the possibility of Nell's really starving herself to death; but all concluded nothing could be done about it, it would not be right to do anything against her will, and her provocation was real. The Straw Boss and the naturalist, opposing Edward, said she had a right to her life, she had earned it and she could cast it away. Edward was indignant, sulky; he simply said, "I can't say why, but I know this death is wrong."

They argued about life and death, responsibility and society, for a while and returned to the rooming house for their beds. In the morning, all went on as before and once more Edward brought down his work. Nell was now very ill, feverish, murmuring, tossing. Edward was relieved. He felt that now she had left her senses, he would be excused for calling a doctor. However, he telephoned Nan-Mann at her work and begged her to come to the house. If she thought it right, they would get a doctor. Nan-Mann said, "She would never forgive you; and what you are doing is wrong according to her view of life."

"But I shall be held criminally responsible!"

"Oh, if that's what's worrying you, go back home to your neat little roost, my lad."

Edward went back to his work on the kitchen table. At a certain moment, finding her very feverish, he took a glass of sugared water and, holding her head up, put it to her lips. She drank it. He gave her a little more and later a little more. She smiled slightly, slept and woke about five, seeming more sensible. He said, "Nell, you have drunk water, you know. You didn't know, did you? You can't starve any more, can you? Get up, darling. Come get up? You'll feel better soon. Your back must be aching lying there."

She said she was very weak and he must help her. He brought her to an old armchair and sat looking at her with a satisfied air. Then he went to her, took both her hands, looked into her face, knelt beside her and pressed her to him, looking up at her. All his grace moved him. She looked far away, abstracted. He put his arms round her and pressed her to him again, full of love and grace. "Nell the Belle!" He went back to his chair and looked at her, pleased with himself and her. Her eyes were large, her face pale. She said hesitatingly, doubtfully, "Do you think my life was wasted, Edward?"

He came and embraced her as before. "Nell, don't think along those lines: that leads nowhere. We mustn't ask too many questions."

"Have you anything to live for, Ned?" she said, looking his face over carefully, when he went back to his chair.

"No." He laughed.

"Then it doesn't matter, does it?"

"No."

"My sister, the one who's in the Third Party movement, told me I'd wasted my life. She said if I'd got into politics I'd like them. She said, if Phil had got into something he wouldn't have died like that. She said it was my fault."

"If she had been there—!" said Edward ironically.

"Then you don't think there's anything in it?"

"The things people say in families!" He laughed. He took both her hands and pulled her up, "Come on, do a little bit and then I'll give you lunch."

She reflected a moment. At last she said, "All right, boy."

"Oh, how calm and pleasant it is here! I suppose that's a sweet truth: to know there is nothing to live for? To have the sense just to live? But when I'm older? How is it that I feel old already?"

"It's a long way to go, from thirty-three to seventy or eighty," she said anxiously, still looking at him.

"I know: I must get married," said Edward, very seriously.

"I never felt old till you came here; you did that for me. A person should live in reality."

They looked at each other, calmly, in a pondering way before each turned to work.

DARK
PLACES
OF THE
HEART

Dark Places of the Heart was originally published in England as *Cotter's England.* It appeared in this country in 1966. The story is set in England in the period just after World War II. The dominating figure is Nellie Cotter, a reporter for a radical newspaper in London. Brought up in the poverty of Bridgehead, a mining town in the North, she was attracted by political activism while still in school.

Nellie is married to George, a failed Socialist. She has a half-crazed sister, Peggy, who keeps house in Bridgehead for their senile mother, Mary, and their Uncle Simon; and a brother, Tom, a loving man with a great attraction for women.

The story moves between Bridgehead and London, where Nellie has turned her house into a shelter for unsettled women whom she makes her protégées. One of these is Caroline, a naïve social worker who has separated from her husband, Barry, and is having an affair with Alan, a co-worker in her office.

The first excerpt, which begins right after the death of Tom's friend Marion, gives us a view of Cotter's England and the kind of poverty that leaves its indelible mark on so many of Stead's characters. The second and third excerpts show the relationship between Nellie and Tom and her jealous manipulation of his women—a theme that dominates the story. In the next passage Eliza, George's first wife, gives us a picture of Bridgehead and of Nellie in her youth. In the last two, Caroline, drawn to Tom, is destroyed by Nellie.

I

. . .There was a train leaving King's Cross near midnight. He sat in a café till it was time, and had an interesting conversation with a man counting pennies in heaps, perhaps a newsboy. He was able to stretch out in the second-class carriage. Now that he was on his way, the last terrible days at the farm became real to him; and yet seemed weeks away. He was very tired. There were moments when he felt he had been happy there. "But the man's a fool who expects happiness or the happiness to last; I'm grateful for what I had."

One of his first thoughts was that he must look for another woman at once, who would take him and hold him, so that he could turn his back on the past eight years and begin again. But where should he look?

The train rattled along in the night and he thought for a while of the dark trains he had traveled in during the war and after he got the car, the dark roads, a hooded glimmer all that was allowed; but he had never driven into the ditch. How one's senses developed! And then it was to Marion he had traveled, by train and by car.

He slept as well as he could, waking not long before Bridgehead. "Back to Bridgehead gray," the color of his youth. It was a dark morning, the docks, bridges, ships were lighted. Different shifts were going to work and coming away; and he passed a stand where he got a cup of sour gray tea, "stewed water." He got to his old home before seven. The boy hadn't been around; the empty milk bottles were still standing there. Uncle Simon was some time answering the door; and when Tom heard the old voice, "What d'ye want?" he smiled.

"It's Tom."

Uncle Simon let him in, coughing. "Ye can get in now without that dog tearing the seat off your pants."

"Back home!" smiled Tom. He pushed his grip into the front room and took his parcels to the kitchen. His uncle was too polite to notice them at first, though he cast a few glances under his spectacles.

The fire was not going too well. A newspaper was fastened across the front of the stove and grate. The house was cold but it was warm enough there. The sky was black with smoke fog which had not come down. "If we had a decent government, it would do something about this weather," said Uncle Simon. He was heating his old tea from the night before on the stove and was about to pour some for Tom when he said hospitably, "A'll make ye a fresh pot. Did ye come in your car or off the train?"

"I'm off the train; I sold my car."

"Aye." The old man put one of his three kettles on the gas stove and turned the jet very low under it. The kettle had been sold to Simon as a gas-saver. "It'll be ready by the time the milk gets here." He then got out the bread and his own bit of butter which he set before Tom. "Would ye like some bacon? A haven't touched me bit. Put your washin' on the dresser, ye'll get it spotted."

"That's not washing, that's a chicken I brought for you, Uncle Sime, for Peggy to cook," said Tom.

Uncle Simon said nothing. "It's for you and mother, Uncle, you know Peggy wouldn't touch it."

Uncle Simon looked at the kettle, turned the gas up a little and fussed at the stove. "Thank ye, thank ye." His hands trembled. "A had a bad night: A coughed a lot, A thought A'd die. A ran out of me syrups of quills and me drops." The black coaly sky frowned at him.

Tom said, "How's mother?"

"She's sleepin' too much, not eatin' enough, wanderin' about on the stairs and she sees the dead. Your sister stays in bed till eleven most days; but A wake them with a cup of fresh tea and some bread and butter. Mary needs it. A'll light the back-room fire for ye if ye like."

"I'll sit with you, Uncle Sime. I'll go and see Mother when she wakes."

"She's probably awake now and starvin', but that gel never gets oop for her mother."

When the milk came he prepared the tea, while explaining to Tom about the bread-saw, "They don't know how to coot it: ye move the knife backwards and forwards withoot pressure, it does the cootin; ye can get any thickness ye like." The kettle boiled after a long while and Tom took the tray upstairs.

The dog lying inside the door made a fuss. Peggy said, "It's that silly old man scratching on the door to tease him; all right, Uncle Sime man, wait a bit, can't ye?" and she opened the door. "Oh, lord lovaduck, it's Tom."

"Is it Tom?" said the mother quickly.

"It's Tom: Tom's here. When did you get in?"

He came in, without smiling. "Hello, Peggy, hello, Mother."

The old woman had started to get up and was trying to arrange her little white plaits. She had the brush and comb in her hands and she turned to Tom with a lively amused expression.

Peggy was excited, "Well, the lad's dropped in from the sky."

The old woman observed the young fellow calmly, put back the brush and comb and slid back into bed, "Well, put it there," she said patting the bedside table, "I'm not so hungry."

Tom did as he was told, "How are you feeling this morning, Mother?"

She made a trifling little scoffing smile, "The doctor told me to stay in bed in the mornings, but for all the good it's doing me, I'd rather be up," she said crossly, "up at me work. I don't know what I'm lying here for. Get up, Peggy: aren't you ashamed, in bed, with people here?"

Tom said he'd pour out for her. He sat down on the bedside, but she seemed uneasy and said, "Take a chair, there's a chair there"; and when he held the cup for her, she said, "It's very kind of you."

Tom sighed and looked dispiritedly around, at the plain walls with the children's photographs, the nice dressing table of which his mother was proud, the sickly little tree outside the window, now bare between brick walls. It was still quite dark. "Don't get up yet, Mother," he said, "it's a bitter raw morning, real Bridgehead."

Peggy wanted to know if he was on holiday.

"I'll be here a few days, I came to see how Mother was."

"What struck ye, man?" enquired Peggy sarcastically, "something must have bit ye, ye thought of coming to see your sick mother."

"I expected that kind of welcome."

"What kind of welcome would you be expecting? The flags put out and the fatted calf? After not coming near us at Christmas; it was a black dreary house for me in the festive season. We all stayed in bed all Christmas Day and no one near us. I suppose you had a gay time at Christmas."

"Yes, I had a very gay time."

"Well, it certainly is an unexpected pleasure in a black February day to have a distinguished visitor from London," said Peggy who had got back into bed and was finishing her breakfast. She wanted to know if he had a holiday from work.

"No," he said wearily, "I'm out of a job just now."

"You've not lost that job too?" she cried. "Eh, man, you're hopeless! Well, there's no unemployment round here yet, you'd best try to get a job here and live here. At least we're all paying the same rent and you can help with the house a bit: I'm sick of it. It's not fair a young woman like me never getting out or getting a chance to see anyone."

"I'll think it over," he said; "I don't see why I shouldn't. What else have I got to do?"

"Eh, you're hopeless, just hopeless," cried Peggy.

"Yes, I am," he answered.

"What sort of a future have ye, man?" she enquired anxiously, "if you're such a trifler and so restless at your age?"

"That's a good question."

"Ah, be serious, Tom, I'm worried about ye, man."

"Thanks for that," said he seriously, "that's kind of you: you don't know how kind that is."

"Eh, Tom, I'm not trying to harass you, I'm worried about ye, I don't doubt you have your troubles."

"I'll never forget those words, Peggy," he said getting up to hide the tears in his eyes. "I've had an awful time: it was horrible."

"Well, take it easy, man, don't go imagining tragedies. Pluck up courage, man, try to be like I am. Look at what I have to face every day in this house with no one to stand by me! You had better make up your mind to stay here and the troubles you think you've had will be nothing to the troubles you're going to have with these two crazy old people at ye day and night and not one word of sense from one year's end to the other."

"You're a great consoler," said her brother, going to the door, and smiling faintly, "I had quite an experience once: a friend of mine took me to an undertakers' annual banquet. I'm glad I was there now: I can see there's humor in everything."

"Ye sound like Uncle Sime, now watch out, man, you're getting on in years, thirty-three is not twenty." Tom burst out laughing. The dog rushed out the door and escaped downstairs where he began a savage barking.

When Tom got down there, Uncle Simon was standing in the kitchen near his chair, with bowed legs, looking desperate, while the black dog leaped at him. "He's getting' warse and warse," said he. "He won't let me move. A'd better go to bed. A go back to bed as soon as there's someone aboot, for he doesn't come into me room. A've made up the fire, Tom, and A'd better get to me bed, that's where they want to see me. They don't want me to get up again."

"All right, Uncle Sime," said Tom, "you go up and rest a bit and I'll be muttering to myself down here."

"Don't let the fire go too low and see your Mother doesn't put it out with flingin' food into it." He offered Tom the *Daily Mail,* and though Tom refused it, he left it on the table for him, "It's a good paper, there are some good items in it today. There's another air accident. You mark my words, Tom, they'll give it up, this flyin'. A man is not a bord. Ye've seen it yourself: there's something loose, they haven't time to attend to it, and it goes to pieces in mid-air."

"Yes," said Tom, "all right, and I'll see they cook the chicken for us for lunch or dinner." Uncle Simon slowly made his way through the hall, muttering his thoughts to himself and very slowly got upstairs, being held up halfway by a bad fit of coughing.

Peggy and her mother came downstairs about half past eleven when the house was warm. The street lights were still on; and everyone was coughing. Tom sat in Uncle Simon's chair by the fire, looked at the

Daily Mail and thought how tired, betrayed and unhappy he was. . . .

When Peggy came in, ready to fight if he would not stay in Bridgehead and look after the house and work for them, he shouted that he was not going to spend his life in the back kitchen of a sooty back-to-back, though she wanted to leg-rope him there, "like the rest of the Bridgehead women." Peggy said she had never seen such a thing in her life, a man of his age hanging about a kitchen fire, expecting his tea to be poured for him: she wasn't going to wait on him.

"If you're out of work, you'd better get on relief."

"I've never been on relief yet: not even on the dole in the bad days. I always found something. I did anything; I never got there."

"Don't brag, man, ye'll get there," she said.

He was glad to shout his lungs free and run out into the passage, like a boy again. Uncle Simon hid from the fight. The mother came downstairs with her gentle superior smirk. "Dogs delight to bark and bite," she said in her aged voice, getting distant now as it drew off to another part of the universe: and she looked about for her duster.

"Tom's out of work and he's come home to live off us," said Peggy when he was at the front door. Tom came back and laid on the table all the loose change in his pockets, about twenty-seven and six. He kept only some notes and fifteen pennies for telephones: then he took back some change for cigarettes. The two women quickly and delightedly picked up the money and before he got to the door again, he saw them with joyful secrecy putting the money away in an old sewing box which fitted into the back of the linen drawer. There they kept the money paid by the insurance company and the weekly allowances made to them by Nellie and himself. Uncle Simon's pension covered the rent. He strolled out into the filthy air, full of coughing black smudges which had been born to be men and women; but it choked him after the fresh fields and hills round Market Orange where he had been living with Marion and Connie. He suddenly wondered if his mother had thrown the chicken into the fire. This made him hurry back.

Peggy was sitting by the back room fire knitting, looking very pleased with herself and whistling. "What mischief has she been up to?" thought Tom. His mother and uncle were in the kitchen. Uncle Simon had his felt slippers on the bright fender and was making weak tea. The old woman in a clean apron sat by a clean empty cup.

"Have some tea," said the old man, "I've got some milk of me own, lad, if you're hungry."

Tom said he had eaten a "businessman's lunch," consisting of sausage and French fries.

"A sausage is very tasty sometimes," said Uncle Simon.

Tom found a cup and saucer and poured some tea, using Uncle Simon's milk that afternoon.

"I know ye need the money, lad: ye can share with me," said the uncle.

"Bread's enough for me, I can live on bread," said Tom, "I don't want to get fat; I've been idling for three months now."

"What've ye been living on, relief?" said the mother.

"It's demoralizin' to take the dole, lad, if ye can get work," said Uncle Simon. "Ye can stay here, if ye like and get a good job here. There are plenty of places, and ye're the right age, just the right age; a man of thirty-three is what they want. Ye could get in at Armstrong's. It's not a question of how fast ye are, but how good ye are."

Tom sat down and drank his tea. Three pale, long, blue-eyed Pike faces looked towards the dirty window and the black air. There was a sickly holly bush in the bit of ground round the tree and some bones and crusts at which birds were pecking. "The mice come out and eat Sime's bones," teased Mrs. Cotter.

"There's mony a dead bord in this black fog," said Uncle Simon, "and mony a dead old man and woman, too. It's carryin' them off."

"Did you hear from Nellie, Mother?"

The old woman looked in front of her, "Nellie never coom, Tom never coom: I've got funny children. I washed and scrubbed and cooked and yet they are not grateful: they don't understand. Their wings get stronger, they fly off."

The back-yard bell rang and Uncle Simon got up. "It's Charlie," said the old woman smiling. "He comes for the messages, his mother's very sick and he helps her: he's such a good boy," she told Tom politely.

Uncle Simon returned with a well-grown smiling boy about ten, with shining black eyes and hair.

"Hello, Charlie," said Mrs. Cotter. "You know, Mr.—" she turned to her son, "I'm sorry, I didn't catch your name?"

"Don't be silly, woman, it's your own son, it's Tom."

"Don't you be silly, it's Charlie," she said rocking with laughter. "You'll be the death of me, Simon, you'll be forgetting your own name. He's no son of mine; it's Charlie Rockett, isn't it, hinny?"

"Aye," said the boy smiling.

The old woman went to a drawer and looked eagerly into it. "Who's been turning this drawer upside down?" she asked merrily.

"It's yourself, Mary, and no man else; what are you looking for?"

"For the chocolate for Charlie."

She found the chocolate presently and gave two pieces to the boy, to whom Uncle Simon had now given the grocery list. He impressed upon Charlie the name of his drops, not to forget them and to get them at Burns's, the corner papershop, not at the chemist's; and he carefully counted out the money.

"Eh, give him the money, Simon, don't be an old miser," said Mrs. Cotter, rollicking: "he won't cheat you." She said to her son, "He's a real good boy to his mother; I give him the change for his mother. Now keep a bit of chocolate for your mother, hinny."

She said to Tom, "My own boy Tom used to bring me chocolate when he came home from singing in the choir at Saint Aidan's. He had such a good voice, a real talent; and they always gave him a piece of chocolate and he came running home to his mother; and he used to bury his head in my lap. He was always a mother's boy."

"Don't you know me, Mother?" said Tom. "It wasn't chocolate, Mother. The way it was, was this. We had to be on time and if we came late, we got bad marks, a mark a minute; and if the choirmaster came late, we got pennies, a penny a boy. With my pennies I bought you chitterlings of which you were very fond; that is what I brought you."

She looked at him and laughed, "Chitterlings! They're very good. I like dumplings, too. Mother used to make very good dumplings."

"Aye, she made them in broth and she made them in boiling water: Mother was a very good cook," said Simon.

"I wish she was cooking for us now, I do," said Mrs. Cotter: "I'm hungry, I get really hungry these days, it's the weather coming on to spring."

"It's a fine spring day in Bridgehead, Mother," said Tom laughing; "it is raining black diamonds. I was out; but came back fast."

"Eh," said Mrs. Cotter looking at him, "well, I'm sorry you must go so soon. And look at us sitting in the kitchen!"

"Now gather your wits together, Mary," said Simon indignantly, "ye complain he doesn't come and when he comes ye take him for the grocer's boy. It's ridiculous, that's what it is, A'm ashamed of ye. Ye always were a great one for play-actin' and now it's got the better of ye. Ye want to tell the plain truth all your life, woman, and speak straight and see straight; otherwise ye get to seein' double. Put on your glasses, Mary, don't be ashamed and look in front of you and stop wanderin' among shadows."

"Oh, leave her alone," said Tom, revolted. "What does it matter? I came, didn't I? It doesn't matter if she doesn't know it."

"No, I don't know it," said the old woman to Tom. "There are a lot of things going on in this house I don't know. They're here and they don't come downstairs. I don't know why. It's as if we were strangers. They don't tell me anything; always going and coming. They've got wild since they grew up and Nellie has got them into bad ways. I'm all alone in the house and I don't know what's going on. I don't ask, I don't interfere, but it makes me look funny. I say funny things when people call. People are very kind, very sociable, always visiting; but I'm worried that I'm going to make a fool of myself, put my foot in it. Then they laugh. You see, Mr.—excuse me, my head is so bad now, Mr.—?"

"Cotter," said Tom.

"Mr. Cotter," she said surprised, looking at him; "are you one of the family? You do look like the family."

"Mother," said Tom.

"Don't bother her now," said Uncle Simon; "it's surprisin' how fresh and clear she is often in the marnin' or late at night; but ye mustn't bother her. Peggy's been a very bad lass today and it's got her worried. She can't stand the shoutin' and the cruelty. She was always a timid woman; it's been too much trouble for her."

Tom brought out the chicken and said they ought to have it for supper. The old people were delighted and excited; but Uncle Simon said he'd never cooked a chicken; though he once knew a French woman who cooked a wonderful chicken and he could still remember it. "Though it was thirty-five years ago," said Tom laughing.

"It was thirty-eight," said Uncle Simon, with dignity. "Her husband was a German, a strange sort of man. He went away as a German soldier and he came back after the war. A never did trust him."

"With a chicken cook like that, I'm not surprised he came back," said Tom.

"Now, Simon," said Mary, rocking with laughter; "you're surely not going to try and tell us at this late date that you had a sweetheart who cooked you a chicken dinner?"

"A had a friend who was a good cook," said Simon, straightening himself and looking at his sister. She kept on laughing and gently pinching the plump white flesh of the fowl.

"How do you cook a chicken, Mother? Do you boil it or roast it? Which is better?"

The old woman laughed till she cried; but in the end she said, "I can't remember: it's so long since I cooked one."

"Probably forty odd years," said Tom; "I don't remember ever getting one at home."

"A roast with vegetables is best for the weekend," said Uncle Simon, who did the weekend cooking; "one good healthy man can eat a whole chicken at a meal and crack the bones too. A had a friend who did that, cleaned up like a dog, cracked everythin' with his teeth."

Tom called upon Peggy, who at first screeched at the idea of cooking flesh, but eventually was persuaded, because it was good for her mother.

"I'm hungry, too," said Tom.

Grudgingly she hunted for a cookery book which had belonged to Aunt Lily who had died in their attic five years before and who had lain there for four years before that. Fortunately, the chicken had been cleaned by Connie and the giblets were inside it; but no one knew what to do with them; so Tom asked if he could give the chicken heart to the dog. "Chicken heart? What is that?" asked Peggy dubiously.

"Chicken heart? Heart of a chicken."

"Heart of a chicken? I never heard of that." She was very puzzled. She turned it over, with her rubber gloves on; and at length said that if it was cooked he could have it, she thought.

"What would go with a roast fowl or boiled fowl?" Tom asked. Peggy said it would be better to have whatever was in the larder. They got out two halves of cabbage which Peggy had cut into for raw vegetable salads, and some potatoes. The mother declared a hankering for dumplings; they would boil the fowl and put the dumplings in the water. "And the cabbage?" They could do that in a separate pot, but they were not sure how. Peggy had given up cooking vegetables long ago, having read that cooking took the good out of them. They came to an agreement presently. Tom would try his hand at dumplings out of the cookery book; Uncle Simon would boil the fowl and cabbage; and they were forced to accept his view that all these things would do best on a very low gas; "then you won't lose the goodness." Gradually, the watchers departed, leaving the old man in charge. They could not go to the nearest aunt and ask advice, out of pride and because there would not be enough to invite her. Peggy foresaw that they would give a bone to the dog and kill him. Tom thought they might have potatoes too.

Tom went out to get a beer when the beer shop reopened at six, found dinner was not ready, said he'd take a stroll. When he returned at seven thirty, Mrs. Cotter said she was hungry and they decided to dish up. The water, on Uncle Simon's low gas, had never come to the boil. Assuming command, Tom sent Peggy to lay the table, brought his mother to the kitchen to superintend the dishing up, agreed to divide the fowl himself. Simon said that he would eat by his own fire in the kitchen and remarked that it made a lot of dishes. The old mother wrapped all the necessary forks, knives and spoons in a brown paper parcel and put them with Aunt Lily's book in the sideboard in the front room, just after the potatoes were drained. During the hunt that followed she very slyly, with a pale little smirk, tipped the potatoes into Simon's fire, washed and polished the vegetable dish and put it back in its place. They were recalled to the kitchen by the smell. Tom had to finish the table while Peggy, scolding, stood guard and Simon tried to right his fire. The fine young hen which had been put on in cold water, with no salt, for Peggy thought it bad for the blood, was heavy, leathery; it did not seem cooked. The cabbage when dished up was hard, almost crisp. "You should have turned the gas up a bit, Uncle Sime," said Tom pleasantly.

"And lose all the good juices? A don't hold with the modern way of doin' everythin' fast and tasteless."

"It's better for your stomach if the cabbage is raw," said Peggy.

Mother said it smelled very good, it made her mouth water.

"The dumplin's are very good," said Uncle Simon taking a bit of one. Some had fallen to the bottom, others had spread about in the water. "The taste is very good, ye are quite a hand," said Simon.

"You must be very hungry, Uncle," said Tom, smiling sadly. He carried in the hen to divide up and after ten minutes called to the women to bring in the vegetables. "Surely we can do a simple thing like that without your powers of direction," shouted Peggy.

"Very well," said Tom and sat down to wait.

Half an hour later they were all eating what they could, while the dog constantly had to be threatened with the leash; and when the chicken was carried out, Peggy had to stay in the kitchen to see no one gave him a bone. Meantime, she lectured them on the evils of flesh-eating; but she had eaten a lot of cabbage, onion, cheese and was in a good mood. "You'll not want anything to eat for a couple of days," she said; "such guzzling and gobbling, you'd think it was Christmas." . . .

II

Nellie got up early, washed hastily at the kitchen sink, and went striding over to Ma Hatchard's two streets away. She and the landlady had hated each other at sight. Mrs. Hatchard was in her fifties, like a tree trunk lightning struck, gray, powerful, thick, with a creased face, thin white hair, wearing a very long gray or blue dress with a narrow belt and a small white collar. Her eyes were sea blue. She behaved mannishly, in her strength; except when, vivacious with some tidbit of scandal, she put on a new little flowered hat and high heels and hurried off to neighbors she had known in the bombing, neighbors who for the most part lived in temporary dwellings on a bombed-out site. Hovering in the background of her dark street-level rooms was a good-looking but pale and tired young woman, who appeared to sleep in Mrs. Hatchard's quarters. Ma Hatchard herself slept in a remarkable four-poster bed with canopy and curtains, which reared itself against the back wall, so that the room looked like a stage. Ma Hatchard was fond of cats. She had saved cats from hunger and death during the war and subsequent national starvation; her house, unwashed, unpainted with broken leaking walls and crumbling stairs covered with coconut matting smelled of human and cat urine. But though there were no fastenings on windows or doors and the bedclothes were patched and gray with bad washing, she had fixed her lodgers' rooms up completely, with each a little oven and stove, and good lights, each item on a separate meter. The meters ate up the pennies, sixpences and shillings. There was a regular rake-off for the landlady on each meter.

It was in the best room, the large front room on the first floor upstairs, that Caroline lived; a shabby and dirty room, but cheaper than most to be found and "clean"; that is, free of insect pests. Caroline was deeply ashamed of living in such dirt. She invited no friend there but Nellie. She was afraid of Mrs. Hatchard.

Ma Hatchard let Nellie in without a word. Nellie flung past and ran up the stairs three at a time, with a gay halloo.

"Are you there, love?"

She flung herself down on the armchair with her leg over it and began raging about her brother. How could Tom still go round making experiments with human beings? There was a stormy, seeking time in Bridgehead many years before when they were roaming looking for the road out. "Some people called it Bohemia." That was all right for young people. It was all despair, stupidity and selfishness if they looked home-wards. So they looked outwards and saw depression, the dole, the fourth winter of unemployment, many homes broken up, children wandering for work all over England. They had found the answer, she and Tom; but it had formed them differently.

"I struggled out of it; but he never did. He's remained an adolescent and he's killed souls with his purposeful evasiveness. He's dangerous. I'm warning you. You want to be very sure of yourself to cope with him. It was a bad time, a time of many solutions. There was corruption. Tom and I were in all that corruption together. He's no good."

"But Tom is so gentle and good and so gay," said the young woman.

Nellie said bitterly, "Aye, he's an angel—a gilded angel with rotting wings." She flung herself down and hid her face on the chairback, "I've come for ye. He'll pull the wool over your eyes; he's the spirit of mischief. He'll take you away from me."

"Oh, how can you say that? I know what you've done for me. You've befriended me; and I was so lonely."

"There's no standing water with friendship; it's turn your back on me or come forward and be my real friend. There's no other way. It's me or him. Life or death. He's coming here! I know his tricks. He'll catch a poor bloody innocent like you. And why haven't you trusted me? It should be all right between us, I shouldn't have to worry, after all I've done for you. But you shilly-shally. You married a weak man and you hadn't the backbone to stand by your mistake. You got led astray like a Woolworth miss in Roseland. You fell for that bugger in the office. I know you. I have no faith in you. You have no character. You won't look into yourself and see what you are. You won't confess to what's wrong."

"I know Alan has been strange. I don't understand all he does. I have been very unhappy, very. He was so good to me. I went over everything a hundred times. Why should he be unkind to me? I loved him; he asked me and I told him. I do love him. I always will. Would it be love if I became angry with him the first time he hurt me?"

"I pity you. I pity you from the bottom of my heart. I pity you living in fairy stories like a child. If you even think you love him, I pity you. And you'll be easy game for a prinking thing, a smirking toy like Tom. He'll sing you a song and tell you a tale and you'll go straight to the mountebank and forget everything I've told you and been to you."

"I don't understand you. Why are you so upset?"

Caroline was uneasy at Nellie's pain. Couldn't they all be friends?

Nellie loved Tom, Caroline liked them both. No, no, said Nellie; she had to choose. The ways lay at right angles. Caroline was puzzled and very uneasy at the misery and passion she saw in Nellie.

Nellie was downright, "He has no need of you. He can do nothing for you and I can do everything. He can't offer you friendship, love or any such thing. He's coming over to play cat's cradle with your feelings. If you knew my wild loneliness, Caroline, you'd come to your senses."

"But I thought you had so many friends."

Nellie muttered, "Not one that understands me. In you I thought I had found the perfect understanding. Oh, Caroline, for someone to talk to, to talk into the heart and leave it there and feel peace."

Nellie talked in this distracted way for some time, when they both had to go to work. Nellie went along with Caroline to the station, begging her to be true to her, not to be taken in by the "pink and white illusionist."

"I'm warning you. It will end badly. He can only harm women."

Nellie bought the morning papers, sat on a bench till it was time for the pubs to open and presently went downtown to work.

Caroline came out of the housing office at six o'clock and walked along briskly, thinking about catching her bus, though her head was spinning. She wondered if she would have the courage to go into a pub and have a drink, wishing she were home now, at Ma Hatchard's, so that she could begin the routine of cooking, eating, fixing her clothes. She had thought about Alan so much that she had envisaged even the most unlikely possibilities; even that he would tell her the affair was finished. I couldn't face it, she said to herself; then at once, everything can be faced. And he is too good, too kind and I am no nuisance; and he loves me. She had thought of everything, wondering very much these last few months at his strangeness. I don't know much about men. I have to learn.

This afternoon, after talking to her in a gruff embarrassed way, chopping out his answers and questions, he had mentioned a couple that had been ejected from their one-room home and were now housed in different temporary shelters, wives and husbands separately. The wife was having a love affair with the man's closest friend. The husband couldn't grasp it and was disturbed. "He cries without stopping; he cried for three days."

"Oh, poor man. It's overwork."

"Yes, he was doing two jobs to try to get a home. I told him it will be all right. Temporary affairs have no meaning and don't last."

When he said it, she knew at once what he was getting at. They talked for a while in this way and everything had two meanings. He walked to the door with her and she kissed him as she had been doing, though she noticed he drew back. A car honked at her and there was Tom waiting to take her home. She got in and sat down, quite easeful. He noticed her looks and asked if she were ill.

"I may be, but I'm happy and free."

"Who is happy and free?"

They laughed.

"Would you like a drive in the country?"

No, she had promised Nellie to go straight home.

"Nellie will get along all right."

"No: I promised."

He began to drive. She didn't know where they went; but she realized presently that Tom was talking, talking, the light voice mixing with the street sounds, birds. It stopped when the traffic stopped. He was recounting all kinds of things. . . .

At first there were tears in her eyes: then she fell asleep. He did not wake her up, but she woke when they stopped in front of a Hampstead pub. It was a pretty place, a terrace with benches and bushes.

He laughed, "You say you like me to talk; and you fall asleep."

"I thought I was in trouble; then you were talking and I saw people are living everywhere, and I was glad and I fell asleep."

He looked at her gaily and got her drinks, chatting with everyone.

When they got outside, he said, "To Ma Hatchard's?"

The old woman stood in the door of her den. Tom smiled at her, a light passed over her face, she stood away without a word and let them go up.

"You are not well, you're ill," said Tom.

"I should be ashamed to be ill because of a love affair. I've had plenty of experience."

Tom ran out and up several streets looking for things to eat. He bought food at last in a pub. He came back. He moved about like a cat and seemed beside himself with joy at being able to look after her.

He told her that he thought he could cure people. People believed in him and he wanted to help them. It was a power in him sometimes, not always. Even at moments, he had been able to help Marion.

"Only for a little while."

She asked him what he did.

He got up from his chair, stood near her, leaning slightly forward, spread out his arms a little from his body and began to look straight at her, smiling a deep smile. To her surprise, he seemed to grow upwards and outwards and she felt herself smiling, drawn towards him. His hands and face seemed larger and a feeling of happiness spread through her. He sat down and she began to tremble.

"It is there; but I have to develop it. Marion wanted me to go to India to learn. She said I could be of great use to sick people."

They were sitting quietly by the gas fire, not saying much, a little bored and laughing a little about raffling off the furniture in the dingy room, when there was a discussion downstairs and they heard Nellie's voice. She ran upstairs and burst open the door, looking at them both with a terrible accusing face.

"I knew you were here, Tom. I saw the car downstairs."

"Well, I am here. You were right."

"You must take us all home. I have a room for Caroline. She can't stay here with that harpy. I've explained it to Mrs. Hatchard and I've paid her. Get your things together, Caroline, and come home and I'll look after you."

"Caroline is too tired."

"Caroline promised me to come. She wants to come with me."

"Very well," said Tom.

When he got them home, with the bags, he said he would take Eliza Cook out for a drink. Nellie had not spoken a word to him during the drive and did not speak now.

Tom said, "I'll be back in the early hours of the morning. Don't wait up for me or wonder where I am."

Nellie was pale with rage, speechless; but when Tom clapped the front door to, she flung herself into Caroline's arms and burst into a raucous sobbing.

"It's too much for me, Caroline."

Presently she said that her life was like struggling over a stony hill, stubbing her feet, where the stones were people: that was the Philistine world. Robert Peebles had rejected her article outright. She needed Caroline above all. She kept Caroline up very late talking. George had told her he could not sleep in the house; not only was it that she didn't seem able to sleep at night, but roamed about in the dark hours; it was also her coughing and smoking.

"And that's love for you, Caroline. What the men mean by love is routine and comfort."

Caroline slept at last, in the back room. Tom came home later still and slept late. . . .

III

. . .The next afternoon, a Saturday, he took Nellie for a drive. They had taken a long rising road and were high above the Vale of Aylesbury, which, under a faint vapor, rolled away right and left before them. The road was on a rampart of earth and above it rose an almost naked mound.

Nellie said, "Let's stop here. Let's go up there and get the real fresh wind."

A fair cool breeze was blowing and hissing in the grass tufts.

"It'll be bad for you, Nellie. You shouldn't overexert yourself."

"I'll be fine, chick. Just help me up. Let's sit on top of the world, like we used to on the moors. You always said, I can breathe now. I like to be with you, darling. There's no one like you. You're restful. You help me to believe in things. Ah, darling, it's hard at times. The road is rough."

He held on to her, pulled her upwards.

"Take it easy, Nell."

She had to stop several times; her breath came rasping. She coughed and held her chest while she laughed and protested, "I'll be all right, pet; I'll make it."

He said they never should have come up. They sat down.

She gasped and hawked and said, "Those chimneys spoil the view: see the smoke going into the fresh air!"

"No chimneys and I'd have no work," said Tom.

"Come on, tell me the gossip, Tom."

"What gossip? Nothing ever happens to me."

She said laughing, blowing her cigarette smoke away, "Ah, ye devil! Come chick, let's have your news, don't tease! Tell it in your own deprecating style, at the rate of one hint a half-hour, to be tiresome. Come, what did you do last night, chick?"

"I saw Eliza. We all went to the pub."

"They are a damn dreary lot." She looked restlessly here and there.

"Well, here you are, Nellie, on top of the world."

Said she, musing, "I've come a long way. My life's been an unusual story. In a sense it is clear-cut. The five ages, aye. My childhood up to fourteen when I was a sad serious child, very conscious of my shortcomings and the feeling of guilt. That's salutary. Then fifteen, when I realized the world and myself in it. Then my work in London and the provinces when I brought you all down, out of it, to get into reality; and perhaps I'm guilty. And then George."

"That's four. And then?"

"Then life without George."

He waited.

She wiped a tear off her cheek, "He's leaving me in the lurch, the bastard. He telephoned me this morning. He can't fix it for me for a while. He had a letter from Geneva. He's going to Geneva as soon as he gets his papers ready. They don't want me yet. They want him to settle first. It's the end."

She turned round, clasped his neck, sobbing.

"Chick, I can't be brave."

Tom put his arms round her, and kissed her, "You'll have to stick to me, Nell."

"Ah, bless you, Tom, you're a saint. Would you go up to Bridgehead, lad; and I'll try and get a job there and we'll be back in the old home?"

"Not on your life. Why, you wouldn't stick it three days, Nell."

He chuckled.

She pleaded in a strained yearning voice, "It would do the poor souls' hearts good; and she'd be saner, Tom. You'd take the burden off the poor girl. It's not fair, Tom."

Tom said dryly, "I do what I can."

"Tom, I don't understand you. Our parents are only struggling human beings. They brought us into the world. They're not guilty. We're guilty. Ah, Tom, I feel guilty, guilty. When I stop on the doorstep with the frail bits of parsley by it and see the clean window curtains and put me key in the door, you don't know the awful guilt I feel."

"I don't feel guilty, Nell."

"You're hard, harder than I am, Tom. How can you speak so of that innocent flower destroyed in savagery, in thoughtless egotism and that now has nothing to fulfill itself but in stifled bitterness? What is she, Peggy, the poor darling, but a white flower in a black cloth? What is Bridgehead but the black cloth? She's being slowly suffocated, put away, turned brown and wrinkled in a back drawer. Tom—she's my greatest deepest regret. I feel a horrible guilt. I led the way. I meant to show her life. She was such a rosy white child with that soulless merry laugh. Tom, oh my lad, I remember her as she was, not as the poor Bridgehead lass living a defeated life in a back kitchen as she seems now to you. Men cannot see women. They see them with a purpose, an aim, not with pitiful love and an everlasting tender heart. I see her sitting there in the dark room knitting; to me she's just a white bird with a trailing wing, a bit between spirit and flower."

"You'd say that about a coal barge in the Scotswood muck if it suited you, Nell," he said laughing.

"Ah, Tom, the poor wee lost spirit; why can't I make you see? Will ye go, lad? I'll give up my job and we'll work together for the home."

"I will not."

"They look to us like hungry birds, now that Pop Cotter, bless his heart, has gone. They don't understand it when the money doesn't come in."

"No, they're not getting me back into that trap. I'm no Uncle Simon."

She cried, in a thin failing voice, "But why not? What have you got in your life, pet? I'd understand it if you had a home; but you're just a wanderer. Look at George. Wandering, thinking of his own pleasure, thinking of some new love! What's in the men? You're degenerate— thinking of it and nothing else! No mercy, no pity. I'm disgusted with you all. The first woman that comes along to look at you open-mouthed and everything else vanishes like burnt paper."

"It's a good life," he said, smiling.

"I know you, Tom. You'll begin to spend your money foolishly and it'll end up in some new Marion craze. It's just monkey tricks and mumming with you from end to end."

"I like it."

"And it'll be some harpy again getting the money, when they need it."

"They get more than their share in Bridgehead. Don't nag me."

"Ah, you're bitter, Tom. I'm thinking of what they never had. Have they had the lovely dreams we've had, seen the sights, known the world? Their poor old bodies sitting their lives out in a smoky chimney corner! It's pitiful, it makes me weep. Here we sit on top of a hill in beautiful southern England and we are free to do what we like. They're chained to Bridgehead."

"And they've turned into chuckle-headed gossips and domestic cutpurses and I don't intend to exchange my experience for theirs." . . .

For a while they sat side by side, smoking and looking at the view.
. . . After a silence, she said, "You're angry, aren't you?"

"No, I'm not."

She suddenly flew into a temper, "You'd desert your family and anyone, to stay in London and flirt."

He didn't answer.

She said fiercely, "You're both traitors to me. You'd both desert me for the first harpy that comes your way."

"I wouldn't, Nell," he said calmly.

"You don't sympathize with me: you don't care if he leaves me: it's the League of Men."

"No, it isn't."

"You sit there looking so smooth and fair," she complained, "you know I forgive you everything."

"No, you don't."

"I would even love anyone you asked me to."

"No, you wouldn't."

"You don't think I'd do anything to hurt you, Tom."

"Yes."

"But we're two against the world, Tom: there's only you and me."

"No, there's not, Nell."

"Ah, damn and blast you, Tom Cotter," she said flying into a wild roistering banter, "you've got me by the nose sitting there with your meek smirk and saying, No, I don't, and Yes, you do."

"No, I haven't."

"What do you mean by telling all the women your sorrowing tales and talking about sex and mayflower and saying you feel like the son of Venus's son: and that in the country your feet don't seem to touch the ground and such sonnets?"

"Those are not my words," said Tom.

"Real beams came from Venus all this month: you said that to Caroline this morning: she admired it."

"Those were my words."

"What are you going round telling all the women your poetry for?"

"Because I feel it," said Tom.

Nellie was silent. After a while, she said, "But what's the sense to it, Tom?"

He was looking straight in front, smiling at the red evening.

"What pleasure do you get out of it?"

"No pleasure!"

"Then why do you do it?"

He was silent.

"At your age, Tom, with your experience, you ought to give up this wild dancing in a hall of mirrors."

"This wild dancing in a hall of mirrors."

"And it's an illusion!"

"And it's no illusion," said Tom.

"But you haven't known happiness as I have, Tom: you must grant that. You haven't known the great reality, the one great true experience, the tree of life."

"No, I haven't known it as you have," he said humbly.

"And you never can, it's a one in a million chance."

"No, I shall make another mistake," said Tom.

"Then why try, when you know it's foredoomed?"

No answer.

"Is it right to trouble the lives of these women and go round making mischief?"

He looked slyly at her, a troubling sideways glance.

"If you were honest, you'd tell them to get the hell out of your life and leave you alone."

He looked sideways at her, and she began to tremble with urgency, "Now, Tom, I want you to promise me you won't go and do any more mischief-making."

He looked ahead at the road.

"Eh, Tom?"

"I don't make mischief; I do nothing. I just sit there."

"I don't ask you to restrict your life."

"I don't bother about what you ask."

"What?" she said, astonished.

"Life doesn't restrict itself. It comes and finds you."

"Then you won't make any promise?"

"No."

"I'm ashamed of you."

"To change the subject. My room where I had my last job, Nell, was a miserable bedroom with a light you couldn't read by. The wind howled and blew in the street. The landlord came in and out of the dining room like a dark-colored spook and used to whip the plates at you from behind his trousers like a conjurer. He wore a felt hat and bicycle clips, and his wife used to go to the pub after dinner. I don't blame her. She felt that if they could get away to London they could better themselves. He was interested because the atom bomb didn't injure canned beer. There was a laboratory chemist there who had lost his job and worried because he was getting farther and farther behind. If you're three or four years behind, you're lost, out of it. I used to wake up at night trembling, my heart was jumping about. I knew there was nothing there, but I couldn't help it, I'd lie there without daring to move. It was the loneliness."

"You were born to loneliness, lad."

"And so I think, Nell, I must look around and find a wife."

She said angrily, "You know you're not for women! You can't give. You're a bachelor born. You're cold, stone cold. You're trying to get warm, like poor old Simon at the kitchen fire; but no woman can warm the likes of you; and you can give her nothing," and she said it deep in dialect, "naw-thin."

She continued, "You were born, you will live and die, a lonely man. Ah, isn't it better to accept it, swallow the pill and be yourself, lad? You're out of character, cooing to the women. Be what you were, as a lad. I was proud of ye then. And now I'm ashamed of ye."

"But I think I'll get married. I have my eye on someone."

She sulked. Tom, soon lost in his thoughts, smiled to himself. Nellie, at first absorbed, noticed his expression. She put her thin wrist on his and said sweetly, "You're not going to go where temptation lies, are ye, love?"

"I'm in a mood to be tempted, Nellie."

She reflected.

Along the London road, passing through a large town, there was a wide green, well kept with trees behind and bushes round a convenience in front.

"I feel like a pee, Tom. Let's get out and stretch our legs."

He waited for her and then strolled across the green, half of which was occupied by circus tents.

"Ah, Tom, I love the sideshows, let's walk on sawdust for ten minutes."

It reminded her of Race Week on the Town Moor, when, poor children, bedraggled but whistling and shouting, they had gone up there with a few pence in their pockets.

"Peggy loved it so much, the darling. And now we can't let her go near: it's bad for her. Ah, the bygone days!"

She said as if inspired, "Do you remember, Tom, the day we all went to Whitley Bay and went in the ghost train? Peggy wanted so much to go on the ghost train and we were afraid, for she was always so excitable; and we went in and what was it but a track running in all the curves over bare earth and you could see it too? Poor Peggy! But I was glad. No spiderwebs, no shrieking spooks. The poor devils, aye, they were packing up, no business; but they took our sixpences!" She laughed, "And do ye remember that day, the prawns we ate at Cullercoats! And the bus conductor who fell off the bus and tore me good jacket; and looked at me so angry! He thought I was going to bawl him out and I said, Go on, love, better me jacket than yours; and he still went on up the stairs, looking back so furious."

She went into shrill sisterly laughter, "I was taken for a bloody bourgeois suing dame that day! It was a nice jacket, all new, made to order, me first and in a good cloth. Do ye ever think of those days, Tom?"

"I never had a happy day there but on the football field. I stand now and watch them in Regent's Park, the lads making a thousand goals an hour, but it doesn't get me any more. And like me, the daft lads think they'll reach the big money that way."

"Ah, Tom!" she wheedled. "Eh, look there, Tom! Isn't that a grand one. Let's go in."

They had come along the tents and were now at a large loosely boarded place named Palace of Mirrors.

"I've got such a craving on me for those things, Tom. Let's go in."

"Well, you know what it is: it's distorting mirrors."

"Ah, come, love, let's go in. Let's have a bit of fun, just brother and sister, like the old days. It gives me the thrill of Race Week when I was small. We used to beg petty cash for it."

"Aye and once I stole from Mother's purse. You remember? And you gave me a curtain lecture."

There was no one at the booth: it was between afternoon and evening sessions. They rapped and looked, till they found a man in shirt-sleeves who let them in. The entrance door was a mirror, in which they saw themselves, the short yellow-haired man and the tall wedge-faced woman; they looked earnestly and went in. There was a short corridor with different sorts of mirrors, then a rotunda, it seemed. One mirror showed Tom cut off at the waist and very fat; "A playing-card king . . ." said Tom disgustedly. . . . "And look at me, the spindling hatchet witch," she said, poking out her tongue at herself in the neighboring glass in which her long thin arms, legs and face were fancifully drawn out. Tom looked where it made him a dwarf with a huge head. Depressed, he leaned against the wall and watched Nellie who was looking at herself in every mirror in turn, laughing, posturing, exclaiming, "Eh, Tom, love, I'm a beauty. Tom, look at this black raven! Why, thank god, Tom, it is not the Hall of Truth."

He said nothing. She began to gesture, posture and then dance a strange dance, her own, with knees bent and wobbling, arms akimbo, tufted head going up and down and sideways, like "a crawing creature" she said. Aside and forward she went in the figures of her dance, smiling to herself, beckoning to herself, putting her arms on her breast and with a strut turning the circle. She saw Tom there, stretched out her long thin arms and he came forward in his heavy shoes, took both hands; and they danced a few steps, though he was no dancer, at arms' length, a country dance. Her face bright as metal, triumphant, gleamed and cut into him; very bright, her small eyes peered into his large bursting ones. Then she flung one of his hands aside and began to draw him after her. She stopped a moment, eying a mirror which showed them side by side, shredded, a bundle of dark reeds and a wisp of hay, both with long beaked faces, split like seaweed, on her head a long sprout, on his the dry grass ground birds hide in.

She was displeased, "Not much, is it? They're distortions of human beings! Why do we like it, Tom?"

After eying it for a bit, she screwed up her face, leaned forward and dragged him behind her. "Let's dance!"

So there was a string of them in the dusty narrow corridor, a ballroom of the strangest people, but always the same two. And suddenly, she stopped, dropped to the floor, and leaning on a bent knee and one arm, began to cough. She leaned over, her head to the floor, whooped, almost strangled. Tom stood there waiting. Presently, she climbed up over herself. He helped her up.

She leaned on his shoulder for a breather, "Eh, it's the dust. The floor's thick with the dust of feet," she said.

"Come on, Nell. We'll go home and you lie down."

"It's a drink I need, sweetheart: they must be open now. Take me to the nearest. They're all friends."

"Ye-es, Nell."

"It does me good to have a drink and to stretch me legs in a strange pub. I feel so cosy and so free. Me troubles are outside."

They sat some two hours in the nearest pub, Nellie tossing down one drink after the other, in her own cycle, sherry, whiskey, gin: and Tom taking one glass of wine which made him go red.

Said Nellie, "Must be snobs round here, if they serve you glasses of wine. You'd never get anything as fancy as that in a true workingmen's pub."

After she had drunk two rounds, she leaned her head back on the yellow flyspecked wall, her elbow on the table, her hand turned gracefully outwards, the cigarette smoking into the air; and she said in her weak tone, "If ye only knew, Tom, how it sticks in me gullet. He's dead and he thought that of me at the last, that I was letting the family down. I'll never swallow that black spoonful. I sup with guilt."

"What is it, Nell?"

"Aye, ye weren't there. Pop Cotter in his big bland way, lambasting me, Tom, because I'd dropped ten pounds a week and there wasn't enough food in the house, nor meat for his plate. I'll have it always with me, Tom. If only you had been able to get a job there, darlin'. I know it's work you want, not a name, I wouldn't have this shadow on me shoulders. It's with me in my dreams, it haunts me in the day, that the money isn't coming in and they look to us like pitiful hungry birds."

He did not answer, looking rosily around, noticing everything.

She did not insist then, but grasped his hand, kissed his cheek and said, "Eh, but that was grand, Tom, just when I needed it. You and me together. That's the way we meant it to be; but it can't be. You can't argue with the world. I need the world, Tom and that's why it all went wrong. Let's go; I must get back." . . .

When they sat in the car, driving, looking ahead, she said, "I feel on top of the world, now, because you're the one I've given me real heart to, Tom. Don't let me down ever; or I'll think very little of you."

"You know, Cushie, that you've always got me."

"Bless you, pet."

IV

Eliza was home on Wednesday afternoon for a half-holiday. She was doing Nellie's washing and ironing, Nellie having no time at all for herself. In mid-afternoon she made tea and called Camilla from her workroom to share it. Camilla said that she had not known at first that Eliza was George's first wife.

"There's no point in mentioning it: I'm not his wife now. And I respect Nellie. She's a grand woman."

Eliza said they were all from the same setting, knew each other as children.

"I've known Cooks all my life, his Ma and his brothers and sisters;

and they're as they were before, living in Bridgehead back-to-backs and spending the weekends at the races and owing money to the little clothing clubs. But George had it in him. He was a choirboy till thirteen, then he read something and became an atheist. He joined the union, the party, the county library, evening classes, anything that was going, to get some polish; and then he went into the navy not so much for love of the sea as to get some education while getting pay. I know he's a bright man. I don't blame him. Now I'm fair, fat and fifty myself and I worked, but I didn't study and so I didn't get on much. I'm blaming no one but myself. You must study. He needed one like Nellie. She used to spend all her afternoons in the library at one time when she was about sixteen. You've no idea how they've changed from the Bridgehead lad and lass they were. They've changed each other, too. You should have seen her up there when she was fifteen and sixteen. She left school because it wasn't life she said. Some of us like George and me were at our jobs. Tom was still at school. She got big money, it seemed to us then, writing little bits for a paper; it seemed marvelous to us, her interviewing the nobs. She stood everyone drinks, she bought food, handed out cigarettes and beer. She was there spending her money, making a great show which impressed the youngsters; and others, too, were impressed, I can tell you. There was a man Solomon and others, political types, who expected big things of her. We'll hear from Nellie Cotter, they used to say. I wasn't close to the Cotters then; but I'd see her in real silk blouses and flashing a big sapphire ring she used to pawn every Wednesday when the pay was gone. She was rowdy with opinions she got out of books, perhaps; but for us they were her own; and she never agreed, always disagreed; and she put over her opinions with a lot of them, who were impressed. I didn't know. I did my work. She was not my type. But she made a big splash; and the youngsters there were so ignorant; and wanting to get out of it. . . . She was different then, bony and ugly and wild as a streetboy, ripping out the dirty oaths, with a great charm coming into the drawn lines of her face. Eigh, but that was away above our heads. It was George brought learning into our home." She laughed, "With tomatoes and salad. He taught us to eat them. It was bacon and egg and dripping and the Sunday roast with us and that was all. And they thought it was unmanly and foreign of George, I can tell you, the salad; and I didna like it myself—but I ate it for love."

Eliza became silent, as she spread thick butter and jam on her toast. . . .

"It was a hungry time then, all ways. It was from the slum to the factory, get married early and back into the slum with your first baby, the only recreation to wheel the baby on the moor on Sunday; and unemployment in the factories, the docks and the mines."

She made an impatient gesture, "George said he wouldn't be caught there; so he got out and I followed him. I came to London where I was like a wild heathen; I knew nothing. But I knew him and I went round the bookshops asking for him. I was lucky. I found him working, out the back packing books, in the third bookshop in Charing Cross Road, I asked in. He came out in a khaki workcoat, we walked out that evening, I got a job and we got married. Neither of us could take a Bridgehead future." . . .

. . . Well, the young people all faced a hard future and wanted something better. They were sick of the dull narrow horizons and the meanness of family life, the pools, work talk, gossip and one good time a year, Race Week on Newcastle Town Moor with the sideshows the only news of outside life: mermaids, dog-headed boys."

"I'd like to go up there. You don't know England in London," said Camilla.

"Aye, but not Bridgehead. You should see Newcastle. It's worth seeing. You see the iron of its ribs and backbone when you first look. The reefs of little houses, the iron-ribbed river. It's a great place, a big city, the capital of an old kingdom. They stand against the Scots, they stand against the southerners and the midlanders: they don't even like their neighbors, the Yorkshiremen; and yet they don't think much of themselves. But Bridgehead or Newcastle, it's the same: they feel nothing great ever came out of there. A canna understand it meself."

Eliza dropped back for a moment into the local talk, as they all dropped back when they began to think deeply of their home place.

"If you can forget for a moment the black coal fog and the black coaly river, Newcastle, too, has beauty. But it despises culture. They never mention it. It's pure grind-and-drudge working class and a very mean middle class with butlers, a small town sort; you don't get anything from them. If we had famous men, you never hear of them. Why I heard from George, in London, that one of us, Thomas Belt, made a famous voyage in Nicaragua; and that's us, we go everywhere. But as for mentioning it in school, they don't care for it; only the bread and butter. . . .

V

Nellie tried to sit with Caroline the two nights of the weekend, smoking many cigarettes to pass the time; but it was hard for her to sit without talking. She would go downstairs for tea or brandy, cut a wedge of bread, walk about whistling softly and ruminating. At last, she stretched out beside the sick woman and slept restlessly, coughing and uneasy; she had no covering.

When Caroline woke in the early hours, Nellie made her some tea, cut thin bread and butter and brought them up and put them beside her friend on a chair. She was too heedless to have a sickroom manner; and waited impatiently for Caroline to lie back, which she presently did.

Then Nellie said, sweetly, with a sigh, "I'm glad you're here with me, darling; me poor brother's off gallivanting again. I'm a fool, I must be to trust him. But when he's sweet to me, I trust him again. Aye, we women earn our troubles; and why was it I wonder that Nature gave the men those sweet ways to cheat us to make us the doting weak things we are? Otherwise, we'd see them as they are, no doubt. That must be it. It's the law of survival: aye, it is. For don't we naturally trust each other, more? So there has to be something to lure us; and if the man's your brother, no matter what he is, you can't help the love and pity."

"Yes, I can never forget how nice Tom has been to me, Nellie. You're a beautiful pair; you're a real brother and sister."

"Aye, you feel it, do you, that we're alike, that we have something in common?"

"Yes, goodness and compassion."

Nellie glowed; then lamented, "Yes, I have it, love. But he has not got it, it's a simulacrum: it's the veil of cheating I was talking about. He caught it from me, it's me shadow self, but it isn't him. Any word he says to you is false, for it isn't him and it has no outcome. If he were to say love, it doesn't mean love; things aren't what they seem: things are the contrary: if he were to say marry me, it would be nothing but the joke of a silly, yellow-faced, garlanded clown dancing in a hall of mirrors, but in all these hundred shadows, love, there is not one man. You can't marry him, for there is nothing to marry. If you stood up before the minister or went down to the Town Hall, it's no difference: you'd be the world's most miserable woman. He was married, did ye know that? And the marriage at once fell apart for he cannot play the husband's part; and the poor girl, always a girl, is left to mourn. Did ye not know that? Did he not tell ye? And because the poor simple creature, doomed to loneliness, cannot bear to face the truth, he will play the cat and mouse with all the women. Will ye marry me? Would ye marry me? Could ye marry me? It's a game; and playing the game he knows the women; and there's your lure and dead end of life for you, darling. Don't think of him! Root him out if he's put down root, crush him if he's made a paper flower in your heart, for it's nothing, there's nothing for a woman in him. I can't tell you, love, for it would crush you, the names of the women he has taken in and what has happened to them. Ah, don't let me see you join them. I couldn't bear it with you. I can't bear to think," she said stormily, "that he is doing this to you and to me, when we were so close, close as sisters, we were reaching the perfect understanding, the true love."

Caroline had understood that Tom might propose marriage to her very soon and Nellie's exhortation confirmed it. She became very agitated and said Tom was good and they were fond of each other.

Nellie began to croon, "Marriage is an illusion, it's not the paradise of women as they thought, the poor pitiful mothers and grandmothers. Ah, pet, if ye could have seen me poor mother down on her knees, waxing the lino and polishing the brasses for a man who had eyes only for the harpy's red smile and the fake brilliant in the false gold on her finger, you'd understand me. I see you going wrong. I've seen it before and let it go on, for I'm a great believer in destiny; but I've been punished for it and I'm punished now if ye go wrong. He has no need of you, me weak and wicked brother, Tom. He can do nothing for you and you nothing for him. But I can do everything, I'm the doer and seer. He can't offer you love, not even friendship, he's only playing with your tangled feeling to get relief for a moment, the moment of a cigarette's burning, love, from his own tangled confusion, the contemplation of his wasting and loneliness. I know it's a pitiful thing, I admire you for your kind heart, but it's the kind hearts are taken and consumed."

She leaned forward sharply, bent with her bright fierce little eyes over the sick woman, shaking cigarette ash on the bed, "Heed me, darling. I can see into hearts and I know what is in his and yours. You're not for each other: you're both for the lonely road."

Caroline with a soft and blasted look, lay on her pillow, her large watering eyes fixed on Nellie's, blinking, shutting, opening.

"Nellie, let me rest a bit? I'm so tired and weak feeling, so depleted." . . .

"You'll forgive me, won't ye, love; for warning you about Tom? Let him go and trust me, you'll find peace when you've had it all out, seen it for what it is, rooted it out, confessed and told me everything and faced the music. You've got a long way though to go to get out of your mess, I'm afraid. You're not ready, not willing."

"Why do you say that?" said the woman, feverishly and vaguely.

"Surely you don't think you've succeeded, Caroline? Or are you giving up the struggle?"

"I think the best way for me is not to think about myself and all this trouble, but to get a job in social work as I had before and work for others. And I know I must watch my feelings. I control them and they betray me on a lower level. I never can keep them in hand."

Nellie beamed wickedly, "Muckraking and exposés and the helping hand of the good women are the delight of the Philistine middle class, it's pleasurable pollution and sedative holiness for Sunday: to see the workers rolling in their wallows and pity them so that you can rough-tongue the char on Mondays with a good conscience. There's a gulf between them and us: you can't bridge it over with paper. Is that what you want to do with your life, already wasted so far? The muckraking and social-worker epoch is ended: you've come too late. You can't put ointment on your sore any more with that. The workers understand you. It's your own fate you have to face, not theirs. They know about theirs and they know about you. It's the courage you lack to face yourself. But I'm going to help you. I'm going to make up for what I did to me sister, in my devotion."

"It's hard for me to understand all this," Caroline said feebly, "because I've never really met evil, or I didn't see it, I didn't think there was hate or jealousy or envy in our world; I never saw it. Recently, with your help, I've begun to see it. I know I must face the reality of the world."

"Aye, it's a hard, malicious, lined old face, the world. It's got no smile for you. It's to others, your sisters, to those who understand and pity ye must turn, not to the world."

"And there are things I don't understand even in you. Now you say you love your brother, Nellie. I know you love your sister and family. But you say your brother is selfish and light and only making a game out of his passionate beautiful love for that dead woman, a trifling and skipping you said, a borrowed air on a tin whistle. I can't see it. It's because of that I believe in him. If I can't think that's true, life wouldn't be worth living; I think he's true. That's what I thought existed in the world; and he has it."

"What he's planted in you I've got to tear out bit by bit. He's not what you think, unfortunately, a lover in a poem. He'd like to know you thought that. He never even tried to get you out of that beautiful cell of dream you live in. He's only blown you up with self-importance and vanity, a lot of silly tripe. This sudden whim shows a great weakness in you, you're ready to cling to anyone who'll feed you the moonshine you want. You're clinging to any fairy tale. I'd blush to say such a thing. You have a desire for death and the end; that's noble and true; that's connected with the best and deepest in life, that's realization. It takes courage to face what I see is in you. You're trying to run away. You wouldn't have the courage to make a death pact . . . Would you die for someone who loved you, do this for me because I ask you? Aye, I've heard of such things. I've gone down on me knees in holy humble respect, I've hidden me face for the joy and shining in it, before such a thing. And if ye could do such a thing, I'd go down on me knees before you. But would you? Has my love and respect been misplaced?"

"I could," said Caroline, faintly. "I think so. I wouldn't want the world much if someone I loved in it, died. I don't think it's my fault you don't think me brave. There was the war; I lost Barry; I lost my family. I changed towns and jobs. I poked about looking for something; I had a sort of social consciousness in me; it came from the church perhaps. Now I see that's no use, at least coming from me. But I do believe in something, though I don't now what it is. I love someone, though I'm not sure who it is."

"Ah, no, ah, no; you can't have it both ways."

Caroline was puzzled by this and said nothing.

"Am I keeping you up, when you're not well, sweetheart? Are you tired?"

"I'm a little tired, Nellie. It's the flu."

Nellie put out the light. The faint starlight coming in over the low roofs opposite showed the whereabouts of the hair on the pillows, the sheet turned down. Nellie leaned against the bedhead. . . .

Caroline was beginning to sleep.

Nellie said it was heaven to be talking to someone who understood and who was not afraid of friendship, after Tom's behavior making her so angry, teasing her in her pitiful state, "I'm afraid I blew my top!"

Caroline was grateful for her talking. She was sinking into a sweet exhaustion. Everything was peace now after the strange winds that blew through this house.

"Am I disturbing you, pet?" said Nellie, low.

"No, Nellie."

Nellie was grateful: she sang her praises. There she had been looking for a friend and the gods gave her Caroline.

"But don't you feel the need of a great friendship, the perfection communion, Caroline? Then everything would be clear as morning. You would have joy." . . .

Caroline woke up, Nellie had become excited. Caroline must give her an answer now, whether she believed in friendship. What other answer was there to the loneliness of the human being? Men offered it and tore it away again; aye, it was cruel. You set out to sea with one sail and the first storm blew it away and you were left to your fate.

Caroline, in confusion, listened and fought to understand. Poor lonely woman, sitting up all night trying to stir passions in sluggish souls, singing for herself, a nightingale, the victim of her song. As soon as she opened her throat the same passion poured; ears opened, but she went on twanging in the dark: it did not seem to matter who heard. These sympathetic thoughts fluttered over Caroline but she was too tired: she didn't care now what they both meant, this pair, the singing brother and the singing sister. . . .

Where would it end? The air was becoming unbreathable, filling with the smoke of Nellie's endless cigarettes; ash lay on the bed and pillows, it fell on Caroline's face and hair. Caroline brushed it away, Nellie leaning closer to brush her hair, dropped more ash. Once Nellie hung over the bed, her turnip head down to the floor, while she choked in spasms. But the night wore through and Nellie was wrestling still with her; for everything she said came back to the one thing, to face her loneliness bravely, not seeking pitiable expedients, to listen to the words from a true tongue, not the despicable lies and sensual fantasies of vain, depraved inconstant men, "the shameful expedient, a man's plaything. They made the world; and you believe in them? A woman knows what is in your heart and is your true sister and friend. With them is death, with me your friend is understanding at last, release, a bright morning, the first bright morning of your life." And gradually it began to come out, the story of Venna and the satanic world she had seen. "I'll tell you all—you must know everything."

When morning came, Nellie lay on her back on the bed smoking and listening to the first birds. Caroline lay face downwards with her arms under her, all about her her loose long hair.

"Are you asleep?" enquired Nellie at length.

After a time, Caroline muttered, "Yes, I will die. You are right. That's the thing. You've torn the world away from me. There's nothing else."

Nellie was incapable of saying anything, her face shining with the light of a planet. She asked in an intense low tone, controlling her excitement, "Will you die for me, Caroline? Because you understand death through me? It would be a great triumph. It would set me on my path. Your life would go along with me in me. Have you a great passion for me, Caroline? Will you do what I say? What I need is the confidence your beautiful sacrifice would give me. Then I would be the thing I am meant to be, the great leader—some saw in me. When I was a child, they saw it in me. My brother believed in me then; he knew he had nothing and I had the power. But he wandered away from me, inconstant and incredulous. But you believe. If you made the sacrifice I would look straight in the face of my destiny. Sacrifice, the blood of one dear and devoted—"

Caroline turned on her side away from her friend and looked outwards into the room without any thought in her face. Nellie, short of complete victory, became restless. She changed her clothes, made breakfast and brought it in. Caroline pushed it away. Nellie looked at her, left her to herself except occasionally to ask her questions in a low tone as if to a sleeper.

Caroline said suddenly, "I must go to work. I'm not going to let them down."

"But you're sick, you're feverish."

"You didn't care about that."

"Eh, love! I'll be your slave. Well, go then, but come home here. But you'll come then, Caroline," she said with a sudden pang. "You'll surely not run into the traps and ambushes again."

"Yes, all places are the same: why not here?"

Nellie kept murmuring anxiously and watching her; and in the end they both went off to work at the same time. Caroline had a pale glaring face, but there were many pale skinny anxious staring faces in the city going to work; and the same sort of faces sprinkled among those waiting on the benches in the outer room of the housing office. And all day, when she could hardly read or write, she heard their terrible stories, "two children, my husband and I in one room, and one child tubercular, I make two tents out of sheets to close in the children's cots"; she listened, with bent and burning head and it was just as if she saw these things for the first time.

"In a way Nellie is right; it's what I'm going through myself for the first time—if I'm to live to sixty, seventy and only then find out something for the first time, mistaken all my life, ignorant—"

When she got out of the office, Tom was there.

"I couldn't believe it when my sister said you had gone to work. I'm taking you straight home. I just got back. When I heard I drove here."

"I promised Nellie not to see you again. But I must get home somehow."

He said nothing.

"I must get home, I must get into bed."

"I must take care of you."

"That's what Nellie says. I think it's a put-up job between you. I've always suspected it. You work hand in hand."

He listened in silence to her ramblings, and at last said, "None of this is true and I ought not to leave you there; but I'm stumped. I can't take you to Blackstone now."

"I won't let you hurt me again. I won't suffer any more. I don't believe in you or in her or in anyone. Are there just vultures and ravens?"

Nellie had made an excuse and come home early. When she saw them she was speechless with rage and would not look at Tom, took the girl upstairs herself.

"I'll be back to have a talk with you, Nellie," said Tom.

But when Nellie got the girl upstairs, she flung herself into her arms and burst into a loud sobbing, "It's too much for me, Caroline. I do me best. I wish I could go with you, make a death pact and out. But there's something burning in me won't let me. And I haven't the strength for what the flame tells me to do."

Presently she became calmer and told Caroline her troubles at work; and she went on denouncing and fighting against other, darker, unnamed beings who hated her, friends who had turned against her.

"Oh, I thank my stars that I have found you."

Caroline sat listening and shivering.

"I need you, Caroline, above all: now that I have found you; now that I can give you what I need to give, a pure and lovely thing."

Caroline, fully dressed, rolled on to the bed and seemed to be asleep. . . .

VI

One Saturday morning when, having traveled on a night train, he came in for breakfast, Tom found that Nellie had invited a number of friends for a party for Caroline. . . .

"I've taken your advice, Tom: I thought some company and a drink might cheer her up . . ."

There were some women George had never allowed in the house . . . Nellie did not want George to know. George was such a nagging puritan with liquor and fun and so hard on the purse strings that Nellie couldn't have a real party with him in the house.

"So I shall be king of the May," said Tom with a poky little smile . . .

The guests began to come from their work. Some would not be free till the next day. They were all working women. Of them all, only Eliza and Nellie's friend Flo, from Bridgehead, were born in real poverty. There were one or two others he knew slightly whom he didn't like at all, Nellie's rough gang, women of forty or thereabouts, all hard workers, but too tough, even depraved and licentious, who lived like disorderly men. They gave Tom scarcely a glance. Nellie was gay, accommodating, even a little obsequious to some. Good-hearted Nellie! The mother of every stray cat. In her brave bohemian democracy she allowed no questions of morality. Tom dragged a canvas stretcher out of the shed and put it under the trees.

The women sat round talking in the front room or helped themselves to things in the kitchen. They had all brought food and drink. Tom was not regretted, he saw, when he went out to the pub. There was a pub not far away; expensive, but it was worth it. The favorite drink there was gin in beer; and there were some really old fellows who came in regularly for it. Tom liked to see bent old men having some fun, getting a little unsteady. It always went to their heads; they got their money's worth. Tom sat on his bench with his beer and watched them for quite a time. When he re-entered the house, the women all looked as if he had broken in on a board meeting.

"Have a good time," he said as he passed on his way to the kitchen.

They stared at him without appreciation. Even Nellie said nothing and stared. He felt like Uncle Simon.

"But I'm no Simon. Not even for Nell," said he to himself, seeing years ahead in a moment, George lost, Nell aging, the cynical, aging women. . . .

In the morning, Nellie was exhausted but devilishly gay, as the mood sometimes took her, and kept teasing him about his sleeping: a little anxiously perhaps.

"Sleeping like the dead all night. We called you for some brandy, didn't you hear?"

He hadn't heard and he didn't think he'd been called, either.

The women got up at various times and lounged round the house in careless undress, except one, called by her surname of Hardcast, who wore a business suit all the time, and Caroline in a cream blouse and dark blue slacks. He stared at her: his jaw dropped.

"Are you ill?"

"I didn't sleep. I haven't slept for three whole nights. Yet I feel quite lively."

"Oh, everyone sleeps without knowing it."

"No, I couldn't."

She looked it.

Nellie darted sharp glances at them when they were talking, twisting her beak and tufted head all the time.

"And did we keep you awake, pet?" she said to Caroline. "We stayed up a bit late carousing, I'm afraid, like a pack of adolescents, stealing a night out."

"No, I didn't hear you," said Caroline distantly. Nellie looked at her anxiously.

"That's like Nell," thought Tom; "so very tough in her own opinion: but as soon as anyone's cold to her, she can't take it."

He was a little annoyed with Caroline, even in her illness, for being unfriendly to his sister. Nellie worried about her like a foolish mother. It was true she had cost her a few jobs: that was Nell's idea of what was right and wrong.

Caroline had slept in the back attic, not much more than a box-room, with a low ceiling, a half-sized square-paned window looking out over the back yard. Nellie had drunk too much perhaps. She was in an overriding humor. She kept dashing in and out, teasing. She was hard to take in such a mood.

The girl did not want any lunch with them and went out to sit on the grass patch with Tom.

"I've never felt so calm," she said. "I can't sleep and it's as if that's what I've been craving. I manage to get up to go to work. While I'm riding in the bus I look at the others and think, How will I get to be like them: have so little and keep going? Going up the street I feel like collapsing between each step. I see young men like me, too: workmen. They put a foot forward, the body doesn't follow in the ordinary way but it comes forward afterwards. I'm finished."

"When you suffer, you think, I wish I could go back to that moment when it started, I would know how to choose. But what would you choose?"

She didn't hear him. She went on playing with a blade of grass. Her cheeks were thin and glowing, the skin on her neck was drooping; there were gray hairs. Her eyes had fallen into hollows. She looked up and he once more looked through their transparent lenses into her mind. He felt her feebleness, nervous incoherence, himself gave up the ghost for her. At this moment, an idea he had about her slipped loose from him. They knew they were thinking of the same evil thing: he suspected her of depravity, she suspected him of being his sister's accomplice. She drew back and looked meanly, personally accusing.

"Do you think someone has taken advantage of you?" Tom asked involuntarily.

She shrank back farther and he could see that for her he was convicted. Her interpretation was that he and Nell, not to mention the others, had taken advantage of her loneliness, nervous collapse, for an abomination of their own. Shrunk like old age, she looked at him with contempt too.

"What you think is not so!" said Tom.

She turned her eyes away. Then she looked back and said, low, hurriedly, "I'm alone in the world and I've agreed to everything Nellie wants, and I've lost my sense of honor: she can't want any more than that, so I've given everything and what have I to give anyone else? She's taken everything from me. I've ruined myself."

"Would it help you if I made her talk to you? I'll talk to her."

"You must never mention it. Never. You will be the only one to understand. I'm getting old, I'm weak, I'm like the things at Stonehenge that frightened you. I am bad, lost. She wants it."

She again gave him a dark look, indignant.

"Not you, Caroline."

"The others must do the work. I can't."

The light wind played with her wasting hair. Tom went inside and said to Nellie that there was something very wrong with Caroline. Her depression and inanition were not normal.

The women were sitting in the front room eating and drinking, smoking.

"You talk her into bed, Tom, you're good at that," said Nellie.

Tom was filling a glass, stopped with the bottle poised, looked at Nellie enquiringly.

"But what does he do when he gets her there?" said their friend Flo, a short, handsome, plump woman with white arms.

Tom picked up two glasses and a bottle.

"Tom's the darling of the middle-aged women," said Nellie: "he smiles shyly and deprecatingly and buys them bull's-eyes."

"The only bull's-eyes they'll get from him," said one of the others.

Flo sat easily, smiling at him: she liked him: but she was altogether under Nellie's thumb.

Tom went out to Caroline. Nellie entered into a roistering mood. She came to the door and blackguarded him, ordering him to come in. He came in. Nellie then went to Caroline and very roughly ordered her to come in, too. She gave Nellie a strange look, but Nellie took no notice, picked up the things, came in cursing; what did she mean turning down all her guests? What was the new phase? She didn't like masochism. Was she superior to them all? She could drink with Tom? Then she could drink with them. She had been respecting Caroline's feelings and now she found out it was a ladylike pet. None of that here, it wouldn't go. Tom was shocked and acquiescent. He had never known Nellie like this: she was rough and ready as a tart. Was there a woman of that sort among the women? He eyed them. Nellie would do anything in her rough, bohemian democracy: she would never make herself out superior to other people. Once she had lived in a prostitutes' hotel. All the girls were prostitutes. She was very friendly with one.

There was some rough joking going on to which he listened half-surprised, half-amused. He did not believe women could be really rough. "You can take a horse to water but you cannot make him drink," said Flo to Tom; it was a rough joke.

"Don't take any notice of the hags," said Hardcast, the woman in the business suit, in a loud dry voice. It was the first time she had looked at him. Tom was eating, his wind-roughened lank red face bent over his plate. Hardcast always sat stiffly about with a long-distance look; never facing people, riding sidesaddle. She had black hair plastered down. She was head of a very big, city office. She was in a position to take bread from people's mouths. Some of the women there were her subordinates. Nellie had once been one of them.

"Tom doesn't mind: he's used to our style of humor," said Flo. "I suffered enough from him and Nell when we were children. They'd always be running ahead, leaving me behind and throwing back smart cracks over their shoulders. They thought they ran Bridgehead in those days."

"I never said anything unkind to you," protested Nellie shaking her topknot eagerly.

"Everyone did. You gave me a sense of inferiority."

"Didn't I work to get you out of Bridgehead?" cried Nellie indignantly; "you owe it to me!"

"I came of myself," said Flo in an easy-going style. She was very untidy, but her chalk-blue angora sweater blazed round her beautiful arms and neck; her greasy black hair framed a fine white forehead. She was an attractive slut, uneasy when she washed. She had a good nose and missed the numerous familiar scents from her own body.

"I have a lot of the dog in me," she always said; "I like to find my way about my own house by smell. I like to smell my own children. It's healthy and natural. I feel twice the woman. Besides, I'm not strong enough to keep things clean."

Her skirt, slipping from her waist and without a fastening, gaped showing a white hip. She sat next to Tom who glanced at her flesh appreciatively and smiled at what she said. Then he began talking to the woman on his other hand, Binnie, a soft plump reddish woman about thirty-eight, dressed carelessly but in a city style, with tossed well-kept hair. She was a rover, had been all over Europe, visited every danger spot, had lovers there, probably gone there to pick up lovers. She was energetic, headed committees, made speeches, had a number of children, wrote books, spoke languages, met statesmen, gave parties, introduced one circle to another and showed no sign of it at present when she was like an effusive, garrulous, top-heavy girl.

"Tell me how you do it," she said to Tom.

"Do what?"

"Make the women dance, what's the tune?"

"I do nothing."

"Is that it?"

He laughed.

"Perhaps that's it," she said lifting her voice with a slight domineering affected accent.

"We know he does nothing," said Nellie, who with sharp, jealous, glances followed every word of the conversation.

"He flirts, that's enough," said Flo eating big dollops of pie. "He's the darndest flirt I ever met. The playboy of the Western World. Look at the footlights face!"

"A glitter like a Woolworth ring," said Hardcast, looking out of the window.

"Is that your mother's?" asked Binnie rudely of Hardcast, who wore a heavy gold wedding ring.

"My grandmother's, my mother had it," said Hardcast: "my grandmother wanted her to go into a convent."

"Better a mother than a mother superior," said Binnie.

This coarse joke made the women nervous. Binnie began to talk about the health of her children with Tom.

"Don't you ever miss children?" said one of the women teasing, to Tom.

"I have a child," said Tom. "I had one when I was twenty-one years old."

"A summer with but one rose," said the same woman.

Tom was angry.

"Leave him alone," said Nellie, who was watching everything.

"I bet you're happy now, surrounded by seven women," said the same tease.

Tom looked at the seventh woman longingly. She was a startling creature, flat and slender, with flaxen hair that she wore in an unbecoming but surprising style. She was elegant, in a plain Paris silk suit of yellow, stitched in white. Her eyelashes, eyebrows and the skin-hairs were pale. The light bathed her, soaked through her. She kept an unnatural stillness and coolness, sat in a sunny spot when she could, or lay on what golden, yellow, white, mustard, ochre lounges and cushions she could find. She was not saying anything, but knitting. She ate little and dry, at least when in public. She was knitting men's socks of thin natural wool, in a variety of fine stitches. Tom could not keep his eyes off them.

"I think I know something about knitting," he said, rising and drawing nearer. "But I've never seen anyone like you. Why don't you go in for these national knitting prizes?"

"I shouldn't care for that," she said in a sharp chiming voice.

"Stop flirting in your corner," called Nellie.

"I'm not flirting," said the yellow girl, Marilyn.

"Where are you from?" she asked Tom.

"Upstairs," said Tom, laughing.

"Bridgehead? What's it like? Would I like it?"

"In autumn, about October, just before Guy Fawkes Day it's all dark at eight, quite dark. There are a few boys and girls playing quietly round the few street lamps like moths, the rest dark, no lights, all have retreated to the back fire for high tea, curtains are drawn tight across the windows. Go down the backways and you'll see a bright stream of light through the crack of the back gate and hear the yard being scrubbed. The air is sickening, you're right in an aerial coal seam, a slowly blowing, vaguely stirring mist of coal: and the next day will be rain. In the meantime you can see the stars through a ceiling of about ten feet of coal mist."

"Don't let him put you off," cried Nell impatiently, "it's a grand old town, it's our home. It's our mother, we owe everything to it: and they think hardly of us for deserting it. We're very proud of Bridgehead."

Tom did not turn his head but continued to the yellow girl, Marilyn, "And you'll meet a ragged, grotesque troop of children with stockings of flour or sawdust or earth, saying 'A Penny for the Guy.' I always go about with a pocketful of pennies, I don't know if I got it from that time. I always have about a hundred pennies on me. I used to go about myself. I got quite a bit of money. People liked me. I was bashful, my boots were always in holes, I used to sew up the holes in my pockets myself first to be sure not to lose any pennies. The others often had this stocking bludgeon but I never wanted to bludgeon anyone; it's like a big sausage they dangle in their hands," he explained, laughing.

"Are you telling your tales?" said Nellie contemptuously from the other corner of the table. "Quit your flirting there."

"I'm not flirting," complained Tom.

He remained turned to the girl. "They used to get me to sing too: I sang willingly. I had a good voice then. I used to get money."

"Sing now," said Marilyn, looking at him with curiosity.

"It's lost now."

"Come pipe up, brother," called Nellie wildly. "Let's hear the broken pipe."

"It's broken."

"Well, croak it, but let us hear you," she cried jealously.

They were surprised. He turned round, opened his mouth, and sang,

> *"Early in the month of May,*
> *In the taverns slopped with ale,*
> *Broken-footed from the way,*

Loud sing I my threadbare tale,
There I stand, all red and pale,
Clowning in the month of May.
The bramble grows a wild white rose,
Late lay snows in Ilger's plot.
Look, my wreath is heavy with death,
All black beneath with loamy clot.
Sorrow, sorrow, sorrow, sorrow, sorrow till the end!
My heart is broken, none can mend; I must sorrow till the end."

He sang to simple quavering strains he had made up. Nellie laughed loudly and boldly.

"Aye, he can chirp like a bird in a cage: he sings to them, aye!"

"Do you sing to them?" enquired Flo, surprised.

He looked awkward, touching, outlandish. He looked queerer and stranger and twisted his mouth and eyes into odd shapes. He turned round and looked piteously across the room at Caroline who was sitting in a cold sulk by the hearth.

"You are a strange man," said Marilyn.

"Don't flatter him, sweetheart," called out Nellie: "or you'll be hearing nothing else for the rest of the weekend but his heartbreaking tales. He's not all there: there's a part missing."

"It's my heart," said Tom; "you're jealous of my heart."

At first he was angry and then he gave Nellie a splintered smile, very sly. She did not know where to look. Marilyn affected a snowy cold.

"Venus is the star I like most," Tom informed Marilyn in his ordinary tones, "it's like the mooring light of a ship that seems to be moving and isn't. I noticed last night through the roof."

"You write poetry I suppose," said Marilyn.

He assured her eagerly that he did. "In my Logbook. I never show it though. And I have ideas that wouldn't do for stories I suppose. I once knew a woman who wrote stories. She's dead now. This is an idea: a woman tall as the air and white, shaped like bells, and she has chains of rubies: you pull them off and she dies. Then I once knew a man who was fond of spiders, he told me all about them; what they felt."

Nellie began to make a great clatter, bang the china about, pour out wine, shout, swear, roughhouse, like a stableboy. Tom took no notice and went on confiding in Marilyn.

Nellie banged her plate with her knife, shouted, "Eh, young Cotter, throw me that rose, you daft fool, you do look silly in it!"

Tom took no notice but bent his head nearer and went on chatting.

"Thomas is not a good name for you," said Marilyn.

"It's not my name, it's my father's name. I have no name of my own," he replied.

"What do you do?"

"I can heal some people," he said. "I should have been a doctor I expect. If I knew how, combined with my feeling for people, and if I practiced, I could cure people. I'd like to do that."

"What's your brother saying?" asked Flo of Nellie.

"I don't know," said Nellie, "but he's bogus."

"He's saying that he can heal," Hardcast's voice was heard.

"He can give women children, I suppose, that's the kind of miracle he can perform," said Binnie.

"No, pet, he can't, but he can get the women thinking about children. They have only to look at those big eyes sailing right out of his head and they start sighing for a boy," said Nellie, "a boy under a flowering May tree, isn't that so, Tom?"

Tom stopped talking and stared at her.

She cackled, "Eh, eh, I made you stop the sweet drool."

He looked at her sternly.

"Eh, Cushie, you remind me too much of Bridgehead," said Eliza; "don't do it."

Nellie laughed, was so pleased she seemed to fly, eyes winking, hair sticking out like straws, arms akimbo, legs flying about, shoulders waggling, she sketched a fairy hobbledehoy, a woman cut free from the earth.

"Airmen are a great blessing, they can drop in on a woman anywhere," said Flo.

"You can make your selection as they parachute past," said someone else.

"Let them go past," said Nellie; "we're all right."

Tom got up to go out. He stepped through their crossed legs. They were drawn away from the table, close together. Their legs, the stool legs, the chair legs, the bottles and glasses formed a series of circles and the late sun coming through the back, spread its rays through them. He had to cross the empty space to get out. He stopped in the middle, looked round and taking the rose from his ear, threw it to Eliza. Nellie instantly threw her wineglass at his hand as if to stop him. She was half drunk: it was one of George's best wineglasses. A few drops of blood fell onto George's green carpet. He took his hand with the other hand and caressed it, held up the smear of blood.

"You fool," she said.

"Bad thing," said Tom.

"What's that for?" said Marilyn.

"It's just something they do in their family," said Florence.

Tom made his way out.

"I'm sorry, pet," said Nellie, rushing round.

"No, you're not," said Tom.

"Did I hurt you, pet?"

"You didn't kill me."

"Forgive your dumb sister, Tom."

"I don't mind horseplay."

"I'm a beast to you, Tom."

"You're a sweir beast," he said and went out.

Flo laughed and sang from the old ballad, "For Nellie is a sweir beast and canna cross the wa-ter."

Nellie gave her a dark look.

He went for the earliest of his trains, leaving the house about five; and Nellie did not try to keep him back. He was rather angry at being forced out and at the neglect. He had folded up his canvas bed and stood it in the shed, pushing his little tin trunk into a corner of the attic; and put out some canvas shoes, a flying suit and an old leather flying-jacket for Nellie to give to the bazaar. He mentioned these things to Nellie as he was leaving.

"Do you mind if I give them to poor Walter the window cleaner, Tom? I know you don't take to him, but he needs them."

"You know me better."

"You're leaving me in anger, Tom."

"Don't do anything I wouldn't do."

"You'll telephone me tomorrow night, won't you, Tom? Before I go."

"I'll do my best."

"And write to me, pet, give me all the news." . . .

The women in Lamb Street sat round talking, smoking, eating and were, in their relations with Caroline, stand-offish, friendly, curious, reticent, according to what they thought of her. Some of the women were journalists. They were all, but the yellow girl, central London women. They talked about political chances, news of the day, Fleet Street secrets, journalists who had lost their jobs, of special interest to them who were mostly middle-aged or on the verge of it. They were somewhat reserved in this matter towards the yellow girl, who was the youngest of them all and avid and, so it was said by them, unscrupulous: but perhaps that only meant she was younger.

They were least aware of Caroline, but she looked at them as through a block of ice, a woman lost in a glacier and some time after ten, she said she must go up to her bed in the attic: she did not know if she could sleep this night.

"The attic population always goes to bed early," said Nellie.

Caroline did not sleep but was swept along in the deep river of a lucid delirium, and, meanwhile, she vaguely heard noises in the house, music played, voices. After some length of time, she heard footsteps on the attic landing. They stopped outside her door which was presently, after some breathing pause, gently opened and shut. She lay for a while and then got up, went to the door, opened it. There was no one there. The stairs creaked, but the ceiling, stairs and walls always creaked there. The ceiling, for instance, in the attic room creaked all night. She looked over the banisters and saw nothing, though the bottom hallway was light with moon. The attic landing was dark, there being no window at the back there but moonlight fell in the empty room beside her through the skylight. The skylight was slightly raised and a soft air blew through the room. There was a bare grocery box standing under the skylight. A slender, male figure lurked just inside the open door.

"Caroline," said a voice.

She had a moment of excruciating fear. She saw in a moment that it was Nellie dressed in an airman's suit and that her open gash of a mouth was smiling and that her long hand had beckoned her. She had a thought that Nellie meant her some harm in the room, even to kill her. Nellie moved over and was standing stooping under the skylight, and nodded to her to come in: she smiled like a clown in the moon-shade. Caroline went and stood on the box Nellie showed her and looked out from the skylight first at the late light of the sky and then down, down said the nod and the finger, into the back yard. Nellie also struggled for a place on the box: their hands gripped the window frame and the moon shone on Nellie's pointed face. Nellie looked quickly at her, excited, sharp, the clever smirk. The box tipped and Nellie quickly caught her round the waist. Caroline kept looking down with astonishment, and Nellie gripped her harder.

A number of naked women were rounding, breaking, wrestling, weaving together in the back yard between the brick walls, the high fence and the tree. The moonlight showed that some were rosy in the daytime, others were the colors of night-lighted fish and they were like queer fish, a seahorse, an old man snapper, a gar, a toadfish, a puffball and one rather awkward and hesitant was as yet, only a woman: and what was more ludicrous, partly dressed.

Nellie laid her beak and her chin over her shoulder with a sharp penetrating smile, her face wore its highest look of animal intelligence. Caroline looked at this human living and moonflowering wreath in the back yard a moment till she distinguished the creatures, then she disengaged herself from the strong embrace and climbed down while Nellie after a poignant glance looked once more out of the skylight. She clung to the frame, her gaunt snowy face poked forward and with passion, surveyed the tenants of the globular moony night.

She put out her hand to touch Caroline's head, nothing was there; Caroline had gone. She looked still, expecting to see Caroline join them downstairs: she didn't. With a slight smile still she stalked after her like a shadow in the close-fitting and becoming dark suit. Was there a movement just off the stairs? She kept smiling, and followed for she thought Caroline had gone down. She went out and looked about among the women who were not excited enough to keep that slow rhythm up long.

"Where is Caroline?" her clear voice called. She went back and looked in the rooms, beginning with the ground floor. "Caroline, Caroline darling!" The house was still and living. The moon struck the faces of the little houses opposite and shone on the square panes.

"Caroline's there!" said a voice from the back yard.

She went hurrying out with her yearning intense face full of delight. "Ah, pet, where are you?"

But she was not there at all, someone had seen her at the upstairs window for a moment.

Caroline had dressed. She went down one flight and sat on the stairs, thinking she was going to fall because her heart was beating so heavily: she got up again, staggered into the empty front room, and sat down in the armchair. It was dark. Someone stood at the back entry: a voice said, "I'll get her, it'll do her good: we must help her," and footsteps thudded, a strange-shaped naked woman began to appear above the hall floor through the banisters, hank of hair, half-moon face, neck like a can, thickset shoulders, spidery arm after spidery arm, long shank after long shank. The woman complete, some sort of crab, moved past the dark door and went up the other stairs. This sight pulled Caroline together. She heard the fleshy footsteps on the next floor and the voice. In the back yard was a sweet poignant whistling, which to her mind

grew louder and louder, seemed to whistle through the walls and meanwhile upstairs she heard her name. A woman, too, came in from the
yard.

She gently pushed the door to. She was lazy with terror, her heart
bursting. There were steps on the stairs coming up, she heard her name
in various parts of the house. The door came slowly open. Nellie stood
there smiling, her gaunt jaws slightly open. There were some whispered
words. Nellie came in and Caroline groaned. She got up, pushed past
Nellie and went downstairs, while Nellie stood watching. The staircase
came down facing the front door. The soft old lock opened easily. She
began to run, fell down the steps which she had forgotten. She fell flat
knocking her breath out, so that for a while she lay rolling there, and
tried to roll to the road. No one came out, she heard only soft urgent
voices through the door, held to.

She got up and walked clumsily away. She walked about the streets
in that area and then as if the streets unrolled themselves before her
in one direction only, she walked that way, rapidly as if she had an
address in another part of London to go to. Her head was empty and
she knew she was exhausted but found it strange how well she could
keep going. She passed miles, acres. In the streets were the odors of
summer and aged housing. The moon shifted. In these houses were
strangers occupied in struggling for breath, not much more. She did
not want to know any more about them, the wretchedness and fatigue
were too general. There was something else. She had seen the riot,
scandal that was the flowering of the force of nature in some, the strong
wildness, that was anger, the perversity, the nonchalant feeble depravity, the indifference to degradation in others. Though she burned purer
and hotter than ever, and detested vice more than before, she had also
become gentle and indifferent about it: it was their way and they were
human. If people had tuberculosis or cancer they were still entirely
human. Her dislike of all these things, misery, perversity and disease
was stronger than ever; and she knew that she had got into the wrong
circle.

She was sorry she had come to London, but there was nothing to go
back to. Differently from Nellie, she could see that Nellie had an idea
in her constant advice about submitting. It might seem strange in a
beaky, restless, gabby person like Nellie to chatter about submission,
hypocrisy with an aim in it, but Nellie in her blue half-lights lit on
aspects of existence. Was it because she had never submitted and could
not, that she had not kept Barry and never had a friend? "Sink the

turbulent selfish soul," said Nellie, who never did that—or did she sometimes in her excesses? Caroline had no temperament for excesses. "You are afraid of beauty," said Nellie, "you just want grand, impetuous life to provide you with a living; you'll never be an artist."

Caroline had taken submission as a word that Nellie used for her own purposes as she used Introspection and Friendship. By introspection she meant a shameless curiosity and crafty use of her knowledge; by friendship what only a clique meant; and it was dishonest since she trapped people that way. But Nellie was ill, and by submission she might mean death, it might be a preconception of death which only the sick could have. And this chilling submission was what Caroline for the first time was feeling now. Caroline now floated along over-shadowed by the lank, hobbling stride of the woman who had taken her up, haunted her, and ruined her. She was walking away from her, but Nellie was someone she carried with her, as you carry a bad parent always with you; Nellie had got into her being, like the knowledge of drunkenness. There had been nothing in Bridgehead, Nellie said, to satisfy their youthful intellectual and moral hungers, so they had taken to drink, vice, unbridled chaotic speculation and gnawing at each other. Hunger will prey on garbage, rather than be extinguished in death. But Nellie had not called it garbage, she called it knowledge. . . .

As she walked she became aware of someone behind her. She stood still. The moon was still slanting and a faint wind blowing like a drapery, touching her off and on. She heard a giant stride behind her, very soft; it came from up the street towards her. An agreeable nondescript young man with cropped hair was there and wearing something loose, like coolie trousers and coat and a yard or so of uncut pale material over his shoulders. He stood faintly dark against the moonlight which slanted behind him. Caroline knew all this without seeing it. It was behind her. She heard two more strides behind her, an enormous, silent gust and his hand touched her coat lightly, with a wave of air and motion.

"Is it an unknown or death? Is it real?"

She waited but nothing more happened. She walked on, seeing behind her, without looking, the long moonlit and shadowy street. "Three great sighs, three great strides." She began to rest as she walked. Morning was coming into the moonlight, two fluids which did not mix well. There were a lot of people everywhere about at first, and she sat down to have tea in a place full of men. On the dirty table top she wrote a letter to Nellie. She had to write to Nellie, who wanted it and who understood her. Then she wrote a note to the office telling them she was ill and they had better not expect her that day. They gave her envelopes and stamps and she posted the letters outside and began to walk again, though her head was turning.

She went down to the canal and had a look at it. People were about, there were trams full of people going to work and also sightseers. Everything seemed so strange. It was as if she had just come into this world.

Now the men had gone and there were women about. She walked; she could not think. Only to lie down or to climb.

At last she saw an immense apartment building, large rooms, steel girders, brickwork and the frames of windows; everything was rented in advance, a notice said in front. She climbed up a long way through the building and when the first man questioned her she said calmly she was going to see Mr. Whistler, the name of a man in an office she had worked in. "Whistler? Who's he?" were the last words she heard. She went as far up as she could and jumped onto a terrain of the sort she had always liked to play on when a child, clay, lime and sand pits, wheelbarrows, piles of bricks, and plenty of lost nails everywhere. She died that day and was not identified for two days since no one was looking for her; she had at that moment no settled address and she was a long way from Islington.

THE RIGHTANGLED CREEK: A SORT OF GHOST STORY

"The Rightangled Creek" is one of a collection of four novellas published in 1967 under the title *The Puzzleheaded Girl*. Here the author's ability to create ominous atmosphere is as impressive as her insights into the dislocated and fragmented personalities that inhabit the house on Chesapeake Bay.

The road rises steeply from Lambertville on the Delaware, into hill country, bared for planting and grazing, with small old white villages in trees and unpainted farmhouses high on the ridges. The road follows the uplands. Several miles along, entering Newbold Township, a track turns right and down by Will Newbold's red barn, a landmark. The track drops between Newbold's homepatch and the pasture for their famous red and white herd; and, on the other side, some acres of corn and alfalfa. It drops into trees between stony ridges on which live poor Austrian and German farmers, down to a narrow creek. This tiny creek first appears as a meander in a wet place, and then as a wallow, where a broad soft meadow declines into swamp, where Sobieski's black and white cattle lounge all day in a hemicycle of trees, till they are called in the evening, Cow, cow, cow, by Sobieski's little boys. Above, it becomes a creek, falling from a series of rocky saucers from which the transparent water drips between banks of poison ivy, elder and tiger lilies. In the saucers are elvers and other small fish; and where the track and the creek together make a right-angled turn and go east, a trickle from the Strassers' rocky infertile ridge has made a deep cut, passing under a strong wooden bridge in which there is a loose plank. This plank is kept loose at one end to tell who is passing: a footstep, *lunk!* a car, *lonk-lonk!* It is heard in the daytime in the fields; at night, much louder, it wakes from sleep: "Who is that, so late?" But it is above this thin trickle from the hill and going higher and eastward that the creek broadens to several feet, deepens to eighteen inches and more, and threaded with current, planted with waterweed, is lively with eels, fish and watersnake. Now, with a wooded ridge on the right hand, on the left it has turned around a small patch of cleared bottomland, on which stands a double cottage Pennsylvania style, and a big barn. A solid wooden bridge crosses from the road into this clearing, under a magnificent pin-oak and a few other trees, beside the barn; and this clearing of not more than two acres of bottomland, fenced off from Sobieski's rising rounded meadows, with the rightangling creek, coming along a panhandle from Sobieski's cattle-wallow and running east suddenly along another panhandle, turning all around Sobieski's hill, getting deeper and wider under heavier and more tangled bushes, is Dilley's place. For some strange reason, the whole creek in this corner belongs to a piece of land too small to farm; and on this tiny piece of land stands a new barn large enough for a tractor and farm machinery and the well-built house, part stone, with stone cellar and attic, part wood with double porches and upper story.

"That's it," said the taxi-driver to his one passenger, a stubby dark man with bright blue eyes. They passed the cattle-wallow, the car hobbling over ruts and stones, they entered a passage of tall trees, not disturbing two immense affable ravens on the first half-dead sky-searching bough. Low set in the green, below the pouring ivy and lightblow of tiger lilies, ahead through thick leaves, was the cottage, with a set of shining windows. All the other farmhouses bare on the hilltop were blistered and weathered bone-white or raw; this one was fresh in buff and red. Ringed with high fields, waters, trees and overgrown ridges, with its lines flowing toward the brook, low set and like a pumpkin flower, the cottage was spellbinding. The April afternoon was rather quiet. A flock of gold canaries flew through tall weeds. Between the weeds and the creek a lanky soft-molded woman in turban and trousers, with a heavy fork was trying to turn the sods, in an irregular vegetable patch: a fine day, a west wind, a paper-chase of torn cloud blowing over, and coolness with the shadows. The house had two porches, two pitched roofs and, at the back two tall stone chimneys. The spring sun with the birds bathing in it lay on the track. They passed the warning plank, and a large mail box on a post with the name: Laban Davies.

Said the passenger: "Put me down here. I'll give them a surprise. I came straight here from Paris. They don't know I'm in America. I knew Mr. and Mrs. Davies in Paris. We're old friends. They'll be glad to see me. My name's Sam Parsons. If I stay here, you'll see me around, my friend."

"I see Mr. Davies often in Lambertville when he goes to mail his packages," said the taxi-driver. "My name's Newbold."

Parsons crossed the bridge which was the only entrance into the place, crossed the tussocks and stones, dropped his little valise by the open kitchen door, went around the house, creekside; but the woman in the vegetable patch, her tired face turned away, did not hear him above the wind and water. Parsons approached smiling, waited, came closer, walked up to the edge of the fresh sods. The woman went on pushing the fork with her sandled foot, she stooped to pick out a vineroot, threw it on the burning pile.

"Hello, Ruth, hello!"

With her foot on the fork, she looked up, looked into his face with dull anxiety. He was a dark mass against the sun. She took off her spectacles.

"Sam! Oh, my stars! How did you get here?" She began to laugh, showing her strong white teeth.

"I thought you were in Europe! Oh, wait till Laban sees you! Oh, Sam, oh, my brother."

Sam laughed and waved his hands, his wide mouth opened, showing his buck teeth, creamy and broad, and his wide throat: his blue eyes opened and shut.

She was pumping his hand and beginning to weep. He kissed her.

"Here I am, yes, here I am! Not there, here! Ruth, my sister. Ha-ha-ha. What's the matter, old girl?"

"Oh, Sam, you helped us, you helped us. We've never forgotten."

"It was nothing. I was broke that time and couldn't help you much."

"Oh, Frankie has never forgotten. He wanted to stay in Paris, with the man with the money, you remember, the man with the money?"

"The man with all the money—ha-ha!"

"Excuse me calling you my brother, Sam; I feel like that."

"Ha-ha-ha—I feel as if you're my sister. Ha-ha."

"How did you find us? No one knows we're here."

"Don't you remember you sent us a Christmas card last Christmas?"

"Did I? It was a hard winter, Sam," said she. "Where's Clare, but where's Clare?" she continued suddenly looking everywhere, to the porch, the tall weeds. "Oh, she's hiding! Oh, what a surprise," and she began to laugh.

"Clare's in New York: she'll be down. I don't leave my wife behind when I travel."

"Some do, but you wouldn't," said Ruth.

They entered the framehouse by the downstream porch.

"This is a typical way of building 'round here," said the woman. "A farmer builds himself a frame house and when the son grows up, he builds on a stone one for the young couple. You see it more across the river in Pennsylvania than here."

In the wooden house there was only one room downstairs, the big farm kitchen with its two doors, two porches, a long range of windows warm with the sun and warm with the big wood-and-coal stove with its double oven, standing in the center. There was a table, a few chairs, some tubs, a sink and a pump beside it. "We save money here, I do everything," she said in her warm round voice in which there was a strident note. On the stove was a white enamel coffee pot; on the table a thick white cup half full of cold black coffee. There was also a closet; but this turned out to contain a staircase leading to the second-story rooms in the wooden house. Ruth called and explained pleasantly.

"Laban, it's Sam!"

Footsteps irregularly came down the stairs somewhere in the house, though there was no one there. "There's another staircase; it's in the stone house." They went up a step into the stone house.

The sitting-room there had only two small windows and was dark. Laban stood there, a couple of yards from the doorway, looking at them; and then rushed forward with his big hands outstretched, crying, "Sam!" and kissed Sam on both cheeks.

"I couldn't think who Sam was! I'm working and not to be disturbed. Company's not good for me. I mean some company; the sort we're likely to get."

He was a tall thin countryman, in slippers, bare elbows, spectacles, a home-knit waistcoat. His fair hair was thin and turning gray, the large hollow eyes were a transparent blue; he had a knife-edge nose and hollow cheeks. A horrible scar ran from below the ear on the left side of his face up into the scalp which was bare at that place. The flesh had knitted roughly in the old wound.

They sat down at the table and drank black coffee from the white enamel pot. It was on the stove all day for Laban, who drank three or four pots a day—bad for his heart, but it kept him at work. He was working well now. They had taken the farm for two years at twelve dollars a month, a very low rent. They had been lodging over in the artists' colony on the Delaware, New Hope on the Pennsylvania shore, and had seen this place, Dilley's place, advertised in a store. They had rented it from old Mr. Dilley who was retired, they believed, and lived in Jersey City. They lived on country produce, home-grown potatoes, little meat. If Laban's book, a history of European culture, sold, they might buy this place from old Mr. Dilley to have a home in the country for their boy, Frankie, who was now twelve years old, and who was to go to one of the big colleges.

Sam Parsons was a very lively man and had a lot to say about Paris, though Laban himself was in closer touch with literary people over there. He said in a dignified way, "You probably noticed my big mail box."

Sam had no fixed plans. He wanted to look around for a place for himself and his wife in New York City. The Davieses said he must stay with them. They had plenty of room, three bedrooms upstairs, and even a small boxroom with windows that would do, when they got a couch. They bought their provisions in big quantities at the beginning of each month. Sam, who was a writer, and his wife, an illustrator, could work there. "You won't be disturbed." No one had this address but Laban's agent. "Lambertville is too near to New Hope. We never go to Lambertville, where Laban would be recognized. According to Jeroboam's wishes, Jeroboam being our twenty-dollar Ford, we shop each month in Flemington, Hopewell or even Princeton."

It was to Princeton that they hoped to send Frankie, if they could buy the place and if Laban could sell enough. The only true drawback here was that Frankie had to go to the local school, eleven pupils taught by a young city girl, in a small shed. "We take him there in Jeroboam. The pupils are country boys and girls of all ages, mostly rough and backward, destined to be village gossips and wiseacres," said Laban. Frankie had easy victories: he deserved better teaching. But Laban's work came first this year. He had already completed one volume and had sent it off to Paris, asking a celebrated French scholar to write an introduction.

"With typical French negligence and improbity, a rascally, shallow nation, Lebeau, who wrote me such flattering letters in Paris, does not now even answer my letters. Naturally, if I could pay him, I would hear soon enough. But I can't pay; and I think scholars should help each other, without dirty money coming into it. He wrote me a letter recognizing me as one of the leading American cultural experts," said Laban. "Probably he flattered me, expecting me to put him over in this country."

But Laban began to smile. His spectacles shone, he became excited and went out to the barn, got out Jeroboam, took Parsons to get Frankie, all the time talking about his work, his contacts, literary life abroad. Laban was a self-taught man, a ditch-digger's son, become a city desk man, turned to literature. Working with irritability, energy, spite, prejudice and vanity, and a nose for the trends, he had set up a remarkably wide circle of useful acquaintance in many countries. He brought out anthologies of writing in language he could not read, re-translated famous works, wrote introductions to others; had built himself a solid reputation in America. These works were all potboilers; yet Laban had taste, judgment and cunning, and was a literary figure.

When Laban returned he showed his workroom, files, schedules, correspondence; and then the bedrooms. They kept all doors and windows open all the time, merely shutting the downstairs doors at night. The doors and windows all over the house commanded every part of their land; the track, the creek, the two bridges, the Sobieski's cattle. "The Empress Eugenie and her court," said Laban. The cattle lounged handsomely under the trees on the grassy knoll beneath which the house lay. They were sheltered and surrounded by sweet waters and grasses.

No one had ever bothered them. Last winter had been dry and the roads easy. They had gone to distant towns for their groceries. The mailman came twice a day. They went to the Newbolds' to telephone. Frankie had friends at school, especially the fine little Sobieski boys who did all the work on the farm with their widowed mother; and the lively little Tanner boys, two Negro lads, sons of a very fine man who lived in the back-streets and by hereditary right had the business of cleaning the outhouses for the whole community. Sometimes Frankie went with them to the Delaware and along to Trenton; at other times they explored the creeks and woodlands; or they got to know everyone in town; real boys.

"Frankie has got everyone tabbed," said his mother: "he knows everyone in Newbold Township as well as the doctor or the sheriff. He has political genius, Sam."

And the father said that if his books sold, they could have two cars, one for Frankie at Princeton. "We can manage with another edition of Jeroboam."

Laban went back to work. Sam went to perambulate along the grassy track under old trees. He met Frankie with the two Tanner boys. They were all going birdnesting. Sam returned to the homestead with Frankie's thin hand in his short square one; and both talked politics. Frankie, last seen a big-eyed starveling of six, was unrecognizable in this self-confident stripling, with acid prattle, deliberate views. He referred to "the party line," criticized all writers of left literary bent if they deviated, as men will, from his stiff-necked views. But Sam laughed at him, the boy allowed his old charm to flash out; and they laughed, returning like a good-tempered child and a sensible man.

The days passed. The Davieses were poor but would not allow their guest to provide anything. The first item in their budget was tires and repairs to the old Ford; then, flour, potatoes, bacon, coffee, cigarettes, typewriter supplies and stamps; next, milk, eggs, and occasionally a fowl from Mrs. Sobieski on the hill. Mrs. Sobieski was Ruth's only friend in the district. The vegetable garden by the creek, with only Ruth to work in it, had not yielded. Laban went straight from bed and table to his desk. Frankie was being raised as a straight clean American boy, with woodlore and boy's friendships; and ahead of him, his brain, his dizzying future. Ruth, the mother of them both, and now of three, cleaned, cooked and dug, worked the pump, chopped wood, brought coal, collected sticks, heated water and carried tubs, scrubbed linen, spread it and ironed it; fixed blinds, mended doors, carried food to the deep cellar. She had been a strong girl, brought up in jolly health, a success in a small town. Now she was overworked, uneasy and cranky: she saw dangers all around them. The Davieses voted Democrat. Mr. Thornton the rich farmer on the next hill, who collected their rent for the Dilleys, voted Republican. He and Will Newbold were heads of the local farmers' co-operative and charged the rate agreed, fourteen cents a quart for their pasteurized milk. They were all rich farmers, long established; some of the families went back over two hundred years in that district; some had first fraternized with the mild Leni Lenape.

Mrs. Sobieski, poor and a newcomer, like the Austrian and German farmers, did not belong to the co-operative, but sold her uninspected milk for eleven cents a quart. She was a young widow with six boys and a girl to bring up; she had to get rid of her farm produce around the neighborhood. Ruth was preoccupied with these troubles. The farmers might use their own unpasteurized milk. The summer visitors were "typical bourgeois hygienic snobs" and would only buy pasteurized milk from the rich farmers. And there was a well-to-do German family living on the terraced ridge just below the Newbold farmers, who had plenty of water and spoke to no one, "typical Nazis." The Austrian farmers on the ridge opposite were shy, ignorant, peculiar people, too poor to get their cow serviced, so that it had bellowed all last summer rubbing its hungry flanks on the fence; you could see the hairy railings now. There were two black-eyed sulky full-grown sons, who went past without speaking and drove furiously to town on Saturday afternoons.

Ruth, brought up in a town, was quite at home in all the cults and sects of any metropolitan society, and very uneasy here. Laban, bred in a farming community of the Middle West, was knowing and sarcastic about all his neighbors. Frankie learned all these opinions from his parents, and all the local news from the Tanner and Sobieski boys; and the three of them, anxious and hungry, lived in a ferment of distrust.

Sam Parsons was a great one for going to the mail box. He waited for the mailman at the other end of the track near the ravens' tree. Laban said, "If no newspaper comes and no letter, I don't worry. All I love is here. No radio, no local news, I don't care. If the cities go up in smoke, ditto. Nothing can happen to us here. Ruth is here and Frankie is here; and I am here. Ruth has no other interests but Frankie and me; and Frankie when the time comes will have all we can give him." Frankie, listening to this, leaned back in his chair, while his gaunt mother, in her turban and overalls, hustled between stove and table feeding the three men with toast, cereal and coffee.

"I'll have eggs this morning," said Frankie.

"Give him some eggs," said Laban.

"If he asks for them, he needs them," said she.

Frankie remarked, "I was in the post office at Ingalls yesterday with the Tanner boys, when a man came in to buy eggs. Don't buy eggs from Mrs. Smith, the post mistress here, I told him, she overcharges and she gets her eggs form the Strassers, they're Austrian dirt-farmers. Their hens come over into our farm all day and peck our grass. They're not properly fed. I'm always chasing them off. They get drowned in the creek sometimes. Those Strassers don't know how to farm and they overcharge. They belong to the Bund. Do you want to encourage Bundists, I asked him. They stick together, they cheat and they're enemies of the Republic. You must go to Lambertville, or go to Mrs. Sobieski's farm just along the road and you'll get eggs for twenty-three cents a dozen. They're not candled, but no need; she sells all she has. Mrs. Smith told me to get right out and said I had no right to spoil her trade; but I told her very plainly she had no right to cheat the public and that I wouldn't let her get away with it. I told her I'd make people aware. A friend of mine has a printing press in Lambertville, I told her that; and I said, if necessary I can have leaflets printed."

This was greeted with a silence that surprised Parsons. "How do you know the Strassers are Bundists?" he asked.

"They must be Bundists, they're Austrians and sulky bad people, too mean to spend a cent on their farm. The boys go to Lambertville every

Saturday night and get drunk. You'll hear them coming home at two in the morning."

"That doesn't prove that they're Bundists," said Laban; "but they are, in fact, Bundists. I'm sure they vote Republican if they vote at all."

"I'm not going to allow Bundists 'round here to make a living," said the boy; "they've got to be driven out. I told Mrs. Smith I'd close her store if she kept on selling Bundist eggs. At any rate, the man was scared and he went out. Mrs. Smith said she'd make me pay for the lost sale. I said, No, indeed she wouldn't; and it wasn't the last dozen eggs I'd lose her."

Laban was leaning back looking his boy in the face and his own face was shining as if in the sun.

"Well, by gum, Frankie," said Sam, "aren't you ashamed to take the bread out of people's mouths? What crust, my lad! You're a twelve-year-old school kid and you go running about ruining people's business and uttering threats. Supposing Mrs. Smith came to the school and said, Don't teach Francis Davies, he's a numskull, I don't like his looks, put him on a stool in the corner."

Frankie laughed heartily at this. "Oh, it wouldn't work," he cried. Sam Parsons was laughing and the father smiled a little; but the poor mother did not like it. She said that the farmers in the co-op put an unjust price on the eggs, where her poor widowed friend could not get rid of all hers even at a cutthroat price. She was sabotaged; and as for the Strassers who under-sold the co-op, it was not the same thing, for they were European individualists, dirt-farmers, mean, dangerous, vindictive. Embittered by ill-luck, and their hard-won failures, they were ready to join the Bund at any moment: they formed a solid pro-Nazi bloc in spirit. If people did not stand with the Democrats, the Bundists and Mr. Thornton would turn Newbold Township into black reaction.

"But I happen to know that this section has been copperhead since the beginning; they're too durn sly to side with anyone," said Sam Parsons.

When the boy had gone out to play and they heard him hallooing innocently along the track with his friends, Ruth said kindly to Sam Parsons that they were careful not to make any attacks on Frankie's self-esteem; they wanted him to have a perfect sense of security, to be sure of their love. At school he was of course a prizewinner. He had a vivid imagination and he might easily have a nightmare tonight at the scene of disgrace evoked by Sam. "Supposing he dreamed of failure!"

"Surely no boy is as brittle as that!" said Parsons.

But the parents explained that Frankie was not like other boys, but a genius; and all his idiosyncrasy was only that of genius of a high order. He slept feverishly and often called out in his sleep; he dreamed about political enemies, thought he was making speeches. He had a particular ferocity against the "half-savage backward and medieval individualists" of this part of the country. This phrase Laban read from a diary which he kept of his son's remarks.

At each meal, the conversation turned to political matters; and while Laban listened and interjected, both men argued and the boy laid down the law; the mother, always on her feet, hurried from stove to table serving. The child developed his ideas. He listened in silent satisfaction, however, when his parents spoke about his future; but the reality of his genius, the certainty of his eminent future, was so often discussed and as a matter of course, that he had no fatuity. His future was a rather important fact in the future history of the country; he would possibly be President. Afterward he ran about with the children of the hereditary outhouse cleaner and the Polish widow's sons, while the parents listened to his distant voice and yearned after the thin child running like a rabbit in the hills.

Laban said, "We don't feel any sacrifice is too great; we don't need anything ourselves; we have each other."

"You see," said the mother, hastily cleaning up the table and setting a fresh pot of black coffee between the men, "a boy like that especially must not be frustrated in any normal desire or deprived of any normal object. Satisfaction is release of energy, it is victory. That's why we want a good car for him, too. Here it's the symbol of achievement, it's the normal means of personal expression in this country: it's release of power for every individual; it means normal living. We were brought up with older symbols, symbols of poverty. But he must be normal in this age."

"Yes, in a few years Frankie will live in rooms in Princeton or Harvard and have his car and spend money. I would walk to Princeton or hitchhike to Harvard to see him; and if, when I got there, I saw his car parked there and him in good clothes, a leader in his society, I would know that I was right in denying him nothing."

"You see, Laban knew what deprivation was. It didn't do him any good. It doesn't do any of us any good," she said, beginning to weep suddenly, but still hurrying with her work. "We blame Laban's troubles on his early frustrations: the struggle is too hard, too hard." She turned her back to them and began vigorously washing pot and pans.

"And for you," said Parsons, "why don't you go back to town? You mean—the rent?"

"It's for Laban: he's on the wagon," said Ruth, now cheerful again. "Back in town he gets into that drinking set. He wants to get his books done. He needs success: he needs fulfillment. Adversity was always bad for him. He needs recognition. No one knows where we are: and when we come out of the woods, Laban will have his reputation made. That's why we're so glad to see you. Laban has an intellectual equal in the house; and you never touch the booze."

Sam was very happy at this and talked for some time about how much coffee he drank and how it had been in his boyhood; as much coffee as you could drink at Child's, for a nickel; and how he almost bankrupted the place; and probably because of him they had changed the rule; and how, after meetings, when he was a boy, they had all gone to a Greek baker's, and over only one cup of coffee for a nickel, and perhaps a roll, they had talked till two or three in the morning. They could see that though he had been very poor, he had been happy and had fulfillment.

In between his working-spells, Laban with Sam, in Jeroboam, scoured the low Jersey hills, past cornfields and barleyfields, lost farms where the cattle and farmers watered at an outdoor trough, where nothing was to be seen but low long fences, a big barn sometimes broken, a shaky hovel surrounded by children, pigs, dogs. The river was now fat, the tasseled maize turned red, the wheat yellow, the wind blew dry, strong, the air was full of dust, pollen and mites. Laban would often stop halfway in a winding rutted track in a place free of trees in a yellow land, and snuff it up. In the distance, perhaps, would be the Delaware and the Pennsylvania hills turned yellow and red. Laban had then more of the hobbledehoy; he was full of shouting and joy; and in these days he brought out an old manuscript which he had written as a farm laborer. He then wrote of trees, moons, moonlit cornfields, long open stretches of bearing soil where he worked and grew dry; a man, a farm laborer lying dead drunk by the fence, in the silver, in the moon.

The two men would wait for young Frankie outside the school. In the morning, they would wait for Newbold the mailman, walking up and down the sunny track. "See the humming birds sitting on the twig: he's off and back quicker than the speed of sight," said Laban. Sam could not see so fast. Sometimes, they were off somewhere when the mailman sounded his horn for Laban's registered letters. One day when

Sam returned from one of his walks, which always lay along the green tracks where the careless rabbits sat in the ruts, he found the Davies couple very nervous. Laban was drinking black coffee in a determined manner, and Ruth was sitting at the table rucking up the tablecloth with her fingers and talking hurriedly.

"Read it," said Laban, pushing a letter across the table to Sam. It was a scribble saying:

> Ha, old Laban, you old horsethief! We just found out your hideaway from someone New Hope way who saw you scorching up the Jersey hills. We made enquiries of your mailman. We hear you're on the wagon; well we're coming to drag you off it. Expect us: we're on our way. The Rosses are throwing a big shindig Saturday: we all want you there! Tell the good gray mare we're coming to get you off the chain. Nuts to Ruth. What's the idea, chaining up the best drunk in the U.S.A.? Nuts. The Old Bunch.

There followed a dozen signatures.

"I felt something impending," said Laban. "I felt anxiety."

"If you could go out and dig the potato patch," said his wife, "you might work it off; it's the mental concentration."

"I hate digging; I'm an ex-farmboy. If I stop writing and do physical work, I become what I was, as a boy on the farm in Illinois, anxious, troubled, a sort of black sterile perpetual insomnia in the daytime. My mind is awake; the back of your mind which sleeps normally, wakes up in insomnia, is then awake all the time. There's anxiety and a sort of sinister grin too. *I know more than I let on.* Well, you want to drink to shut that terrible eye. They're right in one thing. I know the danger of cutting yourself off from men and living among the *ragged rocks and shivering shocks* of Nature. And society and work go together. Without communication I lose my working ability. The contrast between the world I've seen and those self-satisfied copperhead farmers and the clods on the ridges, is too great. I have to shut my eyes to it. Every psychopathic drunk like me is an intensely dissatisfied and yearning man. He can trust no one and he longs for the simple rest a child or a woman or a dog has. People who can rest, sleep, as they innocently call it, are never fully awake even in the daytime. And life here is vegetation. A man wants more, much more. I have the will power to live as a recluse in this green prison, but I know what I am missing. The life of cities. The mind is like a city; it isn't like a clod. You don't know the agony of living by will power. What will power do you or Ruth need to stay off drink? I don't want to make out that I'm a moral hero. There's the physical and mental sickness to help you, the awful paralyzing weakness, the feeling, How can I ever get back to shore? I'm in the shallows only a few yards from shore, where I could lie down and drink in strength from the sun, but I can't get there; I'll never make it. If I ever get there, I'll do anything, live on bread and water for the rest of my life. And then there's the hate of drink! I loathe it. I must smoke," he continued stridently, "and smoking dries your throat and turns your tongue to pemmican; and I drown all that in black coffee. A man must turn out work, living like that. And we're eating badly now, saving for the boy. That's another reason I mustn't drink. Drink's a matter of physical need, that's what you don't know. You have a certain temperament, highstrung, hungry and your cells, your enzymes I don't know what, are crying out for the one thing that will satisfy the one desire; and we haven't even enough food."

Sam Parsons, exceedingly embarrassed, said he ought to go to New York and look for a place for himself and his wife, see about getting some work; he oughtn't to be there. They had a little money still which they must not waste, but keep in reserve.

Laban hectored him, "Sam, you stay here and keep me from thinking about New York. I get the idea at times that they are all drinking and kidding around there and calling me names, saying I'm tied to apron-strings; and so I am, but I bless them for tying me." He paused, got up and kissed his wife. "My blessed chains. I bless you." He turned to Sam. "That's what they're saying when I'm there. They insult Ruth and I'm too cowardly to defend her. I agree with them; 'damn cow likes to graze.' They're a lousy lot. But I fool myself into thinking that if I were there I could sit on them, stop their sneering. This is a refuge, an asylum in both senses. I'm always glad when I get into hospital after a bout; I wish I could live in one. Once I wrote to an asylum to take me in; they wouldn't.

"The country is so damned dull with their quarrels and animosities over five cents, and who's a Republican. Who cares? Ruth and Frankie are getting sucked into it, too. That young fellow up at Strassers' skulking 'round that dry rock farm often looks as if he's going crazy. If I went to town I would worry about leaving Ruth here alone. He might go nuts in the middle of the week and start burning our house down. I know what's passing in his mind; it passed in mine. You know they've got no water. We're hogging it. All the water they use must come from that spring house that drips across the track back into our creek. I've dreamed that I've seen this place in flames, a fiery honeycomb," he said, exalted; "all we have is a leaky pump, although we own three quarters of a mile of creek. It's the inconsistencies, stupidities, the smug imbecility of the country that gets an intelligent man down. It's all right for women and children if they've got a defense. I often thought of getting a big dog here to defend Ruth and Frankie; but if I did so, do you know what," he said with a bright smile, "I might go off to town. This way I stay here to look after them. That's what irritates me about Ruth's attitude. She quite openly thinks that I'm straining to get off the string. She doesn't understand that I'm thinking of her and Frankie day and night. She doesn't realize that no decent man would go away and leave them in a place like this, without a gate or fence, with all those doors and windows; with the crazy Strasser boys and trucks full of farm workers going about on the road and the hot summer coming. The other day a truck full of boys about seventeen, eighteen, sex crazy youngsters stopped by our bridge and three of them walked right into our kitchen and took a drink of water. They stood there by the sink pumping water and drinking pints of it, pouring it down their throats. I was on the track, Frankie was at school, Ruth was upstairs making the beds. You know Ruth. She's not afraid of men, used to be a good time gal. But she was afraid. She came down and asked them what they were doing there. They looked her over for a long minute, and they walked out without saying a word. When I came home she cried on my chest. Ruth!"

"Well, I have to hang out the washing," said Ruth; and she went out with the basket.

Laban laughed and said, "It would drive you to drink! It's all a worry to me. But the city's hopeless for us. I go along seven or eight months and hate the sight and sound of it; and then I backslide and hell opens. I'm a pathological drunk like Poe, you see; one glass—you think I'm weak-willed probably."

"No, I don't, Laban. I assume there's a factor unknown to me."

"I'm not an ordinary sot. It's another dimension. One glass—and I'm off on those joyrides you dream about as a child, up the airy mountain, down the rushy glen, in an airborne toboggan, flying, the rushing frightening joy that people buy for ten cents on the loop-the-loops. One glass of ordinary red ink and no one knows how long it will last; as long as it takes to make me a sodden, spineless, helpless imitation of a human being, unable to use his tongue or his legs, crawling about the floor like a child of two."

Sam said nervously, hearing the ring of triumph in Laban's voice, "Love of drink is a strange thing. But there must be a great joy, release, excitement in it, when you feel superior to your troubles and to other people, I suppose."

Laban's voice, metallic, hurried on, "In the beginning, as a boy doing the farm chores, I drank greedily and with a certain amount of vanity and pleasure." After a pause, he said, with an underlit smile, "You see, I don't remember many things, many weeks, many months—long periods of my life don't exist for me. If I were under oath and after due reflection, I'd probably say something incredible. I loathe alcohol and I always did. I get an infernal brutish feeling that I'm injuring everyone and everything I ought to like and love, I'm a brute; and then, to hell with it. I never had any joy or excitement or release. Maybe I did. I get to a point where I'm above all such petty considerations as decency, morality, family, fame and even success. I know why they egg me on, they don't want me to succeed. I'm a comment on their living when I escape and get to work." After a moment, he looked friendly toward his wife and said more cheerfully, "I never allow Frankie to taste it. In Europe they let children have beer or watered wine, but Frankie never had it. As a child I was terribly greedy for it. I drunk a whole quart of homebrew on the way home one day and was picked up after a storm, senseless, frozen, wet through. It wasn't the only time; but you only die when your time is up; I survived everything. I've been able to make something of myself even with the curse, because I read a lot as a boy and I realized that I wasn't alone. So many great men have had a hankering or lust for liquor or whatever other artificial paradise: some such terrible blemish usually goes with genius. So I'm afraid for Frankie: because of the father in his blood."

Sam Parsons said he wasn't a genius, but he had read somewhere, some Frenchman had said that genius was the control of disorders and blemishes, just as Laban himself thought.

"Well," said Laban, "you are right, that thought helped me. And I think America's a land to live for. I naturally believe in the future of men; and I believe in myself; and I have the youngster, I believe in him. So what have I to worry about, except an accident of temptation, which I avoid? And I thank God every moment for Ruth. She did more for me than my own mother."

Parsons tried to bring the conversation back to America's future; but Laban laughed poignantly, to say, "My mother's old folks were very religious people; but they took their moonshine and their Bible in equal parts. Religion wasn't my brand. I have got to believe in society, social destiny in our people. That gives me something to give Frankie. My poor father had nothing to give me. He was not much better off, and not as well regarded as Mr. Tanner in Lambertville. When he found out what a present I had got from the old folks, blood ninety percent cornjuice, he just gave me up."

While this conversation had been going on, the men had risen from the table, and had walked up and down the track from the ravens to the rabbits.

When they returned, Ruth was looking for them, as she sat with Frankie in her lap, on the southern porch facing the rustic bridge. She beamed.

Laban kissed her and his son, and remarked, "Boaz has got his Ruth. Whither thou goest there will I go. What did I ever do, Ruth, to deserve you and Frankie? In all my dreams as a young country poet, I never thought of such a perfect afternoon as this, *so cool, so calm, so bright,* this green paradise, this home. I labored in the stormy seas, but I got a toehold on good land at the other side: I am safe home now."

He went upstairs and began writing. Ruth walked out to dig in the vegetable garden. Parsons stood beside, watching.

Ruth said, "I am going to bake our own bread, to save money. I can manage better than I do. Laban is such a good man, such a good man! I never knew there were really good men till I met Laban. I knew there were good fellows, friends, but Laban was something else; almost a saint, I assure you, Sam. He writes me such beautiful letters when he's away. I'll get them out and show them to you. One day they'll be printed. He's never written me a cruel word."

A moment later, she said drily, referring to the time Parsons knew of, "And yet, Sam, that same summer, when you had to buy my boat-ticket home, he went to my father and borrowed six hundred dollars to bring us over; and he used up all that money in six weeks and was destitute when I found him in the hospital. I had to borrow another hundred dollars to start again. He knew when he came over, that Frankie and I were starving in Europe, in a ruinous stone hut in a village no peasant would live in. We had not the money for eggs or milk."

The next afternoon Laban wanted to walk with Parsons to Lambertville to mail letters and get newspapers. It was a good two-mile walk, up and down, either way; but they went by the back way, the green road, past Thornton's, as the bulls were then dangerous up by Newbold's and Sobieski's.

Laban broke into their usual political comments, "You asked me about the pleasure of drink only yesterday; and today I can give you a good picture of it. Last night I dreamed I had taken a glass of the old poisonous slop I used to get as a boy on the farm; and the bottle was standing just out of reach, on top of the outhouse among the wild grapevines; it was the very image of desire. I held the glass in my hand. It was full and glowed like a jewel and the bottle when I looked at it with such desire, delightful, hopeful and hopeless passionate desire, glowed in blue and yellow, absinthe jewels. The drink was very real: it's real to me now. The way I am now, the mere sniff of a dirty old Third Avenue saloon with its mixed smell of sawdust, lethal alcohol and piss would send me raving with delight. Yes, delight and horror; there's delight in it and the utmost limit of horror. Most people don't know what horror is. They talk of it—the horror of the Nazis, the horror of crimes; this is loathsome, that is terrible: they simply don't know. In fact, I wonder how can you be a poet and know the just measure of words and emotions without being a drunkard—a hopeless drunkard like me. I'm glad you're here; and I'm here. As soon as I'd taken that fatal glass in my dream last night, I heard voices shouting, and hissing and singing like a thin musical saw, a saw about two inches long. I saw a cornbin on a bare hill; and this bin was done in rustic style, with a rustic railing round the porch and pieces of wood fitted together to read M—A—D; and voices were singing away over the hill, down the sky in a shouting chorus, 'In-sane, in-sane, in-sane.' I woke up and looked beside the bed and there saw a nest of fluorescent snakes coiling where Ruth had put her stockings. You know the barmen are very clever to put bottles on glass shelves with glass behind them. It's fascinating. If even a drop of water had touched my lips then, it would have turned to whisky, just from my burning desire and I should have been out raging today."

"You had the D.T.'s just from a dream?" remonstrated Sam.

A cold bitter smile was on Laban's lips. "You people call that the D.T.'s. As you can imagine, I'm a specialist. That's a very light hallucination. Why some bad drunks are committed to the madhouse without knowing genuine D.T.'s. There's no imagination in the bottle that you didn't put there. Naturally, with my temperament and visions, a poet, I have very out of the way hallucinosis."

"Don't let's talk about it," said Sam: "It's not good for you."

"The dream's in me: let me talk it out."

"Don't dwell on it."

Laban took his arm in a hard grip, "No, no, it drives me on. Ruth must never know I'm in this condition."

"Let us talk about literature and history: it's better for you. Try to control yourself."

Laban laughed and pointed to his scar. "Ruth told you I got this scar in the First World War. She used to believe that too. One cold Christmas I was out with a friend, from one place to another where they made their own stuff, during prohibition, and we came to a country druggist's who had a kind of general store. He had the stuff in barrels. He was always half-blind, not with liquor but from drugs from his own store; and he loved people to come to him, he loved to destroy others. There he sat like a blind barn owl and motioned us inside. Inside was a cabinet where I knew he kept his homemade whisky. Our host couldn't move; we helped ourselves. I don't know what happened after that, but we heard howling and screaming about the countryside that night; and next day I was picked up beside a barbed wire fence along which I had been dragged." After a pause: "Not that this is my only scar. Hard work on the farms such as I did not only as a boy younger than Frankie, but all the time I was working my way through college—and the fact that I felt obliged to drink because I soon became famous for it—well, that accounts for my obsession. It's like the obsession of a mother like Ruth with her children: I am one of them. What she has gone through for us has turned her from a normal woman into a sort of lunatic, part prison warder and part village sibyl. You know how madhouse warders are all of turned wits. And every year it grows in me, getting bigger like an oak, stronger. I want you to see what I have in me, my will power. It's abnormal, like my vice. How can a man like you who doesn't care if he never sees a drop, understand the need I have to talk about it? Mustn't a lover talk about his love?"

Sam was silent with disgust and fear.

"If I wrote down my dreams, or rather my hallucinosis," said Laban, "they would rank with the stories of Poe. I once thought I saw my mother standing in the doorway in grave-wax, her gray and white hair around her woven into a coat and crying that I had killed her. That's hackneyed, isn't it? I once dreamed——"

"Do me a favor, Laban, and don't tell me any more of this graveyard poetry. I'm not quite the pachyderm you think. I can't take it. My mother is dead, too."

Laban smirked. Neither made an attempt to lengthen the walk, but returned straight to the house. Laban took a jugful of coffee upstairs, shouting to Ruth to put on more. They had a gay supper, and Frankie was allowed to sit up late talking politics. Everyone was happy, Laban in his best mood, penetrating, considerate, balanced. He condemned the Fascists and their "watchdogs and lapdogs of the pen," and he named names—all those who sold their pens. He showed how the ideas of the corporate state and of the brown-shirted horde were essentially incompatible with true writing. Of the four at the table, only Frankie did not know that upstairs in a velvet-lined case in a box was the jeweled cross on a ribbon; and that with it the former farmboy, following Ezra Pound to Italy, dreaming of glory, and flattered by the empty-heads around Mussolini, had acquired a title in a Fascist order. The honest radical scholar, the poor farmboy could not give up this secret jewel.

In the morning, Laban came down from his workroom with spectacles on, looking fussy and saying that his agent had written a ruinous contract, giving fifty percent of Hollywood sales to his publisher.

"That's quite normal," said Parsons: "that is in my contract too."

Laban withered him with a glance. "These ten percent bastards are working for the publishers, though we pay them out of our thin purses. They get into a huddle at cocktail parties, kill themselves laughing at the pretensions of authors. What chance do I stand living in the back of beyond? I am classed with the other daydreaming hicks."

"Write him a sharp note," said Ruth.

"I'll have to go to New York to straighten things out: they throw your notes into the trash basket. Author equals moron." Ruth and Laban had rancorous words. In the end Ruth won. Laban went up to Newbold's and telephoned his agent.

The next evening, a Wednesday, after dark, they were having a light meal in the kitchen, when they heard a car bumping along the track; and shouting and whistling. It was all quite clear, at a distance, in the still gully. The car stopped below Strassers', men got out and there was a lot of shouting, which sounded like "Laban! Laban Davies!" A man evidently fell into the bushes by the creek, was pulled out and the car struggled forward. "A bunch of drunks," said Parsons. Laban was sitting upright and still, his odd long round-eyed face staring at a window which faced the creek.

Ruth cried, "They've come!"

Laban remained motionless, excited, staring.

"All of you go upstairs at once," said Parsons; "I'll say you're not here." He got up, pulled down all the blinds, starting with the ones facing the creek. When they were down, the family hurried through the door into the stone house which was dark and so up the enclosed stairway of the stone house. The house was now in midsummer screened from the road by the trees. The taxi with the visitors had to make the full turn around the rightangled creek to reach Dilley's wooden bridge, the only entrance to the property. Sam observed the car from the door. It had stopped at the very beginning of the Dilleys' place and with pocketlights the visitors were surveying the creek for an entrance. The banks were smothered with poison ivy, an effective barrier. "Sit still and don't make a sound," said Sam, shutting every door of the stone house. The car started up again and was cautiously making its way over the track, avoiding the creek. Presently it thumped over the bridge with the loose plank and the shouting went on, the voices calling for Laban, all very clear in this hollow. Laban on the way upstairs had recognized voices. There was now not a sound from upstairs, where all was dark. Parsons had no more time than to partly clear the table, leaving only one place, his own, and push away the chairs, when the car which had taxi lights, found its way over the Dilleys' bridge, and stopped by the barn. The men, all drunk, were arguing. The taxi-driver refused to go farther. There was nothing but tussocks and holes ahead. Two of the passengers got out, and, cursing and stumbling, shouting for Laban, they made for the house. Several others milled around the car, took a few steps, saw the creek, hesitated. Parsons stood at the door.

"Put on the porch light, you so-and-so," shouted one of the drunks.

"There's no porch light," called Sam in his resonant Mid-Western voice: "what is it you want, my friend?"

"What's the matter, you damn so-and-so, who are you? Where's Laban? The taxi-driver won't come any closer. What the hell sort of a dump is this?"

"What's the matter? Whom do you want, my friend?" cried Sam.

"Shut up, it's someone else," said the man behind, not so drunk.

"Where's Laban, Laban and Ruth?" asked the first drunk, arms spread to help him over the tussocks and stopping a short way from the porch.

Cheerfully, jolly Mid-Western Sam Parsons declared: "They've gone away, my friend. I'm sorry you had the trouble. Sorry to put you out. They've been gone two days. Went to stay with Ruth's people, in Springfield, Ohio. Where are you from, my friend?"

"Took a goddamn taxi all the way from New York," answered the drunk sulkily.

"Is there anything I can do for you?" cried Sam affectionately.

"What did they go for? Why the hell didn't they stay? Who are you anyway?" said the crestfallen merrymaker. Sam kept up his out-of-date jolly style, while one drunk argued with the other and with the taxi-driver, who said he was going to turn around and get back home.

"Well," said the drunk, "have you got a drink anyway?"

"I'm sorry, my friend, I never touch liquor."

"What the hell sort of a dump," muttered the drunk to himself; but he was so fuddled that he allowed himself to be taken by the sleeve and headed back to the taxi. A cheerful drunk shouted, "Where can we get a drink round here anyway?"

"Wait till I get the lamp," shouted Parsons with overwhelming good nature, "watch out or you'll be in the creek."

"This damn creek is everywhere," said one.

Taking the storm lantern, Parsons now hurried after them, apologizing comfortably and he reached the car, where the rest of the crew, all drunk, were pushing each other into the seats. "Go to Lambertville, go to Trenton, plenty of drinks there," cried Parsons cheerfully. "Go to New Hope, lots of friends of yours there I expect." The car began backing and filling, the taxi-driver began grumbling and cursing, doors slammed and the car hobbled towards the bridge, Sam stood gaily waving the lantern and shouting, "Good-by, boys, good-by: better luck next time. Mind the turn, mind the creek." They got away. This time the little red lamp went faster and winked engagingly in and out of the greenery. Parsons took his lantern, went in and locked all the doors. What luck that they had been so drunk! What luck that not one knew the house. They could have taken it by storm. What luck that his breezy, plainsman manner had thrown them off. He went up the wooden stair into the second story and found the mother, father and child sitting hand in hand on the iron bedstead in Laban's workroom, silent, their thin stomachs tucked in, their thin forms only visible by the pale light from the summer fields.

"We did not move the whole time," said Ruth. The child was silent. They went down, ate a few scraps of food, Laban drank only one cup of coffee and for once they went to bed early and almost in silence. Saying goodnight, Ruth wrung Sam's hand and kissed him on both cheeks, "My brother!" She turned in the dark doorway, on the step to the stone house, and said, "You saved our family tonight."

"They would have taken me away by force," said Laban, pallid behind her and standing in the dark; "I'm strong but there were how many of them?—five or six?"

The next afternoon he walked with Sam and talked. "Have you had any more nightmares?"

"Oh, that phase is ended. Seeing the gang last night brought it home to me."

In the morning of the following Saturday, that is, two days later, Laban came downstairs new-washed, shaved, in his best tailormade light gray suit, his shoes polished, his hat on and his satchel in his hand. The hat was pulled down to partly hide his scar and he had a smooth superior smile. He said he was taking the ten-thirty bus to Trenton to catch the New York train. He had to see his agent. They were not to worry. He would be back not later than six or seven. Ruth, wiping her hands on her sacking apron, looked with worry at her husband, now an attractive New Yorker. Had he money, this and that, she asked.

Ruth was quiet all day, prepared a good evening meal; and Laban did not return that night. They locked the doors, but left the blinds up, with both kitchen lights on. Next day, from Newbold's they telephoned the New York agent. He had not seen Laban. They waited while he telephoned others; no one had seen him. "I cannot telephone that crowd," said Ruth, "and let them know he's away. He may have stopped over somewhere and be back this morning." All day, as they waited, she talked about those men who had come in the taxi; and past events. "I met Laban at his own engagement party. As soon as he saw me, he knew the other affair was off; but he used to see that girl and I didn't feel I could stop him. I had taken him away from her." She showed Sam a letter she had got in Paris, when Laban was wandering around the countryside, lost, memoryless, brainless, a dreadful raving thing, eating nothing and craving any kind of alcohol, an obscene insulting letter signed by Laban and his friends. "Why did you keep it?" "He came back from there. That was our low point." Some of the names were those of well-known New York writers, some talented men. "But they're unable to quit because they're empty and cynical and they can't let anyone else get out. They love to see Laban changing from a man to an animal and from an animal to a log. They can talk about it for months."

The letter said:

"Dear Ruth, As Laban says, Ruth my truth, you should have been with us last night though no one missed you, least of all your dearly beloved Laban. He was hugging Jenny tight but as usual paying even more attention to the bottle. As for the bottle, he had it bad. When he was going to drink out of the bottle he groaned out that it was blood and when he spilled it he tried to drink the blood off the counter, my blood, Ruth, my truth's blood, he said. How's that for a beginning? He groaned, I'm drinking blood! Oh, boy. We all had a time. Don't be counting the minutes baby: he's going to be good this time—"

and more

Pinned to this faded letter was a note from Laban written in pencil:

"Oh, Ruth, borrow the money and come over and save me. I love only you and Francis but I am on a spree and cannot stop. I am sober now, but it is not over and I need you. You are my angel, oh, thousands of angels say your name around me; but save me. I don't know where I was last night. My father came through the ceiling and walked slowly past me, looking at me with disgust and irony. He went on moving and moved past me. I heard sobbing and I don't know if it was I. Perhaps it was you. There was a vague face in front of me and I heard voices of all kinds. You see what has happened to me because I am alone. Take no notice of what you hear. Remember I love only you and Francis."

Ruth looked on with dry eyes as Sam read these documents and she remarked, "You see, I know he loves me; and so do they. And it's inhuman joy to them to take him away from us and to kill him with drink. They know he'll die of it some day. They want to be there when Laban Davies dies."

They waited, in all, ten days. There was no news from any quarter. "Let me go to New York and look for him." "Don't leave me, Sam. There's something peculiar about this place. Do you know I have an obsession that there's someone in the attic, a huge hairy man."

"No one could live in that attic," said Sam laughing.

"It's big enough: there's a huge room up there," she said.

"There's no one there!"

"When you go out for walks on the track, Sam, in the morning especially, I feel sure he's there. I feel sure I'll hear him coming down the stairs." For the enclosed staircase in the stone house, which opened by glazed doors into the first and second stories, went on up to a clean and roomy attic, a well-lighted attic. "It's foolish of me to have such fancies; I'm not the type of woman."

In ten days Ruth did not weep and Frankie, though subdued, asked no questions. She encouraged her son to go out each day with the boys. The lights in the farm-kitchen blazed all night. They sat up late, with the blinds undrawn, talking. Ruth explained that they had never seen the owner, Mr. Dilley, a man about sixty-eight, a baker in Jersey City. He had put two thousand dollars' savings into the farm and borrowed the rest from a bank; total price four thousand dollars. It had come cheap because it had been run as a berry farm for a year or two by a brother and sister and had failed. She did not know who the original farmers were who had bought the creek and the fringe of Sobieski's land and built the double house on two acres. The Davies wanted to buy the place but had not yet the money. They paid the rent to Thornton, who knew Dilley, and now considered himself the estate manager. "He's always snooping around. He takes the rent but I'm not sure he gives an account of it to poor old Mr. Dilley."

"Is he poor?"

Ruth was puzzled. "I don't really know. Someone was ill, the wife I think. They don't want the place, but they hang on to it. It's hard to give up something you've acquired with your life savings."

"Thornton's pleasant to talk to, he's a shrewd modern man. He was telling me about his ten sons, all farmers."

"Oh, yes, he's very hail-fellow-well-met," said Ruth furiously; "but he always has an object."

Sam laughed.

Ruth snapped, "There's a lofty attitude in his friendly smile. You don't know how the yokel, the clod looks at city intellectuals."

"All I know is, he's very pleasant to me."

"Beside Laban, you're the only angel I know among men," said Ruth, and suddenly began to cry.

The ten nights passed and no figure came along the track. The thicketed meadow in which they lived led a simple life of its own without terrors. It was a hot fertile summer. The fireflies walked up all the windowpanes putting their lamps on and off; and with their sparks outlined the branches. One day Parsons went to New York and returned, without having found a trace of Davies. Ruth stayed there because at any time Laban might return and she was his truth. The boy, at first oppressed, soon began to treat Parsons as a father. They walked out, hand in hand, talking eagerly. They sat up late every night; till dawn the lights streamed out to leafy creek and track.

On the morning of the eleventh day, young Newbold the mailman blew his horn. Riding with him was a boy from the bus company. A man had been riding back and forth between Trenton and Lambertville for the last ten days, sometimes getting off at Trenton, sometimes coming straight back. He had slept a few times in the Lambertville bus-barn. He kept saying at first, that he had to get home. He had been seen yesterday morning last. The boy went down with Ruth and Sam in Jeroboam; but when they reached the big bus-garage they found only a bus-conductor. He said the man in question, who did not know his name, was dressed in a cotton shirt and gray trousers, bareheaded and barefooted now, had gone off yesterday to see old Doctor Young, "the old doc who drinks." When they called upon Dr. Young at eleven this morning, the door was opened by a strong thickset man, amiably drunk.

Dr. Young said,

"You see I am fond of liquor myself and I recognized how ill your husband was. He told me the sidewalk was—" He checked himself and continued, "I knew he needed a little rest; and I gave him a sedative. But his spree was not over. If I'd locked him in, you see, he might have gone out of his mind. He would have been locked in with his hallucinations. I had to go out to my patients and when I came back he was gone."

The next morning Ruth left with her boy for New York. After she had left Frankie with a friend, she borrowed money and set out on her search for Laban, who might be anywhere in the States or might even have left the country. Sober, he would not borrow money; drunk, he was very ingenious.

Sam Parsons closed the farmhouse and gave the keys to Farmer Thornton. On his way, he looked back at the place through the first trees. Set back beyond the great pin-oak, the grasses, the round meadows, with old trees beyond, and by the potato patch, with weeds and native flowers grown shoulder high, and flocks of birds, gold, blue, red, feeding there, folded in by green hill, deep summer trees and dripping creek, Sam thought.

"I must remember how pretty it is; it's really enchanted; it smiles: it's a dream cottage. Clare would love it."

He went along the track and into the sunny stretch beside the blackberry bushes where there were this morning seven cottontails. They waited for him to come right up to them before they scattered. He passed Thornton's heavy-headed fields along and up the hill.

·   ·   ·

The next summer Sam and Clare Parsons took the cottage from the Davieses who were now living in California. Mr. Dilley offered the cottage to them for a year for $150 and this they accepted. On a sunny June morning Mr. Thornton met them in front of Dilley's farmhouse with the keys and went around the place showing them with pride how clean it was. He had gone to the expense of putting new paper shades on all the windows. He soon left, saying he had ploughing to do, but they could call on him for everything—and if they wanted it, he had milk for them at fourteen cents. "You will find it every morning and cream, too, in the springhouse," and he showed them his duckpond, his springhouse, his chicken run. The springhouse was a fresh little cave with ferns in it. A long letter was waiting for them from Ruth Davies, asking them to take Frankie for the summer, for Laban was working on his book. They had had a very difficult winter; the boy was pale and over-excited. The next year he would go to a camp "reserved for children of leaders" but this year he was too keen on politics, he couldn't sleep for thinking of politics; and they wanted him to roam the country with the Tanner and Sobieski boys again. "Let him be a barefoot boy with face of tan." Ruth enjoined them not to have any dealings with Thornton, but to get their dairy produce and chickens from Mrs. Sobieski, who was so cheap. She had, indeed, already written to Mrs. Sobieski about it.

They went up the hill to visit Mrs. Sobieski, a young good-humored gold-haired plump slattern; and said they would take poultry and eggs but no milk. She was sitting in her kitchen, a wooden leanto, peeling potatoes for her boys, and the farm-lad. She remarked joyously, "Don't worry about it. Sit down, have some lemon tea. I had a letter from Ruth, but don't think about it. Take the things from Thornton: he's not so bad; he'll like it better. Ruth always wanted to help me because I'm a widow with so many boys; but I'm a happy woman with all my boys. No hard feelings with anyone. I can sell all I grow; I sell it 'round. You don't have to buy my chickens; perhaps you don't like chickens." They parted on excellent terms. "We'll visit you—become friends," cried Sam Parsons. "Eh! You mustn't visit me, I'm too busy," she cried standing at last in the shaky doorway and waving her hand. "If you want to see me, drop in, but I can't visit." Off they went.

Parsons said, "So we are friends of everyone; and we will be left alone. You'll be happy here. Last summer I was thinking all the time, Clare would like it here, this is a nature-lover's ideal, a house sitting on the grass, completely open but inaccessible, neighbors on every hill but invisible, trees and fields all round, and as rich in birds and animals as a Breughel painting."

Clare laughed. "A Breughel painting! Well, not only the sleep of reason, but nature breeds horrors; and this is where you feel the multitudes, the creeping and running, the anthills and wasp nests, the earth breeding at every pore, there's a sort of horror in fertility and rioting insanity in the hot season. I love it."

"Yes, it is the place for you: you will be close to nature."

"But you don't like nature?"

"Why do you say that? I've learned to look at things and recognize a few. I'm not the bookish man I was."

"What I like about the house is it's so lowset that nature comes in on all sides, you see nothing else—the track only, but it's like occasional people passing behind the scenes. We're sitting on the stage and what's happening is animal life, faint sounds, the shrieking of the birds, trees cracking; you could be thousands of miles away from people and yet fields that have been ploughed for two hundred years are a few yards off and they can hear what we say in Strassers' springhouse."

The warm spring air was thick damp and breeding. There was no wind in the hollow. Sometimes it roared over them. Occasionally a car, boy or heavy animal passed over the bridge and the plank flopped. Though they were city people they had confidence in this silent sunny spot, beautiful from all angles. "It's spellbound." "You mean you are?" "No, it is." "Spellbound." "Joy and trust breathes out of it. And it's a bird sanctuary here, they say in town. Every bird is here that's been chased out of ploughland and uprooted woodland." "It's pure happiness here."

In the evening they unpacked. Clare opened a drawer in the kitchen table for the tableware; but there found a large assortment of cutlery. She spread all this on the big kitchen table; many carving knives, and many unshapely, blunt, notched, tarnished, ill-assorted and meaningless blades. She rolled all the knives into an old red cloth, pushed them to the back of the big old bread oven and set in front of them two old iron casseroles. Then there were quite usual objects, an ax and a hatchet for chopping the wood, behind the stove, then an ax that no doubt Mr. Thornton had put on the porch for them with the new wood and a boy's jackknife thrust into a crack in the porch. She took all these to the barn and locked them in, sticking the jackknife into a crack in a joist. Then she locked the empty barn and ran to the sitting room of the stone house which contained very little furniture. There was an upright piano, a small table, a short wall cupboard cut into the wall and painted to resemble a curtained window. It contained part of a dinner service, and behind a large serving dish were a carving knife, fork and steel and several dinner knives. It looked as if everyone who had used the house had come fully equipped with knives. The wife was nervous and began to hurry, to get all done before Sam came in.

He was out on the track taking his last walk of the night. He would soon be in, certainly; for the mourning dove had begun his grieving and sobbing, a desolate sound in this sunken place now quickly filling with the dark. To Sam the mourning dove was horrible. She looked everywhere now, up the chimney, in the grate, under the divan, under the piano—nothing anywhere. Sitting in the kitchen, once more, hearing how someone trod on a loose plank, hearing the mourning dove, she thought of something. She lifted the piano lid and looked in. In fact, there was a hunter's knife in its sheath; the sheath was moldy, the knife rusted. Clare thought it might be useful, so she put it with her own to polish it. That was all. Except that a few minutes after they went to bed, she remembered that she had not looked behind the divan or behind the piano. They had locked the doors and windows. She went down, unlocked the staircase door, went into the stone house and looked. Behind the piano she found another ax. She took it out to the barn, locked it in and came back. Out of doors she had no fears; it was a cool, slightly breathing night with many powdery stars. It was three nights later that she told Sam, as a joke. Sam was untenanted by premonitions and grisly fancies and feared them the more. But to Clare they were an unrecognized part of nature, like the faint sound of a spider scuttling under leaves, or a cat's footfalls. Few heard them; they were there.

The days passed; nature thickened around them. "The grass and the weeds need a-cuttin'," said Mr. Thornton, one fine summer morning. "I'll come down later with the scythe, or send Johnson." "Oh, leave them: we're not making a garden; we like things wild," said Sam. The weeds, white, yellow, purple, wild flowers and plants were so high that Sam could walk into them and be hidden. Here the birds clung and hunted. Plenty of small things ran about the ground in the shade. There were several woodchuck families in various parts of the Dilley creek banks, especially in the long strip of wild land along the Sobieski fields. The creek still was hidden there and there boys fished and swam all hidden, and the mocking birds had their nests. There were large and small burrows opening around the Dilley house, right at the porch and farther out. There were skunks; a weasel like a big swift worm dived and doubled into his hole by the steps. The birds reared full families and started again. Under the separated planks of the bridge was a black spider so large that it could be seen from three hundred yards away. It also was far sighted. It spied the Parsons coming at a distance and it ducked under the bridge, looked out, ducked in. The creek was full of life. Along the sunny track in the fresh mornings, little green snakes took the sun on the low green branches. A dozen little rabbits or more, played on the track. Sam Parsons walked there talking to himself and switching the dust. Up and down he tramped. It was so silent, so fertile, so safe. No vehicle passed there, but the mailman at about nine, the Tanner boys on their bikes, or children after school. Sam Parsons thought over his past business relations, books he might write, about the Spanish Inquisition, the Forty-Five, the Commune; he looked at the flowers, remembering that he ought to learn about outward things too—this was a chicory, this a goldenrod, "our national flower, I should know it." That was poison oak and this poison ivy and that poison sumach. Clare had taught him those first. "Don't touch them." He was a big city boy. He was very proud the first time a bird answered his whistle. Sometimes a friendly but puzzled bird followed him along the track. "It was talking to me, we had quite a conversation," he would report.

At night they went to bed early and sometimes slept badly. They barred the house downstairs but the second story was lower than the hill. They could hear animals passing above them on the hill, birds lower than they were, in a tree. At times the loose-plank bridge solemnly plonked; the owls howled; and there was the restlessness of the magnificent corn nights, the very sensible restlessness of the fast springing harvest, heads weighed down; and the lowing cattle. The house must have been full of field mice. Each night a skunk and its family passed under their window. The woman was awakened each night by the pungent smell and the knowledge that animals were moving around them; she loved animals. It was a lake, a deep pool of animals, a deep pool filled to the top with air and in it animals, not fish. When the skunk smell came, all the mice within the walls, scampered in a multitudinous rout down or up the walls. And often in the night now there were footfalls. These footfalls came from the landing outside their door and went down the stairs, one by one, to the bottom, thoughtfully, clumsily, almost reluctantly; and later would return one by one to the top, crossing the landing. But the door at the bottom of the stair they kept locked. It led to the kitchen.

She heard these footfalls several times without waking the man; but once when she heard his waking breathing, she said, "Listen to the footfalls. Of course, it is the mice! Or rats, do you think?"

"Yes, it is like footfalls; it must be mice, mustn't it? What else could it be?"

They listened for several nights. Downstairs the doors to both stairways, all the outside doors and windows were locked. The knives and axes were put away. They had no fear at all of intruders or assassins coming to them through the woods and fields, the lonely roads; they were happy and safe. But they always, at night, felt agitated, though not lonely. And there were the dreadful doves, driving Sam in before sunset, out of the damp, into the house to light the lamp; and so the nights began too early.

The days were perfect summer and still. The tiger lilies sprang all along the creek and in patches around the house. Sam walked to town every day to shop, talk to Thornton and "the boys"—acquaintances he had made in town; they heard the farmers and their lads at work behind the thick curtains of trees. Clare at home, did her work, tried the piano with the broken keys, heard the Strassers a few feet away on the ridge, noticed the many small birds rearing broods in the porches, woodpiles, weeds and trees. The house was a shed, a roof in which they ate and slept and into which the air and sun poured. They knew the house, the deep cellar under the stone house and the stone house's high attic, full of sun and dust, with old trunks—whose?—bikewheels, rubbish, a blameless place, looking out on the Sobieski pastures. At night the skunks, the cataracts of mice, the plonking plank, and the footfalls.

But where did the mice lodge, they idly asked, that went hopping downstairs every night; and what did they eat in the kitchen, where all the food was put away? Or had they some other purpose? "I believe they come out of that little locked room: they cross and recross the landing from there."

"Leave it alone," said Sam; "they do us no harm." "But listen to that thumping!" "Let's sleep." *Plonk!* "Who's coming over the bridge so late?" "It's not late."

One day when Sam was in Lambertville, Clare found a key to fit the lock of the little room. It was an engaging little room, the prettiest in the house. The roof sloped to the floor. Two small windows set at floor-level, surveyed the sweetest part of Dilley's acres: they looked down upon the green, the weed patch, in which birds flashed; and the clear shallow saucers of the brook surrounded by orange and white flowers could be seen; all swimming in the hollow full to the top with sun and the invisible but thick and moving damp. If you are an underwater swimmer and have visited rock-cities, floated over weedy and sandy bottoms which the fish know, looked down like a fish, that is the liquid sort of scene you see. It was scarcely twelve o'clock. It was still. The world was at work, men, beasts, plants; all was well; an unforgettable hour; the smiling heart of that ineffable house.

After a while, Clare looked at the room. In the center of the bare floor was an old-fashioned leather trunk with a domed lid, attached by leather hinges and straps. The leather was discolored, worn and scaly with age. There was a hat tree behind the door, an old locked wardrobe and a kerosene lamp. She was going out again when she noticed a leather belt hanging on the hat tree. It was of soft leather, with notched edges, about two and a half inches wide, awkwardly hand-embroidered with red, green and yellow wool; and red, green and yellow glass jewels had been let in, in a simple design: a stage property. She tried it on and put it back. She locked the door again.

There were many insects about now and in the silence their multifarious life could be heard: wasps scraping wood off the rough wooden seat on the porch, some insects singing perhaps in their nests, bees humming, the immense horseflies droning, the interminable whipping chatter of the house-wrens and other tiny sounds about the house, half invaded and possessed by wild life; they poured out of the sun copiously on the earth, richest in this manidle dell. There was one other sound which now Clare heard very often in the daytime, in the sun, when she was upstairs or downstairs, or had come close to the house from the fields, a singing or faint twanging in one of the corners of the porch or in the kitchen corner. It was larger than a mosquito's voice, not much more at first, but when she became accustomed to it, it became louder and more insistent; like a brass spider twanging on its brass web. The insects were so thick and noisy that the Parsons did not trouble themselves any more about them. They no longer sat on the porches, for there was, that year, a plague of flying mites, and in the evening, the mosquitoes. So they sat without lights till the light faded, and then went indoors, while up the windows crawled thick the winking fireflies. But she came to listen for the creature singing in a corner of the house, at its work or in its nest. Now she could hear it halfway from the creek, her ear sharper and sharper for the world of beasts and leaves.

In a few days, alone in the sunny silent morning, she returned to the little room upstairs. She undid the buckles and set back the heavy leather lid. The trunk was full. On top was a leather headband to match the leather belt, with stitching and glass jewels. With it were berets, headbands, short skirts, cloche hats, fashion magazines from many years before for out-of-date bridal dresses and baby clothes. There was a life-size celluloid doll dressed in baby's clothes; and with this a pale brown cloth tunic roughly stitched. Underneath these was a white silk dress with lace and pearl beads sewn on it, a simple net veil and pearl circlet. The brown tunic was a fancy dress, unfinished. It was slashed into fringes around the opening and skirt and the skirt was decorated with the same glass jewels. Underneath these, several large feathers dyed, a man's khaki shirt, a Sam Browne belt and other relics of war days. Clare closed the trunk and locked the room. She sat down on the porch teasing the wonderful sensitive plant that grew there. It took it but one hour to move from one side to the other, as she moved an enticing walking stick; toward the stick its corkscrew tendrils vibrated. On one side was a skunk's hole. The sensitive plant, after only a quarter of an hour, began a slow swoop upon the walking stick, which she held out for it. "Yes, plants too live, the Hindus are right: this plant is thinking. But here in this hot-bed, everything lives and thinks. The house itself—" Idle, fascinating days. The catbird clucked in the bushes by the creek or sat on the bare wire of the porch trying to imitate Sam's voice; a cat sneaked through the grass. In a storm a wolfish dog mad with fear, rushed under the house and howled. The little insect in the porch-roof sang loudly.

Mr. Thornton came down bringing the milk, and placidly going backward and forward over the tussocks with him, Parsons talked about simple ways of improving the house. "I suppose Dilley would be glad to sell, if things are the way I've heard. Mr. Davies told me he was in financial difficulties, that he has a sick wife and daughter and he finds it hard to meet mortgage payments."

"I don't know if they're in such a hurry to sell," said Mr. Thornton. "The wife, Mrs. Dilley, thinks the daughter will get better and she wants to keep this place on for her. She thinks the country will improve her. She thinks it was a nervous breakdown. But old Mr. Dilley knows better."

"So you think he'd be prepared to sell?"

"I could ask him. I'm always a-writin' to him about the house. You see I manage for him." Thornton fetched a grass-cutter from the barn, and said he would just do a bit now and then he'd send Johnson. "The place needs a-ploughin' and a-smoothin' down first."

Clare through the kitchen window looked out and said, "Yes, then I could grow my own vegetables here and have a chicken run. If you would lend Johnson to do a bit of digging."

Mr. Thornton was silent for a while. He smiled presently and stated, "Some I-talians, brother and sister, deaf ones, had a berry farm here; but they had bad luck, the crop failed. It's not the place. They went bankrupt. It waited a while before the Dilleys took it. And after them, it waited a while—"

Clare, pumping water into the sink, said, "But what is the matter with Miss Dilley?"

"Mrs. Grace, Miss Dilley that was," he said gently. "Well, I couldn't say. I don't think she'll recover. She's a-lingerin', it's a long business."

"Is it tuberculosis?" said Clare.

"No; I don't think it was that; but it might have been. Was somethin' catchin'."

When Clare had left the sink, he said to Sam, "Come up by the barn. I'll start a-cuttin' there and I'll tell you somethin'." When there he stopped work, and standing strong and tall in his sixty years, his hand on a hoe, he said, "I wouldn't like your wife to hear this. You can tell her after, if you think it's right. I never told my wife or daughter about it; and 'round here with people a comin' and a goin' on this farm, they hardly remember anythin'. Perhaps Rudolf, that Strasser boy, remembers; but he wouldn't say."

"Is the girl dying?"

"She's a-dyin'; I don't think she's dead. I don't know. I saw her myself about eight months ago. I'm the only one knows all about it. I guess I know more than her poor mother. I never told Mr. Davies, for Mr. Davies was a sick man. Well, since you ask me, I think I can say the daughter isn't dead. I think they'd tell me if she'd died. She's right near here. And that's what the Dilleys think; that some day soon, she'll be back here, a-waitin' for them; or the mother thinks. She's not far away. She's very bad. She's in the madhouse over in T. and she'll never get out. The mother thinks she's a-gettin' better, but she's a-gettin' worse. I went to see her at the request of Mr. Dilley about eight months ago and she's nothin' like herself. She didn't recognize me, though she always liked me; and she's not like a woman, she's like a sick animal or a baby, worse; and she doesn't know who she is. They haven't let the mother see her for three years.

"It all happened because of a Nevada man. Dilley was a shoemaker and sold leather goods; and durin' the war he got enough together to retire. They bought this place, which was a-goin' beggin', part paid for and part on mortgage; and thought they'd keep it for their only child Hilda for when she was married. Lambertville was better then than now, Lambertville's a half-ruined town. These factories along the Delaware closed down and the place never came back. At that time it was full of life; and the Dilleys often went in in their old car. There was a big army camp near here where they put the young men who were a-waitin' to be demobilized. This young Hilda was about twenty-two and she was full of life. She used to talk to that Strasser boy a-callin' across the creek; but the parents on both sides didn't like it. There was this Nevada man there, a big tall fellow in a uniform who talked a lot and sang a lot and had this gui-tar.

"Well, he got her to fall in love with him at once; and she wanted to marry him. The parents always gave in to her in the end; so they married and the Nevada man thought, I guess, that he was a-goin' to live soft. He moved in here with the Dilleys and never offered to go to work. He sat 'round the whole livelong day, a-talkin' and a-eatin' and a-singin' to the tunes on that gui-tar. Well, he was an ignorant man and he had a disease and he gave it to Hilda. She had a baby which died and that began to turn her mind; she used to cry for it. The Nevada man wasn't cruel; he just was lazy. He'd sit up there in my kitchen many a time, a-playin' his gui-tar and a-talkin' to my wife. She liked him and he liked her; she was in the house then with our baby girl, my only daughter. He'd amuse the baby! That he liked right well; and he liked to amuse visitors; and he'd go to church and talk to the men. But he reared at work like a crazy horse. I said to him, Come on, come out with me and I'll show you how to plough; and he'd go out to the field with me; but he'd laugh and watch me plough; and he'd sit down and begin to strum and sing. The poor girl began to cry and act strange and to amuse her they took her to the movies and to the-ayter that they had at the church hall. Well, it's a funny thing. One of those shows was about Pocahontas and Captain John Smith. Now that Nevadan said he was a captain; I don't know if he was. He said he didn't wear his ribbons because he was a-doin' of some work. I don't know if he was. But this seemed to stick in her mind; and she began to say she was Pocahontas and she was a-goin' to marry Captain John Smith. She forgot she was married sometimes. She forgot about the baby. So they bought her a doll and she seemed to think sometimes it was a baby. It's hard to say just what she thought. Well, they didn't say anythin' to that Nevada man, because they were afraid to hurt her feelin's and he was better 'round the place than away. Then he went away. I don't know where. He wrote one letter and they never heard from him again. The parents hadn't thought much of him, but they set a detective after him; they wrote letters to people they knew; but he was never heard of again.

"After this Hilda was in a bad way. Her mother, who loved her, sewed her a kind of Indian dress. I've seen it myself; and she'd walk with her every day along the track, a-lettin' her wear this fancy dress and a-listenin' to her talk, which was very proud and boastful. I'd meet them very early in the mornin' sometimes when I was a-comin' back from Lambertville; and I've heard her a-talkin' high because she thought she was this Indian princess. I told Mrs. Dilley I didn't think it wise to encourage her; but the poor mother would not oppose her. She said her mind was turned with so much trouble and only kindness would bring her back. Well, there had been talk about this Nevada captain, if he was; and I myself wondered—if somethin' had gone wrong. My wife and the others too saw her, a-singin' and a-talkin' and sometimes she wore flowers and had a tomahawk or a knife and a rope. Once I was frightened to see her costume there a-lyin' on the road and I thought somethin' had happened; but I saw her a-runnin' naked along the track and a-slippin' down into the creek and she had some leaves 'round her neck. I thought that was no sight for the young men up at Strassers' to see, or my young men either; so I brought the girl her clothes and told her to get dressed like a good girl. I was shocked at her, I told her; and wouldn't be her friend if she misbehaved like that. I said to her like I always said, even when her mother was there, But you're not Pocahontas, my girl. It's just a joke; you're Hilda, you know. But she wouldn't have that: and I thought, maybe her mother was right.

"One morning Rudolf the Strasser boy, the elder, came a-runnin' up the hill about nine and sang out to me, Mr. Thornton, come quick, down to the Dilleys'; it's murder down there. I said, What is it, Rudolf? And while we were a-runnin' down he told me Hilda was out here a-throwin' things and a-screamin'; and her father and her mother couldn't get her home. Well, I wasn't too sure, because she'd been funny before; and I thought the boy could get easily scared by her; but I ran down with Rudolf just the same, a-takin' a bit of rope which was a-hangin' on the fence, with me. I thought: I'll bind her up till she quiets down. They were a-shoutin' and a-hollerin' and when I got 'round the corner of the barn here, I see poor old Mrs. Dilley with her gray head bendin' low down over the garden path, her head nearly in the earth, and Hilda her daughter was a-throwin' knives at her. Just as I came along, Hilda flung a tomahawk which struck her poor old mother on the shoulder. Her head was already covered with blood. She collapsed into the dirt and I thought she was dead. What are you a-doin', Hilda? I shouted. She had an ax in her hands now and she was ready to heave it at her mother. I ran right up before she could think, and said, Hilda, put down that ax! What are you a-doin'? Aren't you ashamed? She looked very pale and wild; and she told me she was a-killin' her mother because her mother did things to her. She said, She takes everythin' from me. I said, Shame on you, Hilda, shame on you! Look at your poor mother, a-bleedin' there in the dirt; you've cut her on the shoulder and on the head. I am ashamed of you, Hilda! And while I was a-talkin' and she was a-lookin' to see what she had done, I grabbed the ax. She held on to it, but I got between her and the tomahawk a-lyin' on the path. Then Mrs. Dilley, who had said nothin', was groanin' a little and she started to get up. She leaned on her hands and said to me, The poor girl doesn't know what she is a-doin'! She was always so quiet.

"Well, I went on a-talkin' to her and a-pushin' her into the house: and I found her father where she had driven him with her ax into the staircase and locked him in; because she said she was a-comin' after him to kill him next. I gave her a terrible talkin' to, shamin' her for what she'd done; for her wickedness, and I talked so much, I got the rope 'round her and tied her to a chair. There was no place to lock her but the barn and that was full of sharp dangerous things. Upstairs she could have got to the windows and done harm. Then I sent Strasser up to my place to get them to telephone for a doctor and I waited there till he came. He fixed up the parents and went back to town to arrange for the girl. There was no doubt at all; Hilda was mad and dangerous. The doctor had given her a drug and they put her to bed and locked her in. Well, after I finished my work I went a-back there and found her awake and a-ravin' and a-shoutin', so I stayed there until two in the mornin'. But when she quietened down, I went in there and I talked to her a long, long time; for I couldn't help a-feelin' that if they hadn't given in to her and let her wear that fancy dress and have that baby doll and that tomahawk, she might not have gone mad. So I talked to her sensibly and scolded her and asked her what was the matter, until she got quite quiet.

"She said I wasn't her friend because I had tied her up with a rope; but I told her she was only like a calf or a young horse, she had to learn. I knew she wasn't a bad girl, only selfish with no thought for her poor parents. Well, we talked on nearly all through the night and she told me a lot of her strange ideas. She thought people were her enemies. When she was quiet I gave her the drug again and locked her in and went away.

In the mornin' at eight o'clock I came with my buggy and horse and knocked on the door: Hilda, it's Mr. Thornton. I want you to come and take a ride with me. You let your mother dress you.

"After a bit I went in and said to her, Hilda, do you want to go to a square-dance? Will you come and dance with me? Then you must get dressed up in your best dress. What are you a-doin' like that, Hilda? You said you'd come dancin' with me. For she had torn her nightdress into pieces. Maybe she wanted to climb out of the window. Well, with a-beggin' and a-pleadin' and a-sayin' of fine stories to her, I got her to get dressed and I brought her downstairs. The poor parents were keepin' out of the way, as they had been told, though it was hard for them. We did not dare tell the mother where we were takin' her. I kept a-talkin' about the square dance and a-praisin' her looks and I picked some flowers outside the door to put in her belt. But she was puzzled, too; and she said, It's early in the mornin' to go to a square-dance. I said, No, it isn't, Hilda. We've got to go to dinner at the hotel first; and we have people to meet. I am a-drivin' you in and I want people to see you. She was pleased and put flowers in her hair too; and I said, Give me those flowers, Hilda, to keep fresh; you know what a long dusty road it is to town. She said, Why, are you ashamed of me? Is there somethin' wrong with me? I think there's somethin' wrong with me. I said, No, no, Hilda, but you are so sweet and pretty, I want to see you in the first figure of the square-dance the prettiest there; so keep your flowers fresh till we get to Lambertville. She looked quite pretty, though her face was pale and troubled and she had not been able to smooth her hair right, poor thing. I drove her straight down to the doctor's and he went with us to the asylum. Mr. Dilley took her things there the next day; and she's been there ever since, many years.

"Her mother kept a-cryin' to get her out and blamed the doctors for not a-curin' her; and with a-worryin' and a-blamin', she got worn and tired out herself. So I'm sorry for Mr. Dilley, too. She can't go far enough to lay the blame; one time on the farm, another time on them both for a-lettin' her marry that Nevada man with the gui-tar; and so on.

"That's the story, you see; and I'm a-lookin' after the place for Mr. Dilley because of his hard luck. Mr. Davies thought I was a-takin' of Mr. Dilley's money, I could see; but I said nothin' to Mr. Davies because he is a sick man. Yes, I saw her right here in that doorway a-throwin' axes and mad as a coot. Young Strasser could hear from the hill—on that hill they can hear everythin' you say down here if they listen. And I guess you can hear what they say, except that they never speak on this side of the hill. And young Strasser ran for me, you see, because roundabout here they run for me. Well, I'll send Johnson down to cut down your weeds."

"Oh, no, please don't, Mr. Thornton. Those weeds bring the birds and my wife loves to have them 'round."

"Ah, the only birds you can find for miles are in this creek run. They've been driven out everywhere else. My sons have been to agricultural college and say we need them. But we're not used to them 'round here. You can have too many of them."

"My wife can't have too many. I think she could live all her life here with them and not miss people."

"Well, that's not quite right for a woman: it's too lonely."

"You don't know my wife. She loves all this. She doesn't need anything else. She always wanted to live in the zoo. She'd like to have the animals, including the insects, in the house with her."

"Would she now? Well, they try to oblige her!" he said, with a kind look, and pointing to the large spider which had slipped out from its plank, viewed them and slid back. "Does she like that?"

"Well, she looks out for it from the house. She tells me, There's the spider sunning himself. He sees her, too."

The summer was fat, steamy, heavy-headed, an obsession. Sam went to town to see "the boys," and Mr. Thornton was busy. Clare was happy in the Dilleys' place. She put out food for the animals, and pulled up no plants because each plant is a shelter for some living thing. Once or twice when alone, she herself lay down naked in the center of the weed patch, to get all the sun, lay there drowsy thinking of fertility, surrounded by all the life and love of the beast and plant world, part of the earth life. "Why is the devil called the Lord of Flies? If he is, then we must be close to his hole." Myriads of flying insects shone, flitted, strummed, whined and in the thick air lived. "The woodchuck is quite bold now, he comes nearer the house every day observing us; only his wife hangs in the background; but she too is coming nearer."

The woodchuck who lived in the bank fed in the old vegetable patch. There was a family of skunks now that came for their food by night, hundreds more mice living with them in the two houses. Two weasels flashed in and out by the porch; the house-wrens on the porch singing boldly or creeping mouse-like through the woodpiles all day sounded their rattles; there were more mourning doves making every clouded and clotted evening sky sad; the whistling whip of the sleepy thrushes, the lowing cows and their lost calves, the woodchucks nearly to the house now, the birds invading, the danger-calling catbirds, the strange insect's strumming in the house, immense flies and wasps, the increasing heat and damp, the owls, the insect rabble; and myriads multiplying in this one sacred uncleared hollow. "If we lived here long enough and everything grew thick enough and high enough we would see the world as an ant does among his grass stalks."

Clare cleaned the house and was frightened. "I was on the landing at the top of the wooden stairs and I felt myself being pushed toward the stairs, a force from that little room wanted to throw me downstairs, from the door, like a . . . I was afraid; I came down the stairs step by step sitting on them."

Sam Parsons then told the story of Hilda Dilley. "I forget her married name. But that was Poky—Pocahontas—after you."

"Is she still capable of such strength? The house has accumulated a great ousting power. But how can it oust me? I am for it, I am for all here."

The catbirds' catcalls and mewing ran through the bushes. Eels went downstream. Clouds of insects came from the cornfields. A large ball of soot sat watching on the bridge and bobbed down when it saw them move. At night the fireflies burned like a net of sparks through the wild plants. If they turned out the light this curtain of fire made a faint glow around them. In bed, they saw them still, for Dilley's place was an underearth, lower than all the green around; and there around them burned the world of flies, so that the distant skystars, obscured by night insects and waving vines and leaves as if by smoke, were unnecessary. It was a kind of infant lightning.

The air grew heavier; unusual streaked and mottled skies appeared. "I never knew we had such large flies in the U.S.A. I thought that was for South America."

"The ants and spiders have come in everywhere. It is going to rain."

"I never lived in so much nature; I never knew I could," said Sam, laughing, tenderly, helplessly.

"Poky is singing much louder now," said Clare referring to the insect that strummed in the corner, and which they had never located. "This morning I heard it when I was near the creek; and I looked for it again."

"I suppose there are more of them. Whatever it is, has had a family. Everything 'round here has had four or five families this summer."

"I read in the Lambertville *Gazette* that this and the wood on the cliff, in the film-star's estate, is a refuge for birds and all wild things, everything driven from the farms."

The owl hooted. "That's a dreadful sound."

"Yes." To comfort him, she remarked, "Where the mice and little birds and insects are, there are owls; and mice and little birds where corn and insects are."

"Oh," said Sam Parsons, "I have gotten used to them. Not so long ago I would have taken the first train back to New York."

They listened awhile to the footsteps, which now began to go downstairs, with a heavy soft irregular tread.

"The mice must enter the kitchen where the step is worn under the door at the bottom."

Presently the footfalls came upstairs again in the same slow soft way and crossed the landing.

"I suppose they get crumbs; I put away everything," said Clare, "but why do they live in the little room here?"

"Let's go to sleep," said Sam.

The plank in the bridge clonked.

"They're coming from the movies."

She heard Sam breathing faintly in sleep. The living sleeping night was all around, close, formless, rich and suffocating as a mother's breast. On the black breast of night she fell asleep, too. The footsteps passed her again; she did not hear them; the bridge gave warning; they slept. The faceless haunter of the stone house moved slightly through the open attic door and down the closed stairs; with the strength of water behind glass, without shape and ready to pour through, it mixed with the moonlight at the locked glass door, mixing as blood with water, smoking, turning. But there was peace in the bedroom; until the skunks came for the liver laid out at the back door, when, at the musky stench, there was a great rain of mice and Clare awoke, listening, delighted. "There you are, friends, animals, children," she thought; and heard many small real footfalls, squeaks and movements.

In mid-July the skies began to cloud. The air thickened and darkened. All day long the wren's wearying clackers rang. Awfully mournful in these oppressive days was the late and early sobbing of the doves; fateful, the sound of the thrush retiring last in the woods. The ants marched thick along their routes. When would the rain come?

Every evening and morning now the Parsons walked out of the brooding hollow, where the Lord of Flies surly sat spinning his flies; and they walked on the upper roads and tracks. Higher up, where the Dilleys' creek parted from the river, was a bridge; brilliant birds, tanagers, orioles, canaries and even bluebirds flew and sat freely here.

One evening they were upon the township road winding around the meadowy hill above the Sobieskis'. Below lay their hollow, the thick trees surging over their red roofs. They were now higher than the Strassers' ridge and the sun was setting over it. There was trouble somewhere, a warning. Something not yet unwound but waiting lay complete under the green stuff in the valley bottom. On this upland the air was easy to breathe; there was still golden light. They started back again, almost with regret. A dead swallow which had been for weeks dangling in the telephone wires, had now turned to skeleton and hung still. The descending road turned south and caught the Dilleys' track which turned west. The sky was sapphire. Looking at it before they went down to their burrow, they saw one cloud forming, one cloud only in the whole sky, in the west directly over the sun going down. It came out in flecks and wisps, became suddenly one curled gold feather, and so stayed, as if beaten out of metal; marvelous, and the only thing in the sky and like an eyebrow right over the sun in the green sky.

"Down came the hurricane," said Clare as the first cold air caught them.

"You would say that is a hurricane cloud?"

"Oh, but it is so still; and the sky is clear. No; that is from the 'Ballad of Carmilhan': the Captain up and down the deck—"

They came down into their trees. It was nearly dark there. There were the solitary liquid notes of the woodthrush beginning to be heard in the brush by the track. "Birds understand music and natural beauty." And then began, miserable, intolerable in this air, the dove who nested by the bridge. For a long time he sobbed; and the birds were restless in the fever of midsummer.

They ate and looked through a book they found on the top shelf of the window-closet in the stone house. They never used the sitting room of the stone house, preferring the stove, the porches and fiery windows of the farm kitchen. But tonight for the first time they sat there, and

read the fat heavy volume, a farmers' encyclopedia, of the sort once sold
at country fairs, miscellaneous reading, advice on farming, cooking,
sewing, illnesses. A nineteenth-century gingerbread murder castle:
"But how could you calculate all the unaccounted-for space in a gingerbread house?" An account of John Wesley and his diary: "You know
when he says he gave up smoking, I believe he meant something else."

The lightning was now forking from opposite the sunset, stabbing
high; and then the sky-creature's blue nervous system, its brain, its
lungs and its nerves like trees lighted up all around, on high, turning
the trees into a black huddle, a pressed herd. Now they did not seem
to be lost in a lowland, but the lowland was heaved up to light and the
hills flattened by the pallid shine.

The rain began, at first only a few drops; and it remained almost dry
all night. Soon they locked everything and went to bed. It was cooler.
The entire sky now quivered with pale light. As well as the perpetual
quivering everywhere and the faint sound, another lightning now rolled
over the sky from east to west in long pale corrugations and thunder
followed its rolling. There was no darkness and no silence. Such a
strange storm they had never seen. They did not sleep; and it was not
the storm, not the light, not the noise, so much as the strangeness. At
length, Clare came and sat on Sam's side of the bed and held his hand;
and the two of them sat all night huddled up, looking with astonishment at a night they had never seen, the combers of light, the continuous irregular rush, murmur and roar.

The next day it rained. The thin glassy creek thickened and washed
from saucer to saucer. In the evening, it could be heard slapping down;
in the night it was gushing. What would the woodchucks do? But Mr.
Thornton had already told them about the good sense of woodchucks.
Old man woodchuck had a dryland exit somewhere up the bank; he
would doubtless save his family. In the morning, with the rain continu-
ing the creek had risen yellow; it poured and curdled along. The
mailman blew his horn. They hurried out. "Are you all right?" At this
they laughed. "Right as rain." In the afternoon, Riondo, the Lambertville butcher, came along in his car and shouted, "Are you all right?"
"What are those planes?" The planes which had been above them all
day were army bombers looking out for marooned farmers. The Delaware had risen; those nearest to it in Lambertville were in danger; they
had drawn all boats out of the river. It was exciting. The birds made
little sound except for the house-wrens and the dove. It was still warm.
In the afternoon, when the rain ceased, the insects and birds began

again; but the woodchuck and his wife did not come to the vegetable patch. It was still raining elsewhere. The creek had risen again and was a yellow pouring in which no life was visible; only the rubbish from the banks and woods. The rain came again at night. Through it, they heard their creek as it tore through the vines and roots. Then it grew quieter and then ceased. In the morning, the rain had ceased and Clare getting up saw that they were surrounded by a gray standing fog, for from all the floor-level windows she could see gray only; but when this gray fog moved slightly, carrying sticks, then she saw it was flood; Dilley's place was underwater. The water had not yet entered the house and it had stopped raining. They took all movables upstairs and prepared to leave. The water spread out over the two acres was smooth and moving slowly; but it rushed and foamed out of the long narrow gorge beyond, where the boys bathed, and had risen to the top rail of the bridge; the spider, the ball of soot, was no more. They waded through the hip-high water at the bridge, climbed the hill and asked Mr. Thornton to get them to town.

His fat fair wife and her fat fair daughter were sitting in rocking-chairs in the kitchen in a jolly mood. They had just received a three-burner kerosene stove from town; they had used a big farm stove like the Dilleys'. Up to this moment they had spent money only on necessary farm improvements and on a small radio. They were not like the Newbolds who had every new electrical improvement.

"My daughter is going to have the money when she marries. When she goes to church on Sundays, all the boys look at her, don't they, Maureen?"

The girl laughed, rocked back and forth. "Maureen is the catch of this township," said the mother, looking back from the stove on which her eyes rested. "We thought you'd be getting flooded out," said Mrs. Thornton laughing and rocking. "Mr. Thornton was saying, They'll have water through the kitchen by this time; that cellar is always full of water in winter."

The daughter laughed and rocked. They talked about her sow which had farrowed three times in a year. Last time it had had seventeen piglets of which she had eaten two and smothered one; but that still made thirty-six living piglets in a year.

"And they're all Maureen's," said Mrs. Thornton. "The sow's hers; she looks after it and they're all her pigs. She sells them and the money's hers."

The fat, small-eyed daughter grinned.

They had sent the boy Johnson, a white-skinned lad of heroic build, for Mr. Thornton, who now arrived, very gay.

Said he, "We've not a drop of water in here; all watertight."

"I always wondered myself why all the houses were built on top of these hills where the lightning can strike," said Clare.

"That house down there is always the same, winter it's waterbound," said the farmer.

"In winter, all you have to do is lean out of the kitchen window and dip in the pail," said Mrs. Thornton.

"Always twenty foot of water in the cellar," said the daughter. "You know that hailstorm we had? Came right up to our fence and turned back, didn't touch a blade nor an ear. Laid everything in Strassers' flat and they're poor, haven't a cent. Everything that side, laid flat. Stopped right at our fence. I wish I had shown you, to see."

They looked brightly at each other.

"You have to have luck," said Mrs. Thornton. "The berry farm failed. I knew it would. One of them got sick; and then the Dilleys had their daughter get sick with the lung-sickness, that's the damp; and then the Davies came. You could see right through that boy when he came and the father's a very weak-looking man," she chuckled, "and the bottle didn't help."

"Mother," said Mr. Thornton, "that's Mr. Parsons' friend."

"Oh, excuse me. Mr. Thornton looks after the house; well—and the —" She began to laugh and poked her daughter in the arm; they both laughed. The daughter could not take her eyes off the visitors. She laughed in a vain way and at the same time her eyes devoured their valises, their town shoes and Clare's light coat.

Mr. Thornton sobered down and said, "There's nothin' to be done with that house. You might as well pull it down and move it farther up into Sobieski's fields. But Mrs. Sobieski wanted money and she sold off that bottom bit of the field that is no good and all the long bit of creek the cows could fall into. It's not much more than a water-meadow. And it was a crazy idea to build that deep cellar; it's just a watertrap. Keep fish there."

At this amusing idea, the mother and daughter went into a gale of laughter. "Yes, fish."

"Couldn't it easily be fixed up?" said Parsons. "There must be a local engineer who could build a dam and there are new ways of treating walls for seepage. Deepen, widen, dam the creek, get permission."

Mr. Thornton thought it might easily cost $10,000. He'd talked to engineers, had one over. "The house and ground is worthless as it stands."

"Well, that wooden bridge stood up to the flood the last three days and is as firm as a rock," said Clare.

"Do you mean to say we can build TVA and not fix a little thing like that," said Sam Parsons.

Mr. Thornton became very intent. He'd had it studied; it couldn't be done. Mr. Parsons, surprised, said that the whole fault lay in the narrow gorge the creek ran through in the panhandle part of Dilley's and the sharp rightangle it turned. Mr. Thornton argued emphatically, while the mother and daughter looked on with rounder eyes, ready to laugh, but aware that Thornton was upset. "It catches all the water from all these hills and you'd need to pull down the house and make the whole place a dam."

He presently took them off in his car. At parting Clare told the Thorntons she would see them in a few days.

"Oh, are you a-comin' back?"

"Oh, yes. We've rented it till the end of October."

Staring, the Thornton women watched them and their valises into the car; and then suddenly again were overcome with fun.

"Well, just send me a line when you're a-comin' back and I'll open up the place for you," said Thornton placably, as he saw them off at Flemington station.

It blew, it rained for two weeks; and in three weeks they returned. As they approached they saw the cottage radiant through the trees. Mr. Thornton was waiting for them on their porch. The creek banks were soiled with floodmarks, the water was not yet clear and all things were grayed by the flood; but the sun shone. They joyously hurried to the house.

Mr. Thornton gave them the key saying, "Excuse me for not a-goin' in with you. I'm very busy now with the farm. If you want anythin', come to me."

They unlocked the door. The floor was muddy. The chairs, tables, benches, windowsills and all downward surfaces were hung with beards of gray-white mold up to nine inches long. "The Spanish moss has migrated from Florida." The stove was rusted. It smelled like a cellar or cave. The cellar of the stone house was full to the opening, the steps ran down underwater, a swimming pool. Thornton's secret; they laughed. They cleaned, aired and sunned everything, keeping one of the chairs to show visitors; but no visitors came yet and in a few days of sun the chair was clean. The birds sang, the woodchuck family reappeared in the vegetable patch; the grapes ripened on the outhouse. The skunks and weasels had gone, there were fewer mice; the wrens had deserted their last brood dead in the nest. After a couple of weeks everything was nearly as before; the insects had returned though they no longer thickened the air; the twanging insect in the house twanged as before. Yet it was a pity to look at the ravaged creekside from which all the delicate plants had gone. The great ravens were still there, one sitting on a naked branch and one picking in the sun on the track.

They looked through the house, peered from the windows of the little locked room. "Oh, why not buy it? It doesn't always rain." The Dilleys' land was only a hand's breadth of riverbank, a woodchuck's backyard. The surrounding hills and combing trees were blameless as before; the sunlight golden through the damp invisible vapors was like a woman's yellow mane thrown over everything; under, her damp warm meadowy skin.

"Poky was singing loudly again today. She sings in that corner of the kitchen that is under the little room. Why don't you come and look at her things, poor woman?" Sam always refused. He had seen nothing but the Indian dress and turned away from that. "I don't want to see it, don't let me see those things." They now always called it, Poky's Place.

"She tries to get rid of everyone: it is still her place."

"Don't say those things."

"Why?"

"It's dangerous."

Bill Jermyn with Clare, and Joyce Jermyn with Sam, were walking along a tree-tufted edge. On one side a crumbling hillside, on the other, private unfenced woods protected by high trees linked and walled with poison ivy and poison oak.

"What do you think of the haunting by knives and axes? It isn't real," said Clare, "but it's astonishing."

Bill Jermyn was a blue-black brunette, with a melancholy nutcracker face, handsome sunk eyes and a strong-set body blanketed in hair; this hair showed through the opening of his blue shirt and on his arms. Clare looked at this hair, glanced away, thinking, Bats fly into women's hair because they don't get the echoes back. I don't get the thoughts back from hairy men. But Clare and Jermyn were close friends. They were interested in things like this.

"I say it's a low hollow where all the water and all the vapors concentrate; not only that, it's protected; things grow faster, breed thicker and then the trees and plants take the air. At night you have no oxygen at all with all those old trees bending over you taking the air from you. It's like sleeping in an old fourposter with curtains and canopy and carpet. And though you're surrounded, it's lonely. You're overlooked. That imaginary man in the attic—you're overlooked by the dark bushy hairy hill. It's lonely here, lonely and timeless, or it has jungle time, millennial time only, dangerous to man."

"Oh, no. It's millennial time we managed very well with," said Clare, laughing; "and I am not afraid."

"Are you afraid of knives?"

"I never was."

"There is something there—the vapors perhaps? This something which also appeared to you as a strong force pushing you downstairs, brought out the idea of ax-murders in Poky; and in you, a fear of knives."

"I wonder you didn't hear the mice in the night," said Clare.

"I wonder myself," said Joyce, a black-eyed impatient beauty, young, rounded. She had a rich, drawling, accusing voice. "Bill's scared of mice; they're nasty symbols to him, sex symbols, horror symbols. He got out of a property deal that way, found there were mice there and got a letter from his psychoanalyst."

When they got home, Jermyn climbed one of the trees and stayed there for forty minutes, his blue shirt visible through the leaves, an attractive blue-black four-cornered bird.

When he came down he said, "What I'd like to do is buy the place away from Thornton; he's after it for that sow daughter of his." He left them for a walk and called on Mrs. Sobieski. He was a young man with a melancholy ingratiating manner. He found out what she thought the Dilleys' place was worth and whether she would sell a bit of her field above the house. He arrived back, smoking his short-stem pipe, with the loping walk of handsome legs and when he got to where they were sitting on the porch, he slung his legs over the balustrade and said he thought he would buy it and rent it or loan it.

"Another thing is the electric light. One thing I noticed about your story was that the electric light being on all night was the storm-signal for Poky's crime down here; and it was the storm-signal for the Davies —Laban went away and the light was on all night; a lighted cabin in all these dark thickets. As in the musicians of Bremen."

And fixing the pipe again in his mouth, he looked toward the bridge and barn, his fine tragic chinchopper face musing.

In a few moments he took the pipe out again to add, "You know Professor Abe Carter has collected funds for a writers' refuge? He's looking for a place. I can make something out of this idea. I'll get Carter to contribute some of the money he's collected, buy Dilley's place, call it Dilley's Place, summer camp for writers, say there's a ghost—you have first option. Give me a few days and I might do something with Dilley's place. Besides, I don't want old man Thornton on his hill to get it; just cussedness; because he's been playing for it. There's something to this place. Easy to work out a dam."

"Get a couple of beavers," said Clare.

"Whoever built this place? In this lap of the hills, a catchment place, a gorge? Naturally anyone who put in a deep cellar was delirious. And insane he who built it in the first place. And then, after winters and summers, he goes and builds a wing in masonry."

"He thought the cellar would take all the water," said Clare.

"Who was the architect, who the engineer? Well, here it is and beautiful as a russet apple. Where's your outhouse? It's that, smothered in grapes? I'll join you with the whole thing worked out." So saying, the handsome young man hopped off the railing, after a while came out again with the farmers' encyclopedia and crossed the yard. They had gone for a walk to see the birds at their stations along the track, especially the buff-and-blue humming birds. When they returned, Bill Jermyn was just returning full of grace from the grape arbor, book in hand. "By the way, what is that strumming or singing that I hear coming from the grapes?"

"That is the ghost."

"It is?"

"Oh, I'm certain."

"That's very curious," said Jermyn, strolling around, climbing, sounding and poking. "Is it a loose wire, an Aeolian harp? Could be an old vine somewhere, some nails."

"The sound has been getting louder for months."

"It isn't flies in a spider's web?"

"Yes, brass flies in a brass web, I always said that," said Clare. There was a wind that night. The next morning Joyce said, "What were you people doing running up and downstairs all night? I was awake. We did our best to get a baby last night; and we overdid it, I couldn't sleep, though he did."

"It was the mice."

"The mice? That?"

"Yes. They do that every night. And fall down the walls."

Joyce looked serious and presently she and Bill Jermyn went for a walk, up and down the track, quite visible from the windows but separated by a palisade of trees, wheeling lights, the impassable barricade of *Rhus radicans*, the creek and its voice. When she came back Joyce said, "There are snakes in the water; watersnakes. Oh, I know I shall get pregnant here; the place is alive," she shuddered, "alive . . . and then I'll get out of here."

The next night she stumbled up the steep dark wooden stairs with a jug of water and a glass. "I may want an aspirin in the night and I wouldn't go down there at night."

She brought up her water and something to eat. "Nothing would make me go on those stairs in the dark hours. I might tread on a mouse. I hate it here. Why is it artists like to live in primitive conditions, with a john a hundred yards away, so that you can step on a snake going to it; or some bull get you or man rape you; remote from life among the farming clods, little boys with sticks driving cows, in a mice-eaten weasel-bitten shack with disgusting little vines that work themselves round your finger while you're reading a book on the back step. Would such hard luck have come to Poky in the city if her parents had had the sense to stay there? All country cottages are mistakes, follies."

At another time she said restlessly, "The trouble with me is Jermyn's not my type. I've got to find my type. I've been too long about it. Now I suppose I'm going to have a baby by him. I didn't have the sense to get out first. Jermyn's a good type for a father and he'll always be able to support the child and me. But as soon as I have it I'm getting out. What I ought to be looking for is a wolf. There are no wolves here. There's nothing here for me."

The next afternoon was warm and close. Lightning the color of fireflies flickered; the south flared, thunder rolled in the distance, rolling iron barrels. Suddenly it roared overhead; and from the sky, violent rain. A gray long-haired animal leapt the creek, and howling, whining in fear, rushed to the porch and crawled under it, where it lay trembling.

"There couldn't be a wolf round here!" cried Joyce. "I saw a wolf!" "It's an Alsatian dog!" "It's a wolf," snapped Joyce. "What a place! It's the backwoods. It's a timber wolf." "Well, you asked for a wolf and it seems that here you get what you want." "A wolf?" "Yes, you asked for a wolf. In Poky's day a wolf was a wolf." "Don't make a joke of it," cried Joyce: "it's too horrible. I'm not staying here tonight."

When the storm had passed they tried to lure the dog from the porch with a piece of meat. He lay close to the earth, in the warm damp narrow space, trembling and whining. "You do have mighty cracks of thunder here," said Jermyn. "It's like the Catskills." Joyce declared she was going back that afternoon. "I wouldn't spend another night here: by the morning you may be invaded by bears and moose. This is just a piece of the great northern world that has got loose. And I know Poky hears every word we say." "You always claim that you're not superstitious," said Bill Jermyn. "I am not. These are facts. I can believe what I see. I said wolf and a wolf came," grumbled Joyce.

When dusk came, but before they put on the light, they looked from the kitchen windows and there almost invisible in the grass emptying of light, ran a pale animal. First he ran crouching, then he began to lope; he sped across the bridge, up the track toward the blackberries. "It's a lost dog: no one 'round here has an Alsatian," said Clare. "It's a specter," said Joyce. She got up early in the morning, packed and came down. "Bill is taking me away. You finish out your summer here if you can. Rather you than me. But I bet you won't finish out the summer here."

"Oh, Poky has done her worst. Now she has made us welcome."

"If you trust her you're mad."

They went. The full dropping summer days passed and trees hung out the golden bough. The Parsons had decided to go to town for the winter and return the next spring. Bill Jermyn, meanwhile, making a sketch of his own plan, was sending down two brothers named Imber to stay, look around, see what could be done to make the cottage watertight, to extend it, make it habitable for a small community. As the villages in this part of the Delaware country declined in workers, and farmers, like the ten sons of Farmer Thornton, went farther out to the plains because of big scale farming methods, the derelict farms and follies were becoming the homes of workers in the arts. Jermyn was shaping up his idea of planting small semi-socialist, self-dependent artistic communities.

The brothers, Frederick and Walter Imber, high school teachers, aged thirty-four and thirty-two, were indistinguishable at a distance, of great breadth and density, large limbed, moving heavily, vain of their strength. They were goodnatured men, timid about their neighbors, about infringements. They did their own housework, and spent the day outside idly, but with an innocent pretense of hard work, while they agreed with each other in long discussions of political theory. They were vegetarians, abstainers and, untrained as engineers or architects or cooks or farmers, they attempted to supply their needs and their friends' needs with their own hands. They made plans for a dam and waterwall to proceed from the dam and protect the house. But, they said, this waterwall would have to be well based in the earth, rocks at the creek's right angle would have to be blasted, the whole creek would have to be dug deeper, thus ruining the charm of its rocky shells and saucers dipping down and the first heavy rain turning the trickle into a torrent would probably flood the road. The whole thing needed planning, not to mention permission from Mr. Dilley, and the Township.

The Imbers decided to go ahead with it at once. They began to dig a new channel for the creek through the old berry patch. The trench filled with water and they were pleased. At once they had another idea. "Broaden and deepen the creek bed all the way along: you'll lose some three hundred square feet of land, but the rest will never be flooded and the track will be safe from flooding." They began on this immense project, with picks and shovels, and at once faced the tangle of elderberry, poison ivy and poison oak and other weeds whose strong woven roots held the soil together. "The creek will be the natural barrier, though we don't want a barrier. The water will keep the Strassers' chickens and stray cattle and dogs away. So we'll get rid of all this spinach," said Fred Imber, sweeping a hand over the vines and bending and thrusting the other hand into the deep tangled green.

"Be careful: you're in poison ivy!" said Clare. At this both the brothers burst out laughing. Walter came running up and Frederick said, "Surely an intelligent woman like you doesn't believe that superstition! It's created by the imagination: it's psychosomatic. You fear it, so you get a rash, or whatever you want to get."

"Well, the country people and the farmers believe it," said Clare: "and I believe it, I've had it." "Yes, they've talked it into you. Surely you know there's no one more ignorant than yokels and farmers. I've heard country people say the mushrooms all disappeared because they were pulled up by the roots." Frederick laughed. "I'll show you," he said. He threw himself down into the poison ivy and rolled about in it. "You'll see, I won't get a spot." He took handfuls of the bright ivy-shaped leaves and rubbed them over his face and neck, laughing, bathed his hands and arms in it, opened his shirt and rolled his barrel chest in the leaves, face and palms down, embracing the ground. "See,

see!" he cried; "I feel nothing. You'll find out it's pure superstition. I don't believe in it, so I won't suffer from it." He turned over laughing and lay back among the plants. All around the poisonous plants moved softly, shone about him. "I'm going to sleep in it, let me have forty winks," he said, smiling. "To sleep, perchance to dream!"

"Good excuse, isn't it?" said Walter. Clare looked, "Don't lie there!" Frederick reached out, plucked branches of the vine and twined them around his neck and face, and put a twig in his mouth. "Now under the vine, in the arms of the vine I sleep," he said.

Sam Parsons could not stir him. An hour or so later, his brother who had kept on with the trench, brought him in to the house, uneasy and somewhat ill. His skin everywhere was marked with a crowded red rash, trails of pinpoint spots marking the places of sprays and lengths of vine that he had worn.

"Don't send for the quack," he said; "I've heard he's an old alcoholic; all he ever knew was washed out long ago; and besides this is a psychosomatic rash, not a real one. What can he do? Let me sit inside for a while till the sun goes down; then the rash will go away; it was brought on by the sun. If you have some water, a fruit drink." He drank and began to walk up and down, through the house, standing in the three porches to get the cool air, keeping out of the sun. "At sunset it will go. I am just dyed by the sun. I'm flushed, I have a sensitive nervous skin," he said.

At night, they sent for the doctor; and that night too, the light was on many hours in the glen, till the ambulance came for the sick man. He died a few days later. His brother went back to the city distraught and deeply puzzled.

One day in September, they posted a letter to Mr. Dilley asking his price for the place. "We may as well have a refuge somewhere."

That evening she was at the leaky pump pumping water into the kitchen sink when she trod on something that felt like a mouse or bird. She moved hastily, slipped in a pool of water and fell breaking her arm.

"Look at my funny arm," she called out to Sam Parsons who was in the stonehouse. He did not reply. She got up and walked to the door of the stonehouse. "Sam, I'm afraid you'll have to go for the doctor."

Sam set out. It was a dark starry night, slightly windy, the full treetops moving. Animals moved, the owls screeched. Sam with the lantern, an uncertain firefly on the track, stumbled and wove his way from the patch to the bridge, from the bridge past lower fields to the hilly track and so to Thornton's. Thornton took him to town and from town he came back with the doctor. All this took two hours. Meanwhile Clare with her arm suspended from the neck in a scarf, walked around the house putting on all the lights: the many bright windows of the cottage shone out like a lighthouse to all sides of the glen; and she sat and drank a bottle of wine. Presently, the doctor came. "And tomorrow you must go into town for an X-ray," he said. He was drunk, but he operated quickly, smartly. The patient was drunk too, and the whole thing passed off very well.

In the morning they sent for a taxi and went to the station with their luggage. Mr. Thornton came early in the morning, a bright warm morning, for the keys. "You can have them any time; I'll keep them up at home," he said cheerfully.

"Thank you. I don't think we'll be back this year," said Sam Parsons.

On the track at the bridge, they turned and looked; the cottage, copper-rose, brick-red, nested close in the green, spellbound, smiling. "Oh, what an enchanting place. We must come back next summer," said Clare. "Look, that is where poor Fred Imber dug his trench." The trench was still there, with a little water in it. "It looks horrible," said Parsons. "Let's get out of here. We are not coming back next summer."

"Look at it now! Oh, how lovely."

"Let the little brass guitar sing to someone else next summer."

"Oh, how superstitious you are after all."

"Yes, I am."

Every summer the cottage enticed some new transient. The Thorntons, mother and daughter, laughed at the strange people; and talked about what they would do with the cottage when it became Maureen's, when she married. "I don't know, I don't know, I'll see," said Thornton. "Remember that poor girl is still alive. We won't touch it yet."

MISS HERBERT (THE SUBURBAN WIFE)

Miss Herbert, issued in 1976, is the most recently published of Christina Stead's novels.

The heroine is Eleanor Herbert, an English beauty who never wakes up to herself or to the latent erotic power which is her only source of authenticity. After years of mean affairs, she marries an unsuitable man and has two children. When the marriage fails she tries her hand at writing and grubs for small jobs on the fringes of the literary world.

In the passage that follows, Eleanor is in her fifties. She has become quite a successful literary agent, but her capacity for self-deception is unimpaired. Dr. Mack, whom Eleanor seeks out unsuccessfully at the end, is a girlhood friend, an expert in tropical medicine who has spent her life helping others.

I

THE GUINEA PIG

. . . Mr. Quaideson received her in the lounge of a small flat furnished with chairs, rugs, divans and a good many bookcases in wood painted white. Putting down her bag and gloves, sitting upright in a tapestry chair, Eleanor got out the manuscript of *Smokeover Farm*, Mary Darling's novel, and asked if Mr. Quaideson wanted to read it—or would she read some of it to him? She had carefully prepared her speech for Mr. Quaideson.

She said, "I have a very simple suggestion, after speaking to Mr. Ambrose and your accountant, that you go in for young unpublished authors of promise; tie them up with a long contract, which they'll be glad to sign, at reasonably low terms, just in case your judgment has had a blind spot, and then just sit back and let your firm build up its own reputation and bank balance."

Eleanor intended this to be an up-to-date, no-nonsense sales talk. She went on talking and Mr. Quaideson sat back looking at her. Light was filtered through a modern skylight from a terrace above. The old hangings and rugs of the flat made a handsome setting for the fine-looking middle-aged woman. Mr. Quaideson, sitting some distance away, with his legs crossed and out from a polished desk, also looked well in that light. He was a tall, fleshy man wearing a silk shirt and scarf and a dark suit of fine material. He had the complexion of a yellow peach, and a rather ecclesiastical dignity; his hair was thick and pale. He had false teeth with an agate shine, handsome pale-red lips and bloodshot eyes in large eyesockets; the face was long with fine cheekbones.

"Don't read me the prose, Miss Herbert," he said when she had finished. "It may be everything you say, but to me, authors merely produce the raw material for my presses. I have always been sorry that we have not a sort of author-machine: press a button, put in a royalty and get out the kind of syrup you want. Does that shock you very much? I am afraid I think that the life of the palest shopgirl or the barber with the emptiest head is worth all the manuscripts ever written: I am afraid I am simply not interested in writers. I bought up a firm very cheap, just as I might have bought a paint-and-varnish shop. I'm rather sorry I didn't, as a matter of fact—I like paint and varnish. I like ironmongery too; do you? It's quite a passion of mine; and I don't know if you believe in cartomancy—I don't—but a woman wrote me a letter saying that a fortuneteller had said that she should eventually make a match of it with a man who liked ironmongery. I thanked the lady for the offer, but I turned it down. She was not an author—I happened to buy an old brass lantern clock from her. I am very much interested in antiques. I just acquired this old Bible box; picked it up in Woking."

Eleanor folded up the manuscript and put it in her bag. Mr. Quaideson, while chattering about his antiques, was watching her with interest; and then said, "What are you going to do now?"

Eleanor told him that she was going to offer the book to several other firms, and that she had decided (on the spur of the moment, but she did not say that) to offer her services with it, as a condition. If she was accepted, she would quit A. & Q's. She rose and went to the door before he could get up.

"My dear Miss Herbert," he said starting from his desk. "Come back! Come back!" She stood with her hand on the door, looking at him proudly; then she returned slowly. "What is the matter? Why do you take such an interest in this young author? It is Miss Herbert, isn't it? Or is it Mrs.? You're not an agent, are you? You're quite new to all of this, aren't you? You see, I am very little of a publisher, also. So sit down, take off your furs, I'll make some tea and we can talk about ourselves—that will be more interesting. I am quite serious when I say that your life or my life as we have lived it is worth more than ten thousand *Smokeover Farms* even if it's all you say it is. I've always had a tremendous craving for life and I'm always irritated with books, they are so far from it. And the only time I am not irritated," he said, with a charming flash of teeth, "is when I am working on my own manuscripts—for I have what is best of all, unpublished manuscripts of my own. That is why, I think, that published books irritate me so much: they are so confident, glossy, hard-faced, pushing. To me, all the juice of the book is in an unpublished manuscript, and the published book is like a dead tree—just good for cutting up and building your house with. Now tell me why you are so anxious to see this book published."

"I must live."

"Ah! You're a widow?"

For the first time in her life Eleanor broke down with a stranger. She suddenly put her hands to her face and with a sob said, "My husband left me. I never thought he would—he had no reason to."

Mr. Quaideson's face brightened and softened. He lost his teasing and callous expression. With a mocking smile, he offered to take *Smokeover Farm* if she wished him to, but said she would do better with a fiction house. "We like curiosities, topicalities—we are more like a newspaper than a book publisher's. It's quite a good idea, and always a paying idea. Authors are a nuisance to us. You peddle your authors elsewhere, my dear Miss Herbert; let us have the benefit of your help and advice, and let us remain friends, but I mean personal friends." He drew his chair beside hers, bathed her in the full light of his smile and glistening eyes and said, "But you yourself must have a story worth anything ever written; I can feel a special flavor in you; I know it would make a story. Did you yourself ever try to write it? For instance, how does it happen that a woman like yourself—a fine-looking and, I can tell, aware, sensually aware, woman, aware of the sensual values—is living alone? You are not the kind of woman who lives alone—your children, your children!" He leaned closer to her, his large face coming nearer to her large breasts. "A woman living with her children is indeed living alone!" When she got up he put a fleshy arm around her shoulders and "propelled" her toward another room. "Come with me, my dear Miss Herbert. I want to see how you react to some of my antiques. I have choice, curious things; I like age, but quality, and I prefer things with strange associations. Do you believe that an idol which has seen many sacrifices is impregnated with the smoke of the burning blood and just as much with the mystic adoration, the mental fumes, steeped in thousands of past lives in dead history? Do you believe you can tell by *feeling* that a rope has taken a man's life? I believe that blood has a voice; the worm has a voice that we can hear if we try, so Blake suggests; and the blood of torment has a voice. Otherwise sacrifice is aimless, the realists win and the rest of us may as well cut our throats."

He had now taken her into an inner room in which she expected to find a bed or divan. But there was none there. There were several cabinets, showcases, a prie-dieu, some masks on the wall (one of those being the mask of an ancient tribal god, so he said), in the drawers of the cabinet some spiced silks once worn by a mandarin who had been murdered, the wrappings from a mummy, poison rings, a photograph of the Paris executioner and his family; and such things. He remarked, "I can imagine many uses in the old days for this prie-dieu: the little maid in the cold garret is saying her ignorant foolish prayers, the master himself comes up to find out whether the maid shouldn't be warmer. Why should he take her away from her prayers?" Mr. Quaideson at first had to emphasize his theme and make his meanings clearer, for Eleanor found antiques distressingly dull, but soon she began to apprehend him, and she smiled in a warm, friendly and almost maternal way; and then she became a little excited.

She laughed and put her hand on his arm. "I see that here you have just the stage props for a book that is being written!"

"Oh, no," he said, "these give life to me. You've no idea how much truer that is. It's the life that's seeped into these things and dried into them that I can imbibe. The other side of dried-in cruelty is love. As a sour grape, dried, is sweeter than sugar."

Such talk, which had never before been addressed to her, enchanted Eleanor; and seeing she was so innocently charmed, Mr. Quaideson showed her a pillory in ivory, a full-size bloodstained whipping post for slaves, a silken swing from a brothel and a curious screen. And then he made her tea. He proposed to take *Smokeover Farm* into his firm to please her, but she at once drew up, faced him earnestly and said, No, she must do her best for her writers. She must find a sedate firm run on classic lines which was interested in starting young writers and keeping them till they were old.

Mr. Quaideson laughed negligently. "That does not sound like me." And they dropped the subject. Eleanor was disappointed. However, she sat through tea, making literary conversation, until Mr. Quaideson touched her on the arm and said, "Well, if that is the way you look at manuscripts, I think I might trust mine with you. Take this home and give me a report exactly as if I were one of your authors. Count me one of your authors. But I must warn you, as a publisher-author— that his bashfulness makes the most modest violet look like a brash peony—a publisher-author's skin is tenderer than any. Spare my feelings. Make it gentle. I'll believe every word you write." He confessed that he had thought of submitting his MS. to *Marco Marvel*, which published horror stories. "But I never had the courage of the most draggle-tailed typist writing her life out to get from behind the desk and be a Writer"; and with many more such remarks he whiled away the afternoon.

However, at the end of it, when a red and yellow sun-spoke shot through the rim of one of his windows, it fell like drops of hot water on the opened pages of his manuscript—a book entitled "The New Curiosity Shop." What Eleanor read there embarrassed her, brought her into a soft general state of excitement, and gave her the sort of alert admiration you have for someone who admires you.

"I have a house down in the country I'd like you to visit," said Mr. Quaideson. "Come soon, and you'll see the trees—I have flowering cherries and producing cherries and apples and plums; come later, you'll see the lilacs or the rhododendrons. I have an oddity for housekeeper. You'd like to see the very special section of my library where my whips hang. As I'm thin-skinned and cowardly, I'm very much interested in cruelty: I have a library of cruelty. Do you know how many ways death has been devised, and how they have schemed to have pain defeat time? No, of course not. But I think we liberal souls turn our eyes from the nasty and painful; I think we should steel ourselves to look it in the face. Where will it get us? That is another question . . . If you'd care to come sometime, I'll arrange it with my housekeeper. Perhaps you can help me too—to give life to old instruments."

Eleanor, without being able to listen to or comprehend all this, had her usual timid resistance and hastily said that she saw little of her children during the week; they expected their Mummy to be with them during the weekends. "I don't want to encourage them to look for love in other homes just yet." She described them—Deborah as a very nervous girl, handsome but distrustful, who went in and out of love affairs as if treading a complicated figure in a country dance. "She is irritable when she's in love and mournful when she's out, reaching a sort of desperation as time goes on which can only be solved one way, I'm afraid," she said; with a slight smile, murmuring, "That is by putting her arms round Mummy and asking Mummy if she knows what it feels like." She could not desert the children now—they had been "hurted" enough by life. Russell, between sixteen and seventeen, was a sweet, obedient, mild boy, absorbed in his friend "The Rev." Jonas, a boy with tirades on all subjects, and in his mother and sister. They had talked over ways and means and decided to make what sacrifices were necessary to give Russell a scientific training so that he could be at least a laboratory assistant—he would then be excused from military training. He was not particularly interested in science, but "The Rev." was, and that was enough for Russell.

Eleanor talked on and on about her children, foolishly maternal, in a warm, affected, oily voice; and she herself, in her elastic maternal roundness was full of sweet affectation, gestures and words worn to a dull luster by use. It seemed soft and natural. She began to talk freely as if to an old friend. Mr. Quaideson did not repeat then or at any other time the invitation to his orchard, but as they sat there in the dimly lighted, darkly furnished flat their two large masses took on supple outlines. They sat as the obese sat, firmly, but their outlines softened sensually toward each other. When Mr. Quaideson took her to the door, he passed his hand over her upper arms and broad back and said, "A real woman's back, what fine firm arms!"

"I need them," said Eleanor.

The story of "The New Curiosity Shop" was about a man who sat all day long among his curios and became enamored of a woman client, elegant, enigmatic, and perhaps dissipated. He courted her, fitting out an apartment for her with a prie-dieu and many other curious things Eleanor had seen. The woman never saw the flat, but in the shopkeeper's fantasy it was because she had died. Once, after she had "died," he saw her in the street. He then tried to lure her to the shop to kill her. The story had a lingering sensuality and sudden whiplashes of unseemly horror. It was not anything that Eleanor could deal with, but she bravely read through it and wrote a long report on it. Quaideson thanked her, but never mentioned it again and never paid her for it as he had promised.

Nevertheless they continued friends, and Eleanor continued to get work from A. & Q's. She went in with the work whenever it was ready or whenever she was summoned, and as a rule, paid one visit a week,

in the afternoon, to Quaideson's rooms over the antiques shop in which
he had a partnership. They had very soon become lovers of a strange
sort, not of a sort she had ever known before; but this affair of "classic
poses" and "love portraits" as he called them, were restful to her—she
found them curious and amusing. She never quite understood "Geoff,"
and he was always able to interest and surprise her. She felt that for
the first time she was beginning to understand "mature sex." She liked
to stand exposing her smooth, powerful body in the quiet old rooms in
some noble or perverse pose; she felt perfectly feminine. Mr. Quaideson had explained to her in the beginning that love and pleasure were
best in the imagination: nothing can disguise the crudity of ordinary
sexual love! "I found it offensive though at one time essential; but I
trained myself away from it and very soon was able to make it lovely
through the obscure senses."

Eleanor's life was now tranquil; she was happy. A publisher had taken
Smokeover Farm, and after its success her literary agency business had
increased so much that she employed a secretary several days a week.
She hoped soon to use one of her rooms in her flat for an office.
Deborah at twenty was working in an office and earning so much
money that she could pay her mother's rent and bank money as well.
Poor Russell had turned out to be tubercular: there was no question of
the army for him, and he had been invited by his grandparents to stay
in Switzerland, where they would provide for him until he could provide for himself. Deborah was businesslike though somewhat reticent,
and "with moods of rain and shine," which made Eleanor twitter a
little asking, "Are you getting ready to leave me, my darling? Have you
met the right man?" Deborah would reply firmly, "I'll never marry till
you're married, Mother! I won't leave you alone. You're my responsibility." Sometimes, when Eleanor was praising Mr. Quaideson, repeating
his opinions, with "Geoff told me," and "Geoff says," Deborah would
say impatiently, "Oh, Mother, why don't you marry Mr. Quaideson
and have done with it? I wouldn't mind. Don't you realize I can't marry
till I've got you off?"

Eleanor would reply with false simplicity, "Geoff and I, dear, are just
friends—very good, very dear, very sincere friends; but it's a middle-
aged comfortable friendship with no future and no strings attached;
and you must remember, my pet, that Mr. Quaideson is over seventy,
and Mummy, though she is forty-five to the world, is, according to the
registrar and to Father Time, really fifty-five. People simply don't marry
at fifty-five. So you must go a-Maying, it's your age—and you must

marry, pretty maid. Mother will be able to manage quite well: she has so far."

Eleanor kept up a busy, cheerful correspondence with all the authors who wrote to her or passed through her hands. She did them favors if she could, apart from her fees, offered them work, asked after their families (though authors don't care much for that), wrote long, kindly phrased criticisms of any manuscript, was playfully modest, deliberately humdrum, "for I never compete with my authors by *languaging,* when I am an editor." Some of these authors, after telling her all their troubles, misfortunes, the injustice done by others to them, proved ungrateful, restive beasts who got away from her and resented the fees they had to pay her; her quaint and kind remarks insulted them. One stopped answering her letters; another was enraged at her remarks about a coal-mining novel—"What do you know about it?" Another drew away because she advised him to take politics out of his novel, although she used exactly the terms she and Geoffrey used in conversation: "We ought not perhaps to make a cocktail of the ephemeral and the basic eternal: how dead old novels seem which concerned themselves with topicalities! And besides, it does set editors against you if they're not of your stripe—unfair of course, but human-all-too-human. We all have our pet corns."

One of her satisfactory authors was Mary Darling, who had sold her third novel and had just signed another good contract for seven more novels, with Rainshelter's, a most unusual affair, but which meant to Eleanor that her ten percents were safe for some time to come, and an easily earned ten percent, too—the author sold herself and made up for the "rough patches" and "disobedient ungrateful children." Another was Huie Dele Casterbridge, an author of several small books about landscape painting and aesthetic pilgrimages, with whom she had been in correspondence for nearly two years. He wished to write a "real novel." He had an income, lived on a small modern farm in Scotland. He sent her portions of a manuscript always conscientiously, painfully reworked and retyped. They had written to each other about farming, and even about Mendel and Darwin. Eleanor knew little about the subject but could write glibly; and she knew the names of Huie's dogs, and pigs and pigeons ("Pigs are very intelligent, they know their names"), and that he had just installed a stove which heated the house centrally and an immersion heater. She knew how the big fireplace was arranged; he had sent her his mother's "old-fashioned recipe for giblet pie," and described his visit to the weekly market in the nearby town—"I'm sure you're an expert at picking up things in weekly markets."

She said of him in her report to Orchard's, a large fiction firm: "This novel is without beginning or end and with splotches of Walter Scott that must certainly come out; or at least, we must clean up the heavy old canvas; and yet he has a kind of intuition of genius and we must put our foot down firmly there, or it will ruin his talent. His characters do not quite come alive, but they retain our interest; but at the end of it we have, I am afraid, a lucubration, he lets himself go, very grand indeed, but which will simply have to come out. However, this author is a lamb, and that is a virtue for which I would trade in many more literary ones."

Huie was enchanted with all she did for him. He knew she worked very hard and was in poor circumstances—he invited her to take her holiday with Deborah at The Bents, his farm. Then they would work together on his novel, as she had suggested, but only if she wanted to. They had already a scheme, a plot, "a likable hero, boy meeting girl early in the day," and he had managed the heroine according to Eleanor's recipe, "someone the male reader at least wants to get into bed with." He had "tightened the writing, casting out superfluous adjectives."

This had been one of Eleanor's most pleasant jobs. She was still working very hard, for she spared herself nothing, reading far into the night, or sitting up all night preparing her correspondence for her secretary. She wrote to Huie, "I luxuriate in work. I glory in all my free time which is putting me so far ahead of the clock-watchers, and I don't regret the guts I put into my job. My agency is not a sub-post-office like most of them." Her coarseness toward Huie seemed to her salutary sternness, she had the fun of putting a man on his feet, leading him, giving him hope and joy. So they wrote and wrote, and a few months before Geoffrey Quaideson's retirement, Orchard's had accepted Huie's novel *Touchdown*, "now a competent job with recognizable people and the author has revealed a natural gift for communication." But Huie wrote to her, "You are really my collaborator and your name is going to appear on the title page; you are not getting ten percent but fifty, for that is what I owe you and more."

Huie had written to her that as soon as he could leave the farm, he was coming to London to meet her, to celebrate and to "make their pen friendship flesh and blood." The editor signed the contract and sent him the money—only a small advance—because Orchard's were niggardly, but for Huie it was a "very great day." No sooner had he got the money than he telegraphed Eleanor that he was on his way to meet her. He booked at a hotel quite near her that she had recommended, and within a few days she "found him on her doorstep." He had driven down in his small car and was "bursting with plans, for both of us."

Eleanor had long ago given him some idea of how she lived. He took her to the theater, to dinner; he excused himself for not dancing—"I can only do the Highland fling!" He was sturdy, square-headed with black-gray wavy hair, about fifty, of a rosy-brown complexion with friendly dark eyes; he talked and smiled eagerly, gestured, had plenty to say and was lively—he would walk up and down thrusting his hands into his pockets, turning to her, thrusting with one shoulder. They seemed to be very old friends. . . .

She was very happy while Huie was in town and promised to think over the summer holiday.

"I want to be frank with you. I don't want you to come up there without knowing what is in my mind," he said. "My idea was, if we hit it off, that we might become real partners—" He looked at her with meaning, then added, "But it is not fair to ask you till you have seen my farm, my home, what other work I have done and so on. You've got a full life of your own here."

Eleanor thought it quaint that Huie should want her to go into farming with him, and she was a little curious about his way of speaking. He could not be thinking of—? She was not at all ready to quit London, which had been her whole life and where she had all her contacts. She told Huie they would wait for everything else till the summer. When she left him at the train, he kissed her. She turned away so that the queer flashing grin of joy disfiguring her face would not be seen by him. "He loves me!" For a few minutes she lived automatically, smiling and waving; she returned to normal, but in the evening and that night, for the first time for many years, perhaps, she felt a normal feeling of love for a man. It was not love, she knew: it was a physical answer. She saw to it that her letters showed no change.

At the end of June she received his formal invitation to the farm, "with Deborah and Russell, I want them too."

But by this time Geoffrey Quaideson had begun the long decline which ended in his death, and Eleanor spent much more time with him. She told Huie that she had promised to go on a walking tour with Mary Darling, and had to put it off for "private domestic reasons." She received an anxious letter from him and answered that "there was illness in the family." She might come later, she needed rest; she had been shocked by unpleasant news, the illness of someone dear to her. "Is it a man?" Huie wrote. She did not reply.

He telegraphed saying that he was making a quick trip to London and would call upon her. He called in one sunny afternoon about three. She was dressed in her old tweed suit, which had been sent to her by her mother-in-law and had already served five years. With it she wore a black-and-white striped blouse a cousin had given her, her walking shoes and some very cheap rayon stockings that had lain in her drawer for several years and that dated from the days she had meant to work as a charwoman. Her thick hair was brushed back into a low knob; she wore no make-up and she showed him no charm—she had wanted to work all the afternoon.

"Well, Huie, my dear, you're becoming a gadabout. I'll make some tea and then tell me your news and then I must get down to work. All I have is what I earn."

She felt Huie was intrusive. She had a pile of manuscripts two feet high on her desk and they called her; she still had an eager, almost lecherous interest in the next book, the next author. Besides, she wanted to think about Geoffrey and her life with him; many of the things he had said casually were precious to her, she repeated them to herself. He was the only man who had ever understood her, and appreciated her, "in every intimate nook and cranny of me, body and soul.". . . When, the first year after she met Quaideson, A. & Q. gave her a contract, making her a kind of outside editor, she realized that she had a very tender feeling for "G.Q." even if she did not love him. A few months later, in the spring, one day when she came in with her hair freshly washed, pink-cheeked and happy, "when I felt very lovely, some boy and girl kisses were indulged in." Early the next morning the thought of those kisses between a man of seventy and a woman of fifty, made her spring from bed as fresh as a girl, pink, soft-eyed, with a curving smile, and she went hallooing down the house, rousing the children, driving them on to breakfast and work—"Oh, I am twice the woman I was, when I have a man." She drew closer to him during the year in respect and a tenderness that seemed to grow quite apart from their rendezvous in his little flat. After a time they had begun to go out to dinner and he would talk about his views, his own work, his hopes. He had, besides his manuscript, a mass of written stuff which referred to "very curious adventures of the human soul, mind, spirit, heart, call it what you like." They might do something with it together.

"I had an idea in collecting all this material," he told her. "I want to leave nothing behind me beside the not very proud name of A. & Q. What if a cheeky young bounder comes along and makes it into another Rainshelter's." They smiled with the same scorn and touched hands lightly. "But I would like to make my contribution to the *curiosa* of this life, a territory which burns with the heath fires, the pure fire of original creation, sacred to Pan and Priapus."

Eleanor sparkled and turned red and white at this academic talk: it was many years since any man had spoken to her of "the grand rites of paganism, and the mysterious fires of tabu."

This clear-voiced strange old man who held her living in his pocket enfolded her with an idea of happiness and safety. They could have married, and at one moment she thought he meant to marry her. . . .

Geoffrey began to be very ill. She saw him for the first time in bed, although he detested bed and would sit up in a swing chair with gowns and blankets on, and tell her about himself. She was strong and tender, a natural nurse; and now her affection became deep, sincere, and her voice took on quite another tone when she spoke of him. She no longer thought about marrying him: her sentiment enfolded him like a soft blanket to keep off the chills and aches; her part was to enfold him.

To begin with, he was a poor sleeper and he had several times said, "I wake in the night, I get up, read, make myself tea (I don't like to drink by myself in the middle of the night), I fix the blankets and my pillows, I take a sleeping pill, rub salve into my aching neck and I use every device I've ever thought up for going to sleep. I remember conversations, try to remember the incidents of the *Three Sisters* or *War and Peace*—a pretty difficult feat, I can tell you—and if that fails, I know I'm in for it. Then, my dear, if only I had you to talk to, I would be well: an hour or two of your calming presence and I'd go to sleep. We must be opposite types, you have such a good effect on me. You restore the tonus. And then you know, apart from your being a charming woman and a sympathetic friend, what appeals to me, if I may say so, is your wonderful strength. You must have been an athlete; you remind me of an old picture I saw, for some reason I can't imagine, in a book of curiosities, 'The Spanish Beauty.' What power and grace . . ." As this was said in a quiet, thoughtful, dreamy tone, Eleanor was pleased and neither giggled nor felt coquettish—she knew she was admired for what was best, for her own sort of woman. He did not make her think but induced in her a purely physical dream, empty, healthy.

In a dreamy and languid tone, he would go on to ask about her championships, the roles she had taken in amateur theater. He looked at her admiringly, would say, "I can just see you as Hippolyta, as Boadicea. If you'd been at the court of Louis the Fifteenth or Sixteenth you would have had your own sort of pleasures. I regret, too, I was not alive then." He would go on to tell her of the pleasures the courtiers had. They might dress up as stags and does and act the part at mating time. There were always two parts to their history. "If they played at milkmaids and farmhands, they also imitated the love life of the farm."

He began to take up too much of her night hours; but the next day she would swab up her desk with a "work, work, my dear."

Without having any feeling for Goeff's curious prints and books, she had now quite got the hang of them and had worked through his catalogue with him. He had many times said he would like her opinion on this and that. "This must be left to some intelligent, sympathetic editor," he had several times said. "Catalogue or no, I don't know what's in my files or these stacks of manuscripts: in the basement are at least four trunks of drawings, some of which are valuable. Someone must take care of them; and, of course, it is not the kind of thing one leaves to one's children—even if they are grown up and married. I shall never forget the fate of poor Richard Burton in the hands of Lady Burton; and of all the men, writers, statesmen and just plain individuals like myself with natural curiosity, when their estates got into the hands of their sons, daughters and lady wives."

"Surely it's utterly wrong to destroy a man's literary estate," Eleanor exclaimed, though she felt uneasy. "But of course, one can understand the position of those wives and daughters. What were they to do? Couple infamy with one's father's name; show that one's husband had a mistress or two?"

"Yes, indeed; that is why, though I except the word 'infamy'—"

"And I withdraw it—"

"That is why one needs a friend, not too involved, who can stand aside and see what has to be dealt with and doesn't want to lay his own hands on the collections . . ."

"It's a very delicate problem."

They both agreed that there was a strong case for the friendly editor. "Supposing a manuscript of the very highest literary value was left, an acquisition to the literature of the nation and this manuscript was marred by coarse sexual digressions or it advocated anarchism or communism, wouldn't we be perfectly right in editing out the excrescences?" Eleanor said. "I would do it without hesitation out of respect and reverence for the author's wrong-headed genius."

"Ah, yes, but here we have a quite acceptable thing, for the things that are tabu are always accepted as part of society, like the dark of the moon . . ."

In his house or in the office at quiet times they talked about his literary estate, and the part that Eleanor could play.

It was at this moment that Huie sent her a short letter.

Dear Eleanor: I didn't get any reply to my last letter, which I know is very unusual with you; and I feel you must be too busy in some direction to have time for me. Well, to be frank, I had hoped you would have time for me always; by that I mean, I have been wanting to ask you to be my wife; and what gave me the hope was, I expect, that I love you and hoped that you might get to be quite fond of me. We seemed to be such friends and I thought more. Will you marry me? Perhaps you don't like the farm: we might be able to arrange something, when the books begin to sell. My dear, dear Eleanor: how happy you can make me.

Huie Casterbridge.

Eleanor showed the letter to Quaideson, who said, "Why don't you accept him?"

Eleanor at once wrote saying that she was afraid her marrying days were over, that she still felt the responsibility of her little family, that recently she had had news of her former husband that had revived too many distressing memories and that, "perhaps it is that I am not in a marrying mood."

Quaideson never mentioned the matter again; but to Cope and others she explained that "a farmer had asked her to marry him, and she would have relished filling her lungs with good fresh air for a month, but that she could hardly give up her London days and nights and count sows' litters."

She dismissed the offer with scarcely a thought then, and some months later, when she realized that she might have been married, a wife, with a new domestic routine and a connubial life, she trembled as if before a horrid mystery—she felt as if she had escaped carrying a wearisome burden for the rest of her life.

One day she noticed that a remarkably horrible ivory had disappeared from Quaideson's wall—a reproduction of a French church monument, a corpse in the tomb with worms writhing on it. Quaideson at first sulkily and then insolently repeated that he had sold it: "Why leave it to the Boeotians to destroy or hide?" Other pieces were soon sold; and before he retired to his country house, all that was valuable was sold. He showed her his will. The "four trunks in the cellar" he left to a nephew, and the money he had recently acquired through these sales went to a seventeen-year-old niece, a foolish creature, so he had always said. Eleanor herself received nothing and had no interest in what was left of the "literary estate." Nevertheless she took it with a good grace, attributing his unkindness to his illness and his "incurable whimsy."

Two years after his retirement, he died. She wrote to some of her correspondents that she had just lost a dear, good friend, one who was very near to her; and then she was silent about him and "laid him away in rose-leaves with the greater and best part of my life." He had filled her life with a tranquil passion just when life was saddest.

Meantime Deborah had been living with her in the roomy flat and they had often discussed getting a lodger. Deborah was against it. "You've always given us a real home, Mummy, without strangers; we've always managed; and now I'm earning, we don't want someone tramping in all hours and listening to what we say. I want a real home to bring a boy to, when I bring him to meet my Mummy."

The question of the lodger was shelved—"until you marry, my pet, and Mother needs the lodger to keep her."

"Mother, why didn't you marry Huie or Geoffrey—well, Geoffrey's too ill—but why don't you marry someone?"

"When you're my age, darling, you'll understand that everything has a time and place and women my age are glad to have had their marriage and their children, and their happiness is in just being themselves, and, of course, seeing that their dear ones are happy. What better thing could I have than just looking at you, seeing you're in good healthy animal spirits, doing a good job and realize that somehow I've turned out an excellent daughter!"

But Deborah was not in good spirits, as she knew. For some time she had been nervous, "alternately purring and slinking darkly about," which indicated that "she had a man on her mind." Eleanor, irritated by some long silence at the dinner table, twitted her and told her to "come out with it. It won't improve with keeping, you know."

Deborah then told her simply and like a grown woman that she had met a man she was mad about but did not quite understand. "I think we're going to get married and yet he worries me. I don't know what's wrong: am I wrong or is he, or is it just that I've never been going to get married before? I don't feel that I'll be happy with him; but I don't want to miss this chance, if he is the right man. You had such bad luck with Daddy and it wasn't your fault—you just married the wrong man. I really want you to look at him, I suppose, and tell me what you think. And then, I suppose, I won't take your opinion. I don't want him to know he's being looked at, either."

The man, Paul Waters, was older than Deborah. He was thirty-five, while she was just over twenty-two. Presently Deborah invited her mother to a performance of *La Forza del Destino*. (For some reason Eleanor always called it *La Sforza del Destino*.) Some of Deborah's friends were music students, actors and radio performers; they were all going to see a young conductor who was one of theirs. Eleanor was wearing a dress she had made "for the occasion of being a possible mother-in-law," a beige material printed with small brown and golden twigs, which she thought went with her "smooth, golden skin and hair the color of chestnut buds." She looked at herself with gratification in the pier glass before she put the finishing touches to her make-up. She was excited at her new role; she thought her dress, "softly draped around bust and hips, with a side panel giving a floating movement," not only flattering, but exactly fitting to the occasion and her new position.

"I do look the understanding mother-in-law," she said to Deborah. "I make a decorative background. The foreground, my pet, belongs to you."

It was a warm autumn evening with delicate air; if not for the look of the leaves, one would have expected to see cherry blossoms out. They drove to the hall, an ample hall with glass walls, staircases and foyers and balconies over the river. They stood about near a large mirror, rather impatiently looking for friends who had not turned up—time was getting on; Paul Waters, too, was not there. Eleanor had brought her glasses to read the program, but she would not wear them yet; she wanted Mr. Waters to see her at her best. She was too excited, she knew she was being foolish, but she could not help making bright little remarks to Deborah's friends. She knew some of them from Deb's schooldays, anyway, and had entertained them at "gay little bread-and-butter parties," which had cost her a great deal of effort, thought and more than she could afford, but which had been a great success. There they were now, grown up, like Deb; one girl was going to Oxford now, one was working in an orchestra. They were polite to her but they did not seem much interested in Paul Waters. Suddenly one said to her, "He's too old for Deb; he's thirty-five or six."

Just then, another said coldly, "There he is!" She saw a tall man swinging round toward them, his nose in the air, looking. His thick chestnut hair was a neat metallic crest, his bronze face was metallic too; he walked like those who spend an hour or two daily in gymnastics, he had a fine athletic bachelor air. He held his face upwards as if to catch the air, he walked so fast his coat opened and the dark red scarf around his throat flew out behind. Eleanor looked at him intently, though not knowing this was the man; all other things were still or faintly moving. It was like standing looking at a landscape when one still tree all at once moves—a branch and then all its limbs. This strange man whom she did not know yet to be Paul Waters came toward them and looked straight into Eleanor's eyes with the glance of a man who understands a woman wants him and who gives himself and means to take all, a dark look that existed long before language. Eleanor looked away, to hide it from the others. They were introduced and smiled like people who had been introduced years before and had flirted and were now hiding their acquaintance. Then they went up the steps of the hall to find their seats. Eleanor looked at his face with wonder, but she avoided his eyes. His face was of that harmony and regularity which gives lifelong beauty, and the eyes apart, had a great sweetness; and yet the sweetness seemed only part of the wonderful mask, for his eyes were not sweet, but dark, veiled, profound, disturbed. He stood up above them, looking round calmly, though he was in the aisle, holding people up. Then he sat down at the end of the row, next to her daughter and one place away from her. While he affected to look away and look at his program, she studied his profile, dark, rather fleshy. There was a swarthiness about him that she considered foreign; his beauty too, fleshy and proud, did not look English. Suddenly Waters looked straight at her and smiled: the smile of smiles! She gave him one of her society smirks and looked coquettishly away; but she did not feel like flirting. Her heart had begun a great circular thrumming, so it felt. Round and round it gadded, making larger swoops, and her head turned, making larger swoops, as if she were floating, with her large body, round the great dome. Her heart began pounding out hard and real thoughts, like pieces of metal, too; and she heard them, forceful, unanswerable: This is love and he knows it; it would be too strong for me, my life would be carried away into a whirlpool, round and round and down, in the center, lost and gone; I wouldn't want to get out of it, I would lose myself; I'd be swept away; I don't want that. I couldn't live, then all would mean nothing. I can't live like that; what of the past and future? There'd be no meaning to the world or time, but this hour and the future hours with him would break into everything, flooding everything, everything would be washed away: I couldn't stand it, I'm not strong enough, I'm too old to go in for it—

Meantime the people had settled, the music had begun and Eleanor, who was somewhat musical, began to be ordered by and drawn into the music. What a terrible, powerful beat the music had, threatening and promising sullenly, something tremendous, nothing good. In it was a life Eleanor had never known, and which frightened her, but now, for the first time, attracted her—a great potency, passion, which she had been always unconscious of; some great thing approached her and for the first time spoke to her, as if a new world came somewhere near her world and she felt its attraction and feared to be pulled away off the earth, out of life.

When the overture ceased, she looked round at the warm masks, turned toward the footlights. She smiled, tapped her daughter's hand to show all was quite normal, she nodded nicely to show she approved of Paul Waters. But she did not; she felt it was hopeless for Deborah to fall in love with such a man; it was all too great for Deborah—or could they love? A pain struck her full in the breast and she thought, Oh, save me from being jealous of a younger woman; I could not stand it, I'd take poison. I must never see him again, that's certain. I'll tell her I don't like him, I'll influence her as I know how. Then she'll see him in secret, they'll become lovers— Music and drama was going on before her; she took part in it, too, but while sometimes in the dark she smiled with intense joy, and clasped her hands at her success at such unexpected romance, at other times she heard nothing but her warning menacing heart, thudding out the news of her gloomy future.

I will not and I cannot, she said to herself.

During the interval, he went away with Deborah, but she ran into them by accident and stood gossiping merrily with him, quite forgetting the girl; when next they sat down, he sat next to her. Afterwards, while they ate and drank something, they took long looks at each other, drinking each other in, and there was something very bitter, cruel— almost detestation—in these glances. She saw in his eyes that he had appraised her, he could not help the attraction he felt but he was trying to repress it, by seeing her as she was—an aging belle, a faded animal; she felt her age, and dropped her eyes. Over his face all his thoughts passed like cloud shadows. Yet he turned his face up or away slightly so that she could still admire the powerful unlined throat and his traits; his eyes looked darker and larger. She could see he was trying to attract her.

When she got home with Deborah, she stood for a moment at the door, pretending to fumble with the key, feeling the great joy on her: I can love him, and he loves me. Then she went in with an ordinary suburban face and ordinary suburban remarks.

In the night, awake, she rose and fell, like a floating swimmer, on easygoing great waves of voluptuous joy, while thinking, Not for me, no, no, it's all nonsense; it's all past, not for me, no longer; how can it come now when it never came? It's an illusion.

She slept well, awakened early and had forgotten everything. She lay awake like a young healthy girl, happy, subdued, listening to the sound of birds outside; she heard the milkman; she was herself and suddenly remembered everything, jumped out of bed like a newly engaged girl, and ran from one thing to another, table to chair to filing case, hugging them—she hugged and kissed small things, she sat down at her desk in her nightgown, put her head in her arms and laughed for joy. Then she dressed to get to her work, and sat down to it, but when she heard Deborah call goodbye and go out to work, she hurried to Deborah's room, where she had installed a pretty dressing table with three mirrors, two of which, at the sides, could be turned all ways. How fresh she looked in the morning! She felt the little joyful waves begin again round her heart, leaping and beginning to swell round it, soon to drink it down in milk and honey. She smiled, looking downwards and picked up her daughter's hand mirror, peered in it, got her glasses and pored over her face and neck in the mirror.

It was a very long time since she had thought about these details. She was surprised to see that she had some small gray hairs; her skin was not so fine as she had imagined. The more she looked, the more disagreeable the looking became. Over the charming image she had carried with her from her girlhood of fine, smooth skin, rosy cheeks and smooth, shining hair, another coarse face had grown, heavy, but strong and real: herself in the present hour. Of course, he was already wishing he had never seen her, never given her that look, it was a ridiculous mistake; and they would meet next time with a cold, insulting play of manners. "Oh, the time will come when we'll laugh together over the whole business," she tried to say, in her old way.

The day went, she worked and forgot the incident. She had manuscripts to send in, and telephone calls to make. She went to bed quite tired and did not think of Waters at all.

In the morning she woke up with a dreamy smile, remembering the opera. She lay for a while going carefully over every moment of the evening, jumped out of bed, and going to the window, looked out at the little grassy field at the back. It had grown on some earth fallen off a little earthy bluff; grass hung over the head of the bluff, too. "Oh, world, oh, life, oh, time," she said, rejoicing. What poem was that? Where did it come from? She did not know what it was or when she had seen it. But soon she forbade the thought, thinking, more healthily now, with a pretty sad smile, How foolish, but how sweet! And so it was for a few days—she awoke each morning like a girl soon to be married and would lie feeling the sun on her arms and body, thinking, Soon not the sun but he—

During the week she began to feel tired, she was doing too much. She would sit at her desk with the work before her, doing nothing, merely annotating, reading, and her lifeblood beat fiercer and fiercer in her, till she found herself trembling, as if something stronger than herself had got inside, a turbine which had started out on a long voyage and was now well on its way churning up the shallow waters, satisfied in the deep waters. On the last day of the week she woke up feverish, after a feverish night, unable to think of anything but this miserable affair of her daughter's lover. She felt no love for her daughter, nor anyone; and hugged only one thought to her, that never, never again must she see this intruder, this man, this god, this tyrant, who had begun to squeeze the life out of her.

She got up slowly, trembling, hardly answered Deborah, who seemed to see nothing wrong with her, and when her daughter had gone, slowly put on her outdoor things, took her purse and went in to the city, each step, each stage seeming like an achievement. She would get to a bus stop and seem to rest; reach a well-known street, pause and feel at rest. Yet she was very anxious, very pressed. Dr. Mack's office was closed. The building was owned by a Greek restaurant-keeper, who was in his restaurant downstairs. He told her that Dr. Mack had gone away to northern India. She intended to "walk into Ladakh in Kashmir and beyond into Tibet; she may stay there. But I talked to her about Mount Athos and she is thinking of trying to get to the forbidden territory." He looked at Eleanor and said, "She has special clothing; it would not be easy to tell whether she is man or woman."

Eleanor went away. She felt she had no one to turn to. She reached home and then something strange happened. It was just as if someone lifted the top off her head for a moment and let air in so that part of her brain blew cold. She lay down on a couch and was found asleep there some hours later by her daughter.

"I've been very, very cold, just as if I'd fallen into a c-c-crevasse in Tibet." She laughed a little. Deborah looked after her. She recovered, though she felt unwieldy, she who had been so limber. But she had her work to do and it was as if somehow she had made a wise decision: she was going to take things easier. A life full of work—good, good, she had accepted life. She could rest. She said to Deborah, "I kept to the rules, but the rules didn't keep me. But I hewed to the line; I cultivated my garden. So let us work, my pet. Soon I will have my pension and then I am going to write the story of my life; then I will really get down to it; and it will open some eyes."